DIVINE
ASSASSIN

Other Novels by Bob Reiss

THE CASCO DECEPTION
SUMMER FIRES

DIVINE
ASSASSIN

by

BOB REISS

Little, Brown and Company
BOSTON ◆ TORONTO

FIRST EDITION

Library of Congress Cataloging in Publication Data

Reiss, Bob.
    Divine assassin.
    I. Title.
PS3568.E517D5   1985   813'.54   85-6802
ISBN 0-316-73969-3

BP

DESIGNED BY JEANNE F. ABBOUD

*Published simultaneously in Canada
by Little, Brown & Company (Canada) Limited*

PRINTED IN THE UNITED STATES OF AMERICA

For a Safe World
for Amit

A VERY SPECIAL THANKS TO ELIEZER AND RINA
ADAR, THE BREAD LOAF WRITERS' CONFERENCE,
DUTCH, THE FBI'S TERRORISM SECTION, JIM GRADY,
KIBBUTZ EIN GEV, ESTHER NEWBERG, BILL
PHILLIPS, RUTH "TARANTULA" RAVENEL, CURT
SUPLEE AND KAREN WILLIAMS

DIVINE
ASSASSIN

CHAPTER

I

THE fat man splashed through the swamp, toward the protection of the trees. He was ten yards from a willow bank, forty from scrub forest at his back. His white suit was drenched, sweat burned his eyes. The marsh merged into blurred green, rancid water and ripping thorns. All to the hammering of his heart and the pounding of a plane taking off overhead.

At a crash behind him he whirled. The blond man burst into view across a pool. Where the swamp met the piny woods, knee-deep in water, the younger man was coming fast, his T-shirt bulging even at a distance, the gun a black mass in his fist.

The fat man groped in his jacket pocket and pulled a silver cigarette case free. He held it up. The blond froze. "Give me," he called. But the fat man threw the case, which arched, end over end, framed by sky and foliage. He didn't hear it hit because another plane was taking off.

He screamed, "Go after the box. Leave me alone."

The blond man kept coming.

The fat man stumbled into the packed forest. His chest was on fire. The trees went in and out of focus. Brambles slashed his face.

Then the path spilled him out of the trees and he was face to face with a woman on a blanket, a picnicker under a willow with a wicker basket and a bottle of wine. Two glasses but one person. Beyond the woman the island ended with black water. There was a bridge across the river, American cars flashed on the road above, moving havens impossibly out of reach.

At eye level and framed beneath a stone arch of the bridge, the fat man saw a building on the far riverbank a quarter mile away. The pilot had pointed it out when the fat man landed in Washington less than an hour ago.

It was the Lincoln Memorial.

He thought, The real dying will start when they find the box. He wanted to yell that the woman should run, but he couldn't breathe; he tore at his collar. The blond man would kill her just because she was here. He fought to remember the right English words.

"You," he wheezed, "must . . ."

He heard pounding footsteps behind him. Her wide eyes shifted from his face over his shoulder.

He did not have to turn to know the pursuer had found him.

CHAPTER

2

PEOPLE still recognized him on the street. It happened rarely now but the signs were unmistakable; the sidelong glance or whisper between companions. Tim Currie read their lips when they said the word *hostage*.

In the early days he had wanted to confront his tormentors. "Yes, it's me, the famous, the mysterious. Take a good look. The man on the news." The *Post* had called him "Hostage with a secret." Reporters phoned constantly. Changing numbers did not help. "What did you tell the President and why did you meet him in private? Are you really an engineer or CIA? Why was the public barred from your Senate subcommittee appearance? What really happened in the embassy? Were you beaten or harmed? How does it feel to be back after a year? How did you feel in that cell?"

In public, at all times, his face had shown the carefully agreed-upon lie of indifference. Only people who knew him well understood the caking lines about his eyes and mouth betrayed enormous pressure, as if his skull were slowly being crushed. But he had never broken his promise to the President, he had never told the truth.

At thirty-four, he was tall, with blond hair like a Californian or an Englishman. He had the imposing shoulders of an ex-athlete and walked with a long-legged stride. Tim Currie favored corduroy jackets and jeans, always freshly laundered. The sureness of his movements implied control, a willingness to battle, and in fact he had been a boxing champion at

Fordham. He exploded his fists when a conversation excited him, the energy traveling his arms and splaying his long fingers. His face was handsome, with a craggy urban ruggedness, youthful when he grinned but otherwise layered, as if his life had gone through profoundly different phases.

He had the deep-lasting tan of a skier, yet there was a stiffness to his carriage, and he combined that purpose and narrow-mindedness found in some self-made men, men who built their world in small pieces, who fixed on a goal early in life and avoided overspeculation in order to achieve it.

Imprinted in his mind, when he awoke in the dark during his first months home, was the face of the black-turbaned fanatic who had imprisoned him; the bearded man with the small eyes of a pig. The face on the poster in his cell.

Or if his ex-wife Anna brushed him in sleep during this time, he shot awake to find himself curled fetally, hands protecting his privates as if expecting a kick. These night visions were more real than home. "We'll take care of everything," the President had told him with Hollywoodish ease. They were in the Oval Office, which was smaller than Currie had imagined, and the President was trying to convince him to remain silent about what had happened in the embassy. He looked at the eagle on the wall and saw hands reaching up, clawing it, tearing it down. He saw the eagle upside down, disappearing into a mob. Currie had said, "Take care of what, Mr. President? Everything is over."

That was the bad time. The State Department sponsored cocktail parties where strangers pumped his hand as if he were a hero, grew disillusioned at his normality and uncomfortable realizing he had done nothing notable. He was merely a symbol of their own failure to rescue him, to rescue all of them, the fifty-three hostages in Iran.

The bad time. During the second week home, Anna, his once shy high-school sweetheart who had become a television

[6]

personality and "hostage wives spokesperson" in his absence, took him to a Georgetown discothèque featuring a shark tank on the dance floor. While revelers gyrated, a lone torpedo shape hung in green murkiness, gills fanning, black eyes staring. Currie had watched the shark for over an hour. He felt as though he were the one in the tank.

"You are depressed," the government psychiatrist announced on his single visit. Currie laughed uproariously. "How much do they pay you?" But he felt like a hostage for a long time. Eating, working, even at midnight, trying to lose himself in mindless television, sitting with the flickering light on his face, listening to the whiny, delighted voices. "My shirts smell fresh. My socks feel clean."

Instead of the screen, he would see the face on the poster in his cell. Or the gaptoothed guard or the jail floor, the looming expanse of concrete close to his face, its coolness rising, as he waited for a kick.

The bad time was over, four years ago. It was just a memory now, able, on rare occasions, to produce savage anger. Mostly it was a shadow he could ignore. Looking back at the whole period, he saw he had never felt so small, so powerless, so weak, exposed and humiliated, before or since. He had been another person, out of control.

He told himself he would never allow anything to make him feel like that again.

Anything.

"Stop kissing. If you're going to lure me out on a picnic during a workday, you have to work."

They reclined on a blanket by the Potomac River, under a willow on the bank of Washington's Roosevelt Island. Beyond the grass and still black water, a bridge hummed with traffic. A plane lifted high. The smell of Indian summer honeysuckle surrounded them.

"You don't like kissing?" he said. He lifted an envelope off a pile, licked the flap and grimaced. "The truth is, I hate it myself. What a relief."

"I'm free all afternoon and all night, mister. We'll see who hates what."

They laughed and he said, "Greedy." She traced his lips with her finger. "Greedy?" she said. "I became greedy the day I met you."

They'd talked about marriage, children. He had not yet offered the ring but felt it in his pocket, a slight pressure, through his jeans, upon his thigh.

"Fifty envelopes for you, I'll take fifty," she said. "The Russians will be furious when they get these."

"To hell with the Russians. Is that chicken I smell?"

"Yes it is, baby, but work. After that," she went into a carnival barker act, "you want chicken, you got chicken. You want relish? You want sweet rolls?"

"I want you."

She was small but lush, full breasted and voluptuous for her size, her waist tiny, almost doll-like, her lean dancer's legs tucked beneath her, arching her back. She wore a blue and crimson peasant dress and a white cotton sleeveless blouse. Her normally straight black hair was piled, cameo-style, above her slender neck, and her profile formed a soft alabaster curve, shadowed hollows and rises. When she turned to smile, her black eyes shone bright with intelligence. She had thin, delicate brows and a full mouth.

A girlhood automobile accident had left her with the single marring slash on otherwise flawless features. A thin scar, a white line which crossed her upper lip diagonally.

She kissed him on the mouth. "I could grow to like this," she said. Never, to Currie, did she ever lose that softness and fragrance, that curve of invitation, in anger or sleep, in furious concentration, in heated argument or girlish dependence, weeping, in black despondency, over some failure.

[8]

Working, he said, "A boy." She understood he meant babies and flashed a cooperative smile. He said. "Two boys. A boy and a girl."

"After we finish these letters."

He had an urge to produce the ring, but they were playing out the last few minutes, savoring the process. That he had met her, that he had climbed out of the horrible hole, was an astonishing miracle to him. He was lighthearted as a teenager. He said, "I'll teach him to box. Building in the basement."

"The shelves you made are fantastic."

"Not just woodworking. Computers. I'll have a whole system down there. A kid who knows computers has a head start."

The corners of her mouth danced. "Suppose Harpo Junior doesn't like computers?"

"We're not naming my kid Harpo!"

She saluted, "Yes sir, sergeant sir."

The envelopes bore the legend "Watchers International." Currie knew the correspondence inside by heart. "Dear Premier Chernenko. Anatole Scharansky has been in a Siberian prison for . . ."

Currie regarded his membership in Watchers as the sole positive by-product of his imprisonment. Upon returning to the States, he had begun noticing small items buried in newspapers. Jailed without a trial, an Argentine professor had been freed after six years. A Russian poet starved himself for permission to leave a country that did not want him in the first place. At one of the interminable celebrity dinners to which his ex-wife had dragged him, a Polish exile photographer told a story of photographing a Mideastern diplomat at a party. Flattered by the picture, the diplomat requested copies. The Pole arranged a trade: two freed journalists for five copies of the photograph.

The Pole had smiled at the disbelief around the table.

"What's so hard to accept?" he said. "The journalists were never important. Important people never go to jail."

The photographer and the articles had both mentioned Watchers International, which worked for the release of political prisoners around the world. Touched by the stories, gripped by kinship for the victims, Currie had attended a meeting, joined, and met Nori too.

They'd taken the afternoon off for the picnic, he from his supervising job at Rockville Computers, she from Watchers.

"Sri Lanka," she said. Now it was his turn to understand they discussed honeymoons. A delicious tension enveloped them, a sweet anticipatory thrill.

He said, "You'd look terrific in a sarong."

"Not only me, mister."

"Me? In a sarong?" They laughed. She said, "Hawaii. Bali." She tested the names on her tongue. She undulated her arms in a hula. "Bali Haiiii."

He said, with uncharacteristic creative humor on the day of his engagement, "I know a place better than Bali."

"Where?"

"A legend. Maybe it doesn't even exist."

"Tell me."

"In all of history only one or two people ever reached it. Their stories were too fabulous for belief."

"I can't stand it so say the name."

"Why," he said, blinking. "Niagara Falls."

In one voice they said, "Finish the envelopes."

He became aware of the breeze on his face and of each strand of grass, of the smallest fold in the blanket, of the island's honeysuckle smell and the deep blueness of the sky. Of Nori's small movements beside him.

Senses bursting, he concentrated on folding the letters, on each phrase — imprisoned without trial . . . ill health . . . brutal treatment — and his job turned to sadness for the lonely stranger overseas. Hostage memories could be triggered by Watchers work. Now his sensitive mood combined with the oddest of catalysts, a waterbeetle lumbering across the blanket's edge. He said, "Arthur was a cockroach who lived in my cell."

"You had a pet cockroach?"

"He was the biggest, the oldest roach in the world. So I called him King Arthur and then just Arthur. I made up his history. He'd come to Iran in a computer crate, an American, like me. He had a lopsided walk. One antenna was shorter than the other. He'd point them at me while I talked. Arthur really looked like he was listening, out there in the middle of the floor. Oh, I know he was waiting for food, but I liked talking. Especially after Zarek got dragged away."

"What happened to Arthur?" asked Nori, who did not like to talk about Currie's human cellmate.

"I've told you about the peephole in the door. Generally I was careful about the guards when I was talking to Arthur. That day I got carried away, telling him about skiing. Vermont. Cold wind. I heard the key in the lock. I said, 'Arthur, beat it.' I could have sworn he screamed when they stepped on him. A thin little noise under the sandal."

"Tim," she said.

"Can you believe I cried over a roach? But the guard was laughing. 'Crazy American. You go crazy in the cell.' "

Nori put down an envelope. "We've talked about this. You couldn't fight all of them, so many of them. Anyway, over a roach."

"Sure. A crummy roach." Frowning, Currie said, "Let's face it. After two years of folding letters, have we even gotten one person out of prison?"

Unfazed, she slid her tongue across a flap. "Takes time."

"It doesn't take any time to put them in prison."

Gently, she touched his face. "You're talking like this because of Arthur. Zarek fought them and they dragged him away. You heard them every night. Beating him in the next cell."

She said, "Would you have felt better if they beat you too?" Currie picked up an envelope.

"Nori, I didn't fight, I didn't get beaten as badly as Zarek. But there's nothing logical about humiliation. The people we mail out letters to, they're like that guard. Laughing."

"So?" She leaned forward, eyebrows plunging. "You and me, we're not rich. Not in the government. How else do we say things if not with letters? If we lick ten thousand envelopes and one person is released from jail even a week early, even a day, isn't it worth it? Wouldn't it have been worth it to you?"

She stopped, amazed. "I made a speech," she said. Struck by her own sophomoric earnestness, she laughed at herself. "In the sun too long," she said. On her knees she walked toward him. The peasant dress floated behind her. She had a hard time suppressing the humor in her eyes. She hooked her fingers into claws and whispered, theatrically, "Tor-ture. Tell us what we want to know." She maneuvered behind him. He felt the massage begin.

"I won't talk," he said.

Her fingers sought the bunched muscles on his neck. "White meat or dark meat chicken for lunch?"

"You'll never get it out of me."

"Vino will loosen your tongue." She pulled a bottle from the wicker basket. "Where's the corkscrew?" she said. "Damn. It must have fallen out in the jeep."

"Love conquers corkscrews," Currie said. "I'll get it."

His last vision of Nori before the forest blotted her out was of a small swooning figure pressing a limp wrist to her forehead. Her exaggerated Southern drawl carried through the dense air even after he could not see her. "Be careful, Rhett. The parking lot is full of dangerous Yankees."

[12]

He sauntered along the wooded path. Sunlight warmed his neck. From overhanging bowers, cooler shadows crossed his face. Cattails and skunk cabbage marked a swamp on his right, the summery vegetable smell grew thick.

He remembered her soft fingertips on his cheeks and her black liquid eyes, her demure glance under curling lashes. She was twenty-five, a former acting student who had acquired a social conscience at American University, the daughter of a delicatessen owner in Westchester, New York, who had thrown herself into the Watchers work with the furious innocence of a suburban convert. Nori Abramoff. Actress, lover, wife-to-be.

From beyond the forest, he heard the screech of brakes from the George Washington Parkway, which ran parallel to the island, and his mind shifted and he remembered the yellow buses. Five years later the memory was still fresh. In his mind he was in the computer room in the U.S. Embassy in Tehran, installing a new "Smart Guy" decoder. "Government wants an expert, government gets an expert, even though a technician could install it," his boss had said. "You'll be home in a week, tops."

Currie saw the blue linoleum floors and white cork walls. He heard the sucking hum of computer air-conditioning units, the rattle of printers and clack of teletype machines across the hall, the murmuring of white-coated technicians who bent like surgeons over the "Smart Guy." He heard bubbling coffee.

Then, superimposed over the other noises, he heard the screech of air brakes.

He thought there had been an accident. Peering from the ten-foot-high second-story window, Currie was struck by the incongruous scene below. Three yellow schoolbuses had stopped outside the embassy's iron gate. Their doors were closed, their windows sheets of sunglare. Puffs of exhaust dissipated in the hot desert air. He almost expected summer campers to appear in shorts, except the sprawling Mideastern metropolis backdrop was all wrong.

Then the doors did open and the mob poured out, the screaming smashing Currie like a blow, driving him back, while from the alleys and avenues surrounding the building a human tidal wave swarmed over the walls and through the gate, chasing a lone marine across the compound.

He saw the hallways filling with frantic secretaries, bureaucrats, businessmen pushing past potted palms and presidential portraits as marines directed them to higher floors. He remembered the tart sweat odor, the souring perfume of cigarettes and jostling bodies. All to the thunder of the horde below, and the shouts, "They're in the lobby! Coming upstairs!"

Then there were no more floors to which to run. The crowd thrust him toward an open door to the roof and escape to the adjacent Canadian Embassy compound. Just out of reach, the sky seemed magically unchanged. He pushed toward the roof but felt someone grip his shoulder.

The woman was twenty, overdressed, bedecked with jewelry, her face a mask of running makeup. She whimpered with hysterical fear.

She stood close to the door but off to one side. She would never be strong enough to fight her way out.

Currie instinctively pushed away from his own freedom against the pressing mass of bodies. He yanked the woman in front of him and propelled her onto the roof.

The door slammed in his face.

At that instant, with escape blocked and the waving staves cresting the banister, he thought, "This isn't happening," the greatest irony of all, since he had warned the embassy about the seizure two days before. While checking the new computer, he had decoded a Libyan radio transmission mentioning a takeover.

"You must be mistaken," the vice-consul had told him.

"You don't understand the Mideast. Libyans and Iranians hate each other. The computer made an error."

This was part of what Currie had promised the President he would not reveal, that American officials had prior warning of the attack.

The crowd slammed him against the closed door and again someone grabbed him, this time a lean stranger who said, "I'm Zarek." Zarek had a bony, narrow face, like a convict or Tennessee cracker. Miraculously, he avoided being jostled by the crowd. "You got my girlfriend Cindy out. I owe you."

Later Currie learned Zarek's girlfriend was one of five Americans to reach home safely. The "I owe you" seemed pathetic, boastful, and as the months lengthened and they found themselves transferred to a cell together, Zarek's promises of a big favor grew tedious. Plus, the more Currie learned about the man, the less he could imagine ever needing his help. Nori had snapped, upon hearing the story, "What do you need from a murderer? I read about Zarek in the *Post*."

He had not seen Zarek for over four years now, not since the hostages landed in Weisbaden Germany. Zarek had disappeared with an army colonel then. He had never been listed on the prisoner manifest, and even the Iranians never mentioned him. Zarek, the President told Currie, had officially never been in Iran.

A narrow footbridge brought Currie across a spit of river onto the parking lot. Beyond the sun-warmed asphalt, cars shot along the birch- and maple-forested George Washington Parkway.

He thought of Nori again and experienced a wave of desire. Nori was daylong hikes in the Shenandoah, she was nights by his fireplace and candlelight dinners at Great Falls. Nori was Sundays licking envelopes at the Watchers office. She was a hundred different people. She had her waif face and her tender face and her furious face. Her petite elfishness imparted to her a magical joy. She was radiant proof of how good and happy ordinary things could be.

"You got me out of the black time," he said to her once, but she had said, "You don't know how strong you are. You climbed out yourself." Currie had merely shrugged. He did not think of himself as strong or not strong. He thought only of tasks he had to accomplish. He broke them into components, like the engineer he was, to examine them and set about mastering them. Nori had said, "You were isolated as hell. You let Anna go because she wanted it. You didn't sue the government like the other hostages. You hated the way the government handled things but you didn't think suing was the right thing to do. You didn't talk to reporters or complain in public, even though you were going crazy inside. You could have made money from the book offers. Maybe you're the last patriot left, whatever that means."

Chuckling, she'd added, "You wouldn't even do the commercial," which evoked hysterical laughter. The commercial was their favorite private joke.

During the first months back, Currie had received a dozen calls from a television personality called The Chicken King. The Chicken King was a millionaire poultry dealer whose commercials had made him famous. He offered Currie a spectacular fee to stand in a kitchen and say, "Ladies, feel like a hostage in your own home? Free yourself! Buy Shake-Them-Chickens!"

The jeep was parked alone, the only other cars a green Triumph convertible and yellow Ford sedan at the far end of the lot. He'd bought the Morosso ten years ago for camping and did all the work on it himself. He'd even modified the engine to improve mileage.

In the spotless interior, the corkscrew flashed silver on the back floor.

How it could have fallen from an allegedly closed picnic

basket was beyond him, but so was Nori's disorderliness. He locked the jeep and turned back, knowing she would have divined his possible irritation and devised tactics for diffusing it. She might ambush him in the forest but he decided she would do an act with the corkscrew, a frequent prop. The corkscrew featured a triangular head and two arms which raised up as the screw bored into a cork. The user would plunge down the arms to pop open a bottle. Nori liked to yank the screw, shooting the arms into the air. "Nixon," she would say. She would pump the screw up and down so the arms would "swim." "Mark Spitz." She could do Superman and gymnast Olga Korbut and ice skater Peggy Fleming, twirling. Using different voices, she carried on conversations between these characters. Nixon and Superman got into arguments. The funny part was, she was shy at bottom. She would never perform for large audiences but would always be an actress for him.

And flooded with happiness, a big man rambling in the Potomac sunlight, he noticed a silver glint where the narrow footpath met the grass. Currie bent and retrieved a silver cigarette box. He issued a low admiring whistle. On the beautifully carved sides, he saw men in turbans, sheep, donkeys, a caravan frozen, the workmanship so fine Currie discerned the lines on the men's faces, the tendons on the wrists. The expressions were haggard but purposeful. The caravan was on an important journey.

Flecks of dirt spotted the box where it had lain on the ground. The side which faced Currie sparkled, unblemished.

Whoever owns this will be happy to get it back, Currie thought. I'll drop it off with the park police.

He reached to open the box.

The scream shattered the forest, coming from beyond the swamp and thick maples ahead.

Crows screeched into the air, in its wake.

"Nori," he said, starting to run.

Unthinking, he shoved the box into his pocket. Overhead, a plane set the island vibrating. He pushed branches from his face.

His heart pounded.

Nori.

CHAPTER
3

THE van lurched, throwing the paramedics together and slamming the back of Currie's head into the wall. "Save her," he cried. In the cramped, rocking ambulance one attendant knelt and pressed fingers to Nori's throat, trying to stop her bleeding. There was blood all over his hand. The second said, "Breathe, breathe, will you?" He'd wedged himself upright between the stretcher and a cushioned bench. He pumped a black leather bag with both hands, almost dislodging the tube which connected it to her throat. The pumping sounded unworldly, like a diver exhaling into a mask.

Seat-belted into the rear of the bench, by the foot of the stretcher, Currie struggled to control his panic. The paramedics would put him out if he got in their way. Suspended saline bottles shook by the ceiling, as did intravenous lines running into her arms. Her fingers curled above the bloodied sheet. She was pale, much too pale.

Watch her nostrils. They expanded and contracted and proved she lived.

"Probable spinal injury," the pumping attendant said. He talked with Georgetown Hospital through a microphone clamped to his head. "Severe respiratory distress."

Clothing cut away and hanging, Nori lay unconscious on a metal spine board on the stretcher, head strapped rigid between bags of sand. Additional straps crisscrossed her body, fastening it in place. It was crucial to keep her from moving.

A loose sheet covered her torso but her legs were encased in black medical trousers inflated by a footpump on the floor. The trousers forced her leg blood into her more critical chest cavity. "Maintaining blood pressure," the broadcasting paramedic said.

The siren sounded far off. White light bathed him from overhead banks and fluorescent tubes lining the walls. "Clearing blood." The paramedic exchanged the pump for a long transparent tube he inserted in her mouth. The ambulance filled with a sickening sucking sound, like the last sip of milk shake coming into a straw. Currie watched the clear tube change color and the liquid wash into a plastic jar bracketed in an alcove.

The images spilled back at him. Galvanized by her scream, he had crashed out of the forest to see Nori toppled sideways, the picnic basket overturned. Oranges and Saran-wrapped chicken garlanded her head. A fat man in a white suit stretched toward her, half off the blanket, belly down, feet tangled in the grass. A red blotch spread along the back of his collar. The bunched pants cuffs revealed monogrammed socks. Neither face was visible.

"Oh, Jesus," Currie whispered, moving toward her. Up close her eyes fluttered. She issued a frothy bubbling sound. He turned her head to see the spilling red hole at her throat.

Cars shot across the Roosevelt Bridge, a hundred yards away. They were so high up they might as well have been on Neptune.

"Help!" Currie cried. He pushed his mind past the chaos of emotions. The practical truth was overriding. Any hesitation could kill her. His reasoning took less than five seconds, coming as concrete fragments. She's dying. She can't be. Carry her to the car. Don't move her — it's dangerous. Run for help. There must be people, yes, people, so run and find them.

Currie yanked a linen napkin from the overturned box. Carefully he pressed it around her neck, aware of the bulging eyes of the intruder three feet away. The man had dark skin like a Turk or an Arab. His lips were drawn back in a rictus of death.

"Nori, I'll be back, okay? Right back, I'll be back."

A single blood rivulet ran out from under the napkin.

He ran.

But the forest, which had seemed so delightful minutes before, had changed. The path twisted, narrowed.

It trapped him in green gauntlet which blocked his view. He was too slow. He beat brambles from his path. Where were the park police? Or a phone line, a crummy wire he could follow to a phone. Had all the people in the world been snatched out of existence?

"Someone!" The invisible riverbank lay only fifty feet away, he knew. And across the Potomac, round rising Watergate, filled with people and medical offices. The Kennedy Center beside it. George Washington Hospital a few blocks away.

"Help! Help us! Help me!" It was the most pathetic word in the English language, an admission of failure, an illusion-shattering cry to a world of strangers, a deafening internal shriek fractioned into four letters and hurled into the void.

Currie bolted around a bend and almost crashed into a tourist family, posing parents with arms entwined, pigtailed daughter aiming an instamatic camera. The father's hand jerked free. Alarm twisted all three faces. Currie gasped. "My girl. Shot. She needs help."

He saw shock, concern. "I know first aid," the husband said. "But I never handled a gunshot." He wore a crewcut and a flower print shirt. He spoke with a flat *a* of a Midwesterner. He said, trying to inspire confidence in all of them, including himself, "I'm a pharmacist."

"She's bleeding all over," Currie begged. But when the

man asked, "Who did it?" he could not answer. The pharmacist hesitated, glanced protectively at his family. The wife said, "Go. I'll get Leslie to the hotel."

Currie left them splitting up but Nori was going to need more than a goodhearted pharmacist.

In the labyrinthine forest the trees spilled him out onto another out-of-place surprise, a marble plaza in the woods, a monument, circular, marble, as vast as it was empty, and he was running, footsteps resounding, under a statue of Theodore Roosevelt, one bronze hand high, Roosevelt's averted gaze passing over Currie's head. The fountains were broken. Across a gravel road ringing the plaza, Currie pounded on the ranger office, an outhouse-sized A-frame. No answer. He wanted to tear the place apart. Running again, he reached the far island bank and saw a Park Service patrol car rolling toward him across the footbridge from the parking lot.

"Save her," he cried again in the ambulance. The paramedic pulled the suction tube from her throat. Blood would collect in her mouth but it was time to use the air pump again. Currie unfastened his seat belt and slid toward her on the bench. He touched her fingers. They were cold. He extended his hand under her nostrils. Her breath felt warm and barely perceptible.

"Move back," the pumping attendant snapped. "You're in the way."

The paramedic had to push him out of the way.

"Nori? Nori? Maybe you hear but you can't open your eyes. We're almost at the hospital." The van lurched, throwing the back of his head against the wall. "You'll be fine, okay, everything's going to be okay."

His last view of Roosevelt Island had been the parking lot filled with squad cars, Washington, D.C. blue-and whites, green Park Service Hornets and Virginia State Trooper Chevy sedans, haphazardly parked, a bouquet of spinning lights.

More cars rolled over the footbridge toward the island, followed by police holding carbines like infantry advancing behind tanks.

The van stopped, throwing him forward. The doors opened and a voice said, "Out. Hurry." In the circular emergency room driveway, Currie rushed beside the stretcher into Georgetown Hospital. Past a nurse's station. Past staring patients in a waiting room.

The paramedics hustled Nori through swinging double doors but an orderly blocked Currie. "No admittance."

He pressed his face to the window. Nori dwindled on the other side as more aides joined the rolling procession. Through the mass of moving white frocks, Currie glimpsed one bare foot.

She was gone then. The hospital light gleamed like liquid film running down yellow tile. Orderlies hurried between rooms.

The intercom said, "Dr. Jacobstein, Dr. Jacobstein to the emergency room."

He felt sick.

"Mr. Currie?"

He saw the silver badge first, then the blue Dacron cuff and maroon tie. The cop had white-blond hair and a smooth face like a Nebraska high-school football captain. You knew you were aging when police looked younger. But the voice was surprisingly deep and measured. "My name is Hansen, Detective Ron Hansen. I know this is a bad time. It would be helpful though. Could you answer questions?"

Currie heard the voice from far away. The shock he'd battled off at the island crashed back at him now that Nori was gone. He saw her on the picnic blanket, the spilled chicken lying near her head. He saw the swaying plasma bottles in the ambulance. He wanted to burst past the "No Admittance" doors and find her.

He was amazed to hear himself say, with a calmness he did not feel, "D.C. police? I thought Roosevelt Island was in Virginia?"

"The parking lot's Virginia, the island's D.C.," Hansen said. "Park police handle crimes in national parks but not murder." Currie must have blanched because Hansen added, "Your girl will be okay. I meant the guy."

He even blushed a little when he said it. He added, "There's a private room. We can talk."

A baby kept screaming behind the "No Admittance" doors. In the public waiting room, through which Hansen steered him, rows of patients raised their faces to a television set, its audio drenching the room in metal sound. Nobody seemed interested. Beneath the bland illusory cheerfulness of a quiz show, a moaning teenager pressed his wrist. Two men in worker's overalls flanked a fat woman in a green tent dress. The woman heaved, her eyes were shut. Everyone was equal under the TV.

Currie muttered as they passed the nurse's station, "I walked back slow. Irritated."

"Angry," Hansen said.

"She forgets where she puts things."

"You argued," Hansen said.

Currie realized where the conversation was leading. "No, we didn't argue. I was talking to myself." The private cell-sized room, set off from a hallway, seemed permeated with the unhappy lingering presence of all who had preceded him. Currie looked over cheap wall-to-wall carpeting, cigarette burns on the chairs, a blackboard, a Hecht company fashion catalogue on a glass table. There was a child-sized chair four feet away. "Tell me what happened," Hansen said, huge beside it.

But Currie could not stop looking at the little chair. It brought back memories. He was in a different waiting room. He was twelve. He remembered the cabbage stench, the slum smell that never left its denizens, even in a hospital. A gray-haired doctor looked down at him, weary, blunt. "Your father's done, Tim. I warned him. Keep out of fights."

"Mr. Currie?" Hansen said.

"Sorry."

The intercom said, "Dr. Jacobstein to the emergency room."

Currie snapped, "Why doesn't he get here?"

Hansen's pencil remained poised. Currie added sharply, "And you, the police. No one on that island! Did you even catch anyone yet?!"

He jerked out of the chair. Hansen remained seated, "They were still looking when I got here." Currie drew the back of his hand across his mouth. "Dry," he said. He sat down. He said, "What do you want to know?"

Hansen copied Currie's name and address off his driver's license, then Currie told the story and answered questions. Where did Currie work? And Nori? Were they married? Ah, engaged. How did Currie's ex-wife feel about the arrangement? Any of Nori's old boyfriends around? Had Currie ever seen the dead man before? Never? Was he sure? Had he heard gunshots? How come he'd heard no gunshots when there must have been shooting when Nori screamed?

The intercom paged Dr. Jacobstein.

Concentrate, Currie told himself. He's asking important questions.

Had Currie stopped somewhere to buy food for the picnic? Had he noticed anyone watching him at the grocery? Did he remember the license of the green Triumph in the parking lot? How much time had elapsed between leaving Nori and finding her again?

Currie stood up. "What's going on out there?" He stomped from the room. At the nurse's station a tall nurse signed in a patient. A nurse wearing wire-rimmed glasses seemed dreamy and unoccupied behind a desk. She issued Currie a disinterested smile and explained in a voice filled with bureaucratic complacency that the doctors would surely have informed her of any new developments. Currie asked her to check anyway. Her shrug made him want to slap her. She might have been a thousand miles from a phone and not two feet.

She said, "Just sit. I'll tell you when there's news." The bland smile never left her lips. Knuckles white on the counter, Currie demanded, "Call!"

The nurse seemed to remember she had to look through a pile of papers. Currie growled, "You . . ." and Hansen spoke up from beside him. "I'll ask."

"I can do it, I can do it, okay?"

"Mr. Currie," Hansen said. "You want the information?"

Under the detective's more gentle semiofficial prodding, the nurse sighed and made the call. "She's critical. They're operating." Now that she'd become involved she'd turned compassionate. "Really, they're doing everything they can."

Dizzy, Currie turned back to see a second extended wallet, another silver badge. He didn't even hear the FBI agent's name. Amid the sense of mounting chaos the words ran together. He looked out at the big waiting room and the faces merged. He was seized with a familiar dreaded sense; all the relentless government machinery was creaking, groaning with inefficiency and swinging in his direction. Plus the agent's presence seemed to escalate Nori's danger.

Back in the smaller room his mind cleared a bit while Hansen and the agent conferred. "The dead man was a diplomat," the agent told Currie. "The FBI takes over." Hansen looked pained. McSomething, the agent had said his name was. McCully or McNally. McGregor. He was balding and neatly groomed, he wore a black suit even though it was late summer. Gravel-voiced, he said, "We ID'd him from his passport. He was Libyan, stationed in France."

[26]

"Libyan?"

Currie flashed on the computer room in Tehran, the humming consoles and decoded message swimming up on the screen, the news he could not convince anyone he had received. "TRIPOLI GUARANTEE FUNDS SEIZE COMPOUND."

The agent said, "His name was Tecala. Taher Tecala. You didn't know him?"

Currie shook his head. How many children had been forced to hear bad news in that little plastic chair? *Stop thinking about the chair.* Look somewhere else, the blackboard. But then Currie was imagining doctors diagramming throat wounds on that blackboard, bulletholes. He told himself the blackboard was for kids, not doctors. Kids amused themselves by drawing on the blackboard.

Oh yeah, he thought. Then why wasn't there any chalk for the kids?

Jesus, who cares about the goddamned blackboard?

Vaguely he answered more questions. McSomething tried hard not to repeat inquiries but it was impossible. Currie picked up the fashion catalogue, flipped pages as he talked, threw it back on the glass table. He thought, *God help her.* But there was something about hospitals which robbed prayer of uniqueness. Maybe he sensed other silent pleas surrounding him. Save my child, my wife. Cure my patients. Save me, help me, I'll be good. At least in church you were surrounded by trappings of solace, soft candle glow and soaring architecture. But in this harshly lit room, staring at the tiny chair and listening to screaming infants outside, entombed by floor upon floor of doctors and dialysis machines and screens which changed heartbeats into blue pumping graphs, Currie felt a chorus of rising supplications as if they constituted the shouting of a desperate mob in which he was a single, ineffectual voice.

He said, "I don't want to talk anymore, not now. Let me sit, get out of this room. Call her parents. Christ, did anyone call her parents?"

McSomething said, "They've been called."

"Dr. Weber to the emergency room," said the intercom. Currie wondered if Jacobstein had ever shown up.

He turned down the offers for coffee or food. He found a pay phone by the nurse's station in the larger waiting room. Nobody answered at Nori's parents' house, or the delicatessen in Westchester. The Abramoffs were probably on their way to the airport.

"Libya," said a TV voice in the waiting room. Currie's head jerked toward the suspended screen. All around him, people who moments before had been lost in their private world swung to look.

The announcer's voice said, "Speaking today via Radio Tripoli, Colonel Qaddafi announced a new wave of reprisals against his enemies."

The frozen full-face photograph pictured the Colonel in a swarthy lockjawed pose of belligerance. The peaked military cap was tilted in challenge. The eyes flashed. Currie heard a harsh wave of foreign rhetoric and watched the translation roll under the gold-starred collar. "In the name of patriotic service to man, we will bring justice to the enemies of the state, no matter where they may be, even Washington."

Qaddafi. The name of the Bedouin Warrior exploded like a bomb in the little room. Not a single person present was not paying attention to the famous, the taut, the oddly beautiful face. The name leaped out at them daily in black headlines. In fact and in rumor. He was an assassin, a tyrant. He had tried to kill the President. They gathered around televisions to learn about him at night. His visage lined book covers. His name was scrawled on street statues and shouted in the incessant student parades which stopped traffic in the city.

Statesmen sought his friendship, corporations, governments and usurpers his largesse. Psychiatrists studied him. Reporters argued how to spell his name. With a *K*. With a *Q*. Was he "Brother Colonel" or just "Colonel"? Thrust into power by a colossal rush of oil, which existed in oceans under his desert land, fixed in power by dollars and yen and marks and francs, it was said he symbolized the new ungovernable forces, titanic global reversal and realignment. It was said he represented uncontrollable intruding force and ruin which spread daily, in the rise of the southern part of the globe and its inevitable collision with the north. He was the most terrible ubiquitous demon of the emerging nations. He was power devoid of moral strength. His whim could crash stock markets and close factories ten thousand miles away, it could fund armed bands which stalked the world's airports or it could kill a single innocent person on an island in Washington, D.C.

So they watched the face, uneasy or fascinated or repelled, feeling, in some small subconscious point of their being, their culture, their freedom, their wealth and progress and self-conception, their greatness, their very past somehow threatened. They stared at the face, at the Colonel frozen and suspended. For the moment it was enough to make them forget their infirmities.

Now the face diminished in size until Currie saw it contained in a smaller screen in a television studio. He recognized the prominent announcer. The man had befriended his celebrity-conscious wife, Anna, after Iran in order to interview Currie, a task he had never achieved. But he had invited them to visit the White House Press Corps, where he worked at the time. Anna had accepted. Currie's primary recollection of the day was watching the allegedly influential reporters herded like a giggling third-grade class toward the Oval Office for a presidential picture-taking session while one famous correspondent played "Hail to the Chief" on a musical wristwatch.

The announcer said, "State Department authorities speculate Qaddafi's words signify a new wave of killings against his opponents overseas.

"In a lighter note we turn to an eighty-year-old jogger who ran the marine marathon backwards."

"Bullshit," muttered a man in a wheelchair.

Currie had heard nothing about Nori, which meant reporters had not yet learned her name or the identity of the dead Libyan. They would descend upon the hospital when they did. In fact they were probably outside already.

A new wave of reprisals, the announcer had said.

For Currie, the Colonel's face seemed to linger, to break out of the television and hang in the air.

The FBI man was growing restless by the exit. He would approach momentarily with more questions.

He realized the man had positioned himself to prevent Currie from leaving. *I'm a suspect.* Currie suppressed the urge to laugh wildly.

In Currie's vision he walked on a Virginia beach with Nori, on an island called Assateague. Wild ponies grazed in weaving grass beyond the dunes. They had gone here on their first weekend trip, an autumn jaunt two hours from Washington, a country inn with a common hallway bath and a delicious sense of sin when they brought champagne and ice into the tub.

Undressed, she had a taut body, almost muscular, with thin shoulders and a gingery smell. She'd looked copper and ghostly with the steam rising between them, coalescing into drops which ran down her breasts.

Banging on the door. Are there two people in there?

He remembered the rising sun breaking through the bay

windows. In the gigantic featherbed, the shadows moved on her rounded back each time the seabreeze ruffled the curtains. He remembered the bacon odor from downstairs. Sex memories of that morning still made him smell peppered bacon.

At dawn on the Virginia coast, they'd watched porpoises in the sea.

Eyes closed in the waiting room, Currie conjured this most pastoral vision and built it piece by piece. He saw the dockside restaurant where they'd sat, feet on the wooden railing, for hours. He remembered the stroll on the dunes, the small out-of-proportion ponies they'd startled by walking into the scrub brush beyond the beach. Six or seven black and browns, stump footed and small rumped, running almost sideways into a piny marsh.

He remembered driving the jeep along the shoreline, watching seabirds wheel.

He was relaxed now, smiling, eyes closed. He felt her heady undeniable life in him, eclipsing his worry, building, steady, a robust joy, a joining, an umbilical life. He sent it out from him, like plasma, weaving it, with his mind's eye, past the waiting patients and the watching police, past the nurse's station. It was more than a feeling, it was a tangible link, a fibrous dancing capillary of love, an artery twisting and extending out from him, seeking her, dancing through the hallway past the "No Admittance" door, like blood for her, strength and sustenance, probing the long corridor rooms, his outpouring, finding her, touching her on the table where she lay, under eyes and masks. He relished her heartbeat. He diffused his feeling and sent it across her body, up her neck past her flat belly, her rounded knees. He felt it between the strands of her hair. He felt himself awakening Nori to his presence. It was a religious certainty, the feeling. To hell with the cinderblock walls and signs and nurses.

He was with her now and he felt, for that bright instant,

that fraction of all remembered time, that she knew he was there, that he could hear her think if he concentrated, could experience her feelings, feel the room. That they could even communicate in dream while the doctors worked on her.

It was true, it was true he felt it.

Then he felt the terrible constriction in his chest. The link was gone.

The two policemen across the room saw Currie's mouth open. No sound came out. He looked like a man screaming underwater.

CHAPTER
4

Hours after Tim Currie left Georgetown Hospital, eight thousand miles away in Libya's Fezzan desert, a military helicopter dipped and descended into a sandstone canyon.

Beside the pilot, the man in the white suit leaned back and gazed with professional proprietary interest at the multitudinous activity below.

Until now he had seen no life in over an hour, not even a thorn tree or Bedouin train, only a wavelike monotony of dead volcanic escarpments. But halved by dawn into shadow and dun-colored rubble, the long parched riverbed crawled with tanks, gigantic insects rumbling in threes. Spewing sulfur clouds, they never crossed, never even touched black lines painted across the desert, forming well-ordered corridors for training. The tanks wheeled speedily in perfect formation.

Cliffs loomed on either side. Traversing soldiers dotted the rock.

Eye level fifty yards to starboard, a black-bored antiaircraft gun swiveled, tracking the copter. The installation was set into a blasted area of sandstone.

The man in the white suit was Arab, forty, lean and hard looking in an elegant, well-groomed way. Beneath a bushy brown Afro and silver aviator lenses, his face was impassive with a hint of brutality in the corded jaw. His mouth was thin, downturned but handsome. What appeared to be vertical scars on his cheeks became furrows close up. A smile would have a long way to go to reach the surface of his face. It was a face schooled in serious consequences.

Two other passengers, bulky and aggressive-looking bodyguards, sat behind and neither conversed or relaxed. They seemed careful not to disturb the mood of the man in the white suit, who remained expressionless when the pilot gasped. They had broken from the narrow valley into a vast bowl-shaped depression, bounded by inverted claw-shaped cliffs which dropped into the distance and rose, undulating in the heat, offering between their copper contoured flanks row after row of immobile tanks, a hundred times as many tanks as they'd seen already. Turrets pointed northeast, toward the heart of the Mideast; there were olive-colored tanks and sand-hued tanks, Libyan bars or Soviet stars on their armor. There were rows of halftracks and field artillery. Missile launchers. Jeeps.

The brown tent city beyond, coming up fast on the west, must house thousands of troops, but there was no way so few men could operate this much equipment. It was enough for ten armies, Armageddon in a crack in the earth, a shimmering white haze of somnambulent readied steel.

The man in the white suit saw the other three helicopters already landed. On a small plateau sixty yards from the gaudiest blue tent, an honor guard lined a black landing area. Descending, the rotors threw sand on the immobile troops.

"Taher Tecala is killed," said the man in flowing robes ten minutes later. Under leaning poles and a color photograph of Colonel Muammar Qaddafi, the four arrivals dined cross-legged in the tent.

The man in the white suit occupied the traditional seat of honor facing east, over the heads of the three men opposite, through the open flap of the tent and toward the khaki stationary backs of the guards, thirty paces away.

The two bodyguards stood off to the side, hands crossed before them, unmoving. There was the droning of a small electric generator outside and the soft hum of an air-conditioning unit. It was cool in the tent.

On blue and white Persian carpets, the men scooped steamy minted lamb from wooden bowls. They munched figs and peeled oranges. Their anxiety was reflected in a tendency to avoid the direct gaze of the man in the white suit.

"He phoned the Syrian in Washington," said the man in flowing robes. "Was told to leave the stolen paper on an island, in a box. We notified a radio station after we killed him."

Hamid Ali, the speaker, pushed back a long sleeve and reached for a fig. He headed the Popular Front for Palestinian Resistance (PFPR), a client group of Colonel Qaddafi's which carried out reprisal murders against anti-Qaddafi Libyans abroad. In return, the PFPR received funding for its publicly avowed purpose, the blowing up of Jewish-owned restaurants in France.

Ali was short, with a chubby baby's face. He said, "Our wording: 'We the Arab brothers claim responsibility for the execution of Taher Tecala for treason against the popular struggle. Tecala sold information to enemies.' " He swallowed noisily. " 'Death to traitors. Death to Satan America.' " He looked at the man in sunglasses, "More or less, that was it."

To Ali's right sat a slug-colored black-suited Westerner with a round head and tiny crowded features. He was a noisy eater who devoured his food with single-minded intensity. Victor Malenkov, highest-ranking Russian arms dealer in the Mideast, had announced the arrival of two antiaircraft missile shipments. The new weapon had never before been allowed outside the Soviet Union.

Next, iron gray and fifty, base commander Selim Muktar spoke little and watched the man in the white suit, who addressed Hamid Ali. "The girl killed, she was meeting Tecala?"

Hamid Ali shoveled lamb into his mouth. "She was a picnicker, nothing more."

[35]

"You mentioned her in your announcement?"

Hamid Ali reached for a goblet of orange juice. "Why should I?"

The man in the white suit had a coppery atonic voice. His face was bland between the sunglasses and comfortless smile. "Brother Colonel is grateful for every loyal service." In a state where authority descends in an uninterrupted vertical flow, Jamal al-Hawaz, chief of the dreaded secret police, spokesman, agent and confidant of Colonel Qaddafi, comprised the second most powerful entity. He rose and the others followed. The Russian experienced difficulty unfolding his legs.

They faced the photograph of Colonel Qaddafi.

Jamal announced, "Gentlemen, our waiting will end in two months." From outside, muffled by distance, came the thud of mortar explosions. Jamal's words heightened the energy in the tent, palpable as a parting of lips or intake of breath. The Russian nodded, once. The major set his lips and Hamid Ali grinned.

Qaddafi's photograph blazed into the distance.

Each of them had met the Colonel, yet isolated under the technically perfect two-dimensional immortality of a photo, and surrounded by mortar whumps and the clanking of tanks, the ferocious unleashed energy of their own defiant progress, personal memory vanished and the picture seemed larger, silencing them with mythical pervasiveness until Jamal toasted it with his goblet.

"To great changes in the Mideast," he said. "To October thirteenth. Israel, Iran and Saudi Arabia."

They drank and Jamal said, "Your readiness is only one small aspect of preparation. Hamid Ali, of course you recovered the paper Tecala stole."

For the first time Ali seemed unsure.

"By now, almost certainly."

Jamal allowed himself a laugh. "Almost? You have the paper, don't you?"

"We must. I'm *sure* we have it."

Jamal frowned. "Tell me plainly. Where is the paper Tecala stole?"

Hamid Ali waved a deprecating hand, conjuring. "Picture it," he said. "Tecala flees through a swamp. He's placed the stolen information in a box, this I already told you. But as he runs he flings the box away. My man must choose, Tecala or the box."

Jamal had stopped smiling. His feet remained motionless but he swayed slightly, giving the impression that under the sunglasses he had shut his eyes.

Quite softly, Jamal said, "The paper is missing?"

A pair of Hamid Alis were reflected in the mirrors, gesturing too quickly. "The box was gone when my man returned for it," he was saying, "but Tecala was more important than the paper. We found him, we'll find the box. It has to be in the swamp. Or maybe someone picked it up before the police arrived."

In gruff, slurred Arabic the Russian predicted, "The police found the box." An aspiring overseer, he loved to collect evidence to justify his country's disgust.

Ali said, "Jamal, listen to me. Even if the Americans found the paper — they didn't, but even if they did — they won't understand it without Tecala to explain it." Despite the air-conditioning, his palms glistened. "Don't give them so much credit."

The two men stood a foot apart. They were of equal height but Jamal was leaner.

The air-conditioning unit clacked, whined and resumed humming.

Pinching his frames between thumb and forefinger, Jamal removed his sunglasses. Perspiration broke out on Hamid

Ali's forehead. Jamal's eyes were creamy milky blue, utterly alien in the coffee-colored face, looking as if they'd been inserted into Jamal's sockets after birth. Glowing disembodied orbs impaled Hamid Ali.

Jamal remarked, "We're not discussing your ineptitude in losing the box but your lying about it."

"Lying!?"

Jamal looked away. Instantly Hamid Ali said, "I didn't want to worry you." He stepped closer, the fat bunching in his face. "I was going to tell you. After we found the box." Nobody said anything. Ali said, "We know who has it. The girl's boyfriend. He has to, his name was all over the radio."

The major had turned away and, hands behind his back, gazed out of the tentflap. The Russian remonstrated, "He *has to* have it? If he found it, he gave it to the police."

The desert wind moaned, the poles creaked.

Jamal leaned closer to Hamid Ali, the world reducing itself to those horrible blue holes.

He donned the glasses again.

"Find the boyfriend," he said.

"Yes, yes, Jamal."

"And the truth about the box. Whatever it is."

"I already told my man, my best man."

Growing thunder cracked overhead. Through the open flap of the tent, MiG and Tupolov fighters slashed the sky white.

Jamal stepped into the broiling sun. The earth was vast with shimmering armaments.

"I'll see the tank exercises now," he said. "Ali, find the American and this is what you will do to him. . . ."

CHAPTER

5

CURRIE swung the jeep off MacArthur Boulevard and onto his rutted dirt driveway. He was immediately surrounded by thick vines which blocked his view of road, houses or neighbors. It was eight o'clock at night. The jeep's bouncing headlights reflected off a slick green wall. He jerked, thinking he saw a face in the foliage, but it was gone when he looked again and he decided he had been mistaken.

A series of replaying images haunted him, the little blood spots on the curb outside the hospital, Nori's folded dress on a table inside. The policeman's pen jiggling when he wrote.

Currie had answered more questions until Nori's parents arrived. He'd broken the news of her death to them and accompanied them to view the body. He'd driven them to the Mayflower Hotel.

His memory of the ride was of an almost catatonic silence. Mrs. Abramoff had broken down in the hotel room, sobbing uncontrollably. Mr. Abramoff had sat in a stupor, staring at his hands.

Throughout it all reporters had dogged them, in the hotel lobby and corridors, shouting questions, grabbing sleeves.

The windows were open. Cool night air washed his face. There was the sense that mighty Washington, only minutes away, had been swallowed by the evening. The isolation had always attracted him to his home. He had no idea how he had gotten the jeep here. Disembodied hands guided the steering wheel. In the rearview mirror, a stranger's face stared back at him, heavy with bone-crushing weariness.

The dirt track spilled him onto a grassy spruce-dotted plateau dominated by the 120-year-old home which Anna had lovingly named "Stonehaven" and which Nori, depending on which theatrical mood seized her at the moment, referred to as "Tara" or "Vampire House." "Ve are all al-one," she would hiss in Vampire House. "Evile waits in ze attic."

Now there would be no more Vampire House. There would be no more walks with Nori through the surrounding woods, no late-night forays to the Kennedy Center, in the jeep, for old movies. None of it, no more.

He leaned against the jeep, listening to his own breathing. Two stories up, Stonehaven stood against the bruised night, crowned by a double granite chimney and the crescent moon which hooked open like a descending mouth.

He had known the instant he saw this house that he would live here. That had been ten years ago, when a property this size, even close to the city, had been cheap enough for a young engineer. Stonehaven was more of a shell than a home then. No one had lived there for years. But Currie had seen the possibilities and Anna, initially uncomfortable with the lack of close neighbors but intrigued with the age and acreage, had agreed to buy.

Currie had done much of the renovation himself.

The bulb over the back door must have burned out. It should have come on automatically at dusk, triggered by a solar energy cell he'd installed. But the sky was full of stars and the moon provided light. He stepped inside the kitchen. Often he came home to a dark house but Nori would be waiting. She would have parked her Toyota across Mac-Arthur Boulevard at the bottom of the hill, would have hiked up the driveway to make and hide dinner where he would not smell it.

She might not come out right away, either. She might be upstairs in the bed or bathtub, might be standing just beyond the kitchen in the sunken living room. He felt her in all these places and a dull ache began in his stomach.

He sat at the pine table with the lights off, boot heels splayed. The kitchen smelled of varnish and oak. A conical wok looked like a Chinaman rising from the gas stove. Banks of hanging ferns, potted touches of feminine presence, hung beside a cut-glass window.

Currie looked into the liquor cabinet. The bottle necks were slick glass minarets, the Cutty Sark label the same yellow color of the child-sized chair in the hospital.

Whiskey, boy! Bring me that wet one!

It was his father's voice; he'd heard it at the hospital that afternoon.

"Insults," his father sneered. Currie was suddenly in a different kitchen, crammed into his obligatory tableside seat. A bare bulb kitchen, scrubbed faded clean. Suspenders on thighs, haunches on sink, Currie's father sucked whiskey from a glass.

"Let me tell you about the Cadillac this morning. In front of me in traffic. Chauffeur driven. I could see the Swell reading. People try to step all over you all the time."

His father's biceps expanded, huge against the sleeveless undershirt. The shoulders and neck were covered with black hair, animal hair.

"Traffic's hardly moving but the chauffeur doesn't care. He takes his time, laughing because he's slowing me down. He gets a kick out of keeping guys from their work."

The tenement filled his pauses with crying babies, Spanish arguments. Currie's mother, sitting in an adjacent chair, spoke timidly. "I'm sure he meant no harm."

"Don't argue with me! I dragged the guy from the limo. You should have seen his face, ha. He never thought a guy would touch him."

Variations: "I say to the guy, *What do you mean, the Yankees stink!*"

Or, "Asshole clerk pretends he doesn't see me. He sees me all right!"

And then the worst part, the "boxing" lesson, his father swaying toward him, fists tucked against chest, rotating elbows hard fighter's points. "Hit me, kid. Try to hit me. How come you never come home from school cut up like other kids? Afraid? You disgust me; kids are supposed to fight. Don't fight and people knock your head off. Belt your old man."

Knocking brought Currie back to the present. Steady. Demanding. Turning, he saw a silhouette against the curtained kitchen door window. A tall form. A man stood outside.

Currie had heard no car drive up.

Let me in, a reporter had pleaded outside the Abramoffs' hotel room today. *One question or I'll lose my job!*

Currie figured another reporter was outside and he ignored him.

The knocking stopped. Footsteps descended the back porch. Currie flashed back to the other kitchen. "No, I don't fight," he told his father. "I'm the biggest kid in class, nobody wants to fight me. I'm strong. I box. You fight all the time and look where it gets you."

Currie poured scotch and left the kitchen, descending carpeted steps to follow a slowly diminishing cone of moonlight into the living room. His father had died twenty-three years ago. He did not often think about that other life.

A second shaft of light knifed down from above. The living room was a two-story vestibule he had created by removing the ceiling and ringing the upper walls with picture windows. The bedroom loft above was reachable by a circular freestanding staircase.

On a shelf, the red stereo clock blinked 8:30. Thick pillows littered the wall-to-wall. In front of a dark TV, Currie downed the scotch between the arms of the "stressless" chair. It was advertised to relieve tension when it leaned all the way back.

He heard a skittering sound two stories up. Sometimes raccoons ran across the roof at night.

"*In layman's terms, she drowned.*" Now he heard Nori's doctor's voice. Blue frocked and thirtyish, the doctor wore her prematurely gray hair in a bun. They stood in the little waiting room. "The bullet severed her windpipe. Blood poured into her lungs."

He pulled on the television to stop the voice. The picture swam into focus, Currie recognzed the black-haired reporter from his return from Iran. Now the man stood in the Roosevelt Island parking lot, police cars at his back. It was night. Across the footbridge, bobbing flashlight beams moved in the trees.

". . . today's twin deaths mark the third time terrorists have struck inside the city of Washington in recent years," the reporter said. The scene switched to Sheraton Circle, an embassy area along Massachusetts Avenue. It was daylight on TV. Cars whizzed past. Uniformed Executive Protection Servicemen, assigned to protect embassies, watched from in front of a mansion's iron picket fence.

The reporter said, "Orlando Letelier was murdered here. A former information minister for the ousted government of Chilean President Salvadore Allende, Letelier was exiled in Washington where he lobbied against Chile's military government until his death. Nine years ago last week, he drove into this circle with two co-workers at the Institute for Policy Studies: Michael Moffitt, a young economist, and his twenty-five-year-old wife, Ronni.

"The explosion cut Letelier in half and killed Ronni Moffitt."

The phone rang in the kitchen.

"The FBI eventually found that Chilean secret police agents had planted a bomb under Letelier's car. Two of the three murderers were convicted but freed on a legal technicality. They jumped bail while awaiting retrial. They live in the Caribbean where the United States cannot extradite them. The third man served a brief prison sentence and was freed."

The phone kept ringing but the reporter seemed to be speaking directly to Currie. Now the man stood before a small ranch house on a suburban street. He said, "A year later, during the overthrow of the Shah of Iran, a militant Iranian gunman murdered Iranian ambassadorial aide Ali Akbar Tabatabai on the front steps of this house. The killer disguised himself as a mailman and shot Tabatabai when Tabatabai answered the door. The killer has never been apprehended."

Currie was sweating.

"So the horror of today's tragedy," said the announcer, magically transported back to Roosevelt Island and speaking with theatrically concerned and professionally detached affectation, "goes far beyond the brutal murders of Taher Tecala and Nori Abramoff. Tonight we must ask ourselves, Is terrorism an accepted part of life in Washington? Something we expect and try to forget? More important, would today's attack even have occurred if the perpetrators of the other three murders had been punished?"

The phone stopped ringing. The reporter said, "Today's lone survivor, Tim Currie, a former hostage in Iran, must be asking himself these questions. If a man can be victimized twice by incidents we prefer to think of as freak accidents, just how freakish can those 'accidents' be?" The reporter paused to look boyishly profound. "Back to you, Ted."

The denial exploded in Currie, blanketing the voices, conjuring Nori. In the kitchen. Anywhere in this house which was to be hers. The cellar. The den. His head pounded with the urge to call out to her, so sure he was that her light joking voice would reply from the shadows.

Then he became aware of another sound over the announcer's babble, a flat rhythmic tapping in the kitchen. *Foot-*

steps. A shadow grew toward him in the doorway. *Someone was in the house.*

Dazed, Currie stood full face to the doorway. He filled with impossible crazy joy. It's Nori.

The light went on in the kitchen. He saw who it was.

From the sunken living room Currie looked up at her. She wore a black cotton dress with a high collar, long silk sleeves, a single gold bracelet. She had always shown a tan well. When she moved to the top step, he saw that her walk, tentative and doelike when he first met her in high school, brash and hungry after Iran, had grown unhurried, worldly, and she exhibited the sensual dry slimness of a woman in her early thirties. Currie said, "Anna."

"I knew you'd be sitting here," she said. She'd extended her black pumps over the top stair like a diver testing a board. Shadow obscured her features. Her voice was husky, her shoulders narrow, as were her hips. Tall and leggy, she still wore her blond ponytail like a girl.

She said softly, "I'm sorry."

Against a halo of light she pinched a key between thumb and forefinger. "I knocked," she said. "You never changed the lock."

Currie felt ill. "Nori did that sometimes," he said. "Walk out of the dark."

She moved face into the light. She'd never worn much makeup and she had a tanned, healthy face, like a cheer-leader. All angles. "Have you eaten anything?"

"No."

"Want me to leave?"

"No, just sit a minute."

There was concern in her voice, nothing else. She had sent a card when she joined the Georgetown public relations firm. Otherwise they had not spoken in over two years.

On the television, Arab crowds danced in a wild street scene. Honking horns. Cheers and fists. Another announcer's voice said, "After the massacre of nine Israeli athletes at the Munich Olympics, Black September terrorists were received like heroes in Tripoli."

Currie said, "A year ago I went to Letelier/Moffitt night at Catholic University. A commemoration of the deaths. Watchers International sponsors it annually."

Elbows on knees, cheeks on palms, she sat on the top step, out of the room. Her familiar posture, rooted in his memory, transformed her back into his old high-school friend.

He said, "People give speeches there. This year two were mothers, Argentineans. The military had come at night, arrested their sons. They didn't know if their sons were alive. They were huddled by the podium, small women." He rubbed his hands. "The other speakers were politicians. A senator. A congressman. These women looked like . . . like . . ." Currie had to stop. "Like they'd been cooking dinner, like they'd been snatched from behind a stove ten thousand miles away, transported to a room filled with strangers. They couldn't speak English. They didn't seem to understand what they were doing there. You could see them thinking, 'I don't know who these people are, but maybe this time someone can help my son.'

"Nori's mother looked like that today. Worse. You don't think mothers here are supposed to look like that."

Bright tears ran down Anna's cheeks.

He said, "There was a radio talk show in the jeep tonight. A State Department spokesman kept calling Nori 'the victim.' He called her 'Ms. Abramoff' and he called her 'the girl.' He said a congressman had proposed paying a kind of victims payment to her parents. How much money? A million? Ten million? Money," he said. "Money."

"Oh God," Anna said. "I don't know what to say."

"They wanted to pay after Iran, too."

"You wouldn't take it."

Currie looked at the blank television screen. "Did you see

those Libyan crowds dancing after the Israelis were killed? People were dead and they were dancing."

"Tim, you did what you could."

He wasn't listening. "All the way from Paris," he said. "Qaddafi's men just walked through customs, strolled in. Isn't there a list? People to keep out when they show their passports?"

She shrugged helplessly. "Maybe there's a list."

"Then how did they get in!"

She went into the kitchen. He heard cabinets opening, glass clinking.

The fireplace was dark under one of Anna's paintings, a Maine coast landscape. It was very good. The shelves were filled with electronics books and Nori's Book-of-the-Month Club hardbacks. Beside them, Currie looked over rectangular, indistinct forms of photographs. His favorite showed him and Nori outside an antique barn in Maryland.

Nori's voice said, "Oh, love." Legs folded, they sat on the bed upstairs, running fingertips along each other's thighs, cool sensation.

He looked up to see Anna offering the sandwich on a plate. She had ventured all the way into the room for the first time. "Tuna," she said. "You'll want this later."

Currie shouted, "Why! Jesus! Tell me why!" He waved his hands wildly. "They'll just go back to Paris, get on a plane. Fly away where we can't reach them! Like the people on the news, the ones who killed Moffitt!"

"Tim . . ."

"And Qaddafi just sits there, no one can touch him . . . Oh shit."

Anna knelt by the chair. She'd put potato chips on the plate beside the sandwich. And little pickle wedges. She said, "They won't get away. The FBI . . ."

"No one did anything after Iran."

"That's not the same."

"No one did anything. I didn't do anything."

In a little voice, she said, "Oh, that's it."

He stood abruptly, a razor glitter in his eyes. "Not this time," he ranted. "I'm not just going to sit here! Kill him! I want to kill him!"

His face was horribly contorted. She backed away in fright but her voice was strong. "You sound like your friend Zarek. You're not being rational. Come back."

Currie's harsh breathing filled the room.

Anna said, "You stopped the bleeding. Called the ambulance." It was a singsong. "Aren't you tired? You should sleep."

She left the plate on the rug. Gently, she drew him by his forearm toward the circular staircase, as if a change in scenery would cure him. She said, "If you don't want to be alone, I can sleep down here."

"No, I'm okay. Thanks for coming."

She hesitated before leaving. It was warm outside, she'd brought no sweater. "I wrote my numbers on a paper. Home and office." *Office* sounded funny. She'd worked with retarded kids when they'd first come to Washington. She'd said "hospital" then, not "office." "Office" completed the transition into the present and made her a stranger he had not seen in two years. She said, "Call any time. The middle of the night if you need me."

When she opened the door, a click sounded out in the darkness. A searchlight went on twenty feet away, blinding them. "CBS, Tim! Cary Feldman from CBS! That's Anna Currie, isn't it?"

She closed the door on them. "I'll take care of it," she told Currie. *I'll take care of it* had been her reaction to reporters after Iran, when she wanted to issue statements and answer questions. For a moment his rage shifted to Anna. She'd shown up for publicity. But then she said, "The cops are down on MacArthur Boulevard. I'll send them up, they'll chase the reporters away." She was the crisp professional, in control.

Anna touched the back of his hand. "I'm not your wife but I'm still your friend. If you need something, call. Don't go back into the hole."

She left. Go to hell, he thought. Don't tell me what to do.

He heard her arguing outside, then more voices, angry. He heard motors starting up. He heard two vehicles drive away.

The starkly lit kitchen seemed devoid of life. He turned out the light.

Currie felt the huge desire to sleep.

He trudged up the staircase, over the little pit of comfort below, the stressless chair and plush pillows, the new stereo, the thick pile, the pale untouched sandwich. At the top he looked out the picture window over a summer canopy. Mist oozed from the treetops and hung suspended in a knife-edged layer. Above that the sky was blue-black. He opened a wooden gate to reach the bedroom. The railing prevented a fall in the middle of the night.

He stood by the bedroom dresser, emptying his pockets, when he pulled out the silver cigarette box.

A barb moved into his belly. He held the box close and stared at it. He remembered the box glinting on the black earth of the island. He would never forget Nori's scream.

In flowing robes, tiny silver figures paraded on the box, trailing livestock. A Mideast scene.

Taher Tecala sold information to the Americans, the killers had announced on the radio.

Currie's heart pounded in his ears. Under a nightlight, he opened the case. He turned the contents onto his palm.

A box of cigarettes fell out and a folded piece of paper.

His heart grew thunderous.

Unfolding the paper, he saw a series of figures:

Lamplight sculpted the tiny figurines. Currie worked with codes for a living, had been decoding messages in Iran before the takeover, and was holding a cipher, he was certain of it. Taher Tecala had carried this paper onto Roosevelt Island, had lost it or thrown it away while being chased. Taher Tecala sold information to the Americans and he had tried to sell this.

The paper seemed alive, filled with malevolence. He might as well be holding the gun with which she had been murdered. Killed because of a paper, an eight-and-a-half-inch sheet, a series of childish drawings, and Nori bled onto a picnic blanket. Nori lay topped by a sheet. He would see her one last time in a box, bigger than a cigarette box, a life-size box for her decomposition. Because of this paper.

He ripped the paper to shreds.

With a sideways swipe of his hand he knocked the cigarette box off the nighttable. It bounced off the wall onto the plush carpet.

It tipped open, an invitation.

Jagged confetti littered the rug.

There was nothing else to tear, to break. He sat on the bed, shaking. His fists gripped the sheets.

At length his features composed themselves, his posture grew rigid.

Currie got on his hands and knees and gathered up the pieces of paper. *Tape them together.* If the message was so important to the Libyans, maybe it could damage them, identify Nori's killers.

Break the code.

It was something to do, a start.

But it occurred to him as he worked that whoever had murdered to get this box would guess he had found it. The whole city knew he had been on Roosevelt Island this afternoon, the television was broadcasting his address.

A noise on the roof startled him, a heavy dragging sound. He opened the window and looked out.

Ticking began in his ears.

The slate roof rose, empty, except he couldn't see behind the stone chimney. The moon went behind a cloud.

Currie remembered the man's silhouette at the door earlier.

He poured the paper bits he held in his hand into the box and clicked it shut. He could hear himself breathing. There was a baseball bat in a bedroom closet. He had never wished he had a gun in the house until tonight. At the open window he could not see the police outside. Anna had probably ordered them back to the foot of the driveway after the reporters were driven off. She knew how Currie liked his privacy.

Currie swung one leg over the sill and gained his balance on the roof. He thought he was being a little foolhardy, but he didn't want to deal with more police and he was mad. Anyway, the noise was probably an animal.

Even with Adidas on he slipped a little. The moon came out, the gray slate gleamed.

He heard a sound to the right and whirled.

A rustling oak brushed the drainpipe.

Currie laughed in relief and went downstairs. Ten minutes later, shoulders lowered, he was taping the note together at the kitchen table. The jigsaw was finally recognizable after midnight. In a substitution code, he knew, symbols substituted for letters.

But *which* letters?

He wrote *E* above the most commonly used figure and all identical figures too. He tried *A* above another man. He erased his letters and tried a different combination. After a while he lowered his head to rest a moment but did not get up. A breeze ruffled the paper under his head. It did not dislodge it.

In his dream he lay face down on frigid white flatness, arms at his sides. He could not move them. Twin suns rose over the earth, only the suns became eyes and the eyes fixed on Currie. The eyes were in a face, bearded, terrible. It was the face from the television, then the face from the poster in his cell. The face rose higher, filled the sky. The air started to burn.

As he struggled to move, he saw another form, distant and crumpled, dwarfed, as he was, by the immensity. Tendrils of smoke wove off Nori's back. She exploded silently, her embers rising over the desolate flatness. Currie tried to scream but no sound came out. Heat engulfed him.

Sunlight poured through the window when he awoke. He was feverish and drenched with sweat. The paper stuck to his forehead where he had lain on it. It stung when he removed it. He folded it into his breast pocket. It seemed to draw his shirt around him, to constrict him. Currie washed but did not change. He was in too much of a hurry, he knew what he must do. He headed for the jeep, chest burning as in the dream. He could feel the paper next to his heart.

CHAPTER
6

WASHINGTON heat is a special kind of heat. It's swamp heat and river heat and body heat a million times over. It's soft. Wet. Thick. Steamy.

The blond man felt as if someone stuffed a pillow over his face. His suit stuck to his back even at 8 A.M. and he wiped his forehead with the back of his hand. His concentration on MacArthur Boulevard was absolute. The first early commuters were materializing out of the convoluted air, cars floating in the dead heat toward Washington. Currie had to pass this way to reach town. The blond man's instructions were rigid.

Find out if he has the box. Get the paper if you can. After you learned if Tecala explained the paper to him, kill him.

But he had missed Currie at the house last night, had knocked but Currie had not opened the door. Then he had been figuring how to break in when the woman arrived. Reporters. Police.

Qaddafi doesn't want an incident. Make sure nobody finds the body.

Now the blond was terrified because if he missed Currie he would have to tell Jamal in Tripoli, and Jamal would send him into the desert for one of his legendary punishments. Any thought of Jamal filled him with a primal terror, which had been reinforced many times since their first meeting.

He had come to the Libyans from East Germany. The blond, whose name was Lipko, had grown up at the huge state orphanage outside Berlin. Through a combination of savagery against children and a winning manner with adults, he had risen to a position of official privilege during the day and brutal overlord of the sleeping quarters at night. But when he was twelve he had maimed a boy so badly the authorities had forced his name from the victim. Lipko had been driven to a windowless building in East Berlin where a rubber-faced major had asked questions about his hurting children. Lipko's arrogance had turned to jelly. When the major finally inquired, "Do you *like* harming them?" Lipko, unable to stand it any longer, had screamed the truth. "YES!"

But instead of being punished he was driven into the country where, at a different kind of school, he spent four years learning more subtle forms of pain as well as languages, Arab customs, shooting, knife use. By age seventeen he was torturing political prisoners. At nineteen he assassinated a turncoat scientist in Switzerland. Five years later, the major returned. "You will work for our ally Qaddafi. You will be the same as a tin of food or cartridge of ammunition we give him. He will own you. Get in trouble, we won't help. Complete your work successfully and you will come home to glory. I have faith."

Across the street, a woman in curlers took the morning milk into her ranch house.

The blond man had ordered a second car to wait on the Maryland side of Currie's house in case he drove in that direction.

Now he stiffened, squinting at traffic. "It's him," he called to three men in a white Chevrolet at the curb.

If Qaddafi would risk the repercussions of ordering two murders in Washington in as many days, the missing paper must be priceless. The blond man had heard rumors of massive weapons depots in the desert, crazy stories of religious war and the Mideast exploding.

It was unsafe to know too much. Lipko still remembered

his first drive into the desert with Jamal. During Lipko's first week in Tripoli, the secret police chief had taken him to a beautiful oasis in the desert. But unlike other oases this one lacked a well, grazing camels and nomads resting between journeys. The blond man had been puzzled until he saw the ants. They were half the size of his thumb, they came out of huge mounds and they were crawling all over the palm trees. While another East German beat them off the wheels of the jeep, Jamal pointed out a bleaching skeleton half immersed in a spring.

"I belong to the back-to-nature movement," Jamal had said. "Your predecessor was an incompetent man. The ants eat genitals first. I guess genitals are an ant delicacy."

Kill Currie. Hide the body. He could feel the ants eating his skin.

He smoothed down his suit. With his beach boy tan and gray cotton suit the blond looked like an athletic government worker. He opened his wallet and checked his false identification. He had a little deception planned to get Currie into the car.

They swung into traffic behind the jeep. The blond man watched Currie's neck bobbing above the driver's seat. It was thin, like the stem of a vegetable. Despite his fear, when he considered snapping it, Lipko felt a little pleasurable constriction in his throat.

Flanked by stunted museums, Currie fought the jeep down wide Independence Avenue through an endless traffic jam of Nigerian cab drivers, tourists too scared to go to New York and Senate aides who would only drive in the middle lane. He inched past the Kremlin-like edifice of the House Longworth Building and the picture postcard Capitol Dome. They looked two-dimensional. Film props like after Iran. The feelings of unreality were starting again.

"The President expressed sympathy for the survivor Tim

Currie and the Abramoff family," said the radio. Antenna to antenna, the great public outpouring of pity was being served up like a turkey to be picked dry. He'd seen fascination in the half-averted stares of the policemen in his driveway, he saw it now in the openmouthed recognition in a car on his right. Uneasy smiles. The radio said, "In Tripoli Colonel Qaddafi said Tecala was an enemy of the state but stopped short of saying he personally ordered the death. . . ."

Currie kept seeing his fingers come away from Nori's wound, seeing the handkerchief flutter from her neck.

He blinked out at sun-drenched high-school students clowning on lawns. Tour buses disgorged packs of lace-hatted Mennonites.

The jeep stalled when he parked. It better not break down today. Mounting the steps to the Library of Congress he felt the pit open before him. The steps wavered, the edges of his vision blurred.

He fought off vertigo. The paper was in his shirt pocket and the cigarette box against his thigh. Breaking the code would tell him why she'd been murdered.

Nori had loved this library. The ornate massiveness sent her into a mother-daughter act she'd stolen from the *New Yorker*. Mother: Honey do you realize *every single book* ever written is in this building? Daughter: Oh boy, Ma! Even *Pokey Little Puppy?*"

Past marble arches and skylights and under an immense spreading reading room dome, Currie made his way past wooden tables filled with law students, retired readers and Library of Congress bums, resplendent in their rags.

"I'm so sorry about your wife," whispered the librarian rapturously when Currie handed him his call slips. The librarian was a willowy thirty-five-year-old wearing tight jeans and a gold earring. "*I* go to Roosevelt Island sometimes," he sighed. "*I* might have been hurt."

Currie xeroxed two copies of the paper; then his books arrived. *All About Codes* and *Codes and Secret Writing*. If he was going to figure out the message, he would need information for his computer at Rockville Electronics. His code-breaking experience was with the more sophisticated electronic variety and he guessed he might need a little help with the more basic type.

He opened *All About Codes* and flipped a few pages.

He caught his breath.

He was looking at three rows of coded drawings like those he had found last night, except instead of little palm trees he saw stick figure dogs, the legs in different positions.

The book said, "This looks like a simple substitution code where each dog represents a different letter. But it could also be a transposition code where the *position* of each drawing in the group determines meaning. Or the letters may be deceptive even when deciphered. 'A' might mean 'K,' 'K' might mean 'C.' To break this most difficult code, you need a key or guide."

Even the computer would have trouble decoding if he needed a key. But Currie was getting excited. The computer would break a simple substitution code easily and a transposition code with slightly more difficulty. Currie told himself either way he would decipher the meaning.

"The most commonly used English letter is 'E,' " said *Codes and Secret Writing*. " 'T' appears most often at the end of a word. Two-letter words generally turn out to be 'of,' 'to' or 'in.' 'Q' is always followed by 'U.' 'N' is the consonant which most often follows a vowel."

Currie felt a prickling sensation on the back of his neck, his finely tuned sense of being a public figure told him he was being watched. He did not look up. He wasn't going to hide away this time and he was going to have to get used to the feelings.

The Libyans might know I found the box.

Currie glanced around the room. No one was looking.

"The most commonly doubled up letters are 'LL,' 'EE,' 'SS,' 'OO,' 'TT,' 'RR,' 'NN,' 'PP' and 'CC.' Four-letter words often turn out to be 'that.' And more than 50 percent of all English words begin with 'T,' 'A,' 'O,' 'S,' or 'W.' More than half end with 'E,' 'S,' 'D,' and 'T.' "

There was a tap on his shoulder. He spun, covering the paper with his hand.

"I hate to bother you," the librarian whispered. He held the day's *Washington Post* in his hand. Currie recognized himself in the front-page picture. Arm around Nori's mother, he steered her past reporters in the hotel.

"I'm so embarrassed," the librarian said, grinning. "I collect autographs."

Outside the September heat was worse. The sun seemed larger and lower, not higher. It looked as if it might fall and burn everybody up.

The FBI building lay in a seedier section of Washington which had never recovered from the riot burnings of the 1960s. Now that Currie had made his own copy of the note he would give the original to the authorities. He left the jeep in the lot and walked. The streets, packed with sweating shoppers, exploded with noise: workmen's jackhammers, Mack truck airbrakes and honking drivers. Currie passed record stores blaring rock music, cheap underwear and wig shops, nurses' uniform shops, third-rate goods for the three-quarters of Washington reporters never write about unless a congressman gets mugged. *BENT GENITALS* said scrawled graffiti on an alley wall. The punk rock clubs in this neighborhood were Washington-style punk rock clubs. They catered.

For the second time he felt the prickling sensation on his neck. Someone was watching him but he could not spot the person when he looked.

Across from an "Adult Films," the FBI headquarters occupied an entire block. Currie had bailed his father out of plenty of police stations when he was a boy, but the J. Edgar Hoover Building felt nothing like a police station. Police stations featured huge doors on the street to funnel people in. FBI building entrances were hidden. Currie finally found an under-the-building walkway which brought him past a uniformed guard, through an enclosed concrete courtyard and to a smoky glass door. "Can't get upstairs without an escort," an Oriental receptionist told him. "Someone has to come down and get you." Turnstyles blocked access to steel doors which cracked open regularly to emit serious-faced people wearing clip-on identification. Another guard looked on.

Beside Currie on a couch a man wearing a cowboy hat and turquoise bracelets whispered, "Are you an agent? I gotta see an agent. I uncovered a sting operation in New Mexico and they're after me there."

A man dressed in plastic bags stared out at the courtyard and picked at his bare feet.

A suited agent in tortoiseshell glasses harangued a black in sneakers who had exited the steel door alone. "How did you get down here without a pass!"

A voice said, "I'm Asher." Startled, Currie looked up into probing eyes of slate gray in a square, suspicious face. Asher was pale and bullet shaped, small but strong looking in a thick teamsterish way, with big hands and forearms. He seemed older and rougher than the collegiate agents Currie had met, but his blunt neutral manner contained none of the hated and debilitating pity or sympathy. Currie's feelings of relief would not last.

"You'll talk to me from now on," Asher said. "I'm head of the antiterrorist unit." He spoke so matter-of-factly that *antiterrorist* sounded natural here. Like *couch* or *shoe*. Antiterrorist.

[59]

Asher's loose black suit bunched at the cuffs. His black shoes gleamed like a policeman's. Under receding cropped hair, his face showed power but hid inclination. It was a face that absorbed more than it volunteered. And there was something implacable in the dogged scrutiny. Currie felt as if he were looking up from an operating table. Asher had locked onto him to the exclusion of everything else in the room. Currie had the conscious thought that he would not want to be on the wrong end of an Asher investigation. His danger sense was mounting but he did not know why.

"We gridded Roosevelt Island and we're still going over it," Asher said. "Divers. Lab guys in the swamp." They threaded a maze of linoleum hallways, scalpel bright but eerily empty. Currie felt like he was inside a file cabinet. Tumbling down a long gullet. He had seen the midnight *Wizard of Oz* show with Nori last week. At the film's end the mighty wizard's curtain had been yanked back and he had been exposed as a tiny, ineffectual man.

In Asher's one window office, which overlooked a revolving parking carousel, Currie said, "I found this box." Asher's thick brows rose. He had pulled two chairs close and crossed his legs in a deceptive relaxed posture. His eyes never left Currie's face. "On the island," Currie added.

Beside the empty hatrack and olive-drab file cabinets Currie saw a child's homemade pencil holder on the wide, immense desk. He saw a photograph of Asher with a gray woman in a housedress. Two files caught his attention. The yellow one was marked CURRIE. The purple, important-looking one was half hidden. All he saw was SE.

"I forgot about the box until last night," Currie said. "When I was getting ready for bed I pulled it from my pocket. There's a note in it, look at it. Look, it's a code."

He'd made sure to return the paper to the cigarette box so the FBI wouldn't guess he'd made a copy, but Asher frowned at the Scotch tape. Currie said, "I got mad, ripped it up."

Asher ran his finger along the tape. Currie said, "I couldn't stand to touch it."

Asher seemed to accept that. Currie told the rest of the story, leaving out the visit to the Library of Congress. Then Asher said, "One thing I don't understand. Why did you wait until now to bring me the box? Why didn't you call last night?"

Currie had expected this. "I was tired, exhausted. I fell asleep."

"You found the box after your ex-wife left. You ripped up the paper in a rage, taped it together and immediately fell asleep."

"That's right."

"I'm asking because I want to know exactly what happened. Little things can be important."

"It happened just like you said," Currie said.

Asher nodded but his eyes remained fixed on Currie's face. There was a plodding, rhythmic intelligence to his voice. "I tried to phone you this morning," he said. "No one answered."

"Oh that, I don't talk to reporters so I don't like to answer the phone."

When Asher blinked it was like a searchlight going off. "Okay, let's go to the island," Asher said. An hour later, when they were back from Roosevelt Island and Currie had walked Asher through yesterday's events, the agent said, "Let's talk about the note again. You fell asleep right after you taped the paper together, isn't that what you said?"

"Yes."

"Boom. Asleep. Out like a light."

"That's what I said," Currie said, but he was starting to feel uncomfortable.

"I ask because I was thinking. A guy like you, who knows code and works with computers, it would be logical for you to try to figure out the code. Maybe you spent a little time looking at it last night."

"Well, I looked at it," Currie admitted. "Of course I had to look at it."

Asher leaned over the arm of the chair. "Did you try to figure it out?"

"I said I looked at it." Currie felt the Xerox copies bulging in his back pocket. He should have left them in the jeep. He'd had enough dealings with the government to know they'd cry "National Security" and try to take away the paper.

"Break the code?"

"No."

"Call anyone to help you?"

"No."

"Not one single person? Not Anna?"

"I told you," Currie said. The office was hotter than the last time he had been here. "I found the paper after Anna left."

"That's right," Asher said. I forgot. You found it *after* she left." He was quiet a moment. "Make a copy for yourself?" he suggested.

Currie said stiffly, "I didn't make a copy."

Asher withdrew back into his chair. He stood and walked to the window. He yawned, but rather than lessening the tension this increased it, as if he had exhaled into an oversized balloon.

The revolving parking garage was moving outside, the carousel of cars seemed to be emerging from Asher's forehead.

"Craziest thing I ever saw," Asher said, indicating the carousel. Currie didn't trust the small talk. Asher seemed incapable of small talk, it was like Nixon trying to make a joke. Asher said, "Hungry? There's a cafeteria downstairs." Currie didn't answer. Asher massaged his right shoulder with his big hand. "Work nights around here and the food places all close around midnight. After a while cafeteria food looks good. Night shifts, you never get to see the family. How come you lied to me? You said you were home when I called this morning, but the police at your house told me you'd left."

Currie felt like someone had punched him in the stomach. He told himself it was ridiculous to feel guilty over making a copy of the paper.

Arms akimbo, Asher leaned against the sill. For a thick man he moved with surprising lightness. He'd probably been an athlete in high school. "Let's see," he said. "I called you about eight. You came in at ten thirty." The gray eyes bored into Currie. "Lost in traffic?"

Currie snapped, "Look, why don't you do something useful instead of bothering me. What difference does it make what time I came here? I brought you the paper, didn't I? Who are you investigating anyway?" He imitated Asher in a nasal, affected voice. "Did you get *mad* when you found the paper? Did you fall asleep immediately after you found the paper?"

Unaffected, Asher said, "We talk to everybody. Parents. Friends. I'm just the agent talking to you."

"Wrong. If you're running this investigation, you chose to talk to me. Why don't you do something useful?"

"Suggestions?"

"Yeah." Currie was really furious now even though he knew Asher was baiting him. "The people who killed Nori called a radio station in Paris. Why don't you go there?"

For the first time Asher looked uncomfortable. Currie was surprised. "We have good contacts in France," the agent said stiffly.

"What's that supposed to mean, *contacts?*"

"I'm sure you realize we don't have jurisdiction in France," Asher said. "But we work closely with the Sûreté and Interpol. An FBI legal attaché is stationed in Paris, a liaison."

"Great." Currie shook his head. "You guys are all alike. You pick some little point and push and prod and puff yourselves up, but ask about something important and you quote some reason why you're helpless. And anyway, what about

Qaddafi, remember him? It's all over the radio. What are you wasting your time with me for?"

Asher answered slowly, as if to a child. "What should I do, Mr. Currie? Fly to Libya? 'Colonel Qaddafi, you're under arrest?' Besides, we aren't even certain Qaddafi had anything to do with what happened yesterday."

"*What are you talking about?* They called the radio station!"

The agent strolled around the far periphery of the room. "All that proves is that whoever made the call was involved in the murder. It doesn't prove that they're who they say they are."

"Who killed her, then?" Currie slammed the arm of the chair. "Who are you going to investigate if you're not going to look in the logical place? You mean you're going to have trouble investigating Qaddafi so you'll look everywhere else?"

"I'm not saying Qaddafi didn't order it, we're looking into that in our own way. Trust me. I'm just saying *maybe* he didn't order it." Asher went back to the window. You'd never think a parking carousel could be so fascinating, but he was looking at it again. "You want a possibility? Okay. Suppose Taher Tecala had a jealous lover. The lover killed Tecala and arranged for a friend to call the radio station to throw us off the track."

"Or Nori had a jealous lover?" Currie asked. His voice was much too low. "And Nori's lover killed her? Maybe I killed her."

Asher said with a certain weariness, "Let's calm down, okay? I've worked here twenty-three years. People are capable of doing things you can't even imagine, no matter what's happened to you. When a guy's got something on his mind, when it's all he thinks about day and night, you'd be amazed the tricks he can come up with. But I'll tell you we found an extra set of footprints on Roosevelt Island. We found clothing strands from a shirt you weren't wearing. So do I think you murdered your girlfriend?" He shook his head. "No. Am I

[64]

so positive I eliminate you from even the vaguest suspicion?" He shrugged. " 'Almost' still means no. We can get this over with quickly. This is the easiest part of the investigation. We can get past you and move on to better things. You can help me find who killed your girlfriend. Don't you want that?"

Asher sat down again. He said, "You told me you didn't look at the code and then you said you did. You said you were home this morning but you weren't. If you were me, you'd want some answers."

Currie let out his breath slowly. "What do you want to know?"

Asher said, "Tell me about Zarek."

Currie looked up slowly. At first he thought he had not heard correctly, then the slam of the cell door echoed in his head. Two guards dragged Zarek in from the corridor. The mercenary's head lolled. The guards dropped him on his cot, cursed him in Iranian and left.

Currie lifted Zarek's arms onto his chest and checked his breathing. Blood rivulets rolled out of Zarek's mouth and oozed from the ears. The eyes opened suddenly, red but sly as always.

"Assholes don't even know how to conduct interrogations," Zarek grinned. "Sloppy bastards."

Asher repeated, "Tell me about Zarek." The FBI man's excitement pushed out toward Currie. Asher had opened the purple file and Currie saw the SE was part of SECRET. He couldn't see the reports inside but a SECRET stamp black-topped each page. Currie realized Asher had been waiting to bring up Zarek all along.

"He's my friend," Currie said. It was far from the truth, but compared to Asher Zarek felt like a brother right now. Currie and Zarek had shared a cell, a situation. They hadn't seen each other in over four years. What kind of friendship was that?

"Your friend," Asher repeated.

"That's right."

"When's the last time you saw him?"

"You're going to ask about everything but anything that has a relationship to Nori's death, aren't you?"

Asher just waited. Currie said, "Not for years."

"No phone calls. No letters."

I never wanted to see him, Currie thought. But he said, "I've had enough of this." The last piece in the *Post* had claimed Zarek had been involved in trying to overthrow some government in the Caribbean. He could still hear the mercenary's hard cracker twang. "You got my girlfriend Cindy out. I owe you."

Asher said, breaking into his reverie, "Let me tell you about your 'friend.'" His composure was cracking. He really hated Zarek. "He kills people for money. We trained him. Our government. Then he took what he learned and went off for hire." Asher poked the open file, hard. "Central America. Haiti. Iran." He turned pages. "Bolivia. Jordan. Libya."

Asher looked up. "Libya," he repeated. "Zarek worked for Qaddafi?"

Currie saw the lean weather-beaten face and whipcord neck. Zarek did pushups in their cell, a hundred and fifty and gleaming with sweat. "Why am I in Iran?" Zarek said, not stopping. He nodded toward the guard's boots passing the window. "I came to get rid of them. Should have come sooner."

Asher said, "He's an assassin. An ex-marine murderer. It's all in the file."

Currie said heatedly, "What are you saying — that Zarek killed Nori? Zarek worked for Qaddafi fifteen years ago, when Qaddafi was supposed to be a friend. Yeah, we liked Qaddafi then. We supported him because he was anti-Communist. Zarek told me about it. He trained Qaddafi's soldiers, not terrorists. If he's an assassin, arrest him. If you know so much about him, you know he's in Washington half the time. You know his address. You haven't arrested him so it must not be so simple."

Asher had turned red. "You fiancée is dead. Your friend trained terrorists for Qaddafi."

Currie stood up. "I've given you enough time," he said. "That's an interesting strategy you have, eliminating easy suspects first. Here are more. A cab driver took Nori to the airport once. I bought flowers for her from a girl on K Street. That ought to keep you occupied, keep you from having to think."

"We'll talk again when you cool off," Asher said. "Consider what I told you. You can't get out of the building without an escort. I'll walk you downstairs."

"Follow me down, you can investigate my shoe size."

In the elevator, Asher wouldn't let go. "By the way, the people who lost that box may have figured out you found it. You might be in danger." He ran his hands through his receding hair. "Want a police guard?"

"I don't need any guard."

"But they might come after you." Asher was a scientist of human behavior. Currie was his bug.

Currie mashed his fist into his palm. "Let them come," he said. He had no intention of returning to the FBI building. "Let them, I want them to come. I want them to try."

The sweat ran as soon as he touched the street. Enraged, he walked north. Horns and hydraulic drills built to crescendo. Asher's voice was a steady echo in the din. "They might come after you." He saw Qaddafi's face on the television, defiant, arrogant. Maybe he should buy a gun. A woman beside him said, "Excuse me?" and he realized he'd said it out loud.

Don't go into the hole, Anna had said. The hole was a chair at midnight. A rolling TV and no sleep. Plates piled in the sink. Another lightening sky outside.

Across the street traffic was held up by a procession of chanting Arab "students" who looked either forty years old or had paper bags over their heads. They waved posters of Qaddafi inside a protective circle of police. The city existed as a chain of transient political ideas. "We demand our rights," the bullhorned speaker bellowed. Back in Syria he probably would have been dead a year ago.

Currie squared his shoulders and marched into an international newsstand across from the parking lot. He bought a copy of the Arab newspaper *Al Ahram*. He bought *Le Monde* in French, *La Roma* and *Der Spiegel*, the German magazine. He spoke a little French, that was his foreign language ability, but he would need the papers to crack the code.

Rockville Electronics, twenty miles north on route 270, had been built as part of the Silicon Valley of the East, the chain of big electronic and satellite research firms lining the Brain Corridor of Washington's Interstate.

At midafternoon the heat broiled cars heading north into Maryland. A winding driveway brought him past forest and manicured lawn and he left the jeep at the shadowy end of the parking lot.

The company occupied a sprawling two-story glass complex. The guard at the front turnstyle expressed sympathy over Nori's death, as did engineers in the hallways. Currie locked the door of his office and turned on the computer.

FUCK THE AYATOLLAH swam onto the screen. He'd programmed the greeting after Iran. Currie guessed the code would be in English or Arabic, English because it had been destined for the United States, Arabic because a Libyan had written it.

Under a photo he'd snapped of Nori while they climbed Virginia's Old Rag mountain, he tried English first. The code books at the library had told him lettering rules for the English language, so now he typed possibilities into the machine.

At the end of two hours the screen was covered with gibberish combinations, which in no way resembled words.

The last was AXBRUOLKKHTYUGVSLG.

"Not English," he muttered.

Currie spread open *Al Ahram*. Painstakingly he copied each Arabic letter onto a yellow legal pad. He went over three pages of stories letter by letter to make sure he'd missed no symbol. His throat was dry.

Next he assigned each of the letters he had copied down a number. Using the corresponding numbers instead of the Arab letters, he typed the first four news stories into the computer. He instructed the computer to pick out which numbers occurred most frequently, and which were most frequently paired together.

When he had those answers he had the computer substitute combinations of Arabic letters (by number) for the stick men.

Finally, on a legal pad, he transposed the answers *from* numbers back into Arab letters.

Currie stared at the Arabic, having no idea if he was looking at more gibberish or real words. His neck hurt and he looked up at the picture of Nori, a Rubik cube and fern beside it, a poster of Gauguin's *Contes barbares* on the wall. There was a stereo and racks of cassettes of Beethoven and Stravinsky.

Suddenly the idea of breaking the code this way seemed foolish. Too much luck was involved without proper knowledge of Arabic. What if the paper *wasn't* a substitution code. What if it just *looked* like a substitution code or was in a different language altogether. Italian because the Italians had once controlled Libya. French because Tecala had been a diplomat in France. Mongolian. Chinese. Russian.

Currie shook off the feeling and marched out of his office. Downstairs, in the basement, where the young engineers designed new computers, he wove through the cramped work cubicles until he found Ali Ben Khalifah, a Saudi graduate student who worked part-time in Rockville.

Ali was a lean, handsome boy with wavy dark hair and a mustache. He was studying microcode listings. When he saw Currie, his look of concentration turned to anger. "She was a beautiful girl," Ali said. "Those animals should be beheaded for what they did."

Currie spread the paper on Ali's desk. "Are these Arabic words?" he asked.

The young man's brows knitted. He stared, then looked up and grinned. "You have a horrible spelling teacher," he said. "But yes, they're countries."

Currie's heart pounded violently. The room spun a little and his mouth grew parched. "What countries?"

Ali said, "First a spelling lesson. This figure here should be written like *this*. And do you see how the proper spelling of —"

"What does it mean, Ali?"

Ali caught on to Currie's seriousness. "Well, this word here, it is Israel. Then Iran. Saudi Arabia." He poked the paper with his index finger. "Then a date. October thirteenth. Then the words, 'By the blood.' "

The playfulness was gone from his face.

"Where did you get this anyway?" he said.

Currie felt the blood roaring in his head. "That's all it says? Three countries and a date? No names? You're sure? Does that date have special significance in your country?"

"No."

"Israel and Iran, is there something that connects them with Saudi Arabia?"

"We don't get along with either of them."

Currie picked up the paper, but Ali held his wrist. "This paper has something to do with what happened yesterday, doesn't it? Why else would you have a message in Arabic. On the news they said the dead man was supposed to be carrying a note."

"This isn't the note," Currie said. "Thanks for your help."

"The Libyans are fanatics; Qaddafi will have you killed. Don't play around with them. Did you take this to the police?"

"Graduate students aren't supposed to goof off during work hours," Currie joked. "Back to work."

When Currie left, Ali picked up the phone, made sure nobody was working in the adjacent cubicle and dialed a number. "I want to talk to the ambassador," he said. "There is big trouble starting here."

Currie walked through the deserted parking lot toward the jeep. He'd left it in deep shadow far from the building, where the asphalt met the woods. His mind churned with excitement and frustration. What did *by the blood* mean? Qaddafi must have some plan involving the three countries. Invasion? Currie knew enough about the Mideast to know little Libya couldn't invade three countries at the same time. Israel alone could probably wipe Tripoli off the earth. And anyway, how could the mere mention of countries be cause for Nori and Tecala to be killed?

The base of his spine began itching, the sense of being observed was back again. He saw no one in the lot. Maybe people were looking out from the tinted windows. But when he reached the jeep and put the key in the door a voice startled him, directly behind. "Mr. Currie."

He spun to face a blond man two feet away. The extended wallet showed a blue-and-white Central Intelligence Agency identification card. He'd seen plenty of them after Iran. He flashed to an airport runway, to the hostages going home. "CIA CIA CIA SPYSPYSPY," chanted a gauntlet of jeering Iranians.

". . . a cigarette box," the blond was saying. Currie was electrified. And instantly wary. Had Asher called the CIA?

They'd followed him here? The man had the jutting jaw of a senator and a beach boy tan. The slickness in his face was offset by the kind of gray two-piece suit Currie associated with government workers.

"My name is Grano. I've been trying to find you all day. When the terrorists called that Paris radio station they told the truth. Tecala *was* selling us information, he was supposed to leave a message for me in the box, on Roosevelt Island. I'm hoping you might have found that box, Mr. Currie. That box will tell us who killed your girlfriend."

Two hours ago Currie might have blurted out he'd found the box, in gratitude. Now he was irritated at being startled. And with the deciphered note in his pocket he knew once again the Agency either didn't know what it was talking about or was giving him a runaround. The note hadn't said anything about who killed Nori.

Currie said irritably, "Who are *you* trying to pin the killings on? I don't think the FBI reached the Baltimore Orioles yet."

Grano's teeth were white and perfect, his smile unstrained. "You know Tecala was stationed in France and you know he was anti-Qaddafi," he soothed. "That much was on the radio. His family had money. They lost it when the Colonel took power. He's been working with us for years. Little things."

Despite his anger Currie was interested. The blond edged closer, he was wearing some kind of lemony cologne. Currie was tempted to admit he had the box, watch the slavering reaction and bargain for more information. But he kept quiet and let Grano go on.

Grano said, "Last week Tecala got a diplomatic pouch by accident. Total fluke, from Qaddafi himself. The Libyans were going nuts because the pouch was missing. Tecala was afraid to stay in Paris with the note. We were going to let him stay here." Grano shrugged. "They must have followed him to the island."

"But why didn't he go straight to the Agency when he landed?" Currie said. "Why the island?"

Grano pursued his lips, amused. "Do you know where the Agency is, Mr. Currie?"

"Everyone knows where it is," Currie said. "I pass it on the highway all the time."

"Right, everybody. It's a public place, like an embassy. It's watched. We need to talk to you out at McLean, Mr. Currie. Urgently." He reached out and touched Currie's forearm in earnestness, but there was something oddly repulsive in the contact and Currie pulled back his hand. Grano seemed not to notice. He said, "Did you find that box?"

The feeling of alarm began as a pulse in Currie's throat. A front and rear door were opening on a white Chevrolet two cars down. Two men were getting out.

"Mr. Currie, did you find it?"

Grano's voice was friendly but Currie detected a cold lack of mercy underneath, the perfect haircut and neat suit windowdressing, a veneer. Yet this was not what bothered him. Currie had been briefed by Agency operatives after his return from captivity. He was no stranger to their business-as-usual smugness.

"Why don't you come with us in the car," Grano said. "We can talk on the way to the Agency."

The first approaching man wore a bulky blue suit and a gold ring that glinted on his pinky. The shorter, more wiry man had a pitted face and eyes like holes in a mask. They fixed on Currie.

The men drifted apart as they moved, opening pincers.

"How did you find me?" Currie demanded, suddenly aware of how isolated they were at the far end of the lot. On the highway the cars floated, far away. The woods yawned open.

An impatient flash came and went in Grano's eyes, his voice grew slightly less modulated. "It was hard, all right," he said.

"Called you at home. No answer. Went to your house. Nobody home. Missed you at the FBI and we called your office. We just got here and saw you in the lot."

Ahead, the forest opened, dark and stubby Maryland woods.

Currie knew abruptly what bothered him: not the blond but his thuggish companions. They seemed almost bored with the conversation. Police types always crowded around to listen. These two exhibited none of the arrogance or obsequiousness he was accustomed to receiving from government employees who wanted something. No one wrote down his answers. He saw no tape recorder. The men seemed bulky extensions of the blond man's will.

The people who killed Nori might come after you, he had thought last night when he found the note.

Without seeming to move, the two men flanked him so that his path back to the office was blocked.

"I'll follow you back in my jeep," Currie said, testing them. If they were really CIA they wouldn't mind him driving alone since they would all end up at headquarters anyway.

Grano's long fingers touched Currie again. "One of my men can drive your jeep," he said. "Or we can bring you back here later. We have to talk as soon as possible. On the way." He leaned close. "I wish I could tell you exactly how important this is." He lowered his voice conspiratorially, reverently. He looked like a prospector about to whisper *gold.*

"National security," he said.

He's lying.

As soon as Currie thought it, he knew it was true.

There was a new smell under the lemony cologne, tart. An electric expectation charged the air. Currie flashed to Iran, to the worst interrogator he had known, a bearded man named Hashemi. A gangling sadist who chewed his thumb between questions. Hashemi's politeness at the beginnings of interrogations had been legendary. At first Currie had believed this was because Hashemi thought prisoners re-

[74]

sponded to kindness. He'd quickly realized the reason was that by waiting to begin beatings Hashemi increased the pleasure of his own expectation.

I'm being paranoid, Currie thought. Grano hasn't done anything to me yet.

He allowed himself to be led two steps toward the Chevrolet but he began the conclusive test. Pretending irritation, he said, "If you read my file you must know I have Blue Level security clearance. You know that, right?"

As far as he knew, there was no such thing as Blue Level clearance. He didn't know anything about CIA levels of clearance and he wasn't even sure the Agency had a file on him.

"Sure," Grano said. "I know about that."

"Then don't pull this national security stuff on me," Currie said. The pounding in his head grew very bad. "Explain what's going on. Now." *He killed Nori.* The rage that swelled his throat threatened to seize control of his fists, to drive them into that beach boy face and smash windows, to crunch bone into glass. The heated-up cars would explode with his anger.

But he'd shown the wrong emotion. The friendly look was gone from Grano's face; the man showed the same predatory stare Currie had seen in the others. It was the frozen moment preceding violence. In the millisecond remaining before the deception ended Currie saw Grano had preferred not to use force in a public place but wouldn't leave without him. They probably had guns. He saw a thin chance.

"Oh hell," he said, forcing himself to relax, "I found the box." He wanted to kill them. "Yes, I have it all right. Why should I get mad at you? You're only trying to help."

Grano's eyes became greedy. "You have the box?"

"Sure." Currie walked toward the Chevrolet. He could see another man in the driver's seat. A puff of exhaust came from the tailpipe, the car was starting up. He forced himself to ignore the men behind him. He kept his hands at his sides.

The neck and kidney were exposed, he was utterly defense-less if they attacked.

Currie bent to get in , jerked upright, away from the door. "Oh God," he cried. "I forgot!"

Grano started. Currie yelled, "She'll throw it out!" His urgency, his tone better convince them. "The cleaning lady! I left it on the table. *Get in the car!*" Pit Face was running around to the other side, the front. Grano said, "What cleaning lady?" Currie could barely hear himself, the blood rushed in his head. "Don't you understand?" he cried. He was saying the first thing that came into his head. "I left the note on the kitchen table! Hurry!"

He was sandwiched between Grano and Blue Suit. Blue Suit opened the back door and started to slide in. Currie said to Grano, "I don't think —"

He kicked the door into Blue Suit's upturned face and launched himself forward, head down, into Grano's solar plexus. He heard a thin scream behind him. Grano's knees folded, his heels rose and he clutched his stomach. The front door was opening. Currie knew he should flee but he slammed his knee into Grano's face.

There was an ugly crunch and a moan. A shudder ran the length of Grano's body.

Currie ran.

He leaped toward the forest, twenty feet away, his mind working with perfect clarity. Running right or left would mean giving a clear shot to men who probably carried guns. If he could get the trees between himself and his pursuers, he might loop around and get back to the office.

He reached the lip of woods and turned left, almost slipping down a ridge to a chain-link fence in the woods. He'd never known it was there. A fence to keep out intruders, which he had no time to climb. Behind him a voice yelled, "I want him alive!" That much was good but footsteps pounded behind him, and he turned right, toward the highway. He charged through the woods and plunged down an embankment to the road. He dared a look back and saw the driver in the lead, then Blue Suit. Slower, but coming, Grano, his face a mass of red, and Pit Face. His four fates herding him. Impossible to double back to the building now.

Cars floated lazily along the Interstate. Grano's driver was fifteen feet back on the shoulder of the road. No cars stopped. The traffic formed an impassable wall. If Currie could negotiate those six lanes of vehicles, he could lose himself in the woods on the other side and eventually find a house. People. Phones. Help.

His shirt was drenched. He prayed for a break in traffic.

And then he saw it, a space between cars, a slot, portal, chance, gamble if he could move fast enough. A sixty-five-mile-an-hour door. He bolted into the highway.

A horn sounded, a screeching blur shot past, the rushing air singeing him. He sidestepped a car, reached the median strip and turned. Grano heaved, watching him over the stream of vehicles. Traffic blocked them both now. Currie could no more easily cross the remaining three lanes than Grano could reach him. But then there was a break in traffic on Grano's side and the men were coming. Currie ran into the road.

There was a skidding brake sound, a Mercedes barreled toward him. He backpedaled, hands extended. The car halted, touching his trousers, the other traffic careening around it, honking. "Help me!" Currie cried. His palms pressed the hood. He could not see the driver because of sunglare on the windshield.

The Mercedes backed to go around him.

Currie threw himself on the car.

His chest and knees hit steel. He dug his fingers into a slot where the hood met the windshield. Eight inches away on the other side of the glass he looked into the openmouthed face of a man in tennis whites. He saw white hair and a gold necklace. A can of Dunlops on the bucket seat, a spilled cocktail glass on the lap. Melting ice and lime smeared the man's legs.

"OFF MY CAR!" the driver screamed. His jaw worked heavily. The car began rolling. Currie had only meant to stop it, to get it to pull over so he could climb inside. He balled up on the hood. Grano might shoot if Currie was getting away. The car accelerated, the driver either out of control or trying to dislodge him. The horn went off near his head. The rush of air grew. His fingers were being pulled off. He was slipping, he couldn't hold on. The driver screamed again but he could not hear over the rushing air and unending horn. "OFF, OFF." The pull was in his wrists now, his elbows. The car rocked. Currie's face slammed into the windshield and the wipers came on, shaving at him. His feet must be inches from the road. He had no idea how fast they were moving.

Over the driver's shoulder through the rear window, Currie saw Grano and his men running for the Chevrolet.

Then the vision was cut off as the Mercedes rounded a bend. Currie's fingers were numb, slipping. What would it feel like when he hit the road? Tearing flesh on asphalt, other cars bearing down on him. He tried to flatten himself to let the driver see, but the wipers wouldn't stop.

And then the massive jolt that smashed his face into the wipers. He let go, he was bouncing on the hood and the whole car tilted sideways, in the air. He struck the hood twice, out of synchronization with it, his fingers bleeding in front of his face. The car dropped away and he fell toward grass, tire skid marks rushed up at him. His shoulder struck the earth. He rolled into the pain, astonished and grateful to hit grass. Tumbling, he came up and saw he was four feet from the highway. The Mercedes had struck the earthy lip separating road and grass: that was what had dislodged him.

His whole body was on fire.

Ten feet off the car had halted, inches from a hickory patch.

It was already backing. Currie tried to stand but his knees would not function.

"Don't go!" The spinning wheels threw up dirt. The car careened into the highway, leaving a black ball of smoke. The receding license read "LUV U."

Currie rolled onto his knees. He groaned at a sharp pain in his shoulder and his ankle burned. His vision was blurred. He wiped his eyes. His breathing seemed loud, the numbness was wearing off in his bleeding fingers and they were swelling, throbbing. He probed the injuries. None seemed serious.

When he stood, a wave of nausea hit him but he fought it off. His clothes were covered with dirt and grass, there was an earthy, bily taste in his mouth. Feeling in his pockets he retrieved the third and final copy of the paper. It was crumpled but legible. He smiled.

Then he remembered his knee crunching into Grano's face, snapping it back, and his savage burst of joy eclipsed his pain until he looked around and his smile faded. He recognized the straight stretch of blacktop. Washington was still miles away. He had traveled no more than a mile.

They'll be coming for you.

He remembered Grano running for the Chevrolet. The Rockville Electronics parking lot fed into an overpass which could put cars on this side of the highway in seconds. Currie might have only minutes until they arrived.

Move. Hobbling, he headed for the protection of the stubby Maryland woods to think how to reach town. He glanced back to where the blacktop met the horizon. A barb moved into his belly.

Alone, a speeding vengeance, the white Chevrolet raced his way.

CHAPTER

7

L IKE most policemen, Asher associated neighborhoods with
the crimes they produced. Washington's Adams Morgan
was filled with illegal aliens. Downtown meant bank robberies
and H Street the riot burnings of the 1960s. Embassy Row
concealed the decadent assumptions of the legally unsuper-
vised diplomats, but Georgetown bothered him the most.
Asher's bosses lived in Georgetown, where even delicatessens
had French names and street musicians wore suits. Asher
associated Georgetown with secrets.

Asher sat on the iron-railed steps of the Georgetown townhouse holding a file marked CURRIE. PSYCHIATRIC. Currie had
lied to him this morning, had been hiding information. Asher
thought the doctor who lived here might know why.

But Dr. Robert Kirst had refused to allow Asher in the
house during a "session" so he sweated on the steps. The
heat continued to rise in late afternoon. All along the cobblestone street, traffic-pulverized dust formed blue haze above
unused trolley tracks, another affectation of the locals. The
trolleys had stopped running years ago.

He wiped perspiration from his face and considered the
chain of events which had led Dr. Kirst to Currie.

In the 1970s, when terrorists began abducting U.S. diplomats, the State Department included psychiatrists in the
"readjustment teams" aiding returnees. Like firefighters or
SWAT squads, the psychiatrists were ready at a moment's
notice to fly to remote corners of the earth and couch down

with victims and families. A whole branch of medicine grew up around hostages. The Stockholm Syndrome was a household word. Patients could continue sessions, free of charge, back home, and the State Department announced medical reports would be private, guarded, utterly confidential.

Asher had obtained this one by asking for it.

He rose at the noise behind him and a gray-suited man rushed past, sniffling, a tissue obscuring the lower half of his face. He threw himself into a green Triumph convertible and rattled off. "Come in," said Dr. Kirst from the doorway.

The most prominent member of the psychiatrist SWAT team looked like a hippie grown twenty years older. Bald on top, Kirst had frizzy brown hair on both sides of his tube-shaped face. He had the kind of gentle Moonie smile Asher saw in airports. He seemed untouched by the heat in a spotless Caribbean shirt and sandals.

He led the way through the "group session room," covered with bright Moroccan throw rugs and into a smaller alcove where they faced off on reclining chairs. The bullet-shaped FBI man and the willowy doctor. Tissue boxes lay everywhere and there were brightly splotched Rothko paintings on the walls.

Asher thrust the file at Kirst. "Does this mean Currie is dangerous?"

The file said:

Regular psychiatric treatment is strongly recommended for Timothy Currie, who is severely depressed over his hostage period and potentially explosive. He is a time bomb of depressive remorse. He has bottled his rage and refuses to take advantage of anger-releasing outlets. He believes he should have fought back more in captivity even though when he struck a guard he was severely beaten. His feelings of betrayal, cowardice and powerlessness are probably traceable to deeper parental difficulties, a brutal father and condoning mother, both of whom

[81]

he will not criticize, and a value system of revenge in his past.
Currie successfully dealt with this childhood problem years
ago but his captivity caused the resurgence of adolescent rage.
His dreams focus not on the guards who abused him but their
leader, the Ayatollah, a distant parental demon who seems all
powerful. Currie may have difficulties with authority fig-
ures. . . .

Asher said, "Explode?"

Kirst leaned back and crossed his feet on an ottoman. The
frown he had worn when he started reading turned back into
the anxious smile. "It's just a phrase, that's all. Currie might
lose his temper sometimes."

Asher said, "Time bomb sounds pretty serious to me."

Kirst's laugh was mocking, a tinkling two-syllable disdain.
"It's merely a way to describe anger. Don't make more of it
than you should."

"I won't," Asher said, "but let's start with the premise that
these words mean something, okay? Explain them to me.
Does 'lose his temper' mean he might get violent?"

Kirst waved a hand. "Anyone might 'get violent,' inspector."

Asher said, "Me, you, Jack the Ripper."

Kirst was delighted. "See? You're losing your temper yourself right now."

There were times, and this was one of them, that even
after twenty-odd years in Washington Asher felt a tug for
his old home state of Maine. He'd come to the FBI "tem-
porarily" over two decades ago as part of an exchange pro-
gram teaching small-town policemen "modern police methods."
He had not known much about "modern police methods"
but his practical doggedness had netted the Bureau the Don
of a Massachusetts crime family. J. Edgar Hoover had taken
a liking to the bird dog of a Maine cop, which had enabled
Asher's rough idiosyncrasies to go unchallenged while Hoo-

ver lived and remain institutionalized after his death. In the world of the police bureaucrat, Asher had had the good fortune to become the token street cop.

Curbing his irritation, Asher smiled. "Not at all," he said. "I just want to know about the report. You said Currie needed psychiatric care. You said Currie might explode. There's a dead girl and a murdered diplomat on Roosevelt Island. Currie was there too."

Fingers laced, Kirst glared out from under a stern frown. "What I wrote," he said slowly, condescendingly, "was simply a way of recommending more sessions. I wasn't calling Currie a murderer and I certainly wasn't predicting violence. How did you get this file anyway? I find it distasteful the way police use psychiatric speculations to persecute people with real problems. If I say 'yes,' you'll be banging down some poor man's door with a search warrant."

Asher crossed his legs casually. "See? I knew if we kept at it we'd arrive at a definition. When you wrote 'explode' and 'walking time bomb,' you meant he was a normal adjusted person who probably had nothing to do with murders."

"I didn't say that either," Kirst huffed. "I'm not a fortune teller, don't expect me to do your work for you."

Asher leaned back in his chair. The wastebasket was filled with tissues. A little digital clock blinked the time in red. Asher ran his hands through his receding hair. "Look, Doctor," he said, "if you think I'm going to arrest someone just because you think he's capable of committing a crime you have an exaggerated sense of your own importance. And if you think I'll cross someone off my list because you say he's innocent, the same is true. Two people are dead. A thousand factors make up the investigation. You can help with one little piece but you'd rather play word games than take responsibility. So why don't I just keep quiet and you tell me what you meant. I'll sit and listen. Off the record."

Dr. Kirst straightened. He blinked and seemed to grow

fully aware of Asher for the first time. Then he slumped.

"I guess I can't turn it off sometimes," Kirst said. "Sorry. You want me to predict how he'll act, but that's impossible. No amount of academic preparation can decipher uniqueness. He's hurt, humiliated. I'll say one word and that word is pressure. Currie's dignity, his self-conception as provider and protector, all have been destroyed. Whatever social contract binds him to the rest of us has been breached. He's been the good citizen, we've failed our part of the bargain.

"He has a violent family background so even more than the rest of us he has to control himself. Oh, he hears the legal and pastoral voices as well, the sermon urging turn the other cheek, the government's paternal pat on the head and the stern admonishment from law officers like yourself. Leave the law to us. These voices are powerful too but they've already failed him."

Asher said, "Doctor," but Kirst waved him off. "Let me finish. I used the term 'time bomb' in my report. But you're a time bomb, we all are. Push a button, switch a lever, the peaceful farmer becomes a soldier, the loving wife a murderer. For five thousand years we've regulated our lives to prevent the switches from being activated. Now, whatever pressure he was under before has multiplied. I wish he'd come back to me but he doesn't believe in psychiatrists either." Kirst smiled ruefully. "Like you."

"But now that you've suffered through my qualifier I'll try to help you. It's an unprofessional guess. Even if Currie snapped, which I'm not saying he did, but if he were to . . . ah . . . become violent, he would lose his temper with an authority figure, not a functionary. With someone he perceived as having nearly life-and-death power over him. Remember, in his dreams of captivity he never saw the guards, the actual people who struck him. He saw the leader. My guess, based on the limited amount I know, is that he had nothing to do with the murders on Roosevelt Island."

Asher said, "Last question. Did he ever mention someone named Zarek?"

"Zarek?" Kirst shook his head. "Who's Zarek?"

Outside, Asher used the telephone in his car. "Put a watch on Zarek's house."

"Open the envelope, now!" "What's in there!" Eight people sang out at the festive table, tan and joyous looking on the hot summer night. The women, in their twenties, looked sleek in high heels and skintight gowns. The men, at least twenty years older, wore tailored French suits and had manicured fingernails. The deceptive smile, the unhappy presence, was Anna Currie.

At the head of the table the birthday girl slit her envelope with red fingernails. Her eyes glowed bright with winey acquisition. Laura was Anna's boss at the Georgetown public relations firm. "Ooooh," she cooed. "Darling, darling, round trip tickets to Majorca and Amman!"

Everyone applauded. White-haired and elegant, the Parisian businessman at Laura's side said, "And now this little traveling companion." He handed her a silver cocaine spoon on a necklace.

The softly lit restaurant resembled an Italian wine cellar, cool and elegant. The leather menus were sealed in gold foil. Under low arched ceilings, red-jacketed impeccably polite waiters seemed to float rather than walk. They carried the highest-priced wine list in Washington.

The hum of conversation was broken by a bellow at an adjacent table. "HAW HAW, SENATOR, YOU SURE ARE RIGHT ABOUT THAT!"

To Anna's right another white-haired senator dined with half-a-dozen twenty-five-year-olds. They possessed one thing he could not acquire through politics, youth.

She recognized the head of the Film Actors Guild gesturing with a fork at a lean congressman she'd seen on TV.

[85]

Laura cried, "I want to play a game! Write down your fantasies but don't sign them. We'll read them at the table."

With shy sexual glances the businessmen began scribbling, covering their papers. Laura's escort pinched one nostril and snorted cocaine. "Wine, wine," he sang. "Whatever you want! Waiters! Whatever they want!"

At a touch on her wrist Anna glanced down to see two manicured fingers resting there. Laura had demanded boy-girl seating. The Parisian beside Anna was handsome as a film star and smelled of talcum powder. He leaned close and whispered, "Guess what I have under my napkin?"

The napkin lay on the table, a thin bulge underneath.

"A pencil."

He roared. "HAHAHA, a pen-ceeel!" Nobody at the table paid attention. "You are ve-ree fu-nee." The Parisians were partners in a luxury Georgetown condominium Laura's firm represented. They flew back and forth to France every other week. They were all married. The pressure on her wrist grew. "No idea?" he said. "No idea what the little gift could be? Could it be a chocolate éclair?" He shook his head. "But no, it cannot be an éclair. An éclair is too large. Clearly what is under the napkin is smaller than an éclair."

Smiling her PR smile, Anna said, "I'm so bad at guessing." She extricated her hand by reaching for the wineglass. A waiter immediately filled it. Platters of veal and pasta littered the table, and wine bottles, red and white.

The Parisian reached under the napkin and dangled a gold watch. It moved back and forth like a hypnotist's globe. It made Anna sick. The Parisian announced, "I am in the office yesterday. I see your lovely wrist." The offering had caught everyone's attention. He said, "It would be so much more beautiful encircled by gold." He kissed her hand. "Mademoiselle."

Across the table Laura cried, "It's beautiful! Oh, Charles!"

"Beautiful," Anna repeated. She had no intention of accepting the watch but it would embarrass a client to refuse it in public. Laura read fantasies out loud. "I dream of hot tropical nights with green satin ladies." Anna wore a green satin dress. Laughing, Laura said, "Who wrote that? Charles, was it you?"

"I'll be right back," Anna said. Her face hurt from smiling. Two chairs down her best friend Elaine said, "Me too." Women in restaurants make a dainty conspiracy of relieving themselves.

Elaine said a minute later, "What's the matter with you?" They sat looking at each other in the powder room mirror, which was encircled by bulbs like a film star's. Elaine was all ovals under wild black hair. Huge black eyes under high round cheekbones. A curving mouth in a red bow. She wore a body-tight white gown with a Chinese collar; she showed bare shoulders. "Cut it out," she said. "The only one who's going to sleep with any of these guys tonight is Laura. I have Bob, Maureen has Ritchie. It's just a silly party to keep an account. And it's Laura's birthday; she doesn't have any friends. You don't have to keep the watch. Enjoy the food, we could never afford it."

Both divorced, they lived in one-bedroom condominiums in the stylishly single DuPont Circle area. Their building was called "The Casablanca."

"I used to read about this restaurant when I was married," Anna said. "I read the 'Front Page People' column in the *Washington Post*. All the senators came here, the ambassadors. When I drove by I looked at the doors. They were so small, almost hidden. I thought the most wonderful things were going on in this restaurant. The funniest jokes. The wittiest people. If I could come here, I would know secrets."

Elaine applied gloss to her lips. "I don't think this mood has anything to do with the dinner," she said. "I think this mood started yesterday, in the office. When you heard about Tim."

[87]

Shoulders slumped, Anna brushed her hair. "You're wrong. I just didn't take this job to make myself a piece of cheesecake in a restaurant."

"Come off it. There's not a business in the world where you don't have to yuck it up with clients. Men do it, too. And we have a lonely boss who would have cried herself to sleep tonight if Pierre hadn't whisked her away to get high." The door opened to admit an elderly blond in a designer gown which did not help her appearance. She looked hard at Anna. Anna turned away. She knew the celebrity look, she had stopped appreciating it some time ago.

"I left him my phone numbers but he won't call," she said. "He'll just sit there or . . ." She shivered. "I swear he was different. I sensed something terrible in him."

Elaine said, "His fiancée was murdered, of course he was acting crazy. He's the same person he's always been. What do you want him to do, sit around and smile? The minute someone becomes passionate you run away — you're afraid of passion, that's your problem. And anyway, he's not your concern anymore. Take care of *yourself*. You're still not seeing anyone two years later. The second anyone starts to like you . . . you don't give men a chance."

Wearily, Anna said, "Later, okay?"

"When later?"

"I'm telling you he was different," Anna insisted. "Stretched."

Elaine said, "You want to go back with him?"

She'd phrased it innocently but Anna grew furious. "Can't I be his friend without going back? I was his best friend once." She stopped brushing her hair. "And I feel bad about last time. He needed me and I couldn't help him. Now I can."

"Charles doesn't look like the type who gives up," Elaine remarked.

They returned to the table and Anna said goodbye. When she stepped outside, she felt free. The moon was behind clouds, there was a vague translucent yellowness to the sky.

Thoughts turned inward, she located her white Volkswagen Rabbit and headed for the home that had once been hers. She drove smoothly, with clean movements of the wheel. The police and newsmen were gone from Currie's driveway. His jeep was not at the house.

High heels on night grass. She clicked up the wooden porch. The leaves were still. There was a moist, earthy smell and a brass electric tang. It was unlike Currie to be absent at this hour.

"Tim?" She used her key, knowing he wasn't there, giving herself an excuse to go in by pretending to look for him. She switched on the kitchen light. The wood on the counter shone. There was a bag of Fritos in a bowl. Elaine was wrong. She only wanted to help him. She had failed him before and now he needed a friend.

But in the eddying night memories came to her with a sudden appalling ache. The touch of his tongue, the wild imprint of their first night in the moonlit vestibule upstairs, the ragged heat-bathed mornings in the young couple's house, the wood shaving and cool granite smells of construction, and the solid comfort of a future where everything is real. There was more in this empty house than that whole packed restaurant. She felt the currents of history embodied between the walls. She'd built this kitchen and had traded it for The Casablanca.

The car door slamming startled her, too heavy to be from Currie's jeep. There were footsteps on the back stairs. Alarmed, she reached the door to see a small man coming toward her on the steps, his pale face upturned in the vaporous light.

"Who are you?" she demanded, then sighed with relief when he held up the FBI shield.

"Mr. Currie isn't here?" Asher said. He sounded like a prosecutor asking questions and looked at her as if he were waiting for a confession.

"I . . . I was married to him. I'm Anna Currie," she said,

[89]

defensive under his scrutiny. She tried the PR smile. He cut her off by walking into the kitchen.

"We'll wait for him together," he announced, and led her into the living room.

After a while Asher brought his questions around to Zarek. They found they had a lot to talk about.

Currie hesitated before reaching for Zarek's knocker. His sweat had caked, his clothes were soiled. Bathed in light from an over-the-door bulb he tasted the brassy metallic tang of a brewing electrical storm. The air was much too still. At nine at night the heat had settled.

He jerked as headlights rounded the corner, materialized into a police patrol and passed. Grano had made him a fugitive in his own city.

But when Currie remembered smashing his knee into Grano's face the fury turned to triumph. He'd seesawed all afternoon, rage and euphoria. His heart still pounded at his narrow escape. He remembered Grano's smile in the parking lot and the clawing flight on the hood of the Mercedes. When he'd seen the Chevrolet barreling toward him, he'd fled into the trees but the car had skidded onto the road shoulder. Currie had crashed deeper into the forest, the pursuers calling to each other behind him. He'd reached a Rockville access road. A hitch, bus and Metro ride had left him in Capitol Hill.

Zarek's two-story townhouse was draped with vined trellises and fronted by a flower garden and waist-high iron fence. Roses lined the walkway to cluster like carolers below curtained French windows. It was not the mercenary's lair he'd envisioned.

The wolf's head knocker hit loud enough to rouse the whole street. "I owe you," Zarek had promised when Currie saved his girlfriend in Iran. "I owe you," he'd repeated daily, endlessly exercising in the cell. Currie had mocked it inwardly at first, impotent bragging from a prisoner helpless as himself. Now he felt the power of the words.

But when he heard footsteps on the other side of the door, he wanted to leave. Four years had passed. Zarek hadn't contacted him, either. Or had been lying about owing a favor. Or had moved.

Or was out of the country, killing somebody.

The overhead light went out, plunging Currie into darkness.

"Yeah?" growled the familiar gravelly voice. "Tim? *Tim!*" The doorway was dark but the flash of heat lightning showed Zarek stakelike, teeth iridescent. Gripping Currie's arm, he drew him into the dark foyer. Cool air enveloped him, a hissing fan spun overhead.

"Don't stand in lighted doorways," Zarek said. With the door closed the hallway blazed, but the man's radiating intensity had been evident even in the dark. Zarek held his lean body with extraordinary grace. The leathery skin came from years in the sun. The lines around his eyes were deep, weathered, the face broad, flat from a Polish mother. The jet-black hair came from Zarek's Indian side, as did the eyes of translucent green. The pupils were black and diamond shaped and made Currie think of serpents, Zarek showed emotion with his mouth only.

"What happened to you?" he growled.

Looking down at his sweatstained clothing, Currie felt the helpless rage return. There was no other way to say it.

"They tried to kill me," he said.

Zarek's natural frown deepened. "The same ones?" He knew instinctively what Currie was talking about: he was asking if the attackers were the ones who had killed Nori. Currie felt as if no time had passed between them. Perhaps that was what had always frightened him. The connection. The sense that Zarek saw inside him. He nodded. "Four of them."

"Four?" The edges of Zarek's lips rose. "Four of them."

He had the deep laugh of a fatter man. "That's good," he gasped. "Oh, that's good. An engineer beats four of them!"

"I kneed one of them," Currie said. Then the laughing made him feel better and he said, "That *is* pretty good." The exuberance returned. "I *kneed* one of them!"

They were both laughing, old friends rejoined. Zarek permitted himself emotion where the manly arts were involved. He sobered. "You tell the cops?"

"I called the FBI from the Metro but I didn't want to see them."

"Nobody's following you?"

"I got away in the woods."

Zarek considered the answer. "How many policemen were in the squad car that passed while you were outside?" he tested.

"Two."

Zarek grunted. "Describe the person sitting across from the house in the Honda Accord."

Currie jerked. Zarek said, "Don't worry. It's just the neighbor's boyfriend. The kid sits out there, afraid to ring the bell. Anyway, you probably did get away. They wouldn't have followed you in the woods if they knew where you were, they would have killed you." Zarek squeezed Currie's shoulder. "The house has more alarms than Fort Knox. Someone tries to get in and I'll know it." He rubbed his belly. "Tell me the story after dinner."

At the word dinner Currie smelled the thick spicy tomato sauce aroma. He had not eaten in two days and he was famished. For the first time since Nori's death he felt calm, safe almost. It wouldn't last.

"Cindy!" Zarek shouted. He led Currie through the downstairs. The garish living room was stuffed with red Ultrasuede couches, red and white Persian rugs, lots of crystal candy dishes and vases on baroque coffee tables. Willie Nelson sang "Georgia on My Mind." Bookshelves flanked the fireplace, the only title Currie could make out was Hemingway's *Men at War.*

She padded barefoot onto the rug through swinging kitchen doors, plump where Zarek was lean, tan where he was weathered, blond where he was black haired and as visibly demonstrative as he was restrained with strangers. She moved with a saucy bounce, red-toenailed in white flowing slacks and matching cotton blouse. A single gold necklace rested above the ample bosom. She had high olive cheekbones and a wide mouth. She'd been a model before Zarek paid for law school, or at least he'd said he'd paid for law school. Currie wondered if she'd graduated by now. Zarek had rarely spoken of her in prison except to include her in monologues on the unreliability of women. Despite the mercenary's tough-guy image, Zarek had feared losing her.

"You took your time," she cried with joyous exasperation. She rocked on her feet, one hand cool on her hip. "Four years!"

He'd only seen her once, on the embassy roof the day she escaped, but every feature remained sharp in his memory. The crowd fought to reach the door. He saw her battling, losing. Pushing back to give her room, he said, "I'll get out after you." The door closed behind her.

Later he found out she'd been visiting Zarek during a law school break.

Cindy said, "I'm sorry about Nori. I saw her on TV, she looked beautiful." Currie wanted to cry. He'd only been here minutes and they were inside his defenses.

Cindy commanded, "You're eating with us."

"I already told him," Zarek said. "If you ever finish making it."

"Shut up, you! You just finished lunch! Take Tim downstairs and stay out of the kitchen."

Zarek said, "Look how she treats me! Who's the squaw and who's the brave?"

"The squaw runs the kitchen when it's her turn to cook, that's who she is." Rolling her eyes she looked to Currie for support. "You like Italian?"

"I'm starving."

She was enormously pleased. "It's just braciola and linguine. I didn't know we'd have company."

The basement was a cross between a safari club and an armory. Rifle cabinets lined dark mahogany walls. Under the low-beamed ceiling and wild game heads, the men stepped over bear and zebra skin rugs. The room issued a smoky, masculine smell. This was obviously Zarek's part of the house.

But as Zarek moved off to pull two Buds from a barside refrigerator, Currie realized he looked unwell. He had not seen it when the mercenary was closer but Zarek seemed smaller somehow, shrunken. The arms were thinner, corded, the marine tattoo oversized on the forearm. A fold of flesh bunched under the chin and the short-sleeved safari shirt was big, odd because Zarek's clothes were tailor-made. In his own shaken condition and with the excitement of greeting, Currie had missed it. He wondered if Zarek had been sick but Zarek rarely talked about health and regarded suggestions that he might be unwell as insults. Currie would make an inquiry later if the conversation offered a chance.

He downed the Bud in one draught. "Hoo boy," Zarek said. "More coming." Still parched, Currie eyed the formidable rows of rifles opposite. He focused on a long steel barrel with a telescopic sight. "Are those for hunting?" he asked.

Zarek said, "Some of them." He's an *assassin*, Asher had said. Currie tried again. "What are . . ."

"Dinner," Cindy announced.

For the next hour he concentrated on the food, the thick spiced sausages and pasta, the green crispy salad, the hunks of thickly buttered bread and the gallon jug of red wine which grew emptier. Zarek kept refilling his glass. A pleasant alcoholic throb began in Currie's forehead. Zarek said, "More wine," and Cindy shook her head. "You're drinking too much," she said. "I told you." Zarek's voice went much too low. "More wine," he ordered.

Currie realized something horrible was eating at him.

Cindy cleared the table and returned with Turkish coffee, heavily sugared and laced with grappa. She offered a plate piled high with creamy cannoli. They'd been eating a long time.

When they pushed back coffee cups Zarek said, "Okay, tell me what happened."

They sat on the low red couch, brandy snifters glowing gold. Zarek's capacity for alcohol seemed amazing, his voice remained strong.

"I found a paper on the island," Currie began. He showed it to Zarek. He explained about breaking the code. Zarek listened intently, scowling when Currie mentioned Grano, grinning at Asher's name. When Currie finished Zarek said, "Grano's hands, did you notice them?" Startled, Currie described Grano's out-of-proportion fingers and Zarek nodded grimly. "Forget the name Grano. Ernst Lipko is his name. Qaddafi's security men are East Germans."

Qaddafi, Currie thought. He saw the powerfully indifferent face on television. The rage collected behind his eyes.

Zarek said, "I know Asher too. Where's the scrapbook, honey?"

Cindy retrieved a looseleaf album filled with newspaper clippings. Zarek's name was underlined on the rare occasions when it appeared. "COUP PLOT UNCOVERED IN GRANADA." Zarek had been leading the aborted coup. "CIA ASSASSIN IN NICARAGUA." No name on that one. Zarek flipped pages while Currie stared in amazement. "BRIDGE COLLAPSES ON AMBASSADOR IN FREAK ACCIDENT."

Zarek and Cindy, the loving couple showing memorabilia. The really interesting articles didn't even mention Zarek at all. "MYSTERY AMERICAN ACCOMPANIED PERUVIAN TROOPS WHO

Killed Che Guevara" and "Antiterrorist Hunts Down IRA Killers."

Currie remembered what Zarek had revealed about himself in Iran. Orphaned, he'd grown up in a series of foster homes. At sixteen he'd lied about his age and joined the marines. He'd been the first marine in Vietnam, where he'd operated alone behind enemy lines, stalking guerrillas in the jungle.

After Vietnam he'd left the army to go freelance, teach martial arts to U.S. Sky Marshals. Once he'd told Currie in the cell, "I do bond retrievals too."

"What's that?" It had been a summer night in Tehran. The temperature in the cell was over a hundred degrees.

Zarek said, "Let's say a couple of businessmen jump bond and run away to Peru. The bailbondsman is out half a million dollars. He sends me to bring them back."

"Suppose they won't come back?"

"I convince them."

"Suppose you can't convince them?"

Zarek had rolled over on his back. "If the businessmen are killed while being apprehended, the bondsman gets some of his money back from the court."

"You murder them?"

Zarek had grown angry. "I never murdered anybody. The businessmen run down there and hire themselves an army. Twenty, thirty guys to protect them. You don't understand how it is. When I go down there I'm working for an officer of the court. It's legal. You have to go through a dozen bodyguards to reach them. Same thing with hostage retrievals."

Currie hadn't been so sure he wanted to know what that was.

"Hostage retrievals?"

"A banana company executive gets kidnapped. He's somewhere in Columbia. Someone has to bring the guy back."

[96]

After a while it dawned on Currie that Zarek told him things he never revealed to other people. Currie never entirely understood the reason. Partially, he supposed, it was because he had saved Cindy from the Iranians. Partially Zarek simply felt an affinity with him, assumed Currie understood him. In the presence of other American prisoners Zarek went sullen and uncommunicative.

But the most frightening aspect of Zarek's monologues was his tone of voice when he told his stories. Never bragging, simply stating answers to questions as if it were an obligation of friendship, Zarek had told tales with the same passion he'd use talking about a trip on the subway.

"Here's Asher," Zarek said.

The headline read, "FBI ARRESTS GUNRUNNER IN BOSTON HOTEL." The corners of Zarek's lips rose. "I walked into that room and saw twenty cops in flak jackets, pointing guns. They looked scared shitless. 'Don't move a muscle, Mr. Zarek.' Asher came out of the bedroom, he was probably hiding there. What kind of a guy wears a raincoat in a hotel room? Desk drivers, report writers, that's the FBI. Waiting for pensions. But Asher screwed up. I wasn't selling the guns that time, someone else was doing that. I'd just been contracted to train the customers. Nothing illegal in that. Besides, they were rebels from Afghanistan. Anti-Communists." Zarek drained his brandy and poured more. He probably had the fastest metabolism in the hemisphere.

He grinned, showing a little gap between his two front teeth. "Asher resented it," he said.

Cindy raged, "They treat Zarek horribly! Oh, if they want something it's champagne and the Concorde all the way, first class. Just wave the flag under Mr. Zarek's nose and he comes running. The rest of the time they give him lie detector tests. I have to meet him at the airport when he comes home, with someone from the Agency. Otherwise you never know how he'll show up on some customs inspector's computer. They might shoot him! He's a patriot, he'd never go against his country! Last time he came in they were afraid he was trying to sho——"

Zarek said, "Cindy," in a voice Currie had not heard before.

She gathered the plates.

"I have a brief to write." She stomped up the stairs.

When she was gone, Currie said, "Asher said you were an assassin." Across the room, the boar's tusks gleamed, curving. Zarek, who had been amused at Cindy's huffy departure, turned his attention full on Currie. He seemed to consider a moment, he turned a page. Currie read, "FIVE DIE IN PARIS AIRPORT BLAST."

"Look, I respect you so I'll tell you," Zarek said. "But I don't explain myself. And I don't care what Asher thinks." He nodded at the headline. "I'll tell you about the people who died. One was an eighteen-year-old girl, an art student. She used to tell her friends she was going to be famous. I don't know anything about art. They found her arm thirty yards from the blast. A dentist and his wife were taking a vacation. They owned a house in Nice. The stewardess was on a new route. A housewife was saying goodbye to her mother."

They're like Nori, Currie thought. They didn't hurt anyone and they died. The throbbing in his head built hugely.

Zarek said, "The man who ordered that bomb set off lived a thousand miles away, on a mountain, guarded. He wanted those strangers to die. That's the way animals like him make points." Zarek closed the book. His intensity grew. "But a month later someone got past his guards, into his bedroom and slit his throat. Tell me," he said, "do you think the two men are the same? The one who ordered the bomb exploded? The one who killed him?"

No, Currie thought, thrilled by Zarek's story of retribution.

Something was about to happen in this room, he felt it growing.

"There are mad dogs in the world who have to be killed," Zarek said. "Carlos. Qaddafi. You can't jail the man on the mountain but you can't roll over on your belly in front of him either. He'll keep coming back. He looks unstoppable but he bleeds. He'll hurt more people if you let him."

Lipko will keep coming back, Currie thought. He felt the coursing truth, he'd known it all along and had come to hear it. He'd already crossed the line into Zarek's world before coming here, he saw. The run-in with Asher and the flight from Lipko had been preparation for this room.

Zarek said, "Suppose someone would have killed Hitler before he came to power. The Ashers would have screamed assassin. But that man would have been a hero."

Currie said, "If Qaddafi lived in Washington, Asher would have picked him up by now. Just because he's somewhere else . . . he *did* the same thing but he lives in a different country . . . Asher can't do anything."

Zarek said, "The cities heap honors upon the slayers of the despot. Xenophon said it two thousand years ago." Zarek said, "Everyone knows it, they agree with me, they say it at cocktail parties. They just don't want to watch."

"The whole investigation is for show," Currie said.

Softer, Zarek said, "Washington is the safest place in the world to kill someone, not the other way around. Because people here convince themselves words are action." He waved the day's paper, which had been beside the bar on a stool. "Look at the headlines . . . 'President *Urges*' . . . 'Senate *Argues*' . . . 'Israelis *Debate*' . . . No one is doing anything in the town." His face was all twisted with anger. "They want to stretch the limits of your suffering and make you a cripple and when they succeed they will pity you. You have to decide for yourself. Do you want to cry or revolt? Do you want to

[99]

be a victim or a fighter? No one will help you. Fanatics change history. Everyone else gets dragged along."

Currie stood. The rising tide of his rage overwhelmed him. Zarek addressed his very soul. Currie passed over the line where daydreams take form and restraint falls away to gut-tearing clarity. He floated high above the room on fury.

Qaddafi was the man on the mountain. Distant. Mocking. Guarded. Untouchable. "An eye for an eye," Zarek was saying. "You can kill anybody and get away with it." Currie, metamorphosed, saw that Zarek was truth. Nori was dead. Zarek said, "History is revenge." Currie's voice went flat and certain. He heard himself say *kill,* he heard himself say, *I'll kill him, Zarek. Qaddafi. You'll help.*

CHAPTER
8

A T midnight Asher worked furiously in the FBI's computer room. Woodcock the electronics genius was there, too. They worked together often. Woodcock called his computer "Phyllis."

"Yes Phyllis yes baby yes yes yes," Woodcock cooed. "Tell us what Currie's note means. Now right now."

He was slight, with wire glasses and frizzy balding hair. His clothes were all too big.

The third agent present, Legg, was an expert in Arabic. They'd already tried to translate the note into English, French, German, Italian, Spanish and Polish.

"The Poles and the Libyans," Woodcock had said, wrapping two fingers together, "are close."

"You think Currie killed her?" Legg asked now.

"I would have said no a few hours ago. But he lied, said he hadn't seen Zarek in four years but he's been at Zarek's house for hours. And what about his phone call? People tried to kill him but he won't see me? What kind of bullshit is that?"

Woodcock strode from the window to the computer, his pupils contracted in vivid black points.

"Bust in on them," Woodcock said.

HELLO WOODCOCK, Phyllis printed on her screen. DARLING.

"ANSWER IN ARABIC. 537758906528058774." Legg started transcribing.

Staring out at the glowing taillights on Pennsylvania Avenue, Asher snapped, "How can I bust in on them? With what warrant? Besides, I want to see who else shows up. We can move in later. Street's boxed off."

"Jesus Christ," Legg breathed. "It's countries." A few minutes later the three of them were clustered by the console, staring at the deciphered note. Legg said, " 'By the blood'? What's 'By the blood'?"

Woodcock shuddered. "I'll stay with Phyllis. *You* find out."

On the phone, Asher said, "I want to talk to the Director. Wake him up. You're damn right it's an emergency."

The Director wanted to see the note right away. Asher said, "I can be there in fifteen minutes."

He slammed the phone down and headed for the door. "This time I'll get that bastard," he said. "Put more men on Zarek's house, keep them at the end of the block. He looks out the window, he'll spot an agent in half a second." Asher was rushing out the door. Half-filled Styrofoam cups littered the desks. Asher said, "We'll grab them when I leave the Director."

"You'll never reach Libya. They'll kill you first."

At 2 A.M., Zarek opened another beer and drank. He leaned forward over the bar in agitation. His safari suit remained as crisp as Currie's shirt was soiled but Currie had found it impossible to borrow clothes from the smaller man. Zarek said, "You listen."

Arms extended casually, legs crossed, Currie watched from the couch.

On the stereo Sinatra crooned softly. ". . . that's what people say . . ."

Zarek said, "Americans can't even get into the country. You don't speak the language. Qaddafi's got the best protection in the world. East Germans. Russians. A fly buzzes and the guns come out." He slammed his palm on the bar. For the second time Currie was struck by the man's lost weight, although Zarek seemed as formidable as ever. "He's knocking people off all the time, he knows guys are after him. And you don't have the slightest idea how to do what you're talking about."

The venom would run out, Currie knew. His grief had disappeared. He was coming down from the height of passion and what was emerging was certainty. Indisputable fact. The assassination already being broken down, in his engineer's mind, into a series of smaller problems. This moment's task was securing Zarek's help.

Zarek hissed, "He lives in a fortress in the desert. Nothing for a hundred miles around it. It's guarded. You'd never even find it. Or he's in headquarters in Tripoli or on army bases, inspecting. How do you think you're going to reach him? You were lucky to beat those four guys today."

That Zarek might dissuade Currie from going to Libya was impossible. The whole process was steeped in logic so primal it was beyond discussion.

"You said anyone was killable," Currie said. "But maybe you're like those newspapers you were waving around. A lot of words.

"You're an amateur," Zarek said.

"You owe me."

"Your life, not to kill you."

"Teach me, just teach me what to do.'

Sinatra sang, ". . . I know one thing . . ."

Zarek came around the bar with menacing fluidness. Above him the boar's mouth ripped open, frozen in attack. "Teach you *what?*" he growled. "Pulling the trigger is the easiest part. It's the little things you need to know. How to talk to a cab driver, hold a cigarette. I need two years just to get you to the point where I can trust you to cross a street without looking the wrong way."

All the curtains in the house were drawn. No one could see inside.

"I have time," Currie said.

"I don't."

"I'll pay you."

"I'm dying," Zarek said.

Currie's hands came off the couch. Zarek had lost weight, but dying? Dying was impossible.

". . . so I don't have two years to train you to do diddly-shit," Zarek raged. He never talked about health. "It's called amyotrophic lateral sclerosis. Gehrig had it. I don't need any crap from you about it. I'm only telling you because I can't train you and I owe you. Tell Cindy and you're dead. She thinks I have a bug."

"I won't say anything."

"I don't need your damn sympathy," Zarek snarled.

Currie heard himself say, "Then come with me if you're dying anyway."

He was apalled at the cruelty of his own thought. Something had snapped in him. He'd said the first thing that came into his mind. Zarek brought out his harsh side.

Sinatra had finished singing. A news announcer said, "Gunmen attacked a Rome synagogue with grenades and machine guns Saturday. A two-year-old boy was killed, thirty injured."

But Zarek's anger was gone. He sauntered back behind the bar, even looking amused. Zarek finished his beer. Currie realized he had made the only offer that could calm the man down: usefulness.

"Knock him off," Zarek said, although he didn't seem to regard Currie seriously. "The two of us."

"That's right."

The folds on Zarek's neck jiggled when he laughed. "Guts," he said. "I always knew you had it." He shook his head. "I'll tell you one thing. Whoever carried out a reprisal like that, it would be the hit of the century. Pit stop," he said.

He slid up the stairs, you could never hear him move.

Zarek traveled with a predatory glide. The radio said, "Authorities in Rome denounced a climate of hatred." Currie shut it off. He had not felt quiet in a long time. Zarek was dying. An image came to him: Zarek stripped to his waist, glistening sweat as he did pushups in the cell. And karate kicks. A health film came to him. Hunched over a sink, an emaciated man in pajamas threw up, racked with palsy.

Five minutes had elapsed and Zarek had not returned.

Currie rose and peered into the weapons cabinet. Zarek's "field work" rifle had a longer barrel than the others. Black and telescopically equipped. A polished stock Currie mentally fitted against his shoulder.

Impaled by crosshairs in the telescopic halo, he saw Qaddafi's face.

Ten minutes passed. Gehrig's disease, he had read, attacked the nervous system. Who could tell what agony Zarek underwent upstairs. But Carrie refrained from looking for him. Visible concern would incense Zarek, and Currie, who was all too familiar with debilitating forms of sympathy, checked his own.

Fifteen minutes. His mind wandered. It occurred to him that Anna might return to Stonehaven and run into Lipko. The digital clock blinked 1:45 A.M. There was a red phone on the bar. Anna sounded groggy when he called. She'd gone to the house already and met Asher, who had asked lots of questions. A barb moved into Currie's belly. What questions? he asked. Her marvelous antenna for trouble was undiminished by separation. Why did he want to know? *No particular reason.*

Anna said the questions had concerned Currie's relationship with Zarek.

Currie, casually: "What did you say?"

"That you were cellmates, that you didn't see him when we were married." Alarm edged into her voice. "Are you seeing Zarek now?"

"No."

"And why aren't you at the house? Where are you, anyway?"

"West Virginia," he lied. "Taking a few days off." It was crucial to keep her from going back to Stonehaven.

But she sounded doubtful. "You shouldn't be alone. You sure you're okay?"

"I will be."

Twenty minutes. At last Zarek glided down the stairs. Currie was surprised. Zarek did not look as if he had been ill. His agitation was gone, he radiated excitement. The suppressed intensity was greater than usual. Currie wondered what had happened upstairs.

"I can't change your mind," Zarek said. "Can I?"

It wasn't a question but Currie said no.

The mood had shifted from combat to appraisal.

"By the way," Zarek said easily. "FBI's got both ends of the street blocked."

Currie's back came off the couch. "Wasting their time on me," he snapped.

"Yeah, well. Look at it this way. Either they come in here with a warrant, find nothing and leave or they stay outside to see what other dangerous killers show up here besides you. Either way you get a good night's sleep. Lipko will never show up with Fibbies all over the neighborhood." Zarek smiled. "But they bring down property values."

Then he said more seriously, "We could go in straight. I could ask for my old job back. Qaddafi needs instructors all the time."

Blood began roaring in Currie's ears. He couldn't believe it. "You're going to do it?" he said.

"All my life I fought guys like him. I said it before. A dog like that needs to be killed. And I owe you." Zarek grew quiet. Currie knew he was thinking he was going to die soon. Zarek said, "I won a medal in Lebanon a couple years back.

Gold medal. I saw it a minute, then they locked it in a safe. No one's supposed to know I won that medal. Our marines were getting shelled. The enemy battery was in the mountains but our guys couldn't go there." He snorted. "Politics. Someone had to disable the battery." Zarek chewed beernuts. "Complaints are for whiners but one time I'd like people to know the truth. Those articles in the album never mentioned names."

"They'll know your name when we're finished," Currie said. "How did you know the FBI's outside?"

"Attic windows. Infrared glasses. Thought I'd take a scan."

Zarek placed two Budweisers on the bar. "You're my assistant, we'll tell them that. They'll expect you to act like a foreigner so they won't be surprised when you do. You'll need less training. Couple of weeks and you'll get by. And we'll change your appearance a little although I don't think they'd know it was you anyway."

"They'll know it was me in the end," Currie said.

Zarek cracked open the beers. "To a couple of suicides," he said. Foam ran down his chin. "Enjoy it," he said. "It's your last one, you're in training after this, we both are." Currie felt enormously thirsty. Zarek grinned. "You little shit," he said. "I didn't think I'd get back in the field." He wiped his mouth with the back of his wrist. "They cut people's heads off in Libya," he chortled. He made a hissing noise and slashed his hand through the air like a sword. The fatigue had gone out of him.

"We're the ones who'll do the cutting," Currie said.

Zarek nodded approvingly. "If we're lucky. Meantime you do everything I say. It's military now. No hesitation, no questions. When I say go you . . . *what do you mean, no?*"

Currie was shaking his head. "That story about being your assistant is for the Libyans, not me."

Zarek was astounded. He reached into the bowl of beernuts on the bar. "You're going to make the decisions?" he said.

"We go together, we decide things together."

Up close, Zarek's green eyes contained steel-colored tendrils, unreadable. "We're going to vote," Zarek announced flatly. Another nut crunched with a pop. "When we're crawling in the desert, we go the wrong way and we dehydrate. We going to vote on how to survive?"

"Common sense. I'd go along with you on that."

"There's a little bay on the Mediterranean. It's filled with hammerheads. We might have to swim it. We going to vote if I tell you to swim?" Zarek's voice was low, with a driving rhythm. "We going to vote if we have to do a standoff jump from an airplane? That's twenty miles by parachute. Maybe we'll vote while we're in the air."

"I'm going to be the one who kills Qaddafi," Currie said.

Zarek jerked. "Oh," he said.

"And I'm not going to sit in a car while you do everything else. You know damn well I'll listen to you when you're the expert. You wouldn't have used those examples if you thought I'd argue them. Technical problems, you decide. The rest of the time we make up our minds together."

"I never worked with anyone, not even a pro," Zarek said.

Currie grinned. "Start a fashion."

"Easy words," Zarek said. "The basement's nice and warm. The beer is cold. You should have seen your face when you came here. You were never in the army let alone the Green Berets. Now you want to tell me how to work."

"Look," Currie said. "I'm not your responsibility, okay? Just train me and I'll take my chances."

Zarek came out from behind the bar. It always surprised Currie to remember the man was smaller. "You only have one chance by yourself and it's that you'll end up with flies crawling on your face. Take your chances? Christ. If it's not working between us," he threatened, "I'll get out."

Currie's euphoria lasted less than two seconds. Zarek said, "Money."

"I have six, seven thousand in the bank."

"Not enough."

"The company gave me a year's salary after Iran," Currie said. "I never touched it. Forty-five thousand. In money funds. Seems right to use it now."

Zarek developed a sudden fascination for the beer can. He slid his index finger around the rim. "We can make a lot more," he suggested. "Half a million. A Zionist in New York will pay."

He looked up. Currie was sick with horror. Zarek had been making phone calls upstairs, he had not been ill at all. That's why he'd given in so easily a few moments ago. Currie sputtered, "No." His voice rose. "No one's paying, we're not making money from Nori's death. It's us, that's all; you call him back."

Zarek argued smoothly. "We have to pay lots of people. Get paper, weapons, a place to train, ammunition. We have to get in and out of Libya. Especially out. It costs. There's another money option. Libyans. Businessmen who hate Qaddafi."

"I can get the forty-five easy at the bank," Currie said. "And the interest. And the six in the savings account. That's what we'll use."

"Presidents get paid," Zarek reasoned. "Generals get paid."

"No."

"Who's the fucking hero of your life?" Zarek said. "Whoever he is he gets paid."

"Dirty money," Currie said.

"If it's not a dirty act it's not dirty money." Zarek blew air in agitated bursts. Zarek said, "Look, I want to leave something for Cindy, okay? It's for her, not me. I don't need it."

"She's a lawyer, not a wheelchair case. She can take care of herself."

"Oh man," Zarek said. Fists lowered, he paced between the rifle cabinet and the boar's head. Currie thought, *He's going to back out. To hell with him.* "Who even told you to make the phone call," Currie raged. "Who even told you you could ask."

Zarek's breathing was audible across the room.

Slowly, he came toward Currie.

Currie looked down at him. They were an inch apart.

"No goodbyes," Zarek said softly. "No phone calls. We get the money at the bank tomorrow. We don't come back to the house. The FBI will be tricky but I think I have a way past them. No suitcases. We don't pack. We get in the car like we're going for a drive. Understand? If the Fibbies haven't come to the house by then, they'll try to follow us. Any more fucking complaints from you?"

His breath smelled beery. "And no money?" Currie said cautiously.

"Yeah, yeah, no money. But we go to the bank first thing. And we'll get you a passport in New York."

Currie nodded dumbly. He'd won it all.

"I'm ready," he said.

CHAPTER
9

O<small>N</small> Connecticut Avenue Zarek left the motor running in his Eldorado and he and Currie disappeared into the bank. "FBI will figure we're coming back to the car," Zarek said. "But you better hurry."

Neither of them looked back at the green Impala which had followed since they left Zarek's.

"They'll come in after us in a few minutes," Zarek said.

The branch president's name was Merkin. He was a heavy man with a fawning manner who had signed Currie's mortgage years ago. He sweated in the presence of celebrities. "We'll get you out of here in no time," he promised. Currie had phoned when the bank opened to make sure the money would be on hand. Merkin had needed an hour to arrange the transaction.

Merkin led them past a line of waiting patrons to his vault-side desk. "Let's have that money fund certificate," he said. "Ruth. Take care of this! Tim, what are you going to do with sixty thousand dollars?"

"New addition to the house," Currie said.

Merkin said, "Coffee?" Through the glass of the teller's cage, Currie saw Ruth, a long-haired blond, flirting with a male teller instead of getting the money.

Merkin said, "It's good you're getting out and making yourself *do* things. At a terrible time like this you have to *do* things. Just a little paperwork; Ruth will be back in a minute, she's very efficient."

Currie glanced past the line of patrons and out the glass front window. Two men were crossing the street toward the bank. One of them was Asher.

"I saw your girlfriend on the news," Merkin said. "Tim, you have our heartfelt sympathy here at Rymal Savings and Loan. If there's anything else we can do, don't you hesitate, not for a minute."

Asher and the other agent reached the Eldorado and split up.

Merkin said, "A healthy savings and loan supports its community." He meshed his fingers. "On this side," he said, raising his right hand, "capital. On this, citizens. The wife and I are throwing a barbecue out in Potomac this weekend. Maybe you want to come?"

The front door of the bank swung open. Two doormen wearing Hilton Hotel uniforms sauntered in.

Ruth brought the canceled money fund certificate back to Merkin. The cash, which Currie had asked for in five-hundred-dollar bills, was neatly tucked in a plain 10 by 12 envelope.

Currie said, "There is a favor you can do. A reporter's been following me everywhere, from the *Post*. I can't get rid of him." Currie and Zarek had made sure the bank had a back door before parking outside. "You don't have a back door, do you, we can use?"

Merkin scowled. "Leeches. They call me at the bank. You'd think they'd have some sympathy for a guy like you. The other exit is for employees but it'll be a pleasure to make an exception. This way."

Moving across the lobby, Merkin waved an officious hand at tellers. A buzzer sounded.

"The exit lets you out on Nineteenth Street," Merkin said. "Don't lose that money, now. For the house eh?"

A cab was passing. Asher and his men walked into the bank two minutes later. By then Currie and Zarek were on their way to National Airport. Merkin was in for a rough day.

CHAPTER

10

ZAREK swung the Lancia off the Milan-Como road and turned northwest into the Alpine foothills. Olive-groved terraces gave way to black piny woods. Clouds massed low, coloring granite peaks purple. It was cold for September. The mountains seemed to be holding their breath.

"His name is Pietro," Zarek said. "Arturo Pietro. He'll supply guns, training ground, information."

They boomed around a cliff road, two days out of Washington. Below, in the cold blueness of the receding Y-shaped lake, Currie caught a glimpse of glass-roofed needle-nosed ferry launches, fragile, dwarfed.

"We sold arms years ago," Zarek said. "Milan Incorporated. He was broke then, now he's rich. Silks. Little old man, that's what he is, elegant, wily, treacherous." But Zarek's warm tones showed Pietro was a friend.

Currie considered the range of Zarek's contacts, said, "How do you know all these people? Lipko? Pietro?" Downshifting for a hill, Zarek shrugged. "Business is business. Cars or reprisals. Tennis. Guns. A few people at the top know each other."

The woods severed Currie's view of the lake. Pines crowded both sides of the road. From the opposite direction a *carabinieri* patrol jeep shot over a rise and slowed to pass. The trooper in front cradled a submachine gun.

"I have to teach you to use a RPG rocket launcher," Zarek said. "A one-man antiarmor weapon. The Libyans use them.

Czech and Polish submachine guns. Barettas. Colt thirty-eights. Without Pietro it would take months to get them. Italy's got the toughest gun laws. Even Italians can't own guns. They catch us with Eastern Bloc weapons, its prison for twenty years. Because of the Red Brigade."

Bomb explodes in Rome synagogue. Currie remembered the news announcement in Zarek's basement. The sense of siege had begun with the first step off the plane, the airport guarded by soldiers. In Milan, where they had rented the Lancia, truckloads of khaki-clad national police were parked at intersections. Black-uniformed *carabinieri,* fingers on submachine gun triggers, protected government offices, synagogues, churches.

And even below, in the pleasure-seeker and silk capital of Como, the defenses, subtle to the point of being invisible at first to Currie, had been spotted by Zarek. He'd pointed the men out amid the stylish strollers on the cobblestone Piazza Cavour, the string-bikini-clad beauties lounging in private boats along the lakefront, in the glittery delicacy shops and even among the oblivious sight-gorged tourists riding the mountain tram to expensive restaurants above the town.

"There's Gullo. So Charlie the Snake's a bodyguard now, what do you know?" He indicated a bulky chauffeur opening the door of a white Mercedes limousine for its elegant high-heeled passenger.

A dark-suited man walked a little girl in kneesocks carrying schoolbooks. A short man in a blue windbreaker followed a laughing young couple with shopping bags. Both men scanned the crowds.

"The Red Guards could ransom half of Como," Zarek said.

The rage was systemized, Currie saw. Dozens of Noris had died in Italy. In airports, in bombing attacks. The corner troops made terrorism palpable. In most of the world it was expected. In France and Israel and Nicaragua. Currie saw it in the Italian papers every day. The United States, in its size, more easily absorbed shock. In its hugeness and splendor it mistook aggression for mistake. But the Italians cried out for revenge. Precautions were a matter of course. Currie felt linked in a battle, connected by terrain.

He forced his thoughts from the bodyguards. "Qaddafi lives in a fortress in the desert, you said. How do we get there?"

"The Italians built it. Serte, it's called. Radar. Guards. Impossible to break in, so we won't. But he comes out for the military day parade each year. Never misses it, the celebration of kicking out the English. That's the day you get him. That's when they killed Sadat, in Egypt. Until then, patience is the hardest part."

Patience. The word closed Currie's throat. Zarek took a turn too fast, righted the car. He'd found a map of the Mediterranean in the Pan Am flight magazine. He'd put his hand on the map and touched Italy and Libya at the same time. Pinky on Milano. Thumb on Benghazi. His heart pounded, he was that close.

"Teach me the weapons," Currie said.

"There are a hundred ways to carry out a reprisal," Zarek said. "Shooting's easiest and most practical in terms of escape. But you're not a marksman, you'd have to be closer than an expert and you'd probably need more time. Qaddafi gets to the parade by helicopter. That's why the rocket launcher; a way. Explosives are possible. There's Astrolite. You can bathe someone's clothing in it then sew an electronic detonator on like a button. Blow a guy in half." Zarek chewed his lip. He was running possibilities over in his mind. "There are poisons. The agency has a kit, a Styrofoam box with vials. Eight or nine chemicals you mix. One compound works in an hour, another in three days. A chart shows how. It looks like a heart attack. We put it on a Russian's toilet paper once. Get a job cleaning the car, or his seat at the parade. Smear it on. It works on the same principle as heat athletes use, like Ben

Gay. A penetrating agent. If you put the agent on your finger and touch wine, you'll taste wine in your mouth, that's the truth. Mix the agent with the poison. But we'll be searched when we reach Libya. Bad idea to carry Astrolite or poisons. Whatever we use we have to get it there. Best thing's probably to rig up a rifle, set it in wood so it can't move. You can get off a long-range shot then.

With the sixty thousand in cash Currie had withdrawn from his bank they'd flown to New York. "Tom Fleeter" was the name on the passport Zarek had stolen. The real Fleeter was a Cleveland doctor who had the misfortune to resemble Currie. Zarek had spotted him in Kennedy Airport. Fleeter had put his passport in a bag and his bag near a counter. Zarek had glided to the spot.

"He'll report it stolen but who cares?" Zarek had said. "Nobody checks passports to see if they're stolen."

A Pan Am 747 had flown them to Rome.

Zarek's wrist jerked on the steering wheel, the car veered but straightened. "Damn squirrel," Zarek growled, but Currie had seen no animal. It was the disease, the first sign.

He flashed to Zarek's guestroom. A single bed and half-filled bookcase. Two titles caught his eye: *Lou Gehrig, Lou Gehrig . . . A Quiet Hero*. After Zarek had gone to his room, Currie had switched on a lamp. *Lou Gehrig . . . A Quiet Hero* was smudged with fingermarks.

"We were in the room a few weeks ago," Gehrig's [best friend] said, "and Lou stumbled as he walked across the floor. I was reading a paper and looked up to see what he had stumbled over but there was nothing there. I was going to ask him what had happened but he had a strange look on his face so I didn't. A few days later he was standing looking out a window and I was sitting behind him, talking to him, and I saw one leg give way, just as though somebody had tapped him sharply on the back of the knee joint . . . ."

The doctors, Currie knew, had told Zarek the scientific name of his disease. Had probably tried to tell him the progression of symptoms and therapy to delay the inevitable. But Zarek wouldn't have listened to any doctor long, not once he knew he was dying anyway. He would have stormed from the room. And he never would have brought a medical journal into the house with Cindy there. So he'd bought the baseball books. Currie pictured him reading them late at night, over and over while Cindy slept, learning how he was going to die.

A smudged page of *Lou Gehrig* had described the great first baseman's goodbye at Yankee Stadium. July 4, 1939.

In the stands were all that he held dear, his family, mother and father seated in a box, unaware of his doom, his wife seated in another. Lifelong friends were in the boxes, cheering and applauding. And as Lou looked out over them gathered there in his honor, he knew he was seeing them for the last time. . . . For he was the living dead, and this was his funeral. . . .

But when Currie coupled that quiet Zarek, reading in his room, with the cool mercenary cavalierly listing methods of assassination, he was baffled as usual, drawn fearful, grateful for expertise and friendship and loyalty, repelled by Zarek's knowledge beyond what he knew, beyond his depth.

Zarek said, "Here's the turnoff to Pietro's."

He swung the Lancia onto a pitted gravel road which pitched the car as it climbed a rocky ravine. A river crashed below. "Secluded and probably defended," Zarek said. "Pietro picks his spots." Canyon walls closed in on them. Zarek had not wanted to call ahead. You never knew who's listening. The road terminated a mile later at a massive spike-topped wrought-iron gate beyond which the canyon walls dropped away to reveal, on both sides of meandering spruce-lined, crushed-marble driveway, luxurious lawn, flowers, sculptured bushes in geometric designs.

A long slate roof protruded from a rise two hundred yards ahead.

An iron fence climbed away from the gate in a *V* shape, up the forested walls, blocking all access to the estate.

"Not bad," Zarek said. A guard approached from a booth ten feet beyond the bars. He held a shotgun ready, finger on trigger like the *carabinieri* in Milan.

A chubby blond Teutonic, he wore hunting clothes and moved with alert caution. Currie had the feeling the man was ready to fire instantly.

A television camera hummed atop the gate. Unlit floodlights aimed in their direction.

"I don't speak Italian," Zarek said to the guard's question. The blond shifted to cold unaccented English. "You are lost?"

Zarek gave a thin little laugh. He was a good friend of Dr. Pietro's, he said. Come to visit.

Unimpressed, the guard said, "You are not in my book. You will go back." The barrels rose a fraction.

Zarek and the guard locked eyes like male dogs or bulls pawing the ground. Zarek took a step forward. It seemed a challenge under the circumstance. He said, "Just let him know we're here."

The guard repeated doggedly, "You are not in my book." He planted himself sideways so as to present less of a target. His gaze flickered between Zarek and Currie.

The valley at Currie's back knifed the wind down on them. Currie added, "We've come a long way from . . ." He caught Zarek's look. "London. Can't you make an exception?" The guard shook his head. Zarek said, "You have a phone in that booth. Use it."

"Don't walk any closer please."

The light was fading. There was a click and the searchlights went on above the gate. Currie had run into bureaucratic doggedness at home hundreds of times. Sorry, sir, the bank closes at three. Sorry, that isn't my department. But in a country where soldiers guarded public buildings and body-guards the rich, in this secluded armed valley impaled by searchlight, and with Zarek and the guard faced off in some primal recognition, Currie felt the shotgun barrels rising even though he could not see them in the glare. Underneath the frozen tableau, the cold warnings, chemical reaction mounted toward explosion.

"Dr. Pietro's 'close' friends," the guard said, emphasizing the word *close*, "have the villa phone number. If you don't have it, call the factory in Milan. The manager gives Dr. Pietro messages each evening. There are accommodations in Como. You can enjoy views."

Zarek growled, "I can think of a view I'd enjoy."

The snarl of an engine grew audible from inside the estate. Headlights bounced over a rise and a jeep braked beside the guard. The new man wore a gray cap and pointed a sawed-off shotgun. The guards conferred in Italian.

The blond said, "You are on private property. The Dottore owns all land back to the main road. You will turn around, now."

Currie tried arguing one last time, then he said, "Let's go, Zarek." Four barrels pointed at them. "We'll drive back to Como and call." Zarek didn't move. Currie said, "Zarek?" Zarek took a step toward the gate.

"Zarek?"

There was a click beyond the searchlights, shotgun hammers thumbed into place.

Zarek slammed the Lancia door shut. The tires spun gravel. When they reached the main road, he pulled onto the shoulder and cut the engine.

"You will turn around," he said, imitating the guard. "*You will turn around!*"

Currie said, "The guns are more important, getting them.

That guard was a jerk but we'll drive back to Como. *I'll* drive. Get out."

Zarek repeated, "You will turn around."

A hard smile spread across his face.

"This is going to be a pleasure," he said.

"Pietro will take care of that guard," Currie said, but even as he spoke he knew Zarek talked about something else.

Zarek said, "It'll be a black night. We can leave the car in the woods."

A ticking began in Currie's ear. "You're not serious," he said. The ticking grew worse. Currie said, "Two guards, two shotguns. Drive to Como with me. Pietro will put us in his book and we'll be back in two hours."

Zarek's eyes glowed with intensity. "Sur-prise," he whispered.

"Surprise?" Currie said. Zarek was another person, he wasn't even listening. Passing cars grew indistinguishable in the dark. Currie said, "What's the harm in making a phone call?"

"I don't have the number."

"Get it from the factory."

"Too much time. Pietro might leave."

"You said he never goes anywhere."

Zarek snapped, "I don't know what he never does. He's there now. It's going to be easy. This is your first test. They won't expect us to hit them on foot." But it was clear from his relish that ease had no part in his decision.

Currie retorted, "You don't want to break in there to test me, you're risking our lives because a guy insulted you."

"It's the worst defended place I've ever seen," Zarek continued. "I figure they have alarms on the villa side of the fence. If we go over the fence, we trip the alarms."

"Sounds real easy."

Zarek got out of the car. "One guard at the gate, the other's probably at the house." He leaned in the window, wagging a finger. "The camera focuses only on the road, and the lens extends *over* the bars. So even if it's a wide-angle lens, it doesn't transmit a picture of the gate itself. Hmmm."

"The *guard's* at the gate."

Zarek opened the trunk and rummaged through traveling bags. They'd bought clothing in Rome. Currie said, "He'll shoot you." Zarek pulled out a black stocking cap and turtleneck. Currie said, "No way we're doing this." But he felt powerless against Zarek's unwinding insanity, locked into a scene in which he was a spectator. They weren't in Zarek's basement now. The man was beyond reason. An animal was coming out, a transformation in the woods.

Zarek seemed to become aware of him for the first time. "If you're afraid," he mocked, "you might as well forget Libya. Go home. Getting into Pietro's villa is nothing next to Libya, it's candy. Never mind why I'm doing it, for you it's a test." He waved off Currie's "That's not the point." He said. "Pietro will be happy to see me."

Zarek fitted the cap on his head. "You want to go to Como? Take the car. Call him." He grinned. "I'll meet you at the villa."

Currie watched the bowie knife come out of the bag. Zarek hadn't taken a gun to Europe, had not wanted to carry it on the plane.

Currie said again, "Two shotguns. Two guards."

Zarek's grin grew wolfish. "How do you think you're going to get to Qaddafi if two guards bother you." He closed the trunk. "This is one vote you lose."

The dull gleam of the bars grew visible through the bushes. It was two hours later. They approached the fence. The moon had not come out. "Never mind your bullshit about a test," Currie had said, "but you'll have a better chance with two of us." At the moment he thought loyalty a horrible joke.

Diagonally ahead, through the gate and thirty feet away,

the guard's head lowered in his booth. Cigarette smoke bathed him in blue shadow. He looked like he was reading.

Currie went over Zarek's plan in his mind.

Zarek had said, half an hour earlier, as they lay on their bellies at the crest of a wooded hill, surveying the estate below, "How would you get in?"

"I'd wait up here to see if there was a regular patrol."

"Good."

"If Pietro really owns all this land, not only the villa but the woods too, he might have some kind of early warning system in the forest around us."

In the dark, Zarek's eyes had widened with approval. "Like that wire over there?" he said.

Currie's ears grew hot. "I don't see a wire."

"It's three feet in front of your face."

Through the dark, Currie discerned a hair-thin shadow disturbance in the light, a dark strand in a straight line an inch above the mossy earth.

"Jesus," he said.

Zarek brushed away a little dirt and dead leaves. "Nothing to worry about. Just a step over . . . ah!" His hand darted out, came back with a tiny struggling toad he'd caught by the legs. He opened the breast button on his safari shirt and dropped in the toad. Currie whispered, "What are you doing?"

"You'll see. Keep going. What else do we do?"

"Suppose the fence is electrified?" Currie said. "We'd have to find the power box, but it would be inside the estate. How do you disable a fence?"

Now at the fence, Zarek dug the toad out of his pocket, held it with two fingers above the inch-long black steel wedge connecting the bars, and dropped it on the steel.

The animal blinked up at them.

It hopped away.

Zarek mouthed the words, "Not electrified."

He lowered himself like an animal drinking, palms holding up his chest, neck extended. He sniffed the bars of the fence, crawling.

"No urine smell," he whispered. "No guard dogs."

The temperature was still dropping.

Both men had smeared dirt on their faces and Currie wore a turtleneck, too.

"Remember," Zarek had said, "this is an easy test. We don't have to kill anyone. We don't have a problem of escape. No police will be coming. All we have to do is come to Pietro's attention, let him know we're here. He'll be glad to see me."

"He better."

Pleasantly, Zarek said, "Any other suggestions for getting inside?"

"Sure," Currie said sarcastically. "Take the shotgun away from the guard."

"Excellent! You really have an instinct for these things. How would you do that?"

"Zarek, what's the point of risking our lives to get to see someone who'll see us anyway if we just call?"

"I know how *I* would get that shotgun. What would *you* do?"

"Drive back to Lake Como and use the phone."

Zarek pushed his face close to Currie's. "The longer we stay up here, the more dangerous for us. There could be microphones in the woods."

"Sure. Microphones."

"Like this one," Zarek said, holding one up.

For a moment Currie couldn't breathe. Zarek said, "Don't worry, I cut the wire a hundred yards ago when you were bitching about breaking into the estate. Every thought that distracts you from the job can kill you. I asked you how to get the shotgun from the guard."

Currie felt his face itching from the mud. "I don't know,

get him close to the fence, make a noise or something and get him close and when he turns back around tell him you have a gun, order him to drop the gun."

"Go on."

"I mean this sounds so simple and —"

"I told you it would be simple. Order him to drop the gun and then what?"

"Well then, if the fence isn't electrified and the camera at the front gate only shows the road, climb right over the front gate, pick up the shotgun, march him to the house."

"Bravo," Zarek said.

The earth felt cold under Currie's fingernails. He said, "But suppose the guard doesn't drop the gun. Suppose he whirls around and fires?"

"He won't do that."

"What's going to stop him?"

Currie hadn't seen Zarek pull out the bowie knife. In a single movement the arm flashed out. There was a *thunk* in a tree trunk twenty feet off. The moonlight gleamed dully off the still-quivering blade.

"You want him to try to fire, don't you?" Currie said, horrified. "That's what this whole thing is about."

"Don't let your imagination get out of hand," Zarek said dryly, wrenching the knife from the tree. His face was emotionless as usual. He said, "That guard won't try to fire. I'll have some pebbles."

Zarek threw them into the blackness beyond the searchlights. They struck the guard booth. The guard looked up.

"I'll get him close."

With a long stick Zarek jiggled a bush a few feet away. The guard came out of the booth and switched on a flashlight. The guard walked toward them. They ducked.

"After he checks he'll turn back to the booth."

The instant the guard did so Zarek growled, "Drop the

shotgun." The shotgun hit the earth. "Push it under the fence with your foot," Zarek ordered. "Now back up against the fence." He had told Currie, "He won't touch it if it's electrified, extra test."

Holding the shotgun on the guard, Currie thought the whole thing too easy, much too easy. Something was going to go wrong.

Zarek landed on the other side of the fence and held the knife to the guard's throat so Currie could follow. In angry mimicry Zarek said, "You will turn around, now! Walk ahead of us, toward the villa."

The guard's shuffling compliance seemed passive, unafraid. Currie didn't like that either. Zarek said, "One two, one two. March, you Heinie." Everything was happening too fast. Their footsteps crunched on crushed marble. Spruce trees lined the driveway like sentries at attention. Since they had left the wind-tunnel valley, the temperature had risen dramatically, it was almost tropical. Currie smelled lemon trees. He sweated in the turtleneck. His face itched from the dirt.

The guard coughed, stopped, coughed again and brought his hand to his mouth.

The cords in his neck bulged.

Suddenly Zarek kicked him, sending him sprawling. "Grab it!" Zarek hissed. The guard's hand was already snaking back to his mouth. Knowing only that the true nature of the evening was finally presenting itself, Currie leaped and ripped a small circular object from the guard. It was a whistle on a chain. His knees went weak. He said, "He could have woken up the whole villa."

"He didn't want to wake up the whole villa," Zarek said. "It's a dog whistle."

The lemon smell grew overpowering. A dog whistle. Sound so high only dogs could hear. Fear clutched at Currie's belly.

Quiet triumph marked the guard's voice. "Doberman pin-schers, eight of them. Dr. Pietro doesn't like barking. In a minute they will arrive."

Currie said to Zarek, "You said there weren't any dogs."

"Not guard dogs. Attack dogs. So, we'll improvise."

The wooden whistle had two holes on its barrel. The guard stood up. "Gate's too far for you. Shotgun won't stop all of them. Give it to me, I'll save you."

"Don't!" Currie said. He meant the guard would kill them. The guard was furious that he'd been overcome.

Currie heard pounding on gravel beyond the rise.

Zarek jammed the barrels into the man's side, arching him in pain. "If the whistle calls them, the whistle stops them. How?"

The pounding grew louder.

Gasping, the guard said, "Cover the first hole and blow, yes, the first hole stops them."

"Lying!" Currie said.

The guard showed his teeth. "Then shoot me. But you won't because . . ." but Currie didn't hear any more because the Dobermans were hurling themselves over the rise, two of them, five, low to the ground, homing, eight now, pro-pelling themselves with leaps. He shoved the whistle in his mouth; sweat bathed him. The guard's voice said from some-where close, "They'll kill you if you choose wrong. Or if you shoot." Currie covered the second hole, and blew as hard as he could. His neck felt as if it was going to explode. He forced his will into the whistle. He couldn't hear anything except the running dogs and the lead Doberman was sixty feet and closing, fifty when he tried both holes, thirty feet and flying and he had only two choices left, the guard had said try the first hole but the guard had been trying to trick them but maybe the trick was that the first hole was the *right* hole or maybe the whistle had even broken when the guard fell, and Currie, feeling the jaws clamping down on him, feeling the

[126]

dogs sawing his tissues like paper, opened both holes and blew. He blew with all his power. The whistle didn't make a sound and he crouched for the leap — he would go down fighting.

The lead dog stopped. Whined. Sat down.

It cocked its head at Currie, four feet away.

Currie's hands were trembling.

Don't drop the whistle, he thought.

In the dark, the Doberman's eyes glowed yellow. Its ears stood straight, it scratched its hindquarters.

Other Dobermans panted and looked from one man to the other. The lead dog shoved its nose into Currie's crotch.

Slowly, Zarek began bringing up the shotgun. The growling came from six directions, gears ready to engage.

The shotgun lowered.

Currie said, "Keep walking!" He took a step. A dog trotted toward him. He blew the whistle and the Doberman quieted. Another step. The lead dog bumped Currie's knee. Currie kept going. "Slowly," he said. "Zarek, slowly. It's going to be easy to get in here, huh? Slow."

The guard, cheerfully and voluntarily moving beside them, said, "That whistle won't stop the dogs long. They know you're not supposed to be here."

Currie had seen a medieval tapestry once. Wolflike devils feasted on a fawn. Bellies flat, snouts extended, they ripped meat chunks off the carcass. From his vantage point above the ridged muscled backs, he thought he looked down at the devils.

Stop it. Dogs sense fear.

The guard addressed the Dobermans. "Wilhelm, you know me. Kaiser, Duce. Good dogs, Smart dogs. Lovely, obedient dogs."

Zarek tried it, "Good, friendly dogs." The snarling worsened.

"You'll never reach the house," the guard remarked. He

disengaged himself from the group and sat on the grass. He petted two of the dogs. "Bad men," he told the dogs, wagging a finger at Zarek. "They want to hurt Dr. Pietro."

"I told you he's a friend."

"Yes, a friend. Drop the shotgun. I'll call the *carabinieri*. You'll go to prison but you'll be safe."

Zarek laughed. "You want the shotgun? You'll probably just give it away again." The guard cursed in German and the Dobermans snapped and leaned at them. Currie blew the whistle. It was getting harder to quiet the dogs. His fingers were slick. He felt dizzy. The house was over a hundred yards away. He had no way of knowing what Dr. Pietro would do if they reached it anyway, never mind what Zarek said.

Recovering his jovial spirits, the guard said, "I have to admit you're progressing pretty well. Unfortunately, the dogs respond to verbal commands as well as the whistle. Let me see. What is that word for attack?"

The big Doberman rolled his head like a bull about to charge. Two others trotted around Currie manically. He did not want to use the whistle unless he had to. It would only work for a while.

The guard cried, "I remember!" He whispered, "Pasta." He cried, "PASTA!" Nothing happened. Smiling, the guard scratched his head. "I was sure it was pasta," he said. "I better try again." The animal smell thickened. They inched toward the house. Zarek said, "Those Dobes won't attack fast enough to save you." He sounded so menacing, even surrounded by dogs, that the guard blanched but his good humor returned again. "Now I remember," he said. Currie could make out the upper floors of the house over the rise. The guard spelled the attack word as if trying to keep it from the dogs. "N-o-o-d-l-e-s. Isn't that funny? No wonder I thought it was pasta. Pasta and n-o-o-d-l-e-s are alike. NOODLES," he shouted.

The dogs just looked at him. "Ach," he said. "I meant to say it in Italian." A stony superior look came into his face.

"Enough games," he said. "Last chance." He reached to take the shotgun.

Zarek purred, "Touch it, touch it. Watch what happens when you touch it."

The guard withdrew, stiffened. His eyes seemed to have grown smaller in the dark. With abrupt certainty Currie knew what must be done, he knew this type of bully from Iran, he'd had a guard like this man and *trust your instincts,* Zarek had said. Zarek who was goading the man the wrong way, toward explosion. Suddenly Currie said, "You can have the whistle back."

They all stopped. Zarek said "What?" and the guard reached triumphantly. As Currie gave over the whistle he said, "The only thing keeping Zarek from shooting you is the dogs. Once those dogs attack he fires." The glitter in the guard's eyes turned to wariness. Currie kept his voice low, not challenging but factual. The whistle paused halfway to the guard's mouth. Currie said, "You understand? We're in no position to hurt Dr. Pietro with these Dobermans here. Your employer is safe. But you'd better protect us, it's your decision what happens to you. Your choice."

The guard remained frozen. He stared at Zarek's shotgun, at the dogs. He did not look so happy to have the whistle anymore.

He looked from Currie to Zarek.

The guard started to sweat.

When he blew the whistle, the dogs relaxed.

Then another voice said, "Zarek, is that Zarek?"

The guard froze. Everybody froze.

Two figures stood nearby in the darkness. The smaller one stepped forward, Currie caught a glimpse of silver hair.

"Padrone," the guard said respectfully. All malice had disappeared from his manner. He was the perfect polite servant. "The dogs caught intruders," he said.

"And you lent them your shotgun so they could defend

themselves," Dr. Pietro said. At least seventy, Dr. Pietro wore a heavy woolen coat despite the temperate air. His hair was thick and elegant. He had a regal posture and the light step of an old man, he moved among the dogs, petting and cooing. "Bruno, Bruno, you calm, be calm. Wilhelm, big baby." The dogs loved it, they crowded around wagging their stumps like puppies. "Oh put that gun away," Pietro told the guard who had accompanied him. "Meet my good friend Zarek, who can't do anything normal like other people, who can't even call me on the telephone to tell me he is here but has to climb our fence like a criminal."

The rifle lowered. Currie's knees were weak. Zarek said, "See? I told you there wouldn't be any problem." But there was respect in his voice.

Dr. Pietro said, "Roberto, dogs to the kennel. Hans, back to your gate." He waved his hand in dismissal. "Good job," he called after the guard. The man lifted his shoulders. "After all," Pietro said, "he's supposed to keep you out. Germans. Ah. Sadistic and unimaginative but wonderful servants. Also, children love him. Come. Introduce your friend. What is that on your face, mud?"

Crossing the lawn, they passed through a sunken garden garlanded with flowers and crisscrossed by shrubs. The moon appeared, bathing nude nymph statues and elliptical free-standing colonnades. There were cracks on the shaggy flanks and leering faun faces. Naked women on goat feet, smooth-bellied, beckoning.

A silver Mercedes limousine gleamed in the semicircular driveway. The house was covered with vines and trellises and spilled golden light from curtained balconies. A baffling geometry of hallway tiles gave way to a Greek sitting room in lavender marble. It was filled with busts, statues and lounge chairs. Liveried servants offered drinks on silver trays.

"Wash that dirt off, you'll have fresh clothes. Alfredo will show you. Join me in the study." Removing the heavy coat, Dr. Pietro wore an old cardigan despite the overheated room. He had a thin, frail face and eyes of extraordinary blue, tight-stretched skin and the hawk nose of a patrician. "No rush," he said. "I always dine late."

Supper was prosciutto and melon, light veal and grilled lemoned crayfish with golden crusted lasagna, washed down with strong local red called "the chatterer." It made you talk.

The study, to which they retired after dinner, was a more ornate version of Zarek's basement. Game heads lined dark mahogany walls. The leather furniture was plush and deep. Smoking his pipe, Dr. Pietro told stories of World War Two.

". . . When my men and I went over to the Allies, the German commander in this area, Protzer was his name, diverted his troops to bring us back. Up in those hills we fought the Germans and beat them. Never heard that story, did you? The Germans ran from us."

And of his career.

". . . I've been a millionaire three times and I'm not ashamed to start over. Bah! Italians! We love intrigue and use it to bring ourselves down! Now we've sold out to the Arabs, they own the country. Arms sales, antibiotics and air-conditioning, the downfall of the West. Wine? Zarek, why aren't you drinking more, are you in training?"

He spoke of fashion models he had known in Rome, kissing the edges of his fingers as he named them one by one. He spoke of the cardinals and politicians who visited the villa. "I always know when I have become rich again because they reappear. Enough of politics. Love, that is what we shall speak of." He turned to Currie. "You are in love?" he inquired. Pietro was on his second bottle of the chatterer. Currie and Zarek drank mineral water.

"Yes," Currie said. Drinking, he felt as if Pietro had punched a hole in him and he ran like wine onto the floor.

"Her name?"

"Nori." Her musky smell overpowered the wood odor and wine and Pietro's Dutch tobacco.

"When you are in love," Dr. Pietro pronounced, "it is not good to travel far from your woman."

"No," Currie said.

"It must be painful to be here when she is elsewhere. Love is precious, I have been in love only once. Why do you go so far from the person you love?"

"I'm not far from her," Currie said. Dr. Pietro beamed. "The perfect answer. You are an Italian. Zarek, since when do you spend time with people who understand the human heart?"

"I need a favor," Zarek said.

Pietro threw up his hands. "Eh-eh-eh! In a hurry! If you want to live long, you must relax and talk of love, but all right, enough of love." He winked at Currie. "As if there ever could be such a thing. We will discuss what I can do for you. Ask."

"I need weapons," Zarek said grimly. The joy went out of Pietro's face. His blue eyes seemed perfectly suited for sadness.

Outside the massive picture window the moon flooded a hexagon-shaped courtyard. Past that, far below, the yellow lunar sheet of Lake Como.

Pietro sipped Chianti. "Zarek, I am no longer in this business, you know that. You should get out too. After Milan I stopped."

"I know, but I only need a few weapons, one of each kind." He listed them. Pietro watched his glass. His cardigan seemed old and frayed, he'd probably worn it for years. The mere mention of weapons seemed unnatural in the elegant villa.

When Zarek finished, Pietro said, "These weapons make up the Libyan arsenal. You will get hurt. Why do you want them?" Zarek went blank. Pietro sighed. "A favor is a favor.

You will have them. What else? A place to stay? One of my companies owns a lodge in Courmayeur, near Mount Bianco. You can have it to yourselves. So! Tonight you will sleep here! Stay as long as you like. The items you request will be at the lodge when you arrive. There's a shooting range downstairs. Why don't you work for me, Zarek, and forget whatever it is you are going to do. Chilly," he said, pulling the cardigan close. In the stifling room, the other men wore short-sleeved shirts.

"You are tired I am sure," said Pietro. It was a gracious dismissal.

The servant escorted Currie and Zarek from the room. When they were gone, Pietro exhaled heavily, took a key from his pocket and unlocked a lower drawer in the mahogany desk. He took out a red phone. He dialed four digits.

"Pietro," he said when someone answered. "I want to speak to Jamal." When he was finished talking, he locked away the phone. Arms behind his back, he stood at the window, looking out at the far end of Lake Como below.

"I'm sorry, old friend," he said after a while. "I tried to talk you out of it. I told you Qaddafi owns everything now."

CHAPTER

11

A SHER stared back at eight pairs of eyes across the conference table. He was in the Director's private dining room. The White House had called an emergency meeting over Currie's note. Asher kept his face impassive but he was in turmoil. His agents had tracked Currie and Zarek to New York, they combed airports and bus stations. Asher felt there was a simple reason why the two men had gotten together but it eluded him, ate at him. Had Currie and Zarek been in contact since Iran or had they only recently hooked up again?

"ISRAEL, IRAN, SAUDI ARABIA. OCTOBER 13. BY THE BLOOD," read the blackboard. "Our experts have studied the message exhaustively," announced Elizabeth Cotter, the State Department representative. "Made inquiries, cross-referenced computers. The Saudi, Israeli and Iranian desks have been working around the clock."

She was a thin-lipped, delicate-featured blond resembling a Scottish fairy Asher had once seen in a children's book. But her tweed business suit destroyed the effect. She said, "If there were the slightest connection between any of these countries and this date, we would have found it. I suspect the note is not genuine."

"Details," snapped Ike Chapman, White House liaison.

"None of the countries have diplomatic relations with each other," Cotter said. "Only two have oil. Israel and the Saudis support Iraq in the Gulf War, Qaddafi sells arms to the Iranians. October thirteenth has no meaning. 'By the Blood' is probably some slogan, but we've found no reference to the term. We tried a military link. The Russians have stockpiled arms in the Fezzan desert but Qaddafi's army lacks strength. He could never take on just Israel, let alone the others too. It's doubtful he even has enough men to operate all his equipment. Suppose Currie lied about finding that note?"

Harold Dine, the CIA man, retorted, "You mean your experts were incapable of making a connection so none must exist?"

Cotter snapped, "The CIA hasn't come up with anything better."

They fell silent as the door opened. Agent waiters served Beef Wellington, hearts of palm vinaigrette, white chocolate mousse. When they left, Cotter said, "If the note is real, look for alternative meanings. Maybe it's a code, the words mean something else." She donned wire-rimmed glasses. "That's the only explanation we can support."

Asher's turmoil went beyond Currie. *Why don't you go after Qaddafi?* Currie had challenged at their first meeting. Asher had batted away the notion. It was impossible, too simple even to entertain.

But increasingly as he sat here he fixated on Qaddafi.

And borders.

Until Asher joined the antiterrorist unit four years ago he had regarded the FBI as a borderless police, formed originally because bank robbers escaped across state lines. States could not coordinate investigations. Federal crime was crime without boundaries.

But now criminals fled across international lines which even the FBI couldn't cross. To Asher it was obscene that an invisible line on the earth could stop a policeman. Qaddafi was unreachable. And the French police, who were supposed to be cooperating in the investigation, had other priorities. The whole frustrating process of dealing with the Sûreté was about as effective as the Massachusetts police trying to tell New Jersey what to do.

"I suggest taking the investigation out of the hands of the FBI," said Harold Dine. The CIA man was a tall, inscrutable, Ivy League type who wore gray-striped suits and launched into cowboy dialects when talking to women. His run-ins with Cotter were legendary. "The bulk of the work is overseas," he said. "Our contacts are better than the FBI's."

"Forget it," Asher said. "Our jurisdiction. But turn over the Zarek file which I've been trying to get for days."

Dine pressed his lips together like a butler scrutinizing a door-to-door mop salesman. "It's classified. Your vendetta against Zarek isn't our problem. Besides, our relationship with him is quite delicate."

"What's that mean, delicate?" Asher said.

Ike Chapman, the White House liaison, said, "I'm sure it wouldn't hurt to hand over the file. Mr. Asher will be discreet."

Dine smiled. "You'll have it tomorrow." Asher knew he'd never get the file.

Dine went cowboy for Cotter, sweeping his hand along the wineglasses in an effort at gallantry. "Beggin' yer pardon, ma'am," he said. "But the Agency has a different view of that note."

Dine counted on his fingers. "We got Cubans in Angola and Russians in Afghanistan. Weapons is how the Communists move into a place. Qaddafi will need help with those Russian arms, he doesn't even have to use them. I'll explain another way, ma'am. You a football fan? There's a quarterback, see? Joe Theismann's throwing a good game but the Cowboys want to mess him up. Now, the Cowboys don't have to tackle Theismann, all they have to do is *reach his wrist!*"

"Dine," snapped Cotter. "Speak English for once."

"It's like the Mideast is Theismann and the Cowboys are

the Russians," Dine persisted. "And if the weapons are his wr——"

Wearily, the Director said, "Dine."

"The Ivans will man the guns," Dine said, all trace of the cowboy gone. "They don't even have to use them. Their presence will destabilize the whole Mideast."

Your vendetta against Zarek, Dine had said. Everyone thought Asher hated Zarek because Zarek had evaded arrest that time in Boston. They were wrong. Zarek was a pirate.

It went back to when Asher was a boy. On the smugglers' coast of Maine he'd read book after book on pirates. In the end, he'd decided, pirates had existed because governments needed them. The Queen of England called them "Sea Hawks" and gave them letters legalizing attacks against Spain. The Spanish offered amnesty to plunder the British. Pirates went freelance between alliances but as long as countries used them they flourished. They were wiped out only when everyone banded against them. The last pirate stronghold, destroyed by a U.S. marine lieutenant, was in Tripoli.

Two hundred years later Americans recognized other country's terrorists but called their own "agents." "Don't be fooled by labels," Asher's Maine State Police captain grandfather had told him. "Just because someone is on your side doesn't make 'em right. See the truth. When you become a policeman, all your life clever men will try to argue their way around the law. The law might be wrong sometimes but it will never make as many mistakes as the clever men." In Washington Asher had had numerous occasion to test the theory. Two senators were in prison because of it.

"The difference between a cop and a statesman," Harold Dine was saying, looking at Asher, "is that a cop only sees his streetcorner but a statesman watches the whole world."

Ike Chapman summed up the White House position. "The President is heartened to see such warm cooperation among agencies. I'm going to recommend a wait-and-see attitude."

Chapman's primary qualification as White House liaison was that he had run the President's reelection campaign in Delaware.

As they filed out the Director motioned Asher to stay. "Coffee?" He poured. He had headed the St. Louis police force before taking over the FBI. They liked each other because they'd both started at the local level.

The Director said, "Any progress?" They'd decided before the dinner to downplay Currie as a suspect. "He's a hero," the Director had advised. "Don't advertise your suspicions until you have hard evidence."

Asher drank coffee black and hot. He rubbed his thick hands over his bullet head. He relaxed with the Director. "You weren't here when we broke the Letelier/Moffitt murders," he said. " 'Seventy-six." The Director nodded. Asher said, "We only arrested Townley in the end because the Chileans shipped him here. They didn't want to, we had to push. They cooperated because they needed good relations with us."

"So?"

"So the Libyans are never going to help us. Even in Townley's case the guy who ordered the killings, the chief of the secret police, went free. Never touched him." Asher drained the cup. "Currie kept asking why we couldn't go after Qaddafi."

"Try the little cakes," the Director said. "They're delicious."

"What is it, chocolate?" Asher said. "Egh, there's coconut in it. Look, Qaddafi's hit people all over the world. Colorado even. He announced reprisals the day Tecala was killed. The Libyans haven't denied they did it. The clothing bits we picked up support Currie's story. The shoeprints in the swamp were too small to be Zarek's. We found blond hair with some kind of German hair oil on it. Currie said the guy who kidnapped him was blond. And a motorist called the Virginia police the day Currie was grabbed. Claimed he saw someone on the hood of a Mercedes on the Parkway. I talked to the guy. He didn't even know who Currie was. A moron, he never heard of the Iranian hostages, all he knew was cars. We've established no previous link between Currie and Tecala. No problems between Currie and Abramoff. Watchers International people. Letter writers."

"You reversing yourself on him?" the Director asked.

"No, I'm just saying Qaddifi's a suspect too and it's bothering me we can't do anything about him. Currie was right, we have the richest law enforcement agency in the world and we can't do anything and it eats at me. As for Currie, he's been lying from the first. They left Zarek's Cadillac running outside the bank and headed for the airport. You call that innocent? But I have the craziest feeling, *two* feelings that keep getting stronger except they're opposite. Did you ever think a guy guilty but innocent at the same time? That's what's going on."

"The rum pastry," the Director said. "My downfall. Asher, you can't see answers in front of your face. Trust your feelings." He chewed with relish. "What do you get?"

"If I trust my feelings he *is* guilty and innocent at the same time," Asher snapped.

He froze the coffee cup in front of his face.

He whispered, "Two separate things."

Empty glasses and plates littered the table. Asher paced, the blood soaring in his temples. "Christ, of course! But if Currie wasn't involved in Tecala's murder what's he guilty *of*? Or maybe the murders happened *because* of what he's doing. Think," he told himself. He passed back and forth in front of the blackboard. "Currie emptied his bank account. Pulled out sixty thousand — suppose it was for Zarek? Why would someone pay a kill . . . oh shit, shit, shit."

The Director pushed himself back from the table. "The blond who killed Nori, who snatched Currie. He's going after him."

"Could be," Asher breathed.

"That's it!" Head down like a football player, palms on the table, the Director leaned into his argument. "Currie's taken fantastic punishment. He's snapped. He's up against a professional so he pays another professional to do it."

But Asher frowned. "If he's paying Zarek to do it, why go along?"

"To watch," the Director said.

"To do it," Asher said. "He's not the kind that watches."

"Son of a bitch," the Director said. "Sure. And why should he trust us, he knows the history. He knows Townley went back to Chile after prison, free. Even while Townley was inside he lounged around writing letters home. How come they weren't cleaning his pool? Damn, I'd love to let Currie do it." His voice hardened. "Find him."

Asher stopped pacing. "Suppose it's not the blond," he said, voice queerly flat. "Suppose it's Qaddafi?"

The enormity of the idea stunned them silent. Asher said, "He kept talking about Qaddafi. All the time. Nothing about the trigger man, not even speculation. Even on the phone it was always Qaddafi. Qaddafi killed her. Why couldn't I get Qaddafi? And the shrink talked about authority figures, he has problems with them."

"That's crazy," the Director said. "Suicide." He laughed uneasily. "Guesswork. Jewish mothers, that's what we are. They're probably taking a vacation." Neither man said anything. The Director said, "I need someone full-time on this. Take your pick. The rest of the investigation or them."

"Them."

"Make up charges, bring 'em in. I don't care how. A U.S. citizen gunning for Qaddafi, Christ. He's not coming here for a visit, is he? Qaddafi? Not coming to the U.N.? That twerp from the White House will go through the floor."

In his office Asher found a message from New York. An agent had traced a stolen passport to the Pan Am ticket computer and a stewardess who'd recognized photographs.

Currie and Zarek were in Italy, across borders.

He slammed his fist against the desk. The FBI maintained a liaison office in Rome. Asher made airline reservations, called for his car and sped toward DuPont Circle. Maybe Anna would have an idea where Currie had gone. He was making the worst mistake of his life. He was going to let her know Currie was in Italy.

In Europe the day turned over. Four weeks remained until October 13.

Currie dreamed of Nori. He was half asleep. It began as recollection. Two months after meeting at Watchers they'd gone dancing on a Saturday night. Nori knew a Southwest Side disco that turned Latin at midnight. She'd met him at the door swathed in red; red slitted dress, red high heels, fingernails, lipstick, earrings.

"Noreeee had to veesit her seek motherr," she said. "I am Chiqueeeeta. Weeeeel I do?"

Back in her apartment the high heels lay by the door. Gato Barbieri played sax on the stereo. Currie had slept with two women since Anna. He'd been physically satisfied but that was all. Tonight the rotating second hand was like a spring winding him. Her perfume, her dancing, every aspect of her heightened her allure. His head was so gorged with blood he could barely hear her talk. He kissed her long and deep on the couch.

"Chiqueeeeta cannot breathe in her dresssss," Nori said. "She cannot reach her zeeeeper. Weeeel you help her with her zeeeeper?"

She had a tiny waist. He'd dreamed about her legs for months. "Turn around so I can get at the zipper," he said. She shook her head. "If I do that I won't see your eyes when you touch me."

Her arms came around his neck. The zipper was cool but her skin burned, she was burning through the dress. The straps slid from her shoulders. The whole room was getting hot. There was a pounding noise like a heartbeat and he heard loud breathing. They were in bed. She raked his chest. Apple breasts rose, muscles touching. She bit his ear when he entered her, her legs came around him and he ran his hands around her body. He wanted all of it at the same time.

This is what I waited for in Iran, he thought, and then he *was* in Iran, hands manacled to the back of a folding chair. He thought, It's a dream I'm with Nori. The cell didn't go away. There was a writing desk and a little cot and a crawling cockroach. He thought, This is silly. I could reach that desk if I weren't tied to this chair. Nobody knows I'm here. The guard's sandaled feet passed the barred window. He thought, I haven't even masturbated in weeks; I don't get hard when I think of Anna. Anna's oil landscapes were on the cell wall now, Anna's antique Raggedy Ann on the writing desk. He was in bed again, a smooth white back rotating toward him. Anna. Moonlight dripped through the night window like rain and spotted her perfectly solemn Nordic beauty, her arms stretched to him alabaster white. She said, "Don't worry, Tim, the State Department man said sex might be a problem at first." He said, "First to last." Anna disappeared and Nori gyrated beneath him, locked to him, saying, "Tim, Tim, like that, Tim," every part of her moving at the same time; tongue, mouth, hips, hands. The curtains glowed red and heat crawled up the walls like fire. The frenzied sheeted aroma of love. He licked her beaded temples.

"Look at that flagpole. Get up!"

Currie opened his eyes. Zarek looked down at him. The

mercenary wore a blue flannel shirt with sleeves rolled. The tattooed marine sergeant with a knapsack on his back. "Move it," he said.

"Go away." Eyes shut, Currie saw her fading. He felt sick.

"I called Tripoli. We're expected in a week. That's seven days to give you two months' training. I'M WAITING."

Currie batted down the grief and swung his legs over the side of the bed. The lodge was cold. "I'm ready."

They burst into the predawn, tourist joggers if anyone looked. They'd reached Courmayeur three days ago. Zarek had been drilling Currie steadily on weapons, strategy and fitness. Early bedtimes. A biography of Qaddafi to read. But seeing the Alps Currie gasped in awe and forgot all else. The immensity defied photography. Towering, the mountains reduced the valley to dollhouse proportions, the low-roofed stucco houses, wooden balustrades and flower-potted Alpine balconies. The lone church steeple pointed at the morning star.

In early half-light the dirt path brought them through a meadow smelling of wild dandelions and foot-high dew-drenched grass, which sloped, a quarter mile ahead, into the evergreen lower tiers of Mount Bianco. Dawn slid down to meet them as a shadow line touching the snowcapped, luminous lavender and triangular upper peaks. But below that the very massiveness of the terrain made it impossible to absorb without breaking it into pieces; huge forest patches, alluvial chutes and deposits, autumn debris of a thousand avalanches. Banded orange and white cliffs. There was a smoky pine smell and the sound of rushing water. Bianco shifting would crush Courmayeur as effortlessly, as unknowingly as a giant sitting on a flea.

"Good skiing when you're not training for trigger time," Zarek said.

Neither man saw the watchers.

◇   ◇   ◇

On the balcony of a two-story pension at their backs the blond man lowered binoculars and went back into his room.

A heavy bearded man and a bald man with gluey brown irises sat on beds cleaning pistols and screwing on silencers.

"They're making it simple," Lipko told them in Arabic. "Heading up the mountain. Five minutes, then we go too."

They were dressed like a lot of other tourists in Northern Italy. Open shirts. Running shoes. The embassy had promised Lipko the men were good.

Lipko remembered Currie's hitting him in Washington, smashing his face with his knee, doubling him with pain and escaping. Jamal had almost called him back to the oasis for that.

Lipko's frown deepened. "There'll be no witnesses up there."

Zarek said, "We'll start easy today. Two, three miles." Following his finger Currie dimly discerned, straight up and past the tree and snowline, a tiny shack beside a blue, unused ski lift. "Easy?" he said, but he felt good drawing air, using his muscles. The air grew cooler as the field ended and they wove into the trees.

Zarek smirked. "Tomorrow you carry breakfast." The knapsack looked heavy but didn't slow him. He showed no sign of sickness. The rage that had marked his attack on Pietro's was gone. The villa assault had drawn them closer. Each man respected the way the other had handled the dogs.

"*Assassination* comes from Arabic," Zarek said. "*Hassa* means exterminate. And *asas* is an iman, he's holy. We'll show them holy. We'll turn the holiness on them. Think of yourself as having finished before you start. Before you pull the trigger. It frees you up. Feel the difference?"

The sun was almost up. High white clouds floated above the mountain. A deep bark echoed in the forest and Zarek said, "Mountain dogs, brutes. Half wolves, smash 'em in the face and they run." He laughed throatily. "You're good with animals." The reference to Pietro's Dobermans raised Currie's spirits.

Zarek said, "We'll fly to Libya from Switzerland. If something goes wrong, the border's closed or we get split up I have a friend in Riomaggiore, a fishing village near Genoa. He's a liquor smuggler to Libya. Sperazza's his name. Has a boat. Named it after a Polack, a war buddy. The *John Kukulka.* Riomaggiore. The *John Kukulka.* He has Libyans on his crew. They speak Arabic, they pay off the cops. Know how to get around in Libya if you need something. Pay Rosario Sperazza what he asks, he'll keep his word. Documents, weapons. Knows how to get anything. He can get us out of Italy and maybe Libya too."

The pain began as a dull tugging in Currie's thighs. They ran more and his temples throbbed and the trail spun a little. At two miles, climbing almost vertically, he felt sharp pricks in his chest. The pain narrowed his focus until he saw only the path and his running feet. Three miles would have been easy in the valley. The altitude thinned the air.

Zarek said, "First wind, you'll be fine. Don't look at your feet, look at the mountain."

Currie looked up and felt the second wind coming. Zarek said, "I'll train the troops, lay out their obstacle course, work the thousand-meter sniper range, build their combat village. Just do what I tell you. We'll make decisions together in private. If I'm not around and you have trouble with them, act like a king. They're afraid of authority, real cover-your-ass people. We'll have a walk-on-water paper from the army, it lets you go almost anywhere. Flash it. If they can't read, use Qadaffi's name. Or Jamal's. He's a mean, murderous bastard, ten-faced and deadly as a cobra, smart and hope you never meet him. He gets hold of us and it's the oasis for sure. Prisoners don't come back. They . . ."

Zarek made a strangled sound and fell, sprawling. The

path had been smooth, the disease had tripped him. Currie turned to help, Zarek was scrabbling to rise, knee down, dirt smearing his forehead and shirtfront. He glared back with murderous hatred. *Don't watch.* Currie kept going. A few seconds later he heard footsteps and Zarek pulled abreast.

"Military bearing," Zarek continued as if nothing had happened. "Communicate with the officers in a military manner. They're brutal so don't be surprised. They beat their men on the heads and shoulders. They punish 'em by making them walk on their knees in gravel, it wears them down to the kneecaps."

Zarek elaborated on Libyan punishments. Currie blinked sweat from his eyes.

"Move it move it."

"Twenty yards to go, stop at the shack."

Panting on the ground, Currie watched Zarek pull a canteen from the knapsack. Bread. Eggs. They were up so high patches of snow glistened. The cool air was delicious; Currie felt like he had not eaten in a month.

Zarek growled, "Fifty pushups, fifty situps. Then you eat." When Currie groaned, he added with sadistic glee, "We have some interesting little exercises next."

Lipko led the Arabs up the trail. They broke into the open and saw Currie and Zarek a quarter-mile up. They left the path to maneuver through the trees, staying out of sight. Only one path led up here, no danger of escape existed unless Lipko showed himself too soon and Currie made for the forest. The killing lust was a fine tingle at this early point. Lipko said, "Currie is for me."

Currie finished his hot coffee. The air grew warmer and he felt a pleasant ache in his legs. Bianco blocked the view of Courmayeur, Currie leaned against the ski lift and looked down into a gorge so steep the evergreens seemed to float within it, free of the earth, their tops like stakes. He heard water far below, but the bottom was out of sight.

Then Currie heard Zarek say, "I knew Nori."

He looked around slowly. "What?" But they both knew he had heard. Zarek shifted to a slight readiness. He reclined on one forearm, ready to move. The black diamond eyes drilled into Currie. Silence extended the meaning of his words.

A falcon rustled, settling on the ski cable. It inclined its head and watched.

"It was nothing important," Zarek said. "But I figured you ought to know."

"What are you talking about?" Currie said. "You never met Nori." Ticking began in his head. He had never noticed the dirty white blotches on Zarek's face, the way one side of the mouth dipped, uneven.

"It was only sex," Zarek said.

"You're nuts," Currie cried. The roaring in his head was thunderous.

Zarek said, "I didn't know she was yours. She never mentioned you." He used a driving cadence and his eyes never left Currie's. But there was something false in Zarek, calculated.

Then Currie understood and his rage turned icy. "You're trying to get me to do something, aren't you? You want me to fight." He stood up. "You never knew her, she wouldn't do anything like that anyway. It's a test, isn't it? One of your fucking tests. You want to see what I do when I'm mad. Hand-to-hand combat, you want to fight."

"Bravo," Zarek applauded, rolling to his feet with a lazy insolent smile which did nothing to dissipate Currie's fury. Zarek leaned close and lowered his voice. "Sharp mind," he said. Currie swung with all his might; he would have driven his fist halfway through Zarek's skull but the man was already five feet off, grinning, weaving, daring Currie closer with incredible snakelike speed.

As they circled each other the falcon began to "eck-eck." Currie's college boxing trophies were in the attic in Stonehaven. Squash kept him in shape. He was the bigger man. He kept his fist high, left poised for the gut opening. His vision cleared and he pushed his rage back inside himself, he couldn't afford to feel it now. But he kept anger on his face because Zarek expected to see it. Zarek seemed to float before him, the mercenary's hands locked into claws. Currie had one chance and it was that Zarek would underestimate him. He hissed, acting, "Bastard." He dropped his left shoulder in a feint as sweet as any he'd pulled off in college.

Zarek wasn't fooled, which was what Currie had hoped for. Zarek's hand moved to block the right-hand blow.

Letting all his anger flood him Currie threw his weight into the left-hand punch.

Moments later Zarek gasped on his back, arms splayed, head in a patch of snow. He moved his jaw back and forth. He shook his head. "Some punch," he said. Hands on hips, Currie looked down on him.

Zarek grinned.

"Not bad," he said. "See what happens when you make one mistake? Doesn't matter how good you are, a single mistake and you're dead. Stop pouting and listen to me. I'm the one who got hit so we're even." He rose, still probing the jaw. "There's hope for you," he said. "I'll say this only once. I owe you your life, not politeness. Two weeks' training is nothing but maybe I can help you if I know what I'm working with. No time to play games, to say 'try and hit me' when we both know it's phony. I need to see how you fight mad. In Libya you're going to be mad. You figured out my trick; that's better than I hoped for. Now understand why I did it."

Currie's face burned. Zarek said, "You don't have to love me, just listen. I'm going to show you strike points." He touched different parts of the body.

"Target areas are anyplace there's a natural depression.

Hollows protect something vital. That's why they're surrounded by heavy bone. Ears, nose, eyes, elbows. Base of the skull and spinal knot. That's where you sever the cord. Both sides of the throat. Feel the hole in the temple, the crease under the nose? For each depression there's a corresponding attacking part of the body. The heel fits in the armpit, the first two knuckles in the temple. The edge of the hand under the nose. What fits the temple?"

"The knuckles, damn you."

"That's good. The fist fits the solar plexus, that's the only place you boxers have right." Zarek's hands were on his hips. "The points where the body joins together can be broken. There's no such thing as an unarmed man. You are armed right now. You are a deadly menace and I want you to know it. Make yourself a hammer. You can break a face, a collarbone is weak and unsupported. A hammer can smash it, you can smash it. Stand up. I'm going to show you new ways to use your hands."

"They're finished," Lipko whispered. He crouched in the bushes inches from the path. He gripped the gun tight.

He'd chosen ambush because continuing to the top would have meant breaking from cover early, warning Currie he was there.

Across the narrow trail a gorge dropped two hundred feet to a boulder-strewn mountain stream. Shattered bleaching timbers thrust upward on the bottom, to crush or impale a man.

"They'll start down now," he said.

The sun shone with dazzling whiteness. The air smelled of pine trees and thyme.

CHAPTER

12

A T 10 P.M. Anna arrived at Zarek's house. She scarcely
remembered the ride there, she was dizzy with fear. The
blinding realization had hit with Asher's words. *He'll die if we
don't reach him first.* Now she knew she still loved Currie. There
was no time to fight the feeling anymore. She had told him
she would never come to this house but she badly needed
help.

Summer fog blanketed Capitol Hill. Along the deserted
street, windows glowed gold through mist, perfect shining
havens of family.

The terrifying image spurring her was Currie barely a
week at Stonehaven where he'd cried for revenge against
Qaddafi. Face mottled purple and white, eyes sunken, he'd
not even seen her in front of him, the pressure in his features
so hellish it seemed he might rip apart.

I'm coming to you because maybe you can help me save him, Asher
had said. *You and I think alike about Zarek's influence on him.
Maybe you know someone he might have told where he was going.*
Anna had told him that until two nights ago she had not
spoken to Currie in two years. *Then maybe you know Cindy Taft,
Zarek's girlfriend. She knows where they are but she won't talk to
FBI.*

I never wanted to meet her, Anna had told him, and Asher
had left not realizing he'd planted a germ. Now the door
opened and Anna looked into the face of Zarek's mistress.
Currie had not mentioned how attractive she was. Slanting

green eyes and high olive cheekbones. Shoulder-length hair in fashionable rings. She wore tight blue jeans and brown leather boots. She wore a white silk blouse that strained at the buttons.

Currie had lain in jail a year because he'd given this woman his chance to escape. Anna batted down a wave of loathing. She was here for help. "I'm Anna Currie, I was married to Tim. They're in trouble, bad trouble with the FBI. We have to let them know."

If you think of something, Asher had said, *call me*.

Cindy backed two steps, but the fear on her face turned to polite guardedness. "I recognize you," she said warily. She referred to TV.

The living room smelled like a perfume factory. They faced off across a glass coffee table piled neatly with *Vogue* and *Time* magazines. Above plush red love seats Rubens reproductions hung on the walls. Plastic fruit filled a Waterford crystal bowl.

Cindy crossed her legs. "Trouble?"

To Anna each second felt tangible, a worsening of Currie's odds. Anna told the story but changed it. In her vision Asher had Zarek's interests at heart too. He'd traced them to Italy, they were up to "something violent," possibly revenge against the people who had killed Nori. The Italian police had been alerted. There had been an attempt on Currie's life. She repeated Asher's words, "They'll die if we don't reach them first," and her control deserted her a little and her voice shook.

"If they pull it off, they'll go to jail the rest of their lives," Anna concluded.

Cindy remained coolly quiet; she was an attorney, Currie had said. Law school paid for by assassination. But Anna revised early appraisals of insubstantiality. There was formidable intelligence in the slanting green depths.

Cindy remarked, "I have a nice Chianti."

She clicked off to a glass rolling bar.

Anna had a flash of Currie at Stonehaven two weeks ago. She wanted to scream in frustration.

"What I don't understand," Cindy said, pouring to the polite gurgle of wine, "is why the FBI came to you." *You gave Tim up,* she seemed to say. *It's late for you to be involved.*

Anna was dumbfounded. Rather than throwing herself into alliance, Cindy was cross-examing her, *her,* gazing down with superior inquisition at the wreckage of Anna's marriage.

"Why shouldn't they come to me?" she said stiffly. "I knew him for sixteen years."

"But they seem to have felt you might have special information," Cindy said. "They only visited me once and I still live with Zarek. I gather you've talked to them before."

Time's cover read, "MANAGUA BOMBING: DOES THE U.S. SUPPORT TERRORISTS?"

"Yes but . . ." It was the wrong thing to say. Cindy's face closed up, a pleasant hostess expression emerged. She'd probably shut the door on the FBI dozens of times. She issued a light cocktail-party laugh, a fetching two-syllable *ah-ah* tinkle. "There really isn't any cause for concern," she said. She might have been consoling a grandmother worried because relatives were late. "FBIs scare people, that's what they're good at. Asher's just upset because he can't persecute them if they're out of the country. He hates Zarek. There's nothing illegal been done. FBIs invent things. Don't worry."

A dismissal. They could talk more, but the subject was closed. Anna flashed to Currie after Iran, in the jeep coming home from a party. "Why should I tell you anything about that cell?" he had said. "So I can hear it back on television tomorrow?"

It wasn't true. "He went to jail for you!" Anna cried.

Cindy jerked. Her arm came off the back of the couch and the bland look was replaced by something more predatory,

[152]

not a look Anna associated with courtrooms. Cindy said, "If you love him so much, why'd you leave him?"

"That's not the point. Didn't you hear what Asher said, what could happen? Don't you want to help Zarek or don't you care about him at all?"

The lines around Cindy's mouth hardened. "I stayed with Zarek. I didn't run away and tell the story on TV."

Anna felt sick. She saw a photo of Cindy and Zarek on the mantel, overly displayed like everything else in this room, too big, embossed with gold. Cindy and Zarek ate hotdogs on a beach. Zarek was sunburned and sauerkraut hung on his fingers. Cindy wore a string bikini out of *Vogue* magazine.

Anna said, "It was a mistake." She was sweating.

She said, "I know you don't believe me. I don't live in your world. It's no crime to talk to the FBI in mine. People want to talk to them, they come to the door and help you. You're supposed to, you like to." The loathing was bursting out. "You think I wanted to come here? I hate what Zarek is. I never wanted to meet you, what you did to me. Who are you to ask questions? In this house. How it's paid for. But it's not important how I feel. Reaching them, that's what we have to do. The divorce was a mistake, okay? A mistake."

Cindy sipped wine. "Honey, it's no crime to talk to the FBI in your world because you don't know the damage they can do. You see them on TV busting mobsters, they look pretty good on TV. So Asher tole you he wanted to help Currie? Did he tell you if Zarek and Tim are planning something violent they can be prosecuted on conspiracy charges? No. Did he tell you *he* doesn't have the power to decide who gets prosecuted?" She shook her head, drained her wineglass. She put the glass on a coaster depicting Greek nudes. "Of course he didn't. He didn't tell you the FBI is at the mercy of the Italian police overseas. Even if he told the truth, that no charges will be filed, he didn't tell you how police orders get screwed up going down the line, or how some tight-fingered third-rate Roman traffic cop could start shooting and kill Tim because of information you gave Asher. You want the responsibility if that happens? You think you blab to Asher and suddenly everything is fine?"

Overwhelmed with horror, Anna murmured, "I hadn't thought of that."

She was burning with defeat. But when she looked up she saw Cindy's appraising look was back. Anna still had a chance, a wedge for getting through. But she was going to have to tell the whole truth, one which she still had not admitted to herself. That she was not just a victim of circumstance when it came to Currie, that she was not just Currie's "friend," that she was not a professional woman of the world doing him a favor. None of those women would get what they wanted here, none of those self-protective faces would work. *They'll die if we don't reach them.*

With the terrible vulnerability that comes from realizing something is valuable she said, "I didn't know what I had." Cindy was waiting for more. Anna said, "I was nineteen when I got married. I met Tim in school, he's the only man I ever knew." The Rubens nudes seemed to be watching. She said, "The first years were great. Fun. Then I got this restlessness. It kept me from settling in. I was missing things. I saw them on TV. Places. Travel. Tim was different, satisfied. He wanted children. I volunteered at Children's Hospital. The funny thing is that I was afraid of what I yearned for. Glamour." She glanced at the *Vogue* magazine.

She felt immensely tired. "If Iran hadn't happened we would have worked our problems out. But suddenly I was alone. All those glamorous people I'd feared, the reporters and politicians, they came to me. Wanting me. Why should I stay in the house? People stopped me on the street. It meant something, distracted me. No, I *liked* it, you understand? It was exciting. Then Tim came home."

There was a soft drumming outside, rain. Light came from

a crystal chandelier and a long skinny lamp in a corner. Cindy said, "I watched you on *Meet the Press* one Sunday. The *Times* reporter asked you, 'How does it feel to have your husband incommunicado?' What a jerk. Incommunicado. 'It's hard,' you said. I started laughing. Shit, hard. Zarek wasn't even listed under his real name. His passport said George Murphy, businessman. He has eight passports. Thinking up names is a game with us. I say, how about Ivan Volcanovich, fishing trawler captain. He says Carlton Fitzgerald Claflin the third, president of Bankers Trust. Tony Redunzo, olive oil, I say. He says you're the wop, not me. Then we go through the phone book for the most innocuous name we can find. Every time I saw a list of hostages there was 'George Murphy, businessman.' If the Iranians had found out who he was, they would have slit his throat. I almost phoned you but what would I say?" She laughed. "Hi, I'm the reason your husband is a hostage? Let's go out and drink stingers?" The rain sound grew harder. "When Zarek got back he said you were all Tim talked about. Home. Anna. Home. Anna."

Anna nodded miserably. "But when he got back we were far apart. He wanted the old way. Give up speaking, I had job offers. Hide in the house with him but he wouldn't talk about what happened, wouldn't go to the doctor. Sit with him, that was what he wanted. It was crazy. I couldn't do it. I tried to take him places, snap him out of it."

She lapsed into silence. What more was there to say?

Anna knew she would never go to Asher now, not only because of Cindy's warning but because she would lose Currie if she did. She believed that Asher had no intention of harming Currie but she could still feel the loathing in Cindy's look when Cindy had thought Anna was cooperating with the FBI. Currie had looked at her like that after Iran each time she went on television to talk about their life together. She would not be able to stand having him look at her like that again.

To Cindy she said, "You don't have to tell me anything,

but at least try to reach them yourself." Her voice cracked. "I don't want him to die."

Cindy said, "Zarek always calls when he goes somewhere but this time he hasn't."

Anna's heart plunged. "You don't know where they are?"

Cindy played with the wineglass. "He sold arms in Milan a few years ago with a doctor friend, Pietro. If Zarek hasn't contacted him we're out of luck. He owns a silk company in Milan but these guys don't talk on the phone transcontinental. Overseas calls are monitored, dishes suck everything out of the sky. You can splice talk."

Anna heard herself say, "How do I get there?"

Looking at her with new respect, Cindy told her. "Zarek might still call me. We have a code on the phone. I'll wait here. The police will never find him. He'll know they're looking for him but it won't stop him."

"I'll stop him," Anna said. "They'll come home."

Delicately, Cindy said, "Tim loved that girl Nori."

"I know."

"If you get him out it's still a longshot, him and you."

"I have to tell him what Asher said."

She was almost sorry to leave. The chill which gripped her when she stepped into the rain had nothing to do with the temperature. Two hours ago she would have dialed Asher, now everything had changed. Always before she had taken refuge by doing the proper thing. It would not work now, not if she wanted another chance with Currie.

Her boss fired her when she said she needed time off. "You've been mooning around, Tim's not your husband. Love the one you're with, remember that song? Charles calls you every day. You won't get another job like this."

Once this job had been the most important thing in Anna's life.

She didn't care when Laura said, "Don't come back."

She tried to phone Pietro from Milan but could not get through. Cindy's directions, an inquiry at the factory and her road map brought her, after many wrong turns, to a forest road, a huge steel gate and a German guard who spoke impeccable British English. She refused to leave when he ordered her to and after a while the *carabinieri* came and made her go.

Despondent, she drove back to Como. She'd found an English-language radio station and she listened to the news.

The announcer said, ". . . terrorists killed in a shootout in Courmayeur. Authorities believe at least one was American. A passport belonging to George Murphy was found."

Through the pounding in her head she remembered Cindy's words. George Murphy was one name Zarek used when traveling.

She waited for more names to be announced, names of the other dead terrorists.

The announcer said, "Now for sports news."

Courmayeur, the map in the glove compartment told her, was five hours north.

Anna rocketed the car back onto the road.

The sun was high, snow patches had melted slightly and a hawk circled the ski lift. Panting, Zarek said, "Enough hand-to-hand for today. You're pretty good." They were on the mountaintop. It was one day before Anna began her drive to Courmayeur, one thousand yards from where Lipko waited in ambush.

Zarek's jaw had swollen blue from Currie's blow. Both men were heaving. During the last hour Currie had learned how to kick a man to death.

"Your turn to carry the knapsack," Zarek said. "And to lead us down. Take out the rope." It was nylon. Coiled. Zarek said, "From now on we don't use the path to get back, we do it the hard way, through the woods."

"Fine with me," Currie said. He wasn't going to admit exhaustion first.

"During trigger time you systemize precautions," Zarek said. "You never take the same route twice if you can help it. You always assume the enemy might be looking for you. You come home at staggered hours. You keep signs around the house to see if you've been visited. Hairs in the door, stuff like that. Some of the best guys in the field screw up when they think they're safe, make themselves a target."

The pack was light without the climbing rope inside. Currie concentrated on finding a new route down. He walked a few feet and checked the drop by the ski lift. Zarek waited on the grass. Currie walked along the edge of the forest. Zarek was not only testing his ability to think when tired, not only testing his judgment in a descent, but was challenging his memory of the mountain. They had run on the same trail for the past four days. The path crisscrossed enough of Bianco's face so that Currie should know the location of the dangerous drops.

Summoning a mental picture of Bianco, he realized that to begin the journey down the easiest-looking slope would bring them to a dead end and chasm five hundred yards down. He returned to the gorge, got on his belly and looked over the edge. The stream below boiled up at him, he saw the bleaching boulders and heard the roar. Ten feet down a solid-looking ledge in the rock seemed to lead around a bend to a wooded section and more solid area of forest his judgment told him might be passable. For all he knew Zarek might have even come up here before and already knew the easy paths down. In fact, suddenly he was sure Zarek knew them.

Behind them the mountain rose into the ice fields.

Currie looped the rope over his shoulder. Zarek would be

waiting to see how early Currie used up this valuable resource so Currie decided he would get them down without using the rope at all.

Using clearly visible handholds in the rock he climbed down to the ledge. It felt solid. He looked over the edge and a wave of vertigo struck him. Leaving Zarek up top he followed the ledge around the bend and saw that as he'd suspected it led into the woods and to a navigable section of forest.

To Zarek he called back, cheerfully, "Afraid to climb down?"

Zarek reached him in a minute. "Lead on," the mercenary said.

Moving slowly, stopping regularly to reconnoiter and fighting fatigue, Currie led Zarek through the forest. He realized he'd formed such a good idea of the contours of the mountain that even in the woods he generally knew where he was going. Periodically they broke into the open to see the town closer.

His confidence grew. He covered the trail behind them sometimes, obscuring their footprints by brushing them with a branch. He led them through icy streams to obscure their footsteps. Zarek nodded at Currie's precautions, he issued a steady stream of facts.

"Even trivial information might save you later."

Qaddafi had come to power at twenty-two. He was moody and subject to depression. In the early days he'd wandered Tripoli in disguise to hear what people thought of him but now he imposed long periods of isolation on himself, in the desert.

He loved parades. He drove a Fiat. He had formed a "Pan African" army from the Persian Gulf and Britain by promising high pay and participation in an Islamic resurgence. He ordered dissidents killed. One had been shot in New Mexico a year ago by a bogus employment recruiter. Zarek didn't add Tecala and Nori.

It seemed that Zarek had been talking for days but Currie

wanted more. Zarek quoted the Bible. "The revenger of blood shall slay the murderer, when he meeteth him he shall slay him." Zarek said the anti-Qaddafi underground leader in Tripoli was named Salhani. Salhani sometimes knew the Colonel's movements and might help them if they needed a hiding place. "A few years ago the Agency considered offing Qaddafi," Zarek said. "But they decided they wanted him alive. He throws monkey wrenches into Arab politics. Destabilizes the region. I saw pictures of Salhani then. Handsome. Rock jaw. He heads one of Qaddafi's 'People's Committees' and tries to get the Agency to kill him on the side." Zarek pulled raspberries off a bush as they moved. He ate one and gave one to Currie. He said, "But his organization's leaky. Only way you deal with a two-face like that, you tell him there's a letter. In Switzerland maybe. It names him. If we die and the letter gets opened. But I'd rather not use Salhani. His own number two's probably out for his ass too."

Zarek stopped. "You hear footsteps?"

Nothing.

They started again.

Zarek's information continued at a steady, random stream. "You know if something happens to split us up in Italy we go to Switzerland, or my friend Sperazza in Riomaggiore. But what if we have to leave Libya separately? Or what if something happens on the sea? Then you go to Malta. The prostitute section is called 'The Gut.' There's a bar there called Neville's. The guy who owns it is Neville Smythe. Got it?"

"Neville Smythe."

"He's a good friend, he's reliable. The Gut is filled with out-of-work guys who can help us. Qaddafi guys on vacation. Tell Neville I sent you." Zarek took off a small gold ring. The insignia showed a parachute and bayonet. "Tell him I gave it to you. Tell him I said you're the type of chap, and say 'chap,' we could have used at Stanleyville."

" 'I'm the type of chap he could have used at Stanleyville.' This sounds a little melodramatic, Zarek."

"Never mind what it sounds like. How's he supposed to know where you come from otherwise? Suppose I get . . . sick? He'll help you. He used to work for the Libyans, too. He hates Qaddafi as much as you do. You going to rest here all day?"

Currie pocketed the ring, the touch of it had given him a chill, a premonition he shook off. Zarek was pale and had lost weight in the last week. They started walking again. Zarek kept listing facts.

Currie thought back to licking protest letters at Watchers International. "Dear Colonel Qaddafi . . . Dear Colonel Assad . . ." The innocence of that effort astounded him. It was not that he was naïve: the most prominent collective memory of his generation was the shooting of a President. But the extent of the *system* Zarek had been describing for days enraged Currie. In France and Italy organized groups assassinated opponents regularly. The right wingers had names like the SS Weapons Brotherhood, Commando Delta, Avan-guardia Nazionale in Italy, Omega 7. In Chile a prize-winning short story writer doubled as a hit woman for the secret police. "First the head, second the head, third the head, fourth the heart," was her motto. And on the left there was Black September, Baader-Meinhof in Germany, the Red Brigade, Peru's Shining Path, Ireland's IRA. The Rumanians sent agents to kill dissidents in London by jabbing them with poison in crowds. A Turk had been paid by Russians to shoot the Pope. The North Korean government had sent people to blow up the president of the South. The United States paid people to arrange bomb drops on Nicaragua.

Now the White House was protected by concrete barriers

because car bomb attacks were feared. Zero, the execution arm of the Cuban nationalist movement, called their murders "political executions." Certain governments in South America had formed an organization called Condor through which they cooperated in eliminating refugee opponents. Everywhere terrorists were systemized, funded, needed, used. Everywhere Qaddafi's influence was felt.

Currie found a shortcut through the forest. The sun warmed them as they came out of the trees. In the meadow cows grazed near shepherd boys. Courmayeur was a cluster of Alpine roofs two hundred meters away. They crossed a wooden footbridge and passed a chain-link compound filled with St. Bernards, swept impeccably clean, each pair of animals sharing an oversized, brightly painted doghouse. "EMIL & MARIA" read one house. Even the dogs lived in couples. The valley hummed from trucks winding north to the Mount Bianco tunnel to France. Church bells rang and Basque-capped workmen dug a drainage ditch.

The lodge was a low expanse of timber and blue shuttered windows with flowerboxes. Using a key, Currie shut the alarm system to get inside and switched it on again when the door closed. The oblong sunken living room was strewn with bearskin rugs, oiled mahogany tables and armchairs of fine Italian leather.

"Shoot or sleep?" Zarek asked. The testing never stopped. But this time Currie recognized the limits of his own fatigue. "A forty-minute nap. Then we can shoot."

Zarek grunted. "What is this, a resort vacation or a training session?" But he said nothing else and Currie knew the mercenary approved.

An hour later Currie bolted the shutters. The lodge plunged into darkness, Currie switched on corner lamps. He followed Zarek into a side bedroom. They moved aside an armchair and throw rug. The hidden door in the floor brought them into a concrete wine cellar where the racks slid away to reveal a second door. A ladder brought them down to the shooting range.

Gun laws in Italy were strict. Pietro had soundproofed the room with seven feet of concrete.

The light, slowly coming on, showed three firing alleys.

They wore hearing protectors around their necks, they'd cover their ears when they were shooting. Zarek walked to a steel rack containing a row of weapons.

He lifted a stubby double-handled gun with a blade-type front sight and a rear sight in a *U*-shaped notch. "What's this?"

"Beretta twelve submachine gun," Currie said. "Nine-millimeter parabellum-type ammunition. The cyclic rate of fire is five hundred fifty-five rounds per minute. Twenty-, thirty- or forty-round magazines. Three kilograms in weight. Semi-automatic or automatic fire."

Zarek tossed it to him. "Field strip it."

Working swiftly, Currie removed the magazine. He pulled the barrel-locking nut catch down and unscrewed the nut at the front of the receiver. He removed the barrel and bolt. He screwed off the receiver cap and pulled the operating spring from the rear of the receiver.

"Put it back together again."

It took less than a minute. Zarek said, "Anything special you want to tell me about this gun? I'm a Libyan trainee."

Currie said, "It's good for the desert because it operates well even if it gets dirty. In sand."

"You forgot to mention the range."

"Two hundred meters maximum to be effective."

Zarek lifted a longer rifle from the rack, with a skeleton stock, a small cheekpad, a sporting-type barrel and a curved magazine.

"Dragunov sniper rifle," Currie said. "Russian made. Seven point six-two millimeters, normal sights graduated to twelve hundred meters. The telescopic sight has a times-four magnification and a six percent field of view. There's also an integral rangefinder, a battery-powered reticle illumination system and an infrared reconnaissance aid. Smooth trigger action."

Upstairs, the house creaked. Both men froze and listened. Currie walked to a fuse box on the wall and opened it and saw a pinprick red light glowing. He said, "Alarm system's working."

"Okay then. It's time for you to pick your own gun. You'll have one in Libya if you're an officer. Which do you like best?"

Without hesitation Currie reached down for the smallest weapon, the Czech-made Scorpion machine pistol.

"Why that one?"

Currie hefted the black steel. The barrel seemed to fit into his hand, the light gleamed dully off the barrel. "I like it because I can fire it with one hand or from the shoulder. It's light, three pounds. Easy to control because it uses a low-powered cartridge, the seven point six-five millimeter short. Any more questions?"

Zarek grinned. "You learn faster than anyone I've ever taught." They donned their earmuffs and Zarek adjusted the distance of the paper targets, silhouetted men. Currie performed a series of firing exercises from kneeling, standing and lying positions. Eyes blindfolded in a hearing and reflexes test, he spun and fired at noises in different parts of the room. He stood with his back to the paper target as Zarek changed the distance again. Zarek tapped his shoulder. Currie whirled and fired.

The room stank of cordite. "Something new today," Zarek shouted. "Turn around again." He went away and returned. "There's something alive on your right. Ready?"

"What do you mean alive? What's alive down here?"

But Currie whirled, at the touch, finger pressing trigger. His reflexes were good, he jerked the muzzle away. The Scorpion bucked, it grew hotter in his hands. A pattern of dust swirled off the ceiling fifty feet away. The beagle, muzzled so it would not bark, must have been smuggled in while Currie slept. It ran back and forth, tethered to the wall. Its leash jerked it back.

Zarek snapped, "You'll be shooting live targets in Libya, not paper. Some people have trouble with live targets."

"Not the right ones," Currie said. The dog grew more frantic as he approached. He spent a long time petting it. Zarek remained silent.

Currie was dreaming again. Sleep time was staggered. Ten years old, he rode in the bakery truck with his father, going to a Yankees game. His father smiled. Currie clutched a mitt on his lap. Autumn gold suffused the air. When he woke the heaviness in his chest was gone.

Following the heavy odor of tomato sauce he left his bedroom and saw Zarek bent by the stove. An apron circling the mercenary's waist seemed incongruous. Zarek's sleeves were rolled to the marine tattoo.

"I was thinking while you were asleep," Zarek said. "Last Thanksgiving I was at the Suez Canal. On the ferry. A guy next to me had a falcon on his wrist. Barefoot kids sold Coke from buckets. I was in the back of a taxi. I thought, Hey, it's Thanksgiving. Not exactly cranberry sauce and stuffing."

"What were you doing in Suez?"

"Not celebrating, that's for sure. So tonight's Thanksgiving, Italian style. Who knows where we'll be when the real one rolls around. Or maybe it's Christmas. You want it to be Christmas?"

"We'll be home Christmas," Currie said, meaning it.

"Home. Right. That'll be a change. Last time I was home for Christmas was four years ago. Turkey, trout, veal, salad. Cindy can cook. She got me a board game, a novelty. 'Assassin.' It had little pieces, guys with guns. Cards saying, 'The assassin is in the bushes outside. Lock windows.' Or, big bonus, 'Extra bodyguards.' *Hahahaha*, bodyguards. Where does she come up with this stuff?"

The mercenary lifted the cover off the pot and inhaled. "Linguine and sausage," he said. "The Pilgrim's pride."

They'd spent hours telling each other stories in Iran although Zarek was deft at avoiding personal subjects. They were chopping onions. Currie said, "How did you get started, doing what you do?"

Zarek gave him an intent sideways look as if gauging if there was criticism in the question.

Blandly, putting dishes on the table, Currie said, "I'm curious."

He added, smiling, "Partner."

Zarek poured mineral water, sniffed the glass and rotated it to the light like wine. "Ah, Château Mineral Water 'thirty-eight," he said. "What bouquet." More serious, he said, "Okay. We're predators, all of us. My father taught me." The open kitchen adjoined the living room, opposite a huge fireplace and a brown-and-white series of photographs of Mount Bianco. "He was Indian," Zarek said. "Obijway. Ugliest Indians on earth. Big noses. Flat heads. I would have looked like that except my mother was Tennessee Polish. A man's a hunter. Stop being a hunter and you stop being a man. That's why my father died. He stopped being a predator. He gave in. A mechanic. He even changed his Indian name to Zarek. I thought of changing it back but I respected my father, you make do with what you have. The weak people wore him down. I was nine."

"A kid," Currie said. "Then what happened?"

One Mount Bianco photograph showed an avalanche. The

[166]

largest plunging boulder, frozen in flight, was big as a Volkswagen.

"Look," Zarek said angrily. He did not like to remember. "I had seven years in foster homes. Ran away to fight Castro when I was fifteen. Cops picked me up in Carolina, hitching. They sent me home but let me keep my father's gun. They thought I was funny. The sergeant said, 'Kid, you want to fight Castro do it next year when we don't get runaway bulletins on you. Then shoot him for me, okay?' This sauce is hot. Next year I joined the marines. Vietnam. Stop the Reds, that's what I'm still doing." He shook his head. "In 'Nam they'd tie up people with wet leather. The leather would dry and tighten. Bamboo shards in it would slash the neck. The victim would choke and bleed to death." Zarek emptied his glass. "Animals," he said.

In a painting over the fireplace, a St. Bernard dug a climber out of the snow.

"Even when I worked for Qaddafi I fought the Reds. He was our ally then, an anti-Communist. Everyone forgets that. The Agency thought it was a good idea to help him, you think I didn't check? Who could tell he'd become a butcher. We didn't know he'd turn on us."

They were eating salad. "I always wanted to ask you: How come you never talked to reporters after Iran?" Zarek said.

They sat in plush leather seats. On the stereo someone named Claudio sang love songs in Italian. He had a high-pitched voice, like a girl.

Currie considered the question, fork poised in the air. "I'm as patriotic as you, maybe in a different way. When I was a kid in New York my father died when I was twelve. No way I could afford college. I had to support my mom. I got a scholarship from the government. I had a job then and that money went to my mom, but with the scholarship I managed night school. I'd be in the slums today without that scholarship. People think they're too sophisticated to talk about loving their country, but it's a beautiful country and it gave to me. I owe it."

Currie chewed pasta. "But I'll tell you about the day we came home from Iran. You were gone then. People lined the Parkway, waving. I remember all these yellow ribbons on the trees."

Telling the story Currie was transported into the back of the limousine. Anna clutched his forearm in excitement on the ride home from National Airport. The ribbons flew on trees and car antennas and boat masts in the Potomac. People didn't forget you, Anna told him proudly. The ribbons are from a song. "Tie a Yellow Ribbon." It's about coming home. People support you so they bought ribbons.

"Ribbons?" Currie said to Zarek now. "I said to her, 'What do ribbons have to do with anything?' After the ride there was a dinner at the Marriot. A Swedish vocalist sang 'Tie a Yellow Ribbon.' There were cheese puffs and barbecued spare ribs and a cake from Provo, Utah. None of it seemed real. Nobody wanted to talk about Iran. If you started to talk about Iran, they'd say, 'Oh, that's in the past now.' "

Zarek poured more mineral water. Currie said, "When I talked with the journalists, all I could remember was the day the guards showed us the *Time* magazine with the Ayatollah on the cover, *Time*'s Man of the Year. The guards laughing and saying, 'See, even your own journalists write he is great.' When I talked to the priests I remembered the ones who had visited us. The guards had stepped on your hand that day, broken your knuckles. The priests saw it but they went back to New York and announced we were treated well. They didn't want to make waves."

Zarek rubbed his knuckles. Currie took another forkful. "The Vice-President was there, crying. Crying! They'd all constructed this little triumph for themselves to excuse that they hadn't done anything, that they'd lied or tried to act 'objective.' Maybe *Time* will make *Qaddafi* Man of the Year this year," he said.

"If it's Thanksgiving we sing songs," Zarek said. They were in a much lighter mood an hour later, caught up in the mock Thanksgiving celebration. "Trooper Thomas was a Rhodesian Pony Express rider. Eighteen fifty-eight. On Christmas Eve he was treed by a lion. He left the mail on the ground. Spent Christmas in the tree while the lion pissed on the Rhodesian mail." They roared. He hoisted his glass. "Here's to you, Trooper Thomas! Sing!"

"Football," Currie said. It was late afternoon. He had not felt so relaxed in a week. He'd been telling Zarek how he became East Coast boxing champion. Lots of "left, right, left." He said, "What's Thanksgiving without football? After the big meal! Alabama and Georgia State!"
"Alabama will take it this year," Zarek said, reclining on the couch.
"You're crazy."
"Ten bucks."
They pumped hands in an ecstasy of distraction. Over the normality they'd lost. Touchdowns.

Zarek's pauses had grown longer. Gorged, he'd allowed himself a brandy. "We finish in Libya, then you and me, we'll go to Florida," he said. "There are limestone sinkholes in the Everglades. We get oxygen tanks, we go down into the sinkholes, you never know how deep they go. It's pitch-black down there. In the caves. It's a test, see? Down there, in the dark, you have to fight against . . . don't you ever tell anyone I told you this . . . solid, raw terror."
Joyfully, Zarek stuffed cannoli in his mouth. Currie always liked the stories. Zarek was lost in reminiscence. "One time

I got lost down there. Couldn't find the right way up. Finally I burst out of the hole and there's this *boar,* what a mother, he was drinking in the hole and I come shooting out of the water. Huge boar, bigger than the one in my basement. He looked like he couldn't decide, run or charge. Ha ha! He ran! Lucky for me, too! We'll go there after I take Cindy to Europe. I always take her when I get mo——." His look flickered with guilt. "Louisiana hunting," he said. "I ever tell you about that?"

"What were you going to say?" Currie said. The shutters were open again, dusk light streamed in. Currie didn't feel so giddy suddenly.

Zarek said, "There's bears in those swamps you wouldn't believe."

"You were going to say 'money,' " Currie said. " 'I always take her when I get money.' "

Zarek's smile widened. "I don't know what I was going to say. I was just running on at the mouth."

A Zionist in New York will pay half a million, he'd told Currie in Washington.

But Currie was surprised to find himself unshocked. A man like Zarek lied for a living. Was it so surprising he'd taken the money in secret?

Currie said, already knowing Zarek's answer, "I'll listen in when you call to give it back."

"What are you so righteous about?" Zarek growled. "It'll protect us later."

Currie drained his glass, considered a refill and decided he was ready for his evening walk. He was going to leave Zarek. "You taught me a lot," he said. "I'm grateful."

"That's the right attitude. I knew you'd come around." But Zarek's smile died as he realized what Currie meant. "You're not going without me," he said. "We leave together."

"Sure. Together."

"Don't be nuts," Zarek warned, getting more excited. "The contacts are mine. You can't take the job in Libya unless I'm with you. I'll track you, find you." He leaned into Currie's face and shouted, "Our chances drop without money! Half's been paid! It's for Cindy, for us! It's not for me!"

Currie was gathering plates. Zarek stood up. "Call the Banque Nationale de Geneva! It's there! Half's for you, I can't touch it. Ask for Herr Schneider, he has instructions, questions to ask you and then he will wire it." When Currie just carried the plates to the sink, Zarek said, "You know what I think? I think after everything Qaddafi did to you you're *still* not sure you have a right to shoot back. You're afraid of the money. You don't trust your own motives. If you really wanted to kill him, you'd do everything possible to make it happen. Money."

"I gave you money," Currie said wearily. "Sixty thousand dollars." He would leave Zarek but he was going to have to get the cash back first; he'd need it. He said, "Half a million, is that your dollar value on Nori? How do you break that figure up? How much do you think one arm's worth?"

Zarek's face grew contemptuous. "It's evening Mass, is it? I was wrong about you, you're like everybody else. You close your eyes and pray for a miracle. You'll need one off by yourself. But remember, even in church they pass a collection plate."

In the living room Currie put on his jacket. "First the money's for 'Cindy' and then it's for 'us.' Why don't you make up your mind? You said sixty thousand was enough last week, so what changed? I'll tell you who the money's really for — you, because you feel guilty you never spend any time with her." His voice hardened. "So you're dying. So we're not supposed to talk about it but we're supposed to take money because of it. Well, we're not taking money for it. You know what I'd give to have Nori alive? Cindy's a phone call away but all you want to do is send money. Why don't you act like a man to her instead of a pimp. And another thing. You're right I'm different from you. You're having a good time here."

Zarek said, "You better get out of here, get out right now." Currie left him at the table, legs apart, hands on his knees.

He went out into the dusk.

Zarek threw his wineglass. It shattered above the fireplace. Mineral water washed down Mount Bianco. "Fuck this water," he said. "I want a real drink." Then he shouted, "You'll take the money in the end, you'll see."

Glancing at the alarm light, which was off, he stood up. "Asshole, you didn't even reset the alarm."

The front door opened. Currie was probably coming back.

"Long time since Libya," Lipko said, entering. Three of them spread by the door, pistols out. "You lost weight."

Zarek was already moving, launching himself left, toward the open trapdoor to the basement. It was a bad time for the disease to manifest itself. His knee buckled, he went down.

CHAPTER

13

CURRIE strolled through the cobblestone streets of the town. The argument had coalesced into a cold anger in his head. Alpine air washed his temples. Shops glowed at dusk; Courmayeur was filled with walkers. He told himself he would get his money from Zarek and tomorrow they would part.

Yet he felt stronger since the fight and even grateful for Zarek's help. Zarek had been driving him inside himself, sharpening his capability. "Every part of you is a weapon," Zarek had said. "Body. Spirit. Emotion. Welded into a single purpose. Other people compartmentalize themselves. You don't have time even for love. Feel the difference. It will make you more powerful."

Watching the village around him, he sensed Zarek's truth. Dusk was the family time. Men went home to families when the sun went down; when warmth left the sky, they sought it in their homes. He thought of people all over the world going home.

In Washington they walked on Connecticut Avenue. In Milan the industrialists went home, the tourists, the white-frocked pharmacists, severe faced in reading glasses, the innocent Mama and Papa storeowners, the youth-faced sword-carrying *carabinieri,* the old men who gathered at dusk in the Duomo to discuss politics, the lawyers in their Mercedes, the artists in Brera and La Scala, the literary agents, the factory workers. Thousands of people going home at night, a chain from which he had been cut.

Each of these people had problems but felt safe enough to occupy himself with salary and rent and school for a child. Billions of humans were going home tonight. They were what he had been, parts of the whole, seeking not greatness but satisfaction. Not kings and not philosophers. Common men linked by five thousand years of organization. But they were threatened now by the new unraveling, the terrorism, the tyranny of the few like Qaddafi.

Currie stopped at a café and ordered espresso.

That threat was his link. Qaddafi's hands had stretched across the sea and crushed Nori, but they could have destroyed any one of these people. The enemy was the same.

But with sudden crushing sadness Currie saw that the distance between himself and the laughing strollers had grown awesome. The first flush of anger had cooled. Now Zarek's words drove back at him. *The contacts are mine. You can't go to Libya without me.* Currie answered in his mind. *I'll find another way to get to Qaddafi.*

But what way? No Zarek would mean no trip to Libya, no training sessions with Qaddafi's troops and no assassination at the military day parade. No Sperazza to take him on his boat. Even if he used the ring Zarek had given him and went to Malta, Zarek would show up too and block an attempt to get to Qaddafi from that direction. Plus Lipko was still after him somewhere.

He paid and left the café. Hands in his pockets, he walked through the town. It grew darker and the lanes emptied. He saw families eating dinner through curtained windows. He saw how much he had learned from Zarek. He knew lots more than he had known even a week ago. He knew how much more he needed to learn. Bitterly he admitted to himself how much he needed Zarek, or at least Zarek's contacts.

But to make a profit from murder, even Qaddafi's murder, was unconscionable. It was funny because in the old days he had feared that Zarek and he might be alike. They were nothing alike. They shared a primal notion of justice but Zarek *needed* violence, he liked it and he could capitalize on human suffering. There was nothing heroic in that.

In an agony of self-loathing for even considering the question, Currie turned off a sidestreet to a footpath which smelled of wild roses and led, two hundred yards away, to the lodge. His breath frosted. Snowcapped peaks glowed purplish in twilight.

He squared his shoulders. If Zarek could lie to Currie, Currie would use Zarek. *You do what you want with the money,* he told the mercenary in his mind. *None of it's for me.* Currie's admiration for the man was gone. Getting to Qaddafi was the most important thing.

A friendship was over. A business arrangement had begun.

Currie reached the lodge, opened the door.

The gun hovered three feet ahead. Lipko smiled over the barrel. "You're letting cold air in," he remarked. "Close the door. You live in a barn?"

For Currie the oxygen drained away. His headache built hugely and his legs went weak.

A silencer extended the barrel. Lipko did not seem so beach-boyish since the fight in Washington. His nose was blue, tilted. His lips swelled. His eyes were obsidian slits in icy blue. Currie felt vengeful triumph rolling off the man.

"Where's Zarek?" Currie demanded. Behind Lipko he saw the wrecked furniture, ripped cushions and shattered photographs off the wall. A bald man slit picture frames in a corner.

Currie smelled the sweet, pervasive reek of blood.

"I said . . ." But then Currie saw the hand, white and inert, protruding from beside a pile of wreckage. Lipko blocked Currie's view of the rest of the body but did not protest when Currie moved to see. The mercenary lay by an overturned

[175]

coffee table, chin in a throw rug and wrists bound behind his back. His legs twisted, tangled. From one shredded knee a wine-colored pool spread on the floor.

Currie fought down nausea. "Christ, Zarek," he said, kneeling by the mercenary. He saw the sock stuffed in the mouth. A gag. Zarek's chest heaved. Currie's jaw tightened, he could barely talk. "I'll kill you," he told Lipko.

Lipko's eyes widened in surprise, then he laughed.

When Currie stood, the silencer grazed his belly. Lipko's breath smelled of mint. Lipko's shoulder dropped, his fist hurtled upward but Currie sidestepped, slamming both hands down. Lipko was strong but Currie stopped the blow in mid-flight. They strained, faces inches apart.

Currie waited for the gun to go off, too enraged to care.

"Muslach," Lipko snapped.

Currie hadn't seen the third man. His arms were jerked back, pinned. When Lipko attacked this time, Currie was defenseless. The fist exploded in his belly. Lipko stepped into the second punch.

Currie doubled. He saw his sneakers over bent knees.

With supreme effort he straightened. He couldn't breathe. But he forced himself not to show it. He smiled.

"Oh good," Lipko said. "You're going to be difficult."

Across the room Currie saw the open bedroom door and raised trapdoor to the shooting range. *The guns are down there.*

The short Arab disappeared into Zarek's bedroom. "We didn't finish our discussion in Washington," Lipko said, seating himself in a red leather chair. A crash came from Zarek's room. The short man emerged holding Currie's leather money case. A bubbling sound came from Zarek's chest. Currie shouted, "Get a doctor for him!"

Ignoring him, Lipko whistled, admiringly looking inside the case. "American dollars," Lipko said. Currie's gaze fell on glass shards on the floor five feet away, bits of broken lamp, razor sharp, triangle shaped. Lipko would fire if Currie reached for them. A crystal ashtray near Lipko's boots could serve as a club. It was too far away. Lipko's long fingers ran over the stacks of money. Zarek groaned.

"Kneecapping, it's called," Lipko said. "Believe me, you'll wish he were asleep again when he wakes up." Zarek's eyes opened in agony, stared into Currie's. The sock gag dribbled from his mouth like a piece of white sausage. Zarek would hate the humiliation as much as the pain. Lipko's voice was a caress. "I'm going to ask questions in a moment, I'm hoping you won't answer at first." Unconsciously, Lipko's thumb ran up and down a bundle of money. Lipko said, "That way we'll work on Zarek more. Then you. Elbows. Fingers. Elbows are full of nerve endings." The thumb rubbed the money harder. "Fingers are full of joints. So don't answer at first. A strong man like you, I may not be able to get what I want for a whole hour."

"If I cooperate?" Currie asked. When he sat on the couch, the biggest glass shard, rose colored and dagger shaped, lay only three feet away. By leaning forward he lessened the distance six inches.

"I let you go if you cooperate," Lipko said. "We tie you up and go to Switzerland. We phone the police and tell them where you are."

Currie repeated, "You let us go."

"My honor on it."

"Free," Currie said.

They grinned at each other, the lie too fantastic to prolong.

"Pretty glass, that," Lipko said, motioning at the shard.

Sweat poured off Zarek but he remained silent. The pain must be unbearable. He stared past Currie, fixing on the trapdoor. Currie thought, *I see it too, but how do I reach it?*

Lipko laid aside the money. "You like jazz?" he said. Innocuous questions, Currie had learned during interrogations in Iran, meant big trouble was imminent. He tried Zarek's drill. *I'm not afraid. It's an adrenaline problem.* Lipko said, "No,

you look more classical. Beethoven. You like Beethoven, right?"
His voice smoothed with anticipation.

Currie said, "We have records in the other room. You want
some Beethoven?" Anything to prolong the conversation.

"I hate Beethoven," Lipko said. "Muslach, put on jazz!"
From an inside room Gato Barbieri came on, playing "Ruby."
The music grew much too loud.

With gentle reluctance Lipko laid the money on the floor.
"Sixty thousand dollars," he said. "What are you doing with
so much money in Italy?"

"Taking a ski vacation."

Lipko sighed with pleasure. "I knew you wouldn't let me
down." He settled back. He looked like a wine taster just
handed an 1857 Château Lafite.

"Muslach," he said.

The Arab strode toward Zarek, stepping over debris.

"Hey," Currie said. "What are you doing! Leave him alone!"
The Arab bent over Zarek. There was a single violent motion
of his arm and the snap of Zarek's finger was audible over
the rampaging saxophone. Muslach stepped away, Zarek
pressed his eyes shut in agony.

Currie said, "It's my money, I had it in the bank."

"That's not what I asked. Why are you here with Zarek?"

Currie hesitated only a fraction of a second. "Muslach,"
Lipko said. Currie cried, "I'll tell!" Zarek struggled but again
came the sickening crack, the grunt of pain.

"Fucking animal!" Currie cried.

The saxophone music dropped to a soft wail.

Lipko crossed his legs elaborately. The shiny expression
was back on his face. "I'll admit I was angry in Washington,"
he said. "I was in trouble, your fault. Israel was ready to call
me home. And when you took a different route down the
mountain today, I thought trouble was starting again." A
snare drum picked up the music. Lipko pointed the gun at

Currie's face. "You don't have time to think here. You only have time to answer."

But Currie's pulse roared in his ears. Israel? The note had said Israel. The world was turning upside down. He wanted to laugh with hysteria. "You work for Israel?"

"No, Qaddafi. You know that. Stalin was 'Iron Ass.' Because of the way he sat. You should hear what they call Chernenko. In select circles and behind his back, of course."

"A nickname," Currie whispered, awed at the simplicity of Tecala's code. The note played across his mind in ten-foot letters. "ISRAEL, IRAN, SAUDI ARABIA, OCTOBER 13TH."

Zarek had not stopped staring at the overturned coffee table. *What are you trying to say?* Currie screamed in his mind. *What's special about the table?*

Lipko said, "You were going to tell me what you and Zarek were doing in Italy. You were going to tell me fast because you don't want Zarek on your conscience." Currie leaned forward, his heart moving in his chest. "Who," he said, "is Iran?"

The reaction was stronger than he'd hoped for. Lipko jerked, the intake of breath audible over the music. "How do you know about that?"

"Iran," Currie pressed. "Qaddafi is Israel, so who is Iran?"

Lipko stood, the blood draining from his face. He whispered, "Iran?" He looked horrified. He'd been searching for the note but had been unaware of its contents until now.

Lipko growled, "I . . . I ask, you answer." But he struggled to keep his voice level.

Abruptly Currie understood why Zarek kept looking at the table. If Currie could maneuver near the trapdoor, Zarek would distract Lipko with the table. Kick it, knock it over. It seemed impossible that Zarek could even move but Currie believed him.

Lipko barked, "Muslach, all the fingers."

Currie spoke quickly to stop the attack. "I deciphered the note." Alarm spread on the Arab's face. Currie said, "Israel, Iran, Saudi Arabia, that's what it said. October thirteenth. What does it mean?"

Currie had inched forward in his chair to within a foot of the glass shard. Lipko and Muslach launched into an argument in Arabic. Muslach was shouting; he kept pointing at Currie. Clearly he was saying, Kill them, let's leave. But Lipko said to Currie in English, "What else did the note say?"

"I told you. Nothing."

Muslach launched into a fresh tirade. Currie had apparently proven his point. Then Currie had his inspiration. A way to reach the trapdoor. He kept the hope off his face. He hit the crucial lie full stride. "I figured the other information was in the second paper but I never decoded it."

"Second paper!"

"The paper with the numbers. I couldn't figure it out."

But Currie had tricked Lipko once already with a lie about the note. Lipko's confusion cleared. A brutal impatience replaced it. His voice quieted with cynicism. "The 'other' paper isn't here, right? It's in a locker. In Washington, maybe. *What are you doing in Italy?*"

Currie leaned back casually. This was his last chance and he knew it. *Everything is a weapon, even your own pain.* He only needed to convince Lipko to let him walk ten feet.

With calculated arrogance he said, "You believe me, all right. If I'm lying, how come I know about 'Iran' and 'Israel'? I have the second paper but I want something for it." Lipko's face was flooding with color. He would send Muslach after Zarek unless Currie offered himself as target. "But you can't get the paper without me," Currie said. "I want a doctor for my friend. You said you'd let us go in the end, so a doctor's nothing extra."

Lipko stared in amazement. "You want a deal?" he said. He stepped toward Currie, the animal was coming out. The gamble was that Lipko needed him coherent so would not hurt him too badly. The blow came sideways, gun smashing collar, knocking him from the couch. A spike of pain drove into his skull. He lost vision, something felt broken in his neck.

When his sight cleared, Lipko straddled him, looking down.

"A deal," Lipko said. The gun swished lightly, like a club. "A deal."

A new song came on. A man was singing to Latin music. He sounded as if he was saying "Babadabadabadoo."

"No, no, I'll tell you," Currie gasped. He pointed to his bedroom, next to the room with the trapdoor. "It's there," he said.

In order to reach his room he would have to pass the room with the trapdoor.

Currie glanced at Zarek. The mercenary lay on his back, no longer looking at the coffee table. They'd synchronized.

But now Currie, rolling to his knees, thought, *Lipko's probably visited the basement. Suppose he's taken the guns?*

Lipko said thickly, "Muslach, get his paper. Currie, tell him where it is!"

The record clicked off.

Acting vague, as if stunned by the blow, Currie said, "Two . . . dressers . . . smaller . . . bigger . . ."

"The paper," Lipko snapped.

". . . dresser . . ."

"The big one or the little one?"

"One . . . wider . . . uh . . ."

"Fuck it," Lipko said. "Show me." He poked Currie in the kidney with the gun.

Wincing, Currie forced himself into a shambling, defeated

shuffle. He heard the bald Arab turning over the record in another room. His neck was on fire. He stepped onto the raised hallway. Looking bored in a chair, Muslach guarded Zarek with a pistol.

Five paces to go. What could Zarek do with the table? The pressure on Currie's back increased. Maybe he'd misunderstood Zarek. What if Zarek didn't do anything to distract the Arabs? Don't tense, Currie thought. You'll give yourself away. The blood odor thickened. Zarek's sudden roar surprised even Currie. How the man had worked the gag loose was beyond him. But the gun pressure slackened. Currie whipped sideways and threw his weight back. He slammed into Lipko. He heard a cry of pain.

He had a fraction-of-a-second glimpse of the gun in mid-air, Lipko stumbling, Zarek up on his good knee with the coffee table over his head as the Arab pumped shot after shot into him. Zarek was crumbling. It had all taken a second.

Then Currie, running, slammed the door behind him. The crash of the coffee table sounded from the other room. Wood splintered off the door to the thud and whine of bullets. Currie screamed. "I have a gun!" but the door was opening. He dropped through the trapdoor; it did not have a lock. Lipko would be steps behind him.

He hit the wine cellar floor and jerked bottles to move the hydraulic rack from in front of the shooting range. A bottle shattered beside him, the air sprayed red. Bullets whined by his ear *but the rack was sliding* and he hurled himself into the darkness of the shooting range, shattering the doorside light bulb with his elbow. Pain sliced his arm. He'd been trained to shoot in the dark. He scrambled on the floor. The AK-47 seemed to leap into his scrabbling fingers. Easily. Naturally. His arms grew longer. They came together and he meshed with the gun.

Then there was a punch in his shoulder. He whirled toward a descending firing shadow in the square block of light from above. He screamed, "Yeah, now," squeezing the trigger. The cellar exploded in noise. He had never fired without earmuffs on and the sound was deafening. He threw himself onto the matted floor, shooting. Something huge, a Christ with hands outstretched, plunged down at him.

He fired. He fired.

After a while he stopped.

Upstairs the saxophone crooned.

Smoke filled the basement; he smelled cordite.

Arms to floor, the bald man hung upside down on the ladder, legs tangled in the rungs. Another man lay heaped on the floor. Currie could not see the face.

Currie squeezed off two bursts. The bodies jerked from impact but he saw no sign of life. He beat down exultation. With the soundproofed door open his shooting must have been audible in the street. Police would be coming. And only two attackers lay dead, not three.

He turned over the man on the floor. It was the shorter Arab, not Lipko.

Upstairs he heard footsteps running and a door slammed.

Currie slid to the gunrack. The AK-47 was too big to take into the street. He groped for the Scorpion pistol and rammed in a clip. He stuffed a silencer in his pocket. Returning to the ladder he saw the bald man had been shot through the chin. Blood fanned across the face past exposed bits of bone. Blood dripped on the floor.

He looked up, past wreathing blue smoke, into the light from the wine cellar.

"Lipko," he called. The footsteps could have been faked. If Currie was wrong about the shooting being audible outside, Lipko would be waiting.

Currie placed one foot on the ladder.

He rose sliding a hand along the bar. He poked his head into the wine cellar. No feet were visible along the wine racks. He reached the bedroom.

No Lipko.

High, keening, he heard the approaching two-note wail of a siren. More quickly, he reached Zarek. The mercenary lay crumpled across the broken coffee table. Slivers of wood jabbed his forearms. He was drenched.

Currie snatched up the leather case with the money.

He closed Zarek's eyes.

"Friend," he said. "Now I owe you."

Then he was running, out the back and in a field, the town at his back, the black cluster of roofs dwarfed by the arcing peaks, colored by copper haze of streetlights and revolving blue eye of the police car. Where was Lipko? A buzz vibrated the whole valley floor, as if the earth were a nerve ending and he trod on it in flight.

The moon hung high, bathing him in visibility. He dropped to the ground. In Italy he was a murderer now. His only way out of the valley was the two-lane road which wound beneath the peaks and could be blocked by a single vanload of *carabinieri*. The meadow could take him to the mountain but he lacked direction in the forest. He was a city man. Stars were conversation pieces and not signposts to him. And the mountains would be freezing tonight. He'd left his jacket in the lodge.

He would circle in the grass and chance the highway. He could run back to the meadow if he saw police.

Then people spilled around the lodge, fanning out, coming at him. He did not think they had seen him because they moved too slowly. Bobbing searchers calling each other. They were the bakers and strollers he had admired an hour ago. They were the fathers and husbands with whom he'd felt kinship. Now they hunted him. He crawled in the grass toward Mount Bianco.

Using the road was out of the question. Each time his knuckles struck the earth pain jolted him hand to shoulder. He touched his fingers to his shoulder and came away with something sticky. He was bleeding and the sweet odor clogged the night. He remembered the punch in his shoulder during the battle in the basement. It was remarkable, he thought, crawling for his life, how a man could be shot and not know it right away.

CHAPTER
14

THE moon disappeared, clouds blotted out the stars. Wind slashed Currie's face with snow. Three-quarters up the trail he staggered, driving himself, his body a universe of pain. The hammering in his shoulder had spread to his left side, he dipped to the left as he ran. He nearly toppled into a chasm. Trees went in and out of focus. He was going to pass out and if he did not reach the ski shack first he would freeze.

Currie had not had time to grab his parka in the lodge. He wore a flannel shirt, jeans and Adidas.

The Scorpion grew heavier, the money bag weighed him down. Drop them, whispered a voice in his mind. He gripped them tighter, hands numb.

But an awful sense of defeat beat in his head. Zarek was dead. Everything was lost. *Keep fighting.* He focused on Qaddafi. Lipko had escaped and Qaddafi remained untouched, giving orders a thousand miles away. Casual. Impregnable.

The air filled with a bird cry, a steady high cackle. Something in the forest was watching him pass. And there was something he must remember about Lipko but the physical agony blocked his thoughts. The air thinned, his feet dragged. *You went down the mountain a different way today,* Lipko had said.

Lipko had been here!

Turn around, he told himself.

Where else can I go?

Then he saw the shack, a dim block on the snow-dusted crest, dark like warmth under covers. Dark like sleep. It beckoned him below the ski cables that rose toward the tooth-edge ridges even higher up.

Jerkily he pushed himself forward. The bird sound stopped when he reached the shack. Steadying himself against the door he aimed the Scorpion at the padlock.

He'd forgotten to release the safety.

He tried again. A misfire.

Wind filled his mouth when he laughed. To reach the shack and not get inside! He could hammer the lock but he tried firing again. A soft *pffft* sounded, he saw the spark of bullet hitting steel. The lock hung broken.

Cold, so cold. He lost vision as he crossed the threshold. He fell against the door, closing it. The cessation of wind was a mercy. Gasoline and steel smell assailed him. He groped, blinked as light flooded the shack. His breathing sounded too loud. In the harsh glare from the overhead bulb the shack spinned in pieces: bulb, shelves, huge blue wheel rising from the floor. It didn't make sense and it was out of focus anyway. But he saw jackets! Ski parkas, smeared with grease, hanging on a wall. The Scorpion hit the floor. A wave of blackness staggered him. He got the first parka on, struggled with the second. He zipped up the second parka. Gloves, he put on gloves. He had never felt so cold. Frost spread from the core of his body, ice filled his marrow, blue jointed with cold. He reached to steady himself and hit air. Toppling, he struck the shelf with his bad shoulder. His cry of pain sounded high and animallike.

Lipko is up here somewhere, came the unbidden thought. The floor rushed toward him and he hit.

The gasoline smell thickened, the bird cry outside pressed his ears.

Currie opened his eyes.

[187]

Lying sideways on the plank floor he was looking at a section of blue curving steel rising out of a pit. He sat up.

His head exploded in pain and he cried out, grabbing his temples. But I'm alive, he thought. And warm! The parkas had saved him, he had even sweated in sleep. Currie had no idea how long he'd been unconscious. The shack was windowless, he did not know if it was night. The wind had stopped. He saw the cramped one-room shack in its entirety. The eight-foot wheel was a gear to work the ski lift. A gasoline engine beside it was probably hooked to a steel fuel tank against an adjacent wall. NO FUMARE screamed a sign over the tank. It showed a smoking cigarette smothered by a red X. The ignition box protruded from the wall beside the door and was fed by two parallel power lines.

Dangerous to put the tank in the cabin, Currie thought. But maybe snow would cover it in winter otherwise. Or the gasoline would freeze.

And now he saw shelves with toolboxes on the third wall, snowshoes, skis, a spaceheater, greasy rags, a paperback novel entitled *Terror!* The cover showed a woman screaming. Terror meant the same in Italian as in English. It was the international language.

He rose dizzily, noting the Scorpion on the floor as he made his way to a medicine cabinet. Inside he found gauze bandage packages and two bottles with Italian labels. Opened, a plastic thin-necked bottle emitted an alcohol smell. A yellowish glass bottle reeked like Listerine.

He removed both parkas and unbuttoned his shirt. Coagulated blood ripped away at his shoulder, the wound flowed. The skin was shredded but the damage appeared to have been done to the outside of his arm. He did not think a bullet was lodged inside but could not be sure. Either way danger of infection existed.

Currie poured the contents of the Listerine bottle on the wound. A wave of pain burned him, he grit his teeth. The

[188]

cold was getting bad again. He tore off a gauze bandage, soaked it in alcohol and cleaned the wound. He taped a crude bandage to his skin. The buzzing outside remained steady all the while. *Carabinieri* would come up here if they were not already on their way. Lipko knew about the shack. Currie better leave.

Dressing quickly he envisioned the Alps rising in a saw-toothed mass dwarfing the cabin even at a mile up. Switzerland lay north, a direction he could calculate if the sun were visible. But a traveler would encounter snowfields deeper than a man up there, ice chasms to freeze a body for a thousand years. Currie had no food or water. Or maps. Compass. Climbing equipment. Tent. An Alpine crossing would be suicide.

Stay in the valley? The woods were dense and treacherous. Plus he remembered the compounds filled with St. Bernards below. Dogs trained to find people buried in snow. If they could track humans in blizzards, they would sniff out Currie in the forest as easily as if he carried a torch.

The ski parkas warmed him. It occurred to him that the police in town might not know what he looked like. He'd spent no time with Zarek in public except for their morning runs. The lodge had been stocked with food so they'd never shopped. The only villagers to whom he had spoken had been waiters in the cafés. They would not connect him with the lodge. Ticking began in his throat. Pretty funny to go back to town to hide.

But suddenly in the brooding hush a feeling of danger seized him. Nothing had changed in the shack but peril, like a living thing, stood in the room.

The bird noise outside had stopped. Just as when *he'd* reached the cabin.

Currie scrambled for the Scorpion, bringing it up as the door crashed open. Twin spurts of light erupted. Lipko was firing too but Currie had known where Lipko would be.

Lipko threw up his hands. He looked like a cheerleader at a football game. He folded at the waist and flew backwards, legs trailing. His pistol dropped sideways, Currie scrambled after it, kicking it away.

On a dusting of snow outside Lipko looked up at him, red web spreading on his jacket. Blood bubbled from the corner of his mouth. Less than ten seconds had elapsed.

Currie jammed the gun into Lipko's temple. "Who is 'Iran'?" he demanded. He was conscious of enormous thirst.

Lipko tried to laugh but the gagging turned to coughing. His eyes dulled. He muttered in German but then said, "Police will come. Dogs. Trackers. Should have stayed in town."

He showed a painwracked bloody grin.

With calm deliberation Currie pushed the gun into Lipko's mouth, hearing teeth shatter. The man was dying. Currie had only minutes to get answers. "Qaddafi is Israel so who is Iran?"

Lipko shook his head clear of the barrel. Bright blood on his lips brought out a grotesque femininity. "He'll send someone else," Lipko said, "to get you. Even in prison."

His fingers uncurled and his chin dropped sideways.

Currie's rage was undiminished. To Currie Lipko had been one of Qaddafi's weapons, a tool like the note he'd ripped up after Nori's murder. An extension of Qaddafi's will.

With the death of his messenger the Colonel seemed suddenly closer.

Currie's racing mind calculated chances. The snow had stopped. From the overhead position of the full moon he guessed the time as midnight. He'd slept three or four hours. The temperature was colder. In the luminous Alpine meadow he saw white snow patches and black earth, swept clean by breezes.

He retrieved Lipko's Ceska and shut the light. The cabin door faced the mountain, not the town. He did not think the glow would be visible from below, but why take chances? He walked to the crest and looked down. A barb moved into his belly. Rising along the zigzag trail, coming toward him, a stream of bobbing lights.

Thirty minutes should bring the police to the shack.

You should have stayed in town, Lipko had said.

He remembered the St. Bernards which could track him and the chasms he could fall into in the dark. The forest would be pitch-black, it would be almost impossible to make the descent without light unless he used the trail.

Concentrating, he watched the lights approach. There was a way out but he had to think of it. Lipko had said, Qaddafi won't stop until he gets you.

Until he gets you.

Currie brightened.

He hurried toward the shack. He lifted Lipko by the armpits and dragged him inside. He was incredibly heavy. He propped Lipko against the fuel tank. The head lolled. In the toolbox Currie found a wrench and wirecutter. With the wrench he unfastened bolts securing the fuel tank hatch. The tank was half empty.

With the wirecutters he sliced two seven-foot sections of wire off the spools. He lay the sections on the floor for later. He crossed to the ignition box and carefully shaved the rubbed insulation off the two wires which ran into the box. The gleam of exposed copper wire rewarded him. Then he brought the spools to the ignition box and fastened one strand from each spool to the wires going into the box.

Unrolling the spools, backing so as not to dislodge the junction of wires he'd created, he reached the door. He wound wire around the latch to reduce pressure on the junction. He backed into the night, fifty yards across the meadow, away from the crest and its view of *carabinieri*. Then the spools ran out.

Once Nori had lost the keys to Currie's jeep. He'd hotwired it. The principle was simple. Two wires lay close but not touching in the jeep. If they touched, electrical current surged to the starter. Normally turning the ignition key started the engine but if you lost the keys you could touch the wires by hand. A spark would jump between points and ignite a mixture of air and gasoline.

Air and gasoline just like in the fuel tank.

The spark would cause an explosion

Breathing hard, Currie ran back to the shack. He retrieved the seven-foot sections of wire he'd left on the floor. He fastened one section to each wire junction. Just beneath the ignition box he had created two junctions of three wires each. From each junction one wire ran to the meadow, one into the ignition box, one would soon go into the tank. Making sure the wires from the two junctions did not touch each other, he draped the seven-foot sections over the tank and dangled them inside. They were an eighth of an inch apart, half an inch above the gasoline.

NO FUMARE cautioned the red sign.

Lipko had fallen sideways against the tank. Propped on one elbow he seemed to follow Currie with his eyes. Terrorists were blown up all the time making bombs. Lipko would be roasted beyond recognition. Or blown to bits. Forensics might miss the bullet in his chest, if they found him in the first place.

Sweating, Currie took the money bag and Scorpion back across the meadow. Lipko's Ceska was in his pocket. He was careful to stay on the black patches of earth and off the snow. No tracks that way. He shaved the insulation off the ends of the wire from the spools. Fifteen minutes had passed since he'd first seen the lights. No time to check on the police.

He lay on his belly. A cloud rolled across the moon.

He touched the wires together.

Nothing happened. Currie started to rise. Then the sides of the cabin imploded and there was a *whomp!* and the roof split open. Half the roof was in the air upside down. The deep rumbling roar came at him, a column of blue flame erupted upward two hundred feet. He hit the ground. A blast of searing air swept overhead to a crack and boom. Debris smashed into trees, hissed on snow. A second blast colored the meadow orange. He pressed deeper into the earth. There was no third explosion.

When he rose the cabin was gone, steady fire burned at the base. Fiery extinguishing clumps of debris lay over a five-hundred-yard radius. A section of door burned in a tree. Glowing cinders swept overhead.

A severed hand lay in the snow, brushing Currie's sneaker.

He collected the wire as he ran back to the cabin. He threw the spools and wire into the flames. The police must not find the wire and guess what had happened.

Back at the crest, the bobbing lights were closer, coming faster now. Six, seven minutes away, he guessed.

Gun and money bag in hand, he started down to meet them.

He moved swiftly, five steps and pause, six and pause, like an animal in the forest. Zarek had taught him. He listened, mouth open slightly to improve hearing. No tension, no fear. He'd crossed a line with Lipko's death. All his senses were magnified. He heard the buzzing again, the crunching of his Adidas, an owl in the trees. He smelled pine and grease on his jacket.

But he did not hear voices. Could he have been wrong about the police? Or had they stopped? He envisioned them beyond the next bend, flashlights off, guns out, waiting. He slowed but kept moving. The forest rose silvery in moonlight. He envisioned the shattered timbers far below to the left.

He heard running feet.

Currie ducked off the path, crouched in the woods back to a ledge. Then police were hurrying past, many men, flashlight beams bouncing crazily on branches, gleaming on evergreen, shining into a pair of raccoon eyes a few feet away. He heard panting. A deep voice yelled, "Pronto!"

The raccoon at his feet was shivering with fear.

One more man approached, wheezing. A fat policeman.

The gasping receded.

Currie's breath formed a long steamy line. He stepped onto the path.

Behind him flames illuminated the sloping meadow and bobbing flashlights pushed up toward the crest.

Currie continued descending.

From what Zarek had told him about the *carabinieri* war on terrorism he expected truckloads of troops below. House-by-house searches. He would need a hiding place until morning. He would find a way out of this valley but not tonight. A lone walker would be stopped, buses did not run at night.

Lipko had said, You should have stayed in town.

Moving, he considered Courmayeur strategically like a general mapping a campaign instead of a casual visitor. The town spread in the shape of bird's wings on both sides of the highway, with pedestrian tunnels linking the two sides of the road. The center of Courmayeur, just off the highway, was a huge parking lot welcoming visitors, skiers, bus travelers, businessmen on their way to France. Then the village rose in tiers. Town hall came first, white steepled and fronted by a statue of a St. Bernard digging someone out of the snow. After that, dozens of pensions and hotels, full in October, a maze of souvenir shops, butchers, bread stores, groceries that filled each evening. And cafés.

Beyond this commercial core Courmayeur quieted into small homes with neat flowerboxes and lace curtains. And past that, the rich, at their required distance, had built their lodges.

Someone was coming. Currie ducked off the path.

Men passed with flashlights.

Five minutes later, descending again, he saw the town blinking up at him. After the shootout and explosion he was surprised Courmayeur remained unchanged, quiet and toy-like, although the streets must be crawling with soldiers. He saw tiny headlights from a lone car on the road. The tunnels would be guarded.

The meadow ended and he slipped into a hedgerow that marked the edge of the village. Hugging the shadows he crept along the rocky uneven mélange of picket fences, gardens and footpaths. Three or four darkened lodges squatted low and heavy timbered. A patrol passed. Currie flattened himself against a wall.

A Fiat sat in the driveway of the first lodge. But the second driveway was empty. The windows were locked. Staying in the shadows, Currie found the padlocked cellar door. He winced at the thud of the silenced bullet striking steel. Inside he breathed easier, although he was taking a chance if police noticed the missing padlock. Staying in the lodge was the best of bad alternatives.

Moonlight washed through a ground level window to whitewash concrete floors. The upstairs was almost identical to Pietro's: square sunken living room, bedrooms in a row off raised hallways, open kitchen area. The house smelled of mothballs. He wolfed stringbeans and cranberry sauce from cans. The refrigerator was empty, the faucets worked and he drank enormous quantities of water.

The beds beckoned him, narcotic against his exhaustion. But vacationers arrived in town late sometimes so he took quilts from a closet to the basement. Piled on the floor they felt luxurious. Maybe police had found what was left of Lipko and called off the search or slackened off. Tomorrow he would steal a car or take the bus. The thought came to him again: he hoped the police did not know what he looked like.

He knew where to go after he got out of the valley. Zarek had told him what to do.

◇ ◇ ◇

As Currie slumbered a mud-spattered police Lancia turned off the highway and sped into Courmayeur. *Carabinieri* on the main street snapped to attention when the car stopped for directions. The Lancia skidded to a halt before Pietro's lodge.

The first passenger out of the back wore the black overcoat and red shoulder markings of a captain in the Servizio Informazione Difesa, the Defense Information Service or SID of Italy, which directs the war against terrorism in that country. He was a severe-faced dark-headed man who carried black gloves in his right hand.

The second passenger, who wore a rumpled American raincoat and no hat on his gray bullet head, was Asher.

Inside the lodge and under blazing tripod lights forensics officers and detectives scoured the living room with tweezers, dusting powder, chemical kits. White tape outlined where Zarek had lain.

Asher watched with a professional eye. The captain took aside the senior *carabinieri* lieutenant on the scene. They spoke in Italian, which Asher did not understand. The lieutenant was blond like many northern Italians. Courmayeur had once been part of Austria. The lieutenant told the captain two men might have survived the shootout tonight.

"We showed photos of the dead men to hotel staff. A clerk recognized them and said they traveled with a third man, German. We have his description. And a neighbor thought two men were staying here. We found two sets of clothes. But no description. A house-to-house search revealed nothing. We've been unable to trace the lodge past a phony corporation in Zurich."

Listening to the stream of Italian, Asher grew impatient. The lieutenant said, "It's probable one of the two men blew himself up on the mountain. Making a bomb, we think. It'll be hell trying to figure out who it is. And I don't understand

[196]

why we only found one kind of each weapon downstairs. Arms sales may have been going on here, the shooting range was a demonstration area. A rival group attacked."

At the window Asher looked toward Mount Bianco but fog had moved in and obscured the mountain. In Courmayeur the weather could be treacherously changeable. "Foggy" seemed a good description of the whole investigation, he thought. The lieutenant was saying, "More troops will be coming in tonight. With the town, the valley and roadblocks, we have a lot of area to cover."

The captain took a sheaf of black-and-white photographs from the lieutenant and showed them to Asher. "It's Zarek, all right," the FBI man said, looking at the first one. He swallowed hard. He'd seen death before but what had been done to Zarek was hideous. The captain returned to the lieutenant, extracting a wallet-sized photo of Currie from his pocket and said, "Look for this man." Asher had provided the photo from FBI files. It was a full-face shot of Currie taken at Roosevelt Island.

Asher was thinking that only seven hours earlier he had been in Rome trying to convince this captain to mount a search for Currie and Zarek. They'd sat in an office filled with Raphael originals, silver coffee pitchers and furniture that could have been owned by the Medicis. The captain came from a rich family. "My dear Asher," the captain had said with maddening Old World politeness, although Asher knew him to be a ruthless and efficient law enforcement officer, "why should the Republic spare you more than a lowly captain for an hour? Our Maoists have bombed Milan again. The industrialists are whispering about coups and it takes talent when to know to take them seriously. You don't even tell me why you want to find these men. 'National Security' will not get you the help you need here."

As a member of an old boy network who had once done a big favor for the captain, the locating of a Sicilian gangster in Florida, Asher exercised slight personal leverage, enough to be asked along tonight when news of the shooting reached headquarters.

But now, seeing Currie's photo in the hands of the *carabinieri*, Asher experienced a stab of misgiving. The dead men, a Syrian and Algerian, had links to terrorist groups. It was possible they had been involved in the murder of Nori Abramoff in Washington. If that were the case, Asher the husband and father felt a savage satisfaction at their demise. Who cared who killed them? More power to the person who did.

In fact, Asher had found himself thinking more sympathetically of Currie since the Washington meeting in which he'd learned how little the other agencies were doing to investigate Nori Abramoff's death. Poor guy, he thought. First the Iranians and then the Libyans. Asher envisioned his own wife and daughter in Washington. He imagined a phone call. Your wife is dead on Roosevelt Island and Qaddafi's on TV taking credit. A wave of rage rose in him. Who wouldn't want to fight back after that.

He quelled the feeling. Common citizens had no business doing police work. Currie would stand trial if he'd shot those men tonight. That was the way the law operated, and if you changed it for one person you asked for trouble.

"To the car," the captain said. "We'll go up Bianco, it will take some hours and you will sleep in Courmayeur tonight." Outside, wet air enveloped them. The car smelled of cigarettes and plastic seat covering. Asher opened his window and let the town wash in. When he pictured Currie in his mind he saw the grief-stricken engineer who had stormed out of his office. It seemed impossible that the same man could have shot it out with terrorists and won.

A surge of admiration interrupted his thoughts but he battered that down too. He would cable Washington and ask how much he could tell the Italians. At the moment he kept

Qaddafi out of it. The Italians were funny, they liked Qaddafi. They thought he was clownish and ineffectual and that Americans focused on him instead of their own problems. They had business dealings with him. He even owned part of their automobile industries.

"Try to take Currie alive," Asher said.

The captain shrugged, leaned back and drove with one hand, smoking. "If he killed two men he's dangerous, my friend. Besides, he might be dead on the mountain."

The bottom line was finding Currie, Asher thought. It was pointless to think of him as dead. Asher would act as if he lived. Which meant he was in this valley, the town or on the mountain. Asher didn't think he would have run into the Alps.

They drove through a meadow which smelled of hay. Asher saw flashlights ahead; guides would be waiting. The captain's English was thickly accented. "Dear Asher," he said. It was a nonfeminine form of address. "For the past forty years we've been at war. That Englishman Orwell said it. Two big powers slugging it out. First World War Two, the acquisition of territory. Then the Cold War, the consolidation of power. Your man Kissinger said it. In the nuclear age there would be little wars, surrogate wars. Both sides arming tiny countries and taking out their aggressions that way." He took a long puff, slowing the car so he could finish what he was saying. "Those little countries were too far away from the centers of power so now we have a new war, a terrorism war. Those dead men back there are troops in an army. And your man Currie might be a soldier for the other side. I arrest them all." He laughed and talked to himself. "Stick to policework, Matteo. Leave philosophy to the politicians. Now you tell me the real story of Currie between us and never mind national security. How did so much firepower come into his hands?"

A long time ago Asher's Maine State Police captain grandfather had said, "There's conscious knowledge and unconscious knowledge. Intuition is knowledge you don't know you have yet." Asher sat back and let the smell of the valley permeate his consciousness. He felt the quiet of the village and the tenseness of the police. He felt the *carabinieri* patrols, the roadblocks up the valley. If he were Currie what would he do?

The captain sighed. "I didn't think you'd tell me anything. The Lancia reached the meadow and stopped. Flashlights surged toward it. Asher sent his intuition out like radar, like antenna. He was trying to find Currie and if he did he would hand him over to the Italian police.

CHAPTER
15

As an influence upon international events Carlo Crespi was completely inconsequential except for the fact that he owned the lodge in which Currie was hiding. And he was on his way to use it.

At nine that morning the Milanese lawyer turned his Peugeot station wagon off the Aosta highway cloverleaf to join a long queue of cars idling outside the Courmayeur parking lot at a *carabinieri* roadblock.

He was furious. The drive had taken all night instead of five hours. Crammed into the back, the nine-year-old had the flue. His wife's simpering art gallery friends, invited along for the week, swooned at the thought of changing a tire. Crespi had blown two near dawn.

Each time he'd threatened to turn around a great wail had gone up in the car. "No, Daddy! No, Carlo!" Now the *carabinieri* had joined the conspiracy against Crespi's vacation: of incompetent mapmakers, faulty tire manufacturers and the Italian parliament which drew up divorce laws.

He glared at the driver ahead, a long-haired blond leaning from her Fiat while a puffed-up sergeant checked her passport. Crespi's window was open and the voices carried. "I'm Anna Currie," the woman said in English. "Yes, I live in Washington. No, I do not want to have dinner with you tonight."

Crespi drummed on the steering wheel. His wife came

awake beside him with a fart that sounded like the theater cannon at La Scala. "Police! What happened!"

"I want to sleep."

"Documentos!" the *carabiniere* snapped, stepping up to the window. His wife leaned over, she was going to start a conversation, she could never shut up. "Trouble, sergeant?"

"Terrorists. One may still be in the area."

This time a different cry arose in the car. "Let's go back to Milan!"

Crespi grabbed his papers from the *carabiniere.* "I don't care if the whole Red Brigade is in the lodge!" he roared. "We're staying!"

Currie leaned back and stared in the bathroom mirror and was amazed. He looked like another person. He'd found the woman's black hair dye in a closet; big piece of luck, he thought. He'd parted his hair in the middle. The wraparound sunglasses turned the room blue.

Other than that he was naked, the overhead heating light luxurious on his bare skin. He felt safe, hidden.

In a little while he would put on stolen ski clothes — blue-striped jacket and stretch pants — and go outside and try to fool the police. In autumn the highest slope on Bianco remained open. A skier would not be noticed.

Now he relaxed and turned on the shower. A powerful stream of hot water spattered the glass partition. Currie grunted with pleasure, soaping himself. The roar drowned out other noise. He would stroll through town to the bus carrying ski boots he'd broken. His story was he needed to repair the boots in Pré San Didier.

He shoved his head under the shower. "Color won't wash out" boasted the English-made hair dye. For once advertising proved truthful. Currie's disguise would remain intact even if it rained.

But it occurred to him, as he used the rose-scented soap

for a final rinse, that he did not have to go outside at all. Why not hide in the lodge? The police would leave town eventually, they might have already done so if the explosion last night had fooled them. He remembered the squad cars pulling away from Roosevelt Island after Nori's death.

As he shut off the shower, a car door slammed outside.

Pain lanced Currie's shoulder. No mistaking the sound. Cursing himself for relaxing he ran for the bedroom, spraying water on the carpet. He scooped ski clothes off the bed as footsteps came up the walk. Currie pulled out the Scorpion, the lock clicked open in the living room and footsteps came in the house. Naked, he gripped the gun, pressed against the wall. Something heavy dropped in the living room.

The door slammed and footsteps receded outside.

Currie peaked out. A suitcase stood by the front door. Improperly closed, it was slowly swinging open.

He leaped the six feet to the basement. Down the stairs. Pull on clothes. There was a back door down there. *Use the gun,* said Zarek's voice. *Tie these people, take their car.* But Currie would not chance hurting bystanders. Nori had been killed during someone else's fight. If he'd found his fatal flaw, so be it.

He shoved the guns in the ski jacket, stuffed the dollars in the boots. He wedged the money in with socks. Skiers didn't carry money-filled attaché cases.

More footsteps came into the house. A man and woman screamed at each other upstairs. *"Tu non, t'interessi di me!"* the woman shouted. *"Pensi solo a te stesso!"* Any second someone would see the water in the bathroom, the empty cans in the kitchen.

He opened the basement door and looked out to see if any neighbors were about. He stepped outside and strode to the footpath. He slowed. He headed toward town.

Currie waited for the shout at his back. The temperature had risen, the ski jacket was warm. Over the rooftops, against slab gray Mount Bianco, two police helicopters swept in circles. So the police had not left. He did not know what kind of emergency powers the *carabinieri* had but the troops he had seen looked tough and efficient. If they checked his passport they would see the photo with blond hair. He'd used the dye thinking the police might know his appearance but couldn't know his name. He'd left no ID at Pietro's lodge. A trace of the rented car would reveal Zarek's false identity, not Currie's. And Pietro, who was probably too smart to be linked to his lodge anyway, would never talk to authorities, since he had ties with the Libyans.

In the distance peaks stood like trenchcoated sentries. Trucks hurtled through the mist on the Aosta highway, heading for the Mount Blanc Tunnel. They moved fast so the road wasn't blocked. Good sign.

Currie swung the boots casually, making sure the money wedging socks stayed in place. Sixty thousand dollars were hidden in the boots. A black Alsatian dog snarled at him from behind a picket fence. A Basque-capped workman passed, pick-ax over shoulder. The *carabinieri* would come charging down this path and he had better be in the center of town by then.

But he reached it and breathed easier, shielded by crowds of workers, businessmen in pinstripes, a couple dressed for skiing which made him feel better.

In two hundred yards the street would widen onto the town hall plaza and pedestrian promenade overlooking the parking area. He would be able to see if the *carabinieri* checked passengers getting on the bus.

He started to think he might get out of town. No sign of patrolmen. Then pain moved into his belly. Diagonally across the street two *carabinieri* in black greatcoats pushed a blond man against a butchershop wall. The blond had Currie's build and haircut. One trooper leveled a Beretta submachine gun and the other frisked the blond. Currie watched sideways, strolling ten feet away. The frisker pulled a sheet of paper from his coat and checked it against the suspect's face. The throbbing sensation reached Currie's throat. *How could they have my picture?* But thirty feet later he stopped to look back in a souvenir shop window reflection.

Shoppers blocked his view, the reflection distorted it. Through the moving crowd he made out a disturbingly familiar bullet-headed man come up to the *carabinieri*, look into the suspect's face and shake his head. The *carabinieri* released the man. Currie's stomach was really hurting. The bullet-headed man turned to watch the blond walk away.

Currie saw his face. It was Asher.

He couldn't breathe. His entrails turned to ice. Asher, who had hounded him, suspected him. Asher couldn't be here, but the FBI man wasn't disappearing or turning into somebody else. Asher had obviously given the *carabinieri* his picture. Currie grew dizzy with rage. How had Asher found him?

And now the FBI man shifted stance, gazing in Currie's direction. Currie could almost feel Asher's eyes sweeping the street, passing like radar. In nature some animals freeze when in danger. Instinct told Currie if he started walking, if he detached himself from the background Asher would notice him. Asher must have traced the cab to the airport in Washington, must have matched the Tom Fleeter passport with the TWA flight manifesto. A heavy pressure began in the back of Currie's head. Asher was looking in his direction.

A woman's voice startled him. "Are you in need of help?" The grinning proprietor of the souvenir shop looked up at him. Blond pigtails. Thin nose. Currie said, "Excuse me?" Beyond her, in the window, Asher's reflection was shorter than the *carabinieri's*.

Currie said, "I'm looking for a birthday present for my fiancée."

The woman showed even teeth. "What a lucky woman,"

she said. How many hours had Asher wasted coming after Currie? A surge of determination filled Currie. He steered the woman into the shop. The relief he experienced out of Asher's sight died. He saw no rear exit.

The aisles were crowded with wooden souvenirs: mirrors and carvings. With hearty casualness, hoping the woman might tell him something useful, he asked, "Who was that man the police questioned across the street?"

The woman was surprised. "You do not know what happened last night?"

Currie laughed. "When I sleep I don't hear a thing."

An illicit sort of pleasure lit the woman's face. She leaned close, palm half covering her mouth. A schoolgirl whispering secrets. "There was a shooting! Terrorists!" Currie feigned shock. "In Courmayeur?" In a mirror behind the cash register he saw a small bit of street outside. He did not see Asher but Currie sensed him moving around outside the shop.

The woman nodded. "The *carabinieri* came by this morning with a photograph of the man. I'll show you." She opened a drawer. Currie said quickly, to stop her, "Take this necklace out of the case, can you?" He didn't understand why the family back in the lodge had not raised a cry yet. Maybe they were still arguing and had not gone into the bathroom. Sweat gathered under his armpits. Asher appeared in the mirror a few feet from the shop, hands in his pockets like a tourist, not a policeman. He looked as if he might stroll in to buy something.

Would Currie shoot a policeman? Currie wiped sweat from his brow, hoping the woman would not notice. How could he shoot Asher?

The woman held up a single gold strand which twisted in her hand, noose shaped. "My friend makes these. Your fiancée will love it."

"And these earrings?"

A nod of approval. "For a man you have taste. I wrap them up, yes? Earrings and necklace?"

A purchase was necessary to keep the shopkeeper friendly. Currie was about to say yes but realized he had no money. His false name was on his traveler's checks. If Asher had circulated Currie's picture, the police must know the Tom Fleeter name too. The cash was in the ski boot. Little things screw you up, Zarek had said. He'd have to bluff it out.

Currie went uncertain. "She's hard, hard to buy for. Particular." The woman's eyebrows dipped to a *V*. Currie realized she'd noticed Asher and was considering going after a potentially more responsive customer. "Take your time," she said, starting to turn away. Picking up the closest piece of merchandise, a hideous glazed pottery urn, he said, looking admiringly at blue cows on the surface, "She loves animals." The woman stopped but would leave any second. He said, "I can't believe I slept through the commotion last night. You know, I live in New York. Lots of noise." She shifted stance. "Hear the story about the New Yorker?" he said. "Slept through traffic every night. Then there's a blizzard, no cars, no noise at all. The guy wakes up shouting, " 'What's that?!' "

"I'll come back in a while," she said.

"But I wonder if it's safe to stay in town," Currie said, putting authority in his voice, willing her back. "Will the police catch those terrorists?"

It worked. The gossipy light was back in her face. "My nephew is a lieutenant," she confided. "A bomb killed two *carabinieri* in Rome Monday. The troops have decided among themselves. They're not going to arrest the terrorist. They're going to kill him."

"What he deserves," Currie agreed. The ski jacket was stifling. He was astounded his voice sounded normal. But the woman wasn't finished. Her chubby Teutonic face twisted into something furious and grotesque. "Animals don't need trials," she said. She changed again, grew thoughtful, appraising. "I've seen you before. Have you been in the shop?"

Currie laughed. "I look like everybody's uncle in the world." But the sweat was running down his back and *Asher was gone from the mirror*. The street had erupted into commotion, *carabinieri* charged past, coats flapping. Currie cried, "They must have found the man!"

The woman said, "It's not that you remind me of someone. It's you I've seen."

Currie called, going out the door, "Don't sell that necklace! I'm going to find out what happened, I'll be back."

In the moving crowd he cursed his clumsy exit. The woman would remember where she'd seen him and tell the *carabinieri* about the ski clothes and black hair. *Get to the bus.* Maybe the *carabinieri* had overlooked the bus. Maybe they were understaffed or distracted.

The troops have decided among themselves. They aren't going to arrest the man, they're going to kill him.

He fought against panic. Someone slammed into him. Oranges rolled on the cobblestones. Currie said, "Excuse me," forced himself to pick them up. He passed the café where he'd calmly sipped espresso last night. Every waiter had his picture, every shopowner and hotel clerk. He maintained his pace. Even the air seemed malevolent. Thanks to the FBI. His own people.

The smell in town had changed. In the bright little tourist paradise vegetable rotting permeated the breeze. The mountains rose like prison walls or walls of a tomb: high, impassive, gray, impenetrable. A fine little drama for the gossipy souvenir shopowners to tell their customers.

Don't be bitter. It wastes energy. In front of town hall the St. Bernard statue appeared to be eating the guide it was supposed to be saving. Currie reached the promenade. Below, beyond hundreds of parked cars two *carabinieri* jeeps blocked the exit. Troops leveled submachine guns and checked drivers.

But Currie saw the bus! Almost directly below, past a stairway. A line of idle travelers, knapsacks or skis on their backs, filed into the pastel-blue vehicle.

Two *carabinieri* by the door checked documents.

The mist was clammy on Currie's forehead. His scalp crawled and he was thirsty. He'd seen a movie in which a man had woken in a bedroom to see the walls moving to crush him. The man had thrown himself against the walls. He'd screamed for help but the walls had kept closing. The Barettas would slice Currie in half. Bright blood had streaked Zarek's face. Currie wanted to scream at the *carabinieri*, "We're on the same side!"

Take hostages, Zarek's voice said. *Find a quiet apartment, tie the people up. Hide.*

And if the police burst in and hurt them? If the people fight back? I can't hurt people like Nori.

Currie took a step toward the parking lot stairs. There had to be an unlocked car among the hundreds below. He could hotwire it and . . .

A hand grabbed his shoulder.

He spun, the Scorpion coming out of his pocket. In the next brief instant time seemed to slow, he spun in slow motion, dropping into the firing crouch Zarek had taught him. He knew, in the moment preceding death, not in words but in a glorious free rush of emotion, a power and giddy fearlessness, that there were worse things than dying and he had conquered them. That the bullets would hurt but not extinguish, that he would not have done any of it differently. There were acts beyond personal consequences. If you had to commit them you went ahead. On one knee, the Scorpion swinging up, he felt the heady multiple impacts of love and commitment freeing him, launching him to roaring defiant joy, the shout building in his throat.

He never voiced it.

"I," he said. "How? Anna."

She wore a white fur jacket cut at midthigh. She wore skintight designer jeans with burgundy boots and cashmere turtleneck. Her blond hair down her back, gold on white. His senses overloaded. After Asher, Anna was impossible. The police chased him, he'd killed three men since yesterday yet Anna could not be in front of him. She was just standing there like some best friend mirage or divine intervention.

"Put the gun away," she whispered. "Someone will see it."

He did so. She was all alabaster skin and clear blue eyes. Hand on hip, she stood cool, confident looking except Currie knew with Anna the stance meant fear.

A tepid breeze touched his face.

He saw a butterfly on her shoulder, blue wings fanning.

"I thought you were dead," she said. "I thought they killed you." It was so good to see her, weakness flooded his legs. He'd almost shot her. Almost killed Anna. He felt like he'd been away from home for years but he snapped out of the mood, a three-man *carabinieri* patrol made its way in trident shape from town plaza, toward the promenade. They had not identified him but their weapons were ready. "Anna, kiss me. The police."

She came into his arms as if she'd been poised. Her lips tasted of sugar. She crushed his mouth. He felt her curves under the jacket and his head swam as they pulled apart. Blue gold flecks floated in her eyes.

"Hair didn't fool you," he said after the patrol passed. Shy, he touched his hair.

"I know your walk." She puffed herself up and tucked in her chin. "The President walk." An old high-school parody. Her giggle had a hysterical edge. "Cindy told me you were in Italy," she said. She saw his shock. She said, "I knew the police were looking for you, I had to warn you, tell you to stop. Then I heard about Zarek on the radio. That FBI man, Asher, told me . . ."

Currie went cold. "You came with Asher?"

"He's in Washington."

He watched her carefully. "He's here," he said. It was an accusation. His senses were bursting and he reeled from multiple shocks. He didn't know whom to trust. Things moved too fast. In Washington she'd always been intermediary for people who wanted things from him. Reporters needing stories. Socialites gathering celebrities.

She backed a step, palms up. "He didn't find out from me." She'd never lied to him, lying simply was not one of her faults.

"Then how . . ." But how Asher had gotten here was inconsequential. He grew aware again of his exposed position on the promenade. Of the *carabinieri* below and the cars he could steal. He was still shaken over almost having shot her. He'd been squeezing the trigger when he saw her face.

"Anna, I have to get away from here, you have to get away from me, it's dangerous."

Pain added blue to her eyes. "I came all this way."

"I almost shot you."

"Some greeting." A little-girl doggishness marked the joke. She was trembling. She said, "I came to help." He could not stay up here; he turned toward the parking lot stairs. She walked with him, arguing.

She said, "I already helped. When I kissed you, you know it. Those police might have seen you otherwise."

"That's not the point. They'll hurt you." He had a feeling if he told her what the *carabinieri* planned to do to him she'd never leave. He just said, "You can help by going."

"They say you shot three people. The Black Coats are all over town."

It was absurd. In the middle of a manhunt he was locked

in some crazy argument with his ex-wife. "I know a way out," he lied. "It's foolproof. No time to explain." She maintained speed. He said, "I'll call you later." It didn't work. Arguing couples attracted attention. He slowed. "Anna, it means a lot that you came but let me go, please."

For a moment he thought she'd listen. She'd not expected the soft appeal. But she said, "Why are you going to the parking lot? Does it have something to do with your *foolproof* plan?"

In Currie's mind he saw himself having hotwired a car. He drove out of the lot, away from the exit, into town. At the edge of Courmayeur he gunned the car through the cow meadow and up the curved embankment to the highway. A thin chance. Of course as soon as he hit the meadow the jeeps would roar out of the parking lot after him but he'd have a quarter-mile head start. A fast car would outrun the jeeps and on the curving mountain roads if he could lose sight of them he could turn off into the woods. It was better than sticking around and waiting to be caught.

"My car's down here," he said. The police helicopter swept against Mount Bianco, half a mile off.

"Which car?"

"That one."

"The Alpha?" She taunted him, testing. "Let's sit in it and talk. No one will see us."

Be master of the little problems, Zarek had said, and the big ones won't arise. Control your enviornment. Easy to say until your ex-wife showed up. How was he supposed to control Anna? Pull out the Scorpion?

But now he saw with horror that two truckloads of *cara-binieri* had cleared the roadblock. The backs flipped down. The troops began jumping to the parking lot, spreading into sweep formations and moving through the lot.

"All right," he snapped, turning back to the stairs. Anna

had gone gray with terror when she saw the *carabinieri*. But she looped her arm through his like a lover. They moved at a happy couple stroll back up the stairs. Anna laughed gaily as if he'd made a joke. She squeezed against him. "Egh," she said, "I feel that gun." He put his arm around her and drew her close. "Go home," he said. "It's dangerous." She ran a finger playfully down his nose. "No." They reached the promenade, the *carabinieri* sweep driving them back into town.

"Christ, Anna, aren't you listening? Nori got shot, I don't want the same thing to happen to you."

She faltered but kept going. He thought, dumbstruck, She's jealous. The police planned to murder him and she was jealous of Nori. He didn't understand her. Was she that guilty over Iran? She said, "They say you shot three men." It was the second time she'd brought it up. Maybe if he answered her she'd go away. A hard, joyless satisfaction filled him. "They killed Nori."

That stopped her. She shuddered. "You really did it?" She paused, traced lines around his mouth with one finger. In town the bright little tourist shops were like cardboard props. He was desperate for a car. One minute she was the tough Anna he had never seen before, the next she changed back, afraid. She'd always feared even slight involvement, had even been rattled when he joined Watchers International and all they did was write letters. Her mere presence here was almost beyond belief.

A man in a pinstripe suit was openly admiring her from a bakery doorway. His head turned as they passed. She whispered, "It's Zarek's fault, isn't it? I knew something terrible would happen if you got involved with him. He did it, didn't he?"

Currie said, "He saved me." They'd moved a little apart and his wrist rested lightly on her shoulder. "Look Anna, what are you doing here? Get out. I don't want you here, you're screwing everything up like you always do." He hated himself for saying it, for being cruel to her. "Go. Leave. Go home and get away from me."

Little boys playing by a bakery made their hands into guns. "Ta-ta!" they shouted.

Anna said, "Turn yourself in."

Her words were so unexpected that his anger turned to astonishment. He looked sharply at her. "Find Asher," she pleaded. "He likes you, oh he does." Her face was softened by fear. He grew suspicious again. How did she know so much about Asher? She said, "He'll explain to the Italians." They left the commercial area and entered the zigzag gravel lanes that passed the hotels. Currie saw parked cars off the road, on the grass. Anna said, "Anyone would understand what you did, you went a little crazy. And you can't go anywhere in a car. The parking lot's blocked."

"Goodbye, Anna."

"Hide in my room. This is my hotel."

"The clerks have my picture."

"Then go in the mountains. I'll bring you food."

The offer rocked him. The Anna he knew would have fled by now. "Dogs and trackers," he said. "And the Black Coats would see someone leaving town. I have to get out now. Courmayeur will close up for siesta in a couple of hours, we'd be alone on the street."

The pattern, in the old days, Currie having rejected her advice, would be for Anna to sigh and disappear to report that she'd done her best. Currie removed her hands from his forearm. Bad Chopin played on a piano somewhere. He said, slowly, emphasizing the importance, "Someone may have seen you with me. Go sit in a café. Talk to people. Get an alibi."

She was leaning against a white Fiat, sad resignation having seeped into her face and he thought, Good, I've won, although it was a poor kind of victory to send away a friend.

But he'd misread her again. She wasn't the old Anna. Her fury took him by surprise. In one swift motion she whipped something shiny from a hip pocket, car keys, he saw. She opened the trunk of the Fiat. "You'll fit," she hissed between clenched teeth.

Before he could say anything she bent and took out the jack. She dropped it on the ground. Boys who had been playing soccer in a grass strip across the lane filed off the field. No other people were visible. She struggled with the spare tire.

"Help me," she ordered, "you crazy man, you filthy man who won't listen to reason. You need more room if you're going to get in here. I'll drive you out." Her voice dropped. "And then I'll convince you to go to Asher."

"What is it with you and Asher?"

She spun, eyes ablaze, lips drawn back in a rictus of rage he had never seen in her. She mimicked him. " 'Anna, go to a café. Get an alibi.' Maybe you think you can just drive away, drive off in a stolen car. Oh, I know you didn't own that car. There's no foolproof way out of Courmayeur. You want to go busting out like a cowboy." Tears coursed down her face. "What do you think happens to the people you cut yourself off from? They forget you, is that it? I sip espresso and listen to machine guns go off in the parking lot? And tomorrow I look at your damn bloody face in the paper?" She stepped back from him. "Don't you come near me. The police aren't checking trunks, only drivers. Get in. Or maybe you don't really want to leave here. Maybe you want to be caught." Her voice broke. "I'm involved whether you like it or not. I'm going to stay involved."

A half-mile off the police helicopter swung and headed toward them, back to town.

It started to drizzle.

Bending slowly to the trunk, Currie pushed the spare tire over to make room. He was numb. Anna said, "Back seat tilts forward, it opens so you can get more luggage in." If he curled fetally he'd fit. She said, "Push the seat forward a little, you'll have some light. No one's coming. Now."

The door slammed on him. Entombed in darkness he heard the metallic echo of his own breathing. The Scorpion jammed his groin, he laid the gun on the floor of the trunk. He still had Lipko's Ceska in his pocket. It emitted an acrid, oily odor. Currie's hip slammed the trunk when the car jerked forward.

They were moving. He pushed the rear seat forward, it tilted slightly into the car. A thin wedge of light fell on the gun.

"We're on the street with those souvenir shops," Anna said. "Lots of *carabinieri* coming toward us." He imagined the *carabinieri* advancing in a line, checking the houses, noticing the car. He should have walked off and left Anna uninvolved, he thought. Then he thought, Who am I kidding? She would have come after me.

The trunk rattled from the cobblestones and Anna sounded thick, muffled. She talked in spurts, obviously quieting each time passersby looked into the car. She said, relieved, "We're past the Black Coats. We're . . ."

The car halted. Currie heard the creak of a door opening, then the chassis swayed as if someone had gotten in or out. He wanted to call Anna's name, but suppose there was a new passenger? A masculine voice said, "Okay, Anna, where is he?" Pain tore through Currie's entrails. Asher was in the car.

CHAPTER
16

"**F**OR the third time," Anna's voice said, "I don't know where he is."

Currie strained to hear, curled in the dark trunk. The cold grew, the chassis vibrated. Currie gripped the Scorpion to keep it from knocking against the floor.

They must have reached the parking lot by now. Currie imagined the *carabinieri* at the roadblock. He tried to shut out the shopkeeper's words: *They've decided not to arrest the terrorist but to kill him.*

"I'll just ride along with you if you don't mind," Asher said comfortably. "These Italians won't let an American cop do anything. A little sightseeing would be nice. That is what we're doing, isn't it. Isn't that what you said? Sightseeing?"

"Yes," Anna said. "Sightseeing."

"Did Tim phone you in Washington? Ask you to come?"

"What's the point of telling you anything when you don't listen," Anna said.

"Or maybe it was Cindy who told you he was here."

Currie had only met the man once but he remembered every feature: the broad face and steel-colored receding flat-top, the fullback shoulders, the gnarled power in the hands. The probing suspicion in the slightest movement. A face hardened by shrewdness, washed of color by years under artificial light. Asher. The investigation machine pointed in the wrong direction by the implacable, malevolent and blundering indifference of Currie's own government.

At least Anna had not betrayed him. Now Currie sniffed. The gas smell was stronger, he heard hissing. Damn, he thought, groping for the leak. Asher's voice said, "Anna, you don't know how much trouble he's in. We can get him home if I reach him first." The stop-and-go pace told Currie they'd joined the line of cars at the roadblock. He pictured Asher's palms outstretched in a gesture of false concern. "The *carabinieri* have a grudge," Asher said. "They could hurt him."

Anna's voice said shakily, "They're opening that man's trunk."

"They do that on and off. Depends on how heavy traffic is."

The throbbing intensified in Currie's shoulder. He wondered if his wound was bleeding again. Anna would be searching for a way to leave the line without alerting Asher.

It was hard to hear over the vibration of the motor.

"They're taking their time," Anna complained. "All day on one car." A pause. "Hey, my camera. I left my camera at the hotel."

"Pull out of line and the *carabinieri* will be here in two seconds. Better to go through and come back."

"Right." The car slid forward and stopped. Two cars ahead? One? Anna said conversationally, but there was a stretched quality in her voice, "You don't think the *carabinieri* would hurt him if you brought him in, is that it?"

A hole in the bottom of the trunk let in a stream of warm gas. Currie pulled ski socks from the boot and wedged them in the gap. Big deal, he thought. The *carabinieri* will be in here in a minute.

Asher said, "You told me you would report to me after you talked to Cindy."

Currie pointed the Scorpion at the lid of the trunk. The car slid forward again and halted.

She said, "I didn't learn anything worth telling you."

"You flutter your eyelids when you lie," Asher said. "It's very cute."

"I'm not lying."

"Of course not. Tim never phoned you. You learned nothing from Cindy. Magically you came to Italy and by coincidence Tim was here."

Gritting his teeth, Currie lowered the Scorpion and slid it away from him in the dark. If firing started, a ricochet could go through the back seat and hurt Anna. Or even Asher. And if the *carabinieri* saw him holding the Scorpion when the trunk opened, they'd shoot for sure.

Dimly lit, the white socks in the hole looked like fluorescent cancer growths. He would play out his luck. Maybe the *carabinieri* would not shoot with Asher present and no gun in Currie's hand. He'd get out of prison somehow. I can wait, he'd told Zarek back in Washington. Okay, he could wait. But every muscle cried out for him to pick up the gun. Asher wouldn't be around when the *carabinieri* got him alone in jail. Lipko had said, "Qaddafi will come after you." Pick up the gun, urged the Zarek voice in his mind.

Anna told Asher, "I can explain that. I remembered something he told me after Iran. A little thing, only a wife would notice. About Italy. Courmayeur. A mercenary Zarek knew here."

You really ought to pick up the gun, the Zarek voice said. Currie was amazed how well Anna lied, although Asher was right about the fluttering lashes.

"What was the name of this mercenary?"

"I don't remember."

The car slid forward and stopped.

"Why didn't you tell me about him before?" Asher said. "Why?"

Asher spelled "W.H.Y."

"Because . . . it's because you wouldn't know how to talk

to him." Anna's voice grew rushed, whether because they were next in line or because Asher unnerved her Currie did not know. She said, "I realized I might be able to reach him, and get him to come back. He hadn't done anything wrong and you told me he hated talking to you. Besides, Tim being in Italy was a longshot. I thought I'd have a better chance alone."

"Fluttering lashes," Asher said.

An Italian voice barked *"Documentos!"*

Currie clenched his fists. He'd be lying here like some sacrifice when the door swung open. The Italian voice outside grew surprised. "Signore Asher, you are with this lady? Go ahead, basta, basta! Let them go!"

Too easy, Currie thought.

A trick, it was a trick. He waited for the key in the lock, the sound of the trunk opening. He heard the grinding of gears engaged. He felt the car accelerate, sway gently left which meant they were climbing the cloverleaf, straighten for the highway, pick up speed.

I'm alive.

He wanted to scream with joy, pound on the trunk. But as quickly as the euphoria rose it died. Asher's voice said, "You came to Courmayeur worried about finding Tim but an hour later you're sightseeing, eh?"

"If I were meeting him you don't think I'd take you along, do you?"

"Good point." There was a single muffled clap of hands as if Asher had determined this part of the conversation. But then the FBI man said, "So! What shall we see in Pré San Didier? A church? Do you like to visit churches? Most tourists don't go this far north in Italy for churches. You go to church, Anna?"

Currie hated the voice, the inquisitor droning. Bullying. Relentless. Currie thought, Leave her alone. Asher used his voice the way a railroad worker wielded a sledgehammer.

"A church would be fine," Anna said.

"Does he have any other phony passports besides the Tom Fleeter one?"

"Look, why don't you get out of the car, okay? Go back to Courmayeur, I don't need this."

Currie screamed at her in his mind. *Drive into Pré San Didier. Walk away from the car, take Asher with you. I'll climb through the seat and get out and be gone when you get back.*

Asher kept pushing at her. "You know what the penalty is in Italy for helping a terrorist? That's what the *carabinieri* think he is. Twenty-year jail term for an accomplice."

Normally Anna drove well, but she grew careless when rattled. Currie imagined her chin tucked low, eyes ahead in combat readiness, steering palms hard against the wheel with dangerous jerks Currie felt in the trunk.

Asher said, "And it's an Italian prison, Anna. Nobody speaks English. No one visits you. Your family is five thousand miles away."

Currie felt the explosion building, a physical presence in the trunk. An ozone taste was in his mouth. Asher's relentlessness had an almost supernatural power, as if the man knew answers before he spoke. A rhythmic drumming began on the trunk and Currie thought, It's raining.

The frayed aspect grew in Asher's voice. "Tim had nothing to do with Nori's death, I'm sure of that now. We can save him."

Anna said primly, "I don't know what you're talking about."

Asher broke. "Turn around, we're going back to the *carabin*——"

Currie lashed out with both feet, kicking over the back seat, uncurling and scrambling into the car, gun up. Asher's head swiveled. Currie shouted. "Hands up, up, touch the ceiling!"

Anna gave a plaintive cry, swerved the car onto the shoulder but regained control.

Currie was surprised to see rain even though he had known it would be there. After the dark trunk the banality of a landscape, any landscape, astounded him.

The wipers slashed back and forth.

Currie smelled lime aftershave.

In wonder and disgust the FBI agent said, "The trunk. You were in the trunk." A silver digital watch circled his wrist. His raincoat needed a wash.

"Keep your hands up." Reaching over the edge of the seat with one hand and pressing the Scorpion with the other against the back of Asher's head, burrowing it under the prickly hairs, Currie frisked slowly, aware of Anna's eyes in the mirror. "Where's the gun?"

"Not allowed to carry one in Italy."

"You're not even supposed to *be* in Italy, you're not a cop here. Pick up your right foot, put it on your seat. Slow."

The cuff lifted to show a surprisingly hairless ankle but no holster. Currie said, "Left leg. Both feet on the floor now. Take off your belt with one hand. Give."

Anna said, "What are you going to do to him?"

Asher said, "You kill those men?"

"Keep that other hand on the ceiling. Loop your right arm behind your seat. Wedge it between the seat and the door. Bend it back so it touches the seat."

Thunder broke outside like artillery. Anna said, "It was self-defense, Asher." Her voice was wild. "Tell him, Tim. Those men killed Nori Abramoff."

"You think he believes you?" Currie said. "He believes what he wants to believe. Asher, I'm going to tie your wrist with the belt."

He looped the other end around a plastic knob by Anna's seat. Not a secure knot, but to get free Asher would need seconds to get his hand back into the front of the car.

Throughout it all the agent remained calm. "The *carabinieri* have your picture," Asher said. "They're going to wonder where I went. And remember this car. Anna's pretty, they'll remember her too."

Pré San Didier was coming up on the left, another quaint town beyond the guardrail. Conical roofs. White church steeple under Alps. Meadows. Cows. Hikers. Tourists.

Asher said, "I meant what I told Anna. I can help you."

"Pass the town," Currie told her. "You have gas?"

The thunder cracked again and became the honking of a semi truck tailgating. "Half a tank," Anna said shakily. The truck filled the rearview mirror. Deep diesel blasts shattered Currie's ears. Anna shouted over the din, "Tim, listen to him. He can help you."

Asher said, "Can I take my hand off the roof now?"

"Slow."

The truck began passing on an incline. "He's crazy!" Anna shouted. The guardrail closed on the right, the semi sucked at them, fishtailing them. A rush of wind and water shook the windshield.

"Narrow road," Anna said.

Asher asked, "Is Aosta where you're going to meet someone?"

"Aosta is where you're going to shut up."

Anna snapped, "You don't have to talk to him like that. He wants to help, for Christ's sake."

"He helped by giving the *carabinieri* my picture."

Currie thought, Six hours to Riomaggiore. I can find that liquor smuggler Zarek told me about. I can still get to Qaddafi. Zarek told me how.

Asher turned to Anna. "You fooled me," he said, "working with Tim all along."

"That isn't true."

"Was Cindy helping too? All four of you?"

Going downhill they closed on the same truck, only now it blocked them, crawling. Currie said, "Fucking truck."

Anna said, "I knew Tim was in Italy, never mind how I

found out. But I swear I didn't know about Courmayeur until I heard about Zarek on the radio. I can get him to give himself up, I know how to speak to him. Let me try."

Wryly, Currie said, "You don't need his permission, Anna."

Half slumped because of the tied hand, Asher had trouble getting his head around to see Currie. "I could understand you better in Washington," he said. "Crazy with passion. Ranting. Now it's cold premeditated murder you plan."

"Who says premeditation can't be passionate?"

"You don't have proof Qaddafi killed her."

Anna said in a little voice, "Qaddafi?"

Gears engaged, turning faster. Asher said, "Oh, we know about it. But now Zarek's dead, your fault. And Anna, Anna could be hurt. Landing up like Nori because of you."

Currie laughed softly. "I love the way you change things around. I got Zarek killed? If you'd been doing your job I never would have come here."

Anna had gone utterly white in the mirror. "You didn't tell me he was going after Qaddafi." To Currie she said, "Not that. Oh God, not Qaddafi. Oh they'll kill you. It's not true."

The rain was a steady pressure. Currie said, "Asher, I'm going to tell you something you can use when I let you go. Yeah, I'm going to let you go in the end, just don't try anything until I'm ready. You know the note I found in Washington?"

"Israel, Iran, Saudi Arabia. We deciphered it." Asher coaxed him. "It's countries. We're working on it. We'll open the Bureau to you. You and me, we'll work together."

Currie pressed the gun against Asher's head. "Too late for that. But the note's not countries. It's people. I found it out. 'Israel' means Qaddafi. Lipko told me. 'Iran' and 'Saudi Arabia' too. A double code. People."

"Jesus, Jesus," Anna said. "Qaddafi."

Asher said, "What people?"

Currie shook his head. "Don't know. But if I can't, can't

get what I want in Libya, well, maybe you can hurt him with that note."

For no reason the truck braked in front of them. Anna hit the pedal, jerking them forward. She moaned, "This road." Sweat ran down her face in the mirror. Currie was going to have to get her out from behind the wheel but what could he do with Asher? They were coming out of the mountains. Asher said, "You'll never get *out* of Libya even if you get *in*. Have you thought of that, where you go when you're finished?"

"I know where."

Anna said, "You're going to Libya?" Her shoulders slumped. Dazed, she said, "You can't. I can't drive you to do this." But she didn't stop.

There were no turnoffs or country lanes Anna could use to leave the main road. Currie was afraid if she pulled to the side in plain view, a passing patrol might stop to help. But her driving grew more erratic, she accelerated stop and go.

Asher said, "Look, maybe I was wrong in Washington. I should have been more sympathetic. Now you have a second chance. I'll back you. You went after your fiancée's killers. Shot terrorists in self-defense. The government will get you home. The Italians will drop the gun charges, they owe us favors. You'll be out of this nightmare."

The land grew flatter, the rain lessened and they saw the familiar Ligurian landscape: foothills and waterfalls. "Feeling guilty?" Currie asked Asher. He was not a talkative man but Currie saw he would have to explain things. Through the mist and in the rearview mirror Currie had a last glimpse of the Alps. They didn't seem so clean now. They were dirty, sullied. Hannibal had crossed these mountains two thousand years before to attack Rome from Carthage, from Libya.

"Tim," Asher began again, but Currie cut him off.

"This country," Currie said, waving his free hand. "Five hundred years ago kings ran it. Absolute rulers. They could do anything. Take your house. Kill Nori." He knew he sounded as if he was lecturing but he didn't care. "There were police too but they couldn't hold kings accountable."

"Kings," Anna said. "What do kings have to do with it?"

"Don't you see? People got tired of not being able to fight back. They killed the king of France, average people did. Shock waves went through Europe but it was the beginning of the end. Qaddafi's like those kings. He sits behind borders, no way to go after him. He's just not included in the system."

At the word *borders* a shadow had crossed Asher's face. Currie pressed the attack. "You know what I'm talking about. You feel the same way, sure, you figure Qaddafi killed her too. Never mind what you say about proof. You *say* where's the proof, but in your heart you know you're doing his work for him, protecting him."

"It's not that I'm protecting him. If I let you go what about the next guy, the guy who has a beef against his neighbor, who wants to kill *him*? What do I do about him?"

"The difference between me and that imaginary guy is that he can be tried in courts, but people like Qaddafi you fight their own way. I'll give up right now, hand you this gun, if you can tell me how you're going to investigate Qaddafi, take him to court." Currie shook his head. "But it sounds stupid even saying it, Qaddafi on trial."

Anna sounded exhausted. "I have to stop driving. This rain."

"Keep going. At Aosta you won't have to worry anymore."

She straightened sharply. "What's that supposed to mean?"

Currie's wound throbbed. The truck finally turned off to enter a village but Currie couldn't take Asher into a town with a gun at his head. At a side road he would stop and force Asher into the trunk. He'd wedge the back seat in place somehow with Asher's shoes or rocks and lock the FBI man in. He told Anna. "You'll get out at Aosta. Take the bus back to Courmayeur. I'll call you at your hotel and tell you where

I leave the car." She was shaking her head. He said, "That way you pick the car up and the police never know you were involved."

Asher cleared his throat. Currie said, "Forget it, you won't tell on her. There's no point sending Anna to prison, even you wouldn't do that."

"Easy for you to risk Anna," Asher said, but Zarek had been right, Currie's instincts had developed. He knew Asher wouldn't hurt her. It wasn't even a question. Getting rid of Anna was the problem.

Grimly, peering into the rain, she said, "You still think you can send me away. Don't you know you can't?"

A yellow and black zigzag sign warned of dangerous curves two hundred meters ahead.

She said, "Why don't you ask me what I want instead of ordering me? And I'll tell you what I want. I want you to come home. I want to talk you out of killing yourself."

Behind the first curve the road disappeared at a ninety-degree angle.

Stiff with anger, Anna threatened, "I'll go to the *carabinieri*, if you make me leave you I'll tell them."

Currie leaned forward. She had used her bottom-line voice which he had rarely gotten past during their marriage. Keeping his eyes on Asher, he said, "Anna, the *carabinieri* will kill me, they decided among themselves." Her eyes widened. Asher shifted but subsided. Currie said, "No arrest. No trial."

She said, "I'm staying."

"I don't want to fight with you," Currie said.

"Staying."

A truck began coming at them around the curve. Currie, Anna and Asher were looking at each other, not the road.

She said, "Maybe the *carabinieri* plan to shoot you and maybe they don't. All I know is if you go to Libya —"

"TRUCK!" Asher shouted.

Currie had a glimpse of the looming cab, the driver waving

frantically through the rain. Anna threw herself at the wheel and Currie's bad shoulder smashed the side window. He saw the gun dropping. The Fiat went up on two wheels. There was a roar as the truck passed. But they were skidding, throwing up gravel and pitching into a meadow. Asher freed his hand from the belt. The skid pushed Currie away from the gun and Asher toward it. Asher's hand closed around the barrel, blue-black steel came up and, as Asher yelled, "Stop!" Currie launched himself at the FBI man.

"What do you mean, you don't know where Currie is?" said Jamal al-Hawaz. He smiled pleasantly beneath his silver aviator sunglasses, a bad sign. Two thousand miles south of Currie, he reclined on the balcony of his Mediterranean villa, looking up at Hamid Ali, head of the Popular Front for Palestinian Resistance. All was sweating profusely.

Russian arms dealer Victor Malenkov and Libyan air force commander Selim Muktar stood watching beside a table spread wide with a plastic model of a city. Houses in red. Army bases in blue.

Iced bottles of Fanta and papaya juice occupied a silver bucket.

Hamid Ali cried, "Lipko was my best man!"

"And Currie killed your best man. Is that what you're telling me?"

Swaying in the sun, Hamid Ali said, "I'll find Currie. I swear to you."

The ocean was blue and beautiful. White rollers touched the beach a hundred yards from the balcony and Libyan soldiers with submachine pistols stood every hundred feet, forming a cordon around the house.

Moving to the table, Jamal said, "You should have let Currie and Zarek alone after Pietro told us where they were. We would have intercepted them, they were coming right to us.

Now we don't know where Currie is. We still don't know what he knows. Hamid Ali, we don't know too much of anything. I'll make up my mind about you later."

Hamid Ali's robe was soaked. At the table, Jamal looked over the model of the city while the other two men looked on anxiously. To silver-haired Selim Muktar Jamal said, "Your timetable, please."

Muktar jabbed his finger at the model of a white compound at the center of the table. "At two P.M. the first wave of jets arrives. Tupolovs. Air-to-ground missiles and machine-gun fire. At two thirty the MiGs attack. Simultaneously two divisions of the Pan Africa Corps launch the diversionary assault to the north." He touched the table near the model. "Here. Thirty minutes later, full-scale attack."

"Excellent. Mr. Malenkov?"

"My government is delighted at your plan and offers every possible assistance. Weapons. A forum at the U.N. Whatever you need."

A cool breeze brought fresh salt smell from the sea.

Jamal nodded approvingly. Reaching for a glass of papaya juice, he said, "New timetable. We do it three days from now."

Muktar started. Jamal said, "Currie could destroy everything if he has the note, if he knows what it means and he's on his way here."

From the railing, where he had not moved, Hamid Ali advanced one step forward, palms outstretched, like a supplicant. He reasoned, "The danger is not as great as you think, Jamal. Lipko found out Currie gave the note to the FBI. The Americans are only making halfhearted attempts to track us in France, no official complaints from Washington have mentioned the note. They can't know what it means."

Jamal stared at him. Hamid Ali backed away to the railing.

To Muktar Jamal said, "We've got to find Currie. Double guards on the beaches. Double pay to agents in Italy especially anyone with the Italian smugglers. If the *carabinieri* are after Currie, he might try to come here with a smuggler. If Currie reaches Tripoli and the note is delivered, we're dead."

Jamal turned to Hamid Ali. "You've displeased me," he said.

Rifles ready, two guards mounted the steps toward Hamid Ali, who did not see them yet. "I'll find him, Jamal, I promise."

Hamid Ali saw the guards. He tried to rush past them, but the first man brought the steel butt of his Polish assault rifle up; it caught Hamid Ali in the belly and doubled him over. The second trooper swung his Kalashnikov into Hamid Ali's collarbone. There was a crack. Ali screamed.

Gulls overhead mewed, swooping.

"You and I will talk later tonight," Jamal said.

The guards dragged Hamid Ali down to the beach. He was screaming for mercy. Jamal, Muktar and Malenkov watched him dragged under the railing. His heels left furrows in the white sand. There was a slam of a door downstairs and the men turned back to the table.

"By the blood," Jamal said, lifting his glass of papaya juice.

"By the blood," the men echoed.

"Do you know where the slogan comes from?" Jamal said after they drank. "Fifth century. Tripoli was ruled by Caliph Ali Bar Ben then. The plotters who killed him adopted as their slogan, 'By his blood.' I changed it. Drink up. In three days we make history." He raised his glass.

"To the death of Qaddafi," he said. "To our coup."

"To the new president of Libya," said Selim Muktar. "To Jamal al-Hawaz."

The Russian, not to be outdone, said, "And to the completion of our deal. To the wars of victory to begin soon all over the Mideast."

The sun was broiling, the sea air smelled sweet. The men drank.

◇   ◇   ◇

The Fiat skidded, throwing up grass. It came to rest in the meadow, twenty yards from a spruce clump, fifty from a farmhouse. Asher faced Currie over the seat, gun in hand.

The hugeness of what had happened — the near accident and Asher's grabbing the gun — stunned them silent. Currie heard his own breathing.

Asher or Anna must have hit the radio button during the skid. A woman sang, "Roma, Roma."

"That village a mile back," Asher said. The knuckles around the Scorpion were matted with gray hair. "We can find *carabinieri*. Anna, you all right?"

She straightened off the wheel, face drained of blood. "Yes."

"Can you drive?"

She seemed dazed. Currie felt Lipko's Ceska in his jacket pocket. Asher said, "Tim, I meant what I said before. We'll get you home."

Then his voice rose and he said, "Don't do that."

Currie had opened the lock on his door. One hand remained poised by the window, the fingernails of the other dug into the palm of his hand. "What are you going to do if I open it? Shoot?"

Asher said nothing, it was an affirmative reply.

Their eyes remained level. Close up Currie noted Asher's right lid dipped slightly lower than the left, creating a bull-doggish asymmetry. He said, "I'm getting out of here, shoot if you want. I'm not going back."

Asher acknowledged the words with a languid blink. The gray expressionlessness did not change.

Currie said, "I'm dead by the Italians, the Libyans too, according to you. To help me you're going to shoot me. That makes you like Lipko, Asher, doing Lipko's job."

Trailing his fingers down the side panel, Currie lowered them toward the door latch.

Asher said, with weary professionalism, "Don't. Really."

Over the idling engine a cow's low sounded. If Currie moved for his pocket, Asher would fire. The agent shifted the Scorpion slightly to indicate Currie's legs were a target too. "I only need to stop you." His tone was low and un-provocative but the hand holding the gun remained steady.

"Wrong," Currie said. "I'll crawl, crawl until you finish it. Hand me to the *carabinieri*, it's the same thing as pulling the trigger.

"They won't harm you when I'm there."

"You won't always be there, Asher. Anna, no."

She'd been gathering herself for a jump, fixing on the Scorpion. When Currie spoke, she'd jerked.

Asher sensed the flash point too. "Anna, why don't you get out of the car." Neither man spoke as she did. With the door open the Fiat smelled of pasture, fertilizer. Cool humid air blew in Currie's face.

On the highway a horn sounded, a million miles away.

Currie opened his door too. Making sure not to move suddenly or in Asher's direction he shifted on the seat until one foot was on the grass. "You can't arrest me. Follow your own rules, Asher. I crossed the border so treat me like Qaddafi. Do nothing. No one has to know you found me."

In a smooth motion Currie rose to his feet.

Asher said, "I can't let you go." He got out of the car also and pointed the Scorpion across the roof. Blue-black steel. An edge came into his voice. "Last warning. Start walking and that's it."

"I'm not walking. I'm taking the car," Currie said. Asher's lips parted in surprise; Currie heard the exhalation. "Funny," Currie said. "According to the *carabinieri, you're* the terrorist. Using an illegal gun in Italy. Makes you the same as me, a guy who thinks he knows what's right and breaks rules to do it. Maybe you think there's a difference between you and me. Explain the difference."

Anna stood nearby Asher, fingers close to but not touching

his forearm. She said, "I'll go with him, he'll come home. You have to talk to Tim, you can't threaten him. He doesn't respond to threats." Asher said nothing. Anna warned, "Don't you hurt him."

Currie moved around the front door. For the first time he detected sweat collecting along Asher's hairline.

"They'll kill you," Asher said.

"Then let them. You don't have to be the one to do it."

"If you pull it off, I can't let that happen."

"Why not?" Currie said. The key hung in the ignition. There was a little whistle charm on the chain.

"Why?" Asher said. The answer was obvious to him. "It would be an international incident, we would be blamed, that's why."

"What the hell does *that* mean?" Currie said. "What the hell's an international incident? What does it mean? Who cares? I'm out of your jurisdiction, leave it be, Asher. I'm the only chance for justice for that man and you know it. You're programmed to do things by the book? Okay, the book says you're not a cop here. The book says you let me go."

He could see the dirt in Asher's fingernails by the gun. He knew it was impossible to beat this investigation machine. The best Currie could hope for was to neutralize Asher.

Asher's sweat bead did not move. Currie got into the car and adjusted the seat and sideview mirror elaborately, with an almost painstaking correctness.

Currie said, "Are you prepared to kill me to save him?"

The Scorpion, which protruded through the passenger window, lowered. Asher whispered, "I always knew what to do before."

Anna slipped into the car beside Currie. No time to get rid of her now. But Asher had asked the question. Even if he fired, Currie knew he'd asked the question tyrants had feared since governments started.

The engine turned over. Through Anna's open window

[233]

the agent was the lower third of a raincoat, black trousers, a left hand with a wedding ring, holding a gun. Currie shifted into first. He drove up the embankment onto the highway. He turned right toward Genoa and Riomaggiore.

Anna's long white fingers rested by the stick shift, on her knee.

In the meadow Asher stood watching the Fiat grow small. It disappeared but Asher stayed where he was, looking. The Scorpion rested against his thigh. After a while a drizzle began, he turned up his raincoat collar. He walked to the road and began the hike to the village.

CHAPTER

17

THE southward journey of the assassin. Currie drove past pine forest, stucco-roofed farmhouses and waterfalls, over two-thousand-year-old Roman bridges, toward the smoky industrial heartland of Italy. The Dora Baltea River surged along one side of the road. On the other, he outraced quarter-mile-long clattering trains.

Currie steered one hand on the wheel, elbow propped on the open sill. Watching for roadblocks, he was racing for Riomaggiore, hoping Asher had not changed his mind and alerted the *carabinieri*. But the certainty which had carried him through the confrontation with the FBI man was gone. there was no specific danger to fight. His relief at escaping had faded into an obsession with futility.

Zarek was dead because Currie had forgotten to set the alarm in the lodge. With the mercenary gone, the plan to get jobs in Libya had collapsed. Plus, Qaddafi knew Currie's false identity, Pietro would have told the Libyans. Currie's false passport would be worse than worthless if Currie reached Tripoli, it would mean death if he had to produce it. He would need another passport. He reviewed what Zarek had told him about Captain Sperazza and how the smuggler could take him anywhere if the price was right. But for the first time since Washington, he felt like giving up.

Then dryness began at the back of his throat. Danger signal. He looked for *carabinieri* on the highway but realized Anna's nearness caused the tension. Her slim fingers rested on her jeaned knee. He felt her staring at him. With the escapes from Asher and Courmayeur his physical need grew stronger.

"Remember Wyoming?" she said. The adrenaline rush was electric. Wyoming meant honeymoon, the obligatory cross-country post-college trip. Currie and Anna in his first jeep, an old army issue he'd equipped with fiberglass top and rebuilt engine. "I remember," he said. In those days she'd seemed the most wildly desirable woman he had ever known. Long-legged, moving at a naked tiptoe through the forest when they stopped to camp at night. Even driving he'd always been aware of her body underneath her clothing. The legs, tapering, V-shaped embracing the seat, the breasts swelling beneath the tight T-shirt tops, the dark blond thatch of invitation a foot away. Magical.

He'd pulled off the road one day, unable to stand it. They were reaching for each other before the jeep stopped. When they made love, his shoulder kept brushing hot steel. She'd worn a lemony perfume he still smelled when he passed women on the street.

When they were sated that day, sated being a temporary condition, they'd dressed and climbed languidly back to their seats to see a Wyoming state trooper leaning against his Chevy ten feet away. The trooper had slid off mirror sunglasses, sauntered to the jeep and wiped his brow with his sleeve. Reverently, he'd whispered, "Son, the Bijou Midnight Show won't be nuthin' after that. Thank you and Amen."

Anna said now, "What do you think he used to watch at the Bijou?"

"The Walt Disney Story." When she laughed, the tension broke. A sudden ache filled Currie. He had a vision of Anna seventeen years ago, eighteen years old the first time he had seen her naked.

They were in college, freshman year. They'd been inseparable in high school but had never made love until one night

[236]

at her dorm at NYU. Her roommate was away that night. He'd stayed past curfew by mutual consent. But shy Anna had insisted the lights be off when they climbed into bed.

Early next morning the phone had rung, she'd leaped from the covers as if afraid the caller would sense Currie's presence if she did not grab the phone. Currie blinked and sat up. He watched her on the rug, ankles crossed, knees drawn up near her chin. Eyes downward as she spoke into the receiver. Saturday morning college call from Mom. Naked, she would not look at him while she talked to her mother. He had seen her crosslegged a thousand times but never naked. He was astounded and captivated by the intimacy of the familiar pose and the casual, daring nudity. Little shadows filled the hollows under her shoulders. A prism rainbow touched the inside of her wrist. A shaft of sunlight angled through lace curtains to slant sideways across blond hair. The pulse built in him. The phone cord spiraled across a breast, reddening a mark.

He'd slipped from the bed and pressed down the receiver. Over her giggled protests he'd made love to her on the floor, her nails on his back, the phone ringing behind them, seventeen years ago.

Now he thought, What happened to us? In Iran he had played her sundrenched image to keep himself sane. He'd woken from their lovemaking a hundred times to see the guard's sandals outside the window or a cockroach the size of a baby mouse scurrying off the sheet.

But later he had grown to despise Anna's beauty. She never would have been put on television had she not been so lovely. The reporters and party givers would not have wooed her, crowned her with remoteness and placed her behind glass. If not for her beauty. If not because she was so beautiful.

They stopped for gas and sandwiches and drove on. Now Currie knew he had been wrong then. After their arguments had stopped and they no longer slept together he had come to see her beauty had never been the issue. If the marriage had been strong, it would have withstood the reporters. Their ignored problems had come back to haunt them. Realizing this made it easier to say yes when she told him she wanted a divorce. They'd shared a childhood and a dream's end.

The rolling land became hills filled with scrubby cactus and vegetation. They approached the coast. The climate grew arid. Currie saw stucco homes with clay tile roofs, olive groves. Towns tiny at a distance hugged rocky crests. The flat purple clouds floated against Mediterranean blue.

Anna said, "A Sunday like today, you'd be watching the Redskins." The danger ticking began again. *I can talk to him,* she'd told Asher. *Get him to come home.* Currie could not tell if she were trying to persuade him to give up or simply shutting out Italy. Either way, the last dance had sounded. The quiet, private dance. There would be no more hysterical arguments like this afternoon's. Something was happening in the car. A time warp.

"That time we went to the Cavalier Hotel," she said. "Virginia Beach. The jazz club? Remember the club in Virginia Beach?"

"I remember."

"That maître d'. Tony . . ."

"Vaccaro."

"From Little Italy."

"New York."

" 'Starlight,' that song," she said. She sang it. "Star-light." Currie remembered the walks on the beach, waves rolling gray and white. From the crest highway the sea was a vast migratory ice sheet. They were so high up the waves were frozen in place. The whole world looked like ice.

She said, "I'd be painting today. In the Shenandoah or near Travs." Travs was a country bar near Stonehaven, where Currie ate chili and drank Budweiser from iced bottles. She said, "Remember when you rebuilt the Bronco? When we used to have kids from Children's Hospital come for the weekend? Remember that girl who got sick the whole time?"

Friends waited for him in Washington, didn't he see? Movies. His work. She said, "Remember when we built Stonehaven?"

Washington rose around him. Home was only twelve hours away, she was saying. Drive to Rome, get on a plane. The nightmare would be over. A phone call to Asher and he could be sitting in his living room listening to Mozart.

She spoke on about the city, and in the rhythm of her banalities he filled in her truths. Going home would be so easy. Qaddafi has beaten you if he can take away Washington and rob you of October. If you give up what you love and turn to hate, that's his victory.

At that moment he understood she still loved him, that was why she had come to Italy. She loved him enough not to be afraid and that astounded him.

He saw the guileless vulnerability in her eyes, and her life in Washington, the mindless chic rendezvous and hollow singles existence in a condominium called The Casablanca. Her bitter realization that she had had what she wanted before the divorce, not after.

Anna held out his city to him in safe and vivid colors as splendid as the landscapes she painted in her spare time.

But he felt as if he listened to two Annas. The first, two feet away, was saying he'd earned the right to come back. Her fingers gripped his forearm. He'd fought honorably. Avenged Nori. He would be the winner if he quit now. And he wanted what she described, he was affected. No doubt about it.

But at the same time he watched her from far away. She was a speck calling him back with a voice weakened by time and distance. The companions beside him were Nori and Zarek, whom Qaddafi had murdered, who could never enjoy Washington again.

To reach Anna's haven he would have to turn his back on them. He could never do it. His spirits rallied, his drive returned. Qaddafi had not beaten him yet. A slight change of plans and Currie could still reach the man. Zarek had told him how. He pressed harder on the accelerator.

A town was coming up, clustered roofs on a seaside cliff. "Monterosso," read the sign. He watched for *carabinieri* as traffic thickened. When Currie took Anna's hand, it was with a friend's touch, not a lover's. "The road stops here," he said. "There's a mule track in the hills to Riomaggiore."

She accepted his answer with grace, he watched his own sadness reflected in the blue of her eyes and flat droop of her golden lashes. She would never turn him in to the *carabinieri* now. Her binding words had affected her too. And he would not send her away, at least not before he boarded Sperazza's boat to finish what he had begun.

Then at the sight of the blue Ligurian sea again something quickened inside him. The blue was like an electric current touching Libya on the other side. And the wind that blew into his face was hot and African. Then the wind stopped and the earth grew still. Perhaps Qaddafi looked back across the water. *He'll come after you until he finds you*, Lipko had said.

Currie parked the car and turned toward the hills beyond the town. The sun broiled the top of his head. Stepping surely, he moved toward the unequal duel.

They traveled swiftly through the coastal hills on a foot-wide mule track, passing lemon trees and cactus growing from rock. At dusk they came into Riomaggiore. Currie was dressed in rubber-soled shoes and a flight jacket he'd bought to replace the ski clothes. Anna had needed sneakers for the hike.

The money was in a green rucksack Currie held by the strap.

The blood-colored sun was sinking into the water. The town clung to cliffs and tumbled down to the sea. Wash hung everywhere. The sour odor of wine emanated from the buildings and heavy-hipped gaptoothed peasant women passed with plastic tubs of local vintage sloshing on their heads.

Darkness was gathering. In the main road, an undulating cobblestone incline rising from beached fishing boats toward the hills, men played poker under a thatched overhang in front of a bar. The sign read, "Cinzano." The fisherman politely avoided looking at Anna, and when Currie asked for lodging for the night, the dealer, a bald man in a green sweater, called up in Italian to closed green shutters ringing the square. Shutters opened and women peered out. After a sharp exchange in Italian one woman pulled back into her window. The bald man said in barely understandable English, "She will take you."

"I'm looking for a man," Currie said. "A friend of a friend. His name is Sperazza."

The game stopped. Currie said, "Rosario Sperazza." Over the top of the cards the fishermen regarded him with narrowed eyes. The man in the sweater shrugged. "I know no Sperazza." But when the woman led Currie and Anna away, Currie glanced back to see the sweater disappearing into an alley.

Then the woman sped up, rushing them in the dark through a bewildering series of alleys, up narrow steps, past jumbled houses. The wine smell thickened. Stars studded a black strip of night overhead between centuries-old walls.

Through an open doorway, framed in the halo from a lone candle atop a barrel, luminous hands picked grapes off a vine.

Anna was tiring. Currie called, "Slow down," but quickening her pace, the woman rounded a corner. When Currie and Anna reached it she was gone.

A hiss came from the darkness ahead. They stood in the glare of a single overhead bulb. Beyond the light steps rose in a *Y* left and right, fading into night.

Currie's senses screamed danger. He called boldly, "Sperazza!"

A gravelly voice growled from the left stairway, "No hands in pockets." It was a flat voice with elongated A's. Currie pictured the largest card player, a bearded man with a flannel shirt. Anna moved close. The voice said, "Why do you look for Sperazza?"

"Come into the light so I can see you," Currie demanded. "I'll tell Sperazza why I came."

Instead, footsteps grew audible on the stairway to the right. Blue leather shoes stepped into view but Currie could not see the owner.

"I have business with him," Currie said.

"What kind of business?"

"Profitable."

"You are English?"

Behind, Currie heard the soft swish of more footsteps. A shadow crept close to the wall at the end of the alley. Currie thought he saw the gleam of a blade.

"United States," Currie said, trying to stay alert to all three men.

"Who is that woman?"

"My wife." People overseas could never fathom the complex social blundering of American relationships. This last question filled Currie with vast irritation.

"United States. United States of Am-er-i-ca," the voice said, playing with him. The shadow had materialized into a dark curly haired man in a knit fisherman's sweater. He held a knife, all right. He looked Arabic. Currie felt a flash of panic. Could Pietro have told the Libyans about Sperazza too? But Currie decided in a fight he would charge the one in the blue shoes. Blue Shoes might be Sperazza. Currie ordered the man in the sweater, "Stop." He was amazed at the authority in his tone. The man halted. At six feet Currie saw the scar crossing the right cheek.

A new voice, clear and deliberate, older, came from Blue Shoes. "Empty your pockets." Reassured by the thick Italian accent, Currie said, "Sperazza?" No response. Time to gamble on whether the Arab worked for Sperazza or not. With the tips of two fingers Currie withdrew the Ceska by its stock and lay it on the ground. A simple movement and unafraid which said see, I'm no danger to you. He tossed his false passport into the darkness and the knapsack too.

The voice said, "Step away from the gun." When Currie did so, the man on the right scurried forward and grabbed it. Currie glimpsed red hair, a black turtleneck and a sawed-off shotgun. He was weak with relief that he hadn't yanked out the Ceska.

Dirty kittens rolled over an alley wall and hit the ground, biting.

Currie heard the swish of the knapsack straps opened. Anna clutched his forearm. The might-be-Sperazza voice said, "Why do you carry a gun?"

"Protection."

"Who from?"

Currie took the chance. "Police."

The voice seemed amused. "And the money, Signore Currie? Or is it Fleeter? Which?"

"That's not my real passport. I want to hire your boat, I'll pay." Behind him the shuffling started up again. Whatever was going to happen would break loose in seconds. Currie said, "Zarek said you would take me."

A sharp intake of breath. The blue shoes descended until a man came into the light. "I'm Sperazza." Currie was surprised to recognize one of the card players, a white-haired square-faced peasant who carried no weapon but seemed capable of handling himself. Up close the face he had taken

[243]

for impassive earlier showed power in the jaw as well as a brutal quality, cruelty, in the mouth, a hard line slanting in the sun-weathered visage. But there was bright intelligence and curiosity in the black eyes and even a hint of half-buried warmth. Currie had the feeling, as Zarek had said, that Sperazza would be a loyal friend and deadly enemy.

"Ed Zarek," Sperazza said.

"*John* Zarek."

"The Englishman?"

"From Washington." The black eyes studied him. Currie said, "Medium height, marine tattoo on right forearm. Martial arts tattoo on his ankle." Exasperated, Currie sighed. "Zarek who used to drink ouzo with you in Crete. Zarek who you hid under a mackerel catch when the gunboat stopped you off Nice."

Tapping the side of his forehead with his index finger, Sperazza smiled with his mouth only. He showed even teeth. "I have a hard time remembering things. Who is Zarek to you?"

The Arab, close now, carried a curving knife like a scimitar. Under brown kinky hair a deep slash crossed the right cheek.

"I was Zarek's cellmate in Iran. Hostages together."

Sperazza started. "*You* were the hostage?" He leaned into Currie's face, smelling of tobacco. "You Americans were weak. Soldiers should have been sent to rescue you. Currie. He told me about Currie." Pursing his lips, he looked Currie up and down. "A professional does not travel with his wife," Sperazza reasoned to himself. The thought seemed to reassure him. "Answer this," he said. "If you are Currie, what is the service you did for Zarek?"

"The service?" Currie was lost and then he knew the answer. "I helped his girlfriend escape."

When Sperazza grinned, there was a sense of air coming back into the world. The Italian threw his arms around Currie. He barked a command and the knapsack was returned, weighty so Currie knew the money was still inside. The gun came back lighter, without its clip.

Sperazza said, "Excuse my precautions. The *carabinieri* . . ." He waved a hand to show how inconsequential the *carabinieri* were. "Zarek saved my life. In Malta." To Anna he said, "Sailors have fun there at night, Signora. Zarek." The smile broadened to a grin of reminiscence. "Three Germans in a bar, they think they own every place. I beat the big one but Zarek took two. Ah. Zarek. How is he?"

"Murdered," Currie said.

The black eyes hardened. The voice went low. "Who did it?"

"I've found three of them so far."

Sperazza looked surprised at Currie's flat tone. Then he bowed his head to offer respect to a blood feud. In his part of the world it was an accepted part of behavior. An honorable trust demanded of real men. At length he said, mournful, "It happens to all the lone ones. No one understands a man who works alone. That is why I stay in Riomaggiore. I have more success than the others but," he shrugged, "you must have your family, your people." He looked at Currie. "Cut yourself off and people never take you back."

Anna seemed shaken. With rough-edged gallantry he added, "You are tired. I show you to your rooms."

Threading the maze of alleys, Currie surrendered to impatience. "Can I hire your boat?" Sperazza waved away the question. He brought them to a dead end booming with the thunder of the sea. He pushed open a heavy door and Currie was surprised to see airy spacious rooms. Open shutters let in the roaring of the sea. The far wall of the apartment was the outer wall of the town. From the railed balcony they looked down on a scene of violent beauty. Beyond the ancient stairways to the beached fishing boats, October waves exploded against the cliffs, sending spumes of spray upwards a hundred feet.

The comfortable brass-railed bed, visible through a beaded doorway, was swathed in quilts. Oranges and bananas filled a bowl on the table. At a knock two men entered, deposited three bottles of red wine on the red-and-white-checked tablecloth. They brought a vase of fresh violets and a picnic basket from which they removed platters of food. Sperazza obviously wielded a great influence in the town and had ordered the lodging and food. There was homemade lasagna and grilled crayfish and calamari from the sea. Tiny golden fish fried in mushroom sauce. Thick tomatoes and fruit.

"Eat," urged Sperazza. Other than one thin sandwich Currie had eaten nothing since the cranberry sauce in Courmayeur. The juices ran into his mouth. The wine was thick and delicious. Sperazza warned Anna not to drink too much, she would talk in her sleep and the whole town would know her secrets. When Currie finished, he mopped mushroom sauce with thick bread. Sperazza lit a cigarette. To Anna he said, speculatively, "Perhaps you would like to walk in the town. One of my men could escort you."

Anna said, "I'd rather stay here."

Currie nodded that she would stay. "I bow to amore," Sperazza said. When amore came up he was like an Italian on TV. But Currie was surprised because amore had not been mentioned between them in years. Serious now that the meal was finished, Sperazza leaned forward, his face half-obscured by smoke from his Camel. He said, "You both want to go in the boat? No? Just you?" Puzzled, he did not inquire further about Anna but said to Currie, "Where do you want to go?"

"Malta," Currie said. *If something happens on the sea go to Malta,* Zarek had said. *Find Neville Smythe at his bar. He's a good friend. Give him the ring.*

Currie fingered the gold band in his pocket, he felt the inscribed bayonet under his thumb. In Malta he could recuperate, get a new phony passport, monitor the news until Qaddafi left Libya. Or find other men like Zarek to help him go in. There was no need to stab straight for Tripoli. *Plan,* Zarek had said. *Improvise.*

Currie repeated, "Malta."

Neither man heard Sperazza's crewman listening at the door in the hallway outside. He was the swarthy sailor with the scar on his cheek, whom Currie had guessed was Libyan. At the word *Malta* his eyes widened, he crept from the house. He headed for the main street, looking for a phone.

Sperazza said, "Why do you want to go to Malta?"

"I'll pay as much as you want."

Sperazza rubbed his cheek and grimaced. "Everyone pays what I want," he said. "Paying what I want is never an issue. I respect your wish to keep your journey secret but I must know my risk." He exhaled smoke through his nostrils. "Malta is halfway to Libya. Mercenaries and anti-Qaddafi people infest the place. I listen to the radio, I heard what happened in Courmayeur. Those men you killed were Libyans. If you're headed for Tripoli, I'm in danger too. You'll probably only go once but I have to return. If you're captured, the secret police will ask, *Who helped you?* You'll say, I won't tell. They'll wet down your belly and prod you with an electric rod. So you see my risk does not lessen when you leave my boat, or even when you reach Malta. My risk peaks next time I arrive offshore Libya with Chivas Regal for my customers."

The cigarette was down to a smoking butt in the corner of his mouth. He propped both elbows on the table. "Why do you want to go to Malta?"

"One of Zarek's killers is still free."

He feared Sperazza might turn him down but the captain nodded sadly. "Of course it was that. I will take you because Zarek saved my life. But it will be dangerous and my business will be jeopardized. In American money, to get you in and avoid the Malta gunboats, since we are carrying contraband . . ." Sperazza looked at the ceiling. "One hundred thousand dollars."

Currie sputtered, "I . . . it's only three days on a boat. Zarek said pay what you want but this is robbery."

The sixty thousand dollars in the knapsack was all he had. With all his planning it had never occurred to him Sperazza might want more than that incredible sum.

Sperazza ground out the butt in a seashell on the table. Soothingly he said, "In Libya a bottle of Chivas sells for three hundred dollars. Yes, yes, this is incredible but true. To drink it means prison. So the price goes up. My share, one hundred dollars. Twelve bottles in a case. Over one thousand dollars. If I squeeze fifty cases on the *Kukulka* for one trip, well that's fifty thousand dollars right there. The price of your one-way journey. Besides, I don't get it all. I have to pay the crew extra. The harbor police and others. And maintain my magnificent engines." Sperazza sounded like any complaining businessman now. "But if I take you to Malta, which I only do because you are Zarek's friend and because I owe him a service . . . a service to a dead man who doesn't know the difference so it is a holy favor . . . I may never be able to return to Libya if you are found out. One hundred thousand dollars.

Anna was in the kitchen still within earshot. She'd been clearing dishes and bringing coffee as if they were back in Stonehaven entertaining a guest. They'd lit candles because the overhead bulb had been too bright and a smoky paraffin odor tinged the smell of the sea. Sperazza said, "Surely you have a means to raise money. If you were with Zarek, there is money somewhere."

Then Currie remembered Zarek's money which had been paid for Qaddafi's assassination. The money he had wiped from his mind. The money he had argued against taking and which Zarek had accepted secretly. Currie had walked out on Zarek because of that money. Had yelled, *Act like a man, not a pimp,* and stormed off. Then Lipko had murdered Zarek. Two hundred and fifty thousand dollars. Hadn't Zarek told him back in Washington, "We need money to get out?" Currie must have looked as bitter as he felt because Sperazza's eyes narrowed.

Currie murmured, "I can get the rest."

Sperazza brightened. The ocean rumbled outside, sea smell washed the room, humid. Currie said, "I'll have to call Switzerland. Someone will send the money."

Zarek had said overseas calls were monitored so he'd have to speak carefully and leave Riomaggiore immediately afterward. Zarek had said the transaction could be completed on the phone. At the Banque Nationale de Geneva Herr Schneider would ask Currie questions and, if he answered them satisfactorily, the money would be wired. Currie had never heard of such a thing but in Zarek's business unorthodox arrangements were a regularity. He no longer doubted Zarek's "facts."

He wondered how long Swiss banks took to release money.

Sperazza said, "We go when I get the cash."

Currie shook his head. "No. Now. You can have fifty now and the rest soon." Sperazza said nothing. Currie argued, "I'm not going to cheat you. You know where to find me, where I'm going. You can get me killed if I don't pay." Sperazza leaned back. Currie said, "The *carabinieri* are after me. Okay," Currie said. "I'll pay extra. A hundred thirty thousand. Shit, a hundred fifty." What did he care. He wasn't going to take any money for himself.

Sperazza repeated, "A hundred and fifty?"

The Italian leaned forward, greed and appraisal on his face. After Currie's protest over the low price this new offer made him suspicious.

He said one word. "Collateral."

And Anna's voice said, "I'll stay here until the money comes."

Both men swung to her. Framed in the kitchen doorway, she had one hand on her hip, one around a wine bottle she'd been taking to the table. Currie said, "I'll pay him extra, Anna. We'll work it out without you." All his ghosts were coming back at him. The people he wanted to protect, the money he'd refused to touch. That he had seen the logic of Zarek's arguments so late filled him with despair. He saw that in his obsession he had endangered loved ones from the first. He loathed his own need for companionship. The price never seemed to stop.

For a moment he teetered again on the brink of surrender, of absorption back into the past, overcome by the sheer bulk of human connection and responsibility. But he shook off the weight like a fighter regaining vision. And at the same time felt part of himself die and he became more like Zarek.

Anna advanced into the breeze washing in through the window. Sea-wind-tossed blond hair. She said. "You'll find another way to go if Sperazza doesn't help you. He's your best chance. He won't hurt me here. And what other collateral can you offer? The house? How are you going to sell the house from here?" She looked at the floor. She was trying to act bold but her voice was tinny with fright. "Maybe you're right about what you're doing. I don't know. I only know I have to help. Maybe you're stronger than the rest of us. Asher. Me. We do things for you. You must be right or we'd stop you. Maybe you're forcing us to understand something we don't want to see."

To Sperazza she said, "I'll stay until the money comes." She raised her arms helplessly. They formed an inverted *V* with the line of her body. There was something so plaintive, vulnerable and devoted about the gesture, that it obscured the talk of hard cash. She had come to commitment late and embraced it with the fervor of a convert.

Sperazza averted his eyes. He was a man who had stumbled

upon a couple's intimate moment and he pretended not to see. He placed another Camel between his lips. "We will go."

An hour later, when Currie and Anna had returned from the village center, where he had placed a call to the banker's special number and answered questions about Iran, and another to Cindy, the already grieving girlfriend who had heard of Zarek's death on the news, they stood at the arched window and looked out to sea. Beyond the spumes of spray the half moon sent light across the water, a beacon south. Currie's throat was dry. A droplet of spray touched it.

Behind them empty places littered the table.

The candlelight sputtered to form shadow bars on the wall from the brass bed's railing. Shadow humans undulating, growing close.

Anna murmured, "Well look at me. I came to Italy to talk you out of it."

She stepped away from him and, facing him, began to undress. The sweater dropped. Her breasts were white and conical, deeply aureoled. Her nipples sprang outward, released. Moonlight sculpted the hollows of her shoulders.

She said, "Don't say anything. Just don't say one word."

Her stomach was flat. She slid the jeans down her long legs. The blond tuft pressed out beneath silk panties. With her unchanged cattish tiptoe she advanced so that their faces were close. He lifted her, carried her toward the bed. She was ripping at his clothes. He tore the buttons off his shirt. Her legs came up, she wrapped herself around him. The need was in his belly and mouth. Her nails clawed his buttocks. They caressed his chest. The furniture was moving. He glimpsed the nighttable which had been beside the bed, only now it was four feet away diagonally across the floor. She screamed his name when she came but they did not stop. She gripped the bars behind her with her fists. Her mouth was wide open in silent screams. Her whole body had not stopped shaking with passion.

The candle went out.

Billowing curtains caressed his back.

After a while she said, "Don't let him kill you." In the morning they were sleeping in each other's arms when Sperazza knocked and woke him up and took him away to his destiny.

CHAPTER
18

T HE *Kukulka* rounded the western tip of Sicily and turned southeast, toward Malta. The cliffs faded into the blue sea. The sun was bright and dazzling. Sperazza came out of the wheelhouse looking worried. "Gunship," he said, pointing.

Currie stopped doing situps and stood on deck. He followed Sperazza's finger, the pulse quickened in his throat. Where the sky met the sea to the southeast, the approaching ship was a busy speck on the water and a black smudge etched against the sky.

Sweat ran down Currie's torso, he was naked from the waist up. The gunship was coming at them from the direction of Malta, seventy miles away. At twenty-two knots the *Kukulka* was making top speed without cargo.

Sperazza said, "Could be nothing to worry about. We pass lots of ships at sea."

"Change course," Currie said. "See what it does."

"She'll chase us if we run."

"Don't *run*, just alter direction slightly."

He went into the wheelhouse with Sperazza, not wanting to be recognized when the two ships came within binocular range.

Three minutes later, holding field glasses to his eyes, Sperazza said, "She changed course too. Still coming at us." On the *Kukulka*'s deck the crew stood looking back toward the wheelhouse, unsure what to do.

Sperazza put down the glasses. "She's Italian."

"Damn."

The engines chugged smoothly. The *Kukulka* was in international waters. Currie said, "Can they board us?"

"A gunship can do whatever it wants. You can piss and moan in court, but if they find something it does no good."

"Can we fight?"

"Pirates, yes. We have weapons. A gunship? They have five crew to my one and at least two heavy machine guns on deck. They might even have a cannon, not to mention a radio to tell the whole navy my boat is fighting them."

Even from the wheelhouse Currie glimpsed hundreds of silver bursts in the sea, fish flashing, leaping south and falling behind. And an hour earlier he had paused practicing kicks and punches to watch a two-mile-long line of starlings driving toward Libya, filling the air with high-pitched cries. It was as if all life was being sucked back into a vortex of beginnings, a rendezvous of cells and flesh.

This time tomorrow, he had thought then, I'll be in Malta. Figuring out a way to reach Qaddafi.

Now he was trapped on a thirty-foot boat. He wanted to scream with frustration. He had not come this far to be stopped by police. Rapidly his mind scanned hiding places, the cramped bunkroom and hallway and mess. There were guns in hollow compartments in the walls but nothing a man could squeeze into.

"I thought smugglers had secret hiding places on their boats," he said.

"In the movies they do."

"I'm going over the side," Currie decided. "Get me a life jacket. Come back for me after."

Sperazza grabbed his forearm. "Too late, they're close enough to see you and they'll be watching if we dump anything into the sea. Besides, we may not be able to find you later. Once we get a half-mile away, you might as well be in the middle of the Atlantic."

The gunship was bigger now, gray and moving fast.

"Somebody here told them I was on board." From the deck, the Libyan crewman watched them. In the sunlight the scar on his cheek looked pale.

The man's name was Mahmoud; now he called in urgent Italian to Sperazza. The captain said, "He says you better get in the hold with the fish. Cover yourself up. My men have been with me for years. Nobody called the police on you. This could be a liquor raid."

"You're not even carrying liquor. And how do they know our position?"

Currie took the binoculars. Sperazza said gruffly, "They don't necessarily 'know our position.' They might have run into us by accident and they're checking us out."

Through the binocular *O* Currie watched the gray prow, the foaming wake. Two sailors stood on the gunship's deck, cradling weapons. Their rifles looked familiar and as Currie fixed on the curving ammunition magazines the blood turned to ice in his veins. He focused on the sailors' faces. His knees went weak.

"Does the Italian navy carry Russian AK-forty-sevens?" he demanded.

Sperazza grabbed the glasses. Currie had never heard an Italian say "Mamma mia" until now.

Currie said, "It's a Libyan boat."

There were more Arab sailors on deck now. Sperazza barked commands and two crewmen disappeared into the hold. The third worked the radio frantically. He looked at Sperazza helplessly. Sperazza spat, "We're jammed. That's why they used the Italian flag. They wanted to get close enough to jam us and not interfere with other ships. Into the hold with you, quick."

But Currie went the other way, crashing out of the wheel-house toward the lower deck. Sperazza ran behind him. Currie was ripping off his clothes. "Hiding won't do any good if one of your crewmen tells them where I am," he said bitterly.

"None of my men tipped them off."

Currie paused by the engine hatch. "Maybe you did, then."

Sperazza went red. "When you leave, you and I will have a talk then," he growled.

Currie yanked open the hatch. "In the meanwhile," he grunted, "make sure your crew keeps quiet." Oil fumes filled the engine compartment. "Get someone to make my bunk. The Libyans will see an extra man slept here."

Sperazza yelled something in Italian. Currie said, "Your knife, quick."

"What are you doing?"

There was a booming sound, an explosion, and the boat rocked. Currie heard water spattering the deck above.

"Warning shot," Sperazza said. He shouted again.

The engine stopped.

Swiftly, Currie sliced off a four-foot section of spare trans-lucent engine hose. "A clamp, clamp," he said to himself, looking for one. He unscrewed a metal clamp from the fas-tened hose, wincing at the touch of hot steel. "I'll give it back later. Where's a hammer? A nail. A nail."

A booming electric voice came at them from over the water. Currie didn't have to speak Italian to know the *Kukulka* was about to be boarded.

A toolbox held a hammer. He found the Ceska beside his bunk where he'd left it. Now he only had minutes until the Libyans arrived. He shook Sperazza. "A waterproof bag," he said. "Quick."

"You're going under?"

"I'm not getting into the hold with the fish. That's the first place they'll look for me — where the hell else would I be hiding? — *give me a waterproof bag!* You have something waterproof on board, don't you?"

They could hear the droning of a powerboat coming toward the ship.

Sperazza said, "In the wheelhouse, there's a plastic . . ." but Currie was already moving. Reaching the wheelhouse and keeping low, he made out the gunship fifty yards off the port bow. A green-and-white Libyan flag had replaced the Italian colors. In shock, Sperazza looked out at his huddled crew. "But they've been with me for years," he repeated. Currie grabbed the black sealskin waterproof bag. He released the Ceska's safety and wrapped the gun in the bag. He felt the trigger. The Ceska would fire at least once before seawater clogged it.

"I'll be under the boat," Currie said. "My only chance is if you keep your men quiet."

Sperazza grinned at him in admiration. "In all the years I know Zarek he never worked with anyone. Now I know why he worked with you. Good luck, watch for the sharks."

Crouched halfway out the starboard door of the wheelhouse, Currie stopped. The crew looked back at him. The sea was calm and blue, at least on the surface.

"Sharks?" he said.

"The boarding party is coming. Hurry!"

"There are sharks there?"

Sperazza grinned again. "Hardly ever. Mostly they leave you alone, but we always carry a speargun when we work on the boat at sea. It's broken."

Currie slipped into the water. "I hate sharks," he said. The bag was around his head with a strap. He held the hammer, clamp and hose in one hand.

With two strikes of the hammer he fastened the clamp to the boat. He dropped the hammer into the deep. The nail would hold at least an hour. He ran the tip of the hose through the clamp and made sure it extended an inch and a half above the water but remained snug against the hull of the boat. In order to see it from deck, someone would have to lean all the way over the bulwark and look hard.

Currie dove under the boat.

From the wheelhouse, Sperazza watched the launch full of Libyans closing twenty-five yards away. He eyed the AK-47s in the sailors' hands.

The deck of the gunship was lined with more men, all pointing weapons. If shooting started, the Italians would be massacred in seconds.

Sperazza called out, "Welcome!"

Under his breath he whispered to his men. "Cocksucking bastards! If I find which of you called these assholes . . . if you talk to them, gesture with a finger to them, even smile in their direction . . . I slit your throat when they leave and do the same to your family. And NOW," he boomed at the sour-faced Libyan navy lieutenant coming aboard, "how can we help you?"

Currie breathed slowly, the end of the hose in a corner of his mouth. The hose had an unpleasant oily taste but the air coming through was clean, the water cool and clear. He could see a long way in any direction.

He moved his feet lazily, maintaining position, pressing both hands against the smooth hull of the boat. Saltwater stung his eyes. He saw a school of slow-moving red and blue fishes. Beautiful.

The bag was slightly buoyant and the weight of the gun negligible, although he kept the strap around his neck. He felt the wooden hull vibrate from footsteps and imagined the boarding party just above. Sharks. Well, don't think about sharks. That was Zarek's trick. Don't think about things you can't control. Think about things you can.

In his mind he saw Sperazza's crewman Mahmoud in the alley last night, knife in hand. Mahmoud had been alone in the pilothouse much of the time they'd been at sea. Currie decided he had probably called the Libyans. If Currie got out of trouble, he would reckon with the man later on the boat. *If.* If Sperazza could keep the crew quiet. *IF.* Depressingly small chance if Mahmoud really worked for Qaddafi. But maybe Mahmoud was more afraid of Sperazza than of Qaddafi, at least on the boat. Or maybe Mahmoud wanted to keep his role as spy secret and wouldn't say anything in front of the rest of the crew.

Or maybe the spy wasn't Mahmoud at all.

Breathe and don't think about maybes. You could be lucky. You could use a little luck, you're overdue. But the maybes started again. Maybe the Libyans will search the boat and leave. Maybe Sperazza will keep his men quiet and a miracle will happen. Miracles have been known to happen and you could use one right now.

Then Currie felt a bump against his back and turned and almost swallowed the hose. The shark hung two feet from his face through the refracted underwater light. A gill fanned slowly. Currie saw one black marble eye. The shark was so close he could only see one eye.

No, a miracle wasn't going to happen.

Slowly, he brought the hand with the waterproof bag up, gripping it tight, because he didn't want to drop it. He could feel the jaws crunching his bones already. His heart beat loud against his ribs. He thought, Now I'll see how far the Ceska shoots underwater.

"There is liquor on this boat and you will tell me where it is," the lieutenant snapped.

His men were everywhere, stomping around the hold with the fish, tearing up the wheelhouse, ripping apart bunks.

Sperazza snapped. "Leave my ship alone! We're in international waters, you have no rights! There's no liquor except some wine and that's for me! Get the hell off!"

The lieutenant wasn't fooled, just as Sperazza knew the search had nothing to do with liquor. Currie had convinced him the Libyans had been summoned. This lieutenant was playing a pathetic comedy to protect his spy. If the Libyans came aboard to look for scotch and "accidentally" found Currie, whoever called them would be protected.

And now, amid the breaking of glass from below, the lieutenant appeared to be tiring of the deception as well. The man was enraged over finding nothing. He stepped to Sperazza, his sailors' AK-47 at his back.

"Enough games," the lieutenant said. "I want the American."

Sperazza rubbed his forehead in puzzlement. "American?"

The lieutenant was young and wore square wire-rimmed glasses. His breath smelled of onions. "He's on this boat somewhere."

Sperazza said, "What are you talking about!"

The lieutenant cursed in Arabic, stomped off and stopped in front of Mahmoud. The Arab stood with the rest of Sperazza's crew in a helpless little circle, under Libyan guns.

"*Where is he?*" the lieutenant said.

Mahmoud walked away from the crew; the Libyan sailors did not stop him. He would not look at Sperazza. When he stood safely behind the Libyans, he pointed at the floor, the deck. "Under the boat," he said.

As the lieutenant gave excited orders, Mahmoud cried out to Sperazza: "Why couldn't you have let them find him in the hold! Now it won't go well for you!"

The boat rocked, water clogged Currie's mouth. Thirty feet off the shark was coming back toward him. He'd read that sharks circle their victims. He blew into the hose to clear it and hoped whoever was on deck wouldn't hear the noise or notice the spray. Deck was a million miles away.

The shark was enormous. Currie had seen sharks in the

New York City Aquarium as a kid and this one dwarfed those eating machines. Black and white, seventeen feet long. He'd read scare headlines in supermarkets for years. "FAMILY OF THREE DEVOURED BY SHARK." The water was cold, he was shivering. Nothing in his life had prepared him for this shark.

The shark veered left, circling closer.

Don't drop the bag. If the shark had attacked right away, he wouldn't have had a chance but now he felt the Ceska through the plastic bag. He tried to work the slack material so his finger could press the trigger. But he'd released the safety on the boat and if he exerted too much pressure the gun would fire early, ripping a hole in the bag, clogging the gun with seawater.

How far could a bullet shoot underwater? Twenty feet? Could it shoot at all?

The hose tasted of gasoline. His shoulder ached unmercifully. This time the shark swung toward him with purpose. *Don't think about how big it is,* but here it came, straight at him, speeding up, mouth opening. Currie brought the Ceska up. He could feel the trigger through the bag. He'd seen the rows of teeth when the shark bumped him before. Fifteen feet and the whole world was that mouth.

Underwater, Currie screamed.

He fired into the open mouth.

The Ceska jerked twice and died. He saw the tiny bullets foam away. But the mouth was still coming, the mouth wouldn't stop.

Then the shark thrashed, turned right. The tail whammed into Currie's chest, smashing him into the hull. The air went out of him in a burst of bubbles, his vision blacked and cleared. I'm dead, he thought. He glimpsed the bag dropping away. But *the shark was moving off,* trailing blood from both gills, streaming red, falling toward the bottom like a submarine.

Currie groped for the air hose, needing to breathe. He wanted to shout with exultation.

From the depths, two dark forms were rising toward him. More sharks.

The first ripped into the dead one, the second kept coming. Currie kicked hard, dodging under the hull toward the far side of the boat. His head broke surface. Someone was shouting in Arabic above and guns pointed at him all along the bulwark.

"Shark," he cried. Sperazza came shouldering through the Libyan sailors, rushed to the railing, leaned way down and grabbed Currie's wrist and pulled. Currie felt himself rising from the water, but Sperazza's eyes went behind him and grew huge. Currie knew the fin had surfaced too. Machine guns were going off all around him.

With a final tremendous kick, he was out of the water.

Heaving, he stood on deck. The sailors were going crazy shooting at the shark. He thought he would vomit. A Libyan navy lieutenant pointed a Beretta at his belly.

"Excellent hiding place," the lieutenant said. "I never would have looked under the boat except for Mahmoud."

Then Currie saw Mahmoud standing with the Libyan sailors, not the *Kukulka*'s crew. Two Libyans by the railing were stripped to their shorts, gripping long knives. Apparently they'd been about to jump in after Currie. Both men couldn't stop staring at the ten-foot carcass floating beyond the boat.

Two more fins broke surface. The corpse shuddered from impact.

Currie thought, Whatever happens to me now, it will be better than sharks.

Sperazza told him "You were right about Mahmoud." To the Libyans he growled, "You got what you came for. Get off my ship!"

"A moment." The lieutenant was young, Currie figured. Twenty or twenty-one. He barked something in Arabic and

Currie's arms were grabbed from behind. He was dragged, struggling, away from Sperazza, behind the line of Libyan sailors.

The lieutenant ordered Sperazza to join his men.

Currie screamed, "No!" He'd realized what was about to happen. He broke free of the sailors and lunged at the lieutenant. Something hard slammed into his back. Currie went down in agony but grabbed a sailor's ankle, pulled hard. The sailor toppled to the deck. Currie screamed, "Fight them, Sperazza!" He scrabbled for the windpipe, the death spot. But the others were around him, pounding. He was pulled off the sailor. He saw a gun butt rushing toward his head.

After he was unconscious the lieutenant told Sperazza, "My orders are to prevent you from reporting what happened. Nothing personal in this." Mahmoud cried out, "I didn't know they were going to hurt you! I thought they only wanted Currie!"

When the lieutenant said "Open fire," Mahmoud tried to stop the Libyans, so the lieutenant shot him too.

The lieutenant personally set explosives in the engine compartment and bunk area. When the gunboat was half a mile off there was a *whump* and a flash of light on the water. A fountain of sea rose and subsided. The *Kukulka* lifted high and slid under the blue waters of the Mediterranean.

There was an oil smell, a rumbling noise. Currie sought escape in sleep but it eluded him. He knew in minutes his body would be screaming. Dull pain spread through his neck and arms.

From somewhere close, a voice said, "Can you hear me?"

Currie opened his eyes.

He was looking at two bare legs, *his* legs, he saw, extending straight out on a steel-plate floor, ankles strapped to a welded hook. The skin was bruised purple and black. His feet looked filthy.

What happened to my clothes?

He tried to bring his hands up but found them strapped behind him.

"Ah, Mr. Currie. Awake at last."

There was a tremendous jolt, the earth tilted viciously and he cried out as the back of his head hammered into steel. His angle of vision changed. Dazed, he was looking into creamy blue eyes a foot away, disembodied orbs with diamond-hard irises. Zarek had told him about Jamal's eyes, Currie had no doubt this was that man.

Jamal's cheekbones were chiseled, his chin narrow, sharp. Mirror sunglasses were perched over his kinky bronze hair. "You should not have fought so hard, you injured yourself," he said. Power washed from him. Even the small straightening movements were precise under the tailored safari suit. Pain sharpened Currie's senses and he saw he was inside a steel-ribbed armored vehicle. A halftrack or a truck. Bright Bedouin tapestries and scimitars had been hung in a half-successful attempt to detract from the stark military aspect. Blue-and-white Persian carpets covered much of the plating. Fluorescent lights lined the walls.

Fresh spurts of pain savaged Currie's temples when he moved his head. Beyond Jamal he saw two bulky and aggressive-looking men wearing cheap suits. They sat cross-legged on the carpet. Probably bodyguards. The first was a broad-shouldered, hollow-cheeked Arab. The second, square headed and balding, had the fish-underbelly color of an Eastern European. Both remained expressionless.

Rolling his head left, Currie was surprised to see another prisoner five feet away, strapped to the floor too. An Arab, maybe forty years old. Black hair. Staring back. The man's red-and-white robe was soiled, his thick wrists blotchy with bruises and his swarthy face a mass of blue black pain. Currie said, "What are you here for?"

The man's eyes narrowed, his jaw worked. When he spat, the spittle landed between them.

"Hey," Currie said. "What are you spitting at *me* for?"

Jamal called him back gently. "Good you are here," he said. His lips were stretched in a rubbery smile. "Your face looks terrible. We will fix it. Bring you to the coast, get you back to Italy. The straps. We'll take them off in a while. You were pretty wild on that boat. Just answer a few questions." He leaned forward. He wore sweet cologne. "Why were you coming to Libya?" Jamal asked.

"The desert is good for my sinuses."

The muscle jumped under Jamal's right eye. When he stood, the guards followed his movements like dogs sensitive to an affront to their master.

"Where are my clothes?" Currie said. "I want something to wear."

The straps were so tight they dug into his wrists. From the pitching motion of the halftrack Currie guessed they were in the desert, but there were no windows. The air-conditioning chilled him. The scimitar on the wall hung six feet away, out of reach. It could slice through Jamal like paper. It might as well have been in Washington.

"This ride can be either short or long," Jamal said. The toothpaste smile was gone, he had a low frustration tolerance. "Opt for short. Time, it's funny. A single second can last all night."

He removed a shiny object from his breast pocket. Cigarette lighter, Currie saw. The flame went on. He braced himself for pain. *Don't think about what it will be like.*

But without warning Currie's mind shifted: he was in Iran, in the basement interrogation room. A rifle muzzle pressed his temple. "Why were you helping SAVAK?" Click. "Answer the question!"

It was incredible. Happening again. Suddenly Currie was

screaming, savaging his wrists on the straps, cursing. Jesus, he thought, I'm losing control. He saw the blue of Jamal's eyes, the cot from his cell, Sperazza's crew huddled on the deck. The Iranian guards stood over him.

Jamal waited until Currie quieted.

Jamal rotated the lighter like a glass of wine. Currie's forehead was covered with sweat. Jamal said, gently and almost sympathetically, "The human body is a marvelous receptacle for pain. Millions of nerve endings. Each one to be cultivated, each yields a truth."

Lowering the lighter to Currie's eye level, he said, "We'll start with this common lighter and work our way up. Save yourself trouble. I offer a second chance, a rarity in itself. Why were you coming to Libya?"

"Blow it out your ass, motherfucker."

In one easy motion, Jamal brought the flame to the underside of Currie's foot.

Currie leaped against the straps, his foot exploding in an agony of fire. Burning, searing pain. He smelled flesh roasting. His leg felt as if it was turning black.

Jamal pulled back.

The secret police chief swam in and out of focus. But Currie had remained silent. Jamal said admiringly, "I like your spirit." The pain was horrible. "A challenge, that's what you are," Jamal said. But Currie saw that defiance for its own sake was stupid. He needed his body in working condition or he'd never get out of here. Talk, lie, keep the conversation going. There had to be a weakness, an angle he could exploit.

Jamal went academic as the halftrack lurched. "In the beginning I believed you an amateur. Felt sorry for you, I really did. Your girlfriend, killed by accident. Innocent victims, you and she." Testing the straps again Currie realized they had loosened since Jamal applied the fire. Not enough to free his hands but a little. He battered down hope. The straps were slick, his hands were probably bleeding all over them.

Jamal was saying, ". . . then you hook up with Zarek. Three of my men are dead, three. You're no amateur. Who are you working for?"

"Nobody." The lighter went on. Currie said, "Nobody! You'd never understand. People like you. Everyone has to 'work for' " . . . but the rest was lost in a scream as Jamal brought the flame to Currie's foot again. Currie arched against the straps, engulfed in a universe of anguish. His body was ripped by convulsions.

"I'm getting bored with the lighter," Jamal said, withdrawing it.

"You . . . don't even know the truth when you hear it."

Jamal shook his head. He couldn't believe Currie wasn't cooperating. He glanced at his watch. Currie had a feeling the ride would be over soon. Zarek had said something about Jamal's taking victims to an oasis. "I'm going to confess," Jamal said, "I am a vindictive man. Impatient and too old to change." He held up his hand to stop Currie's "I told you!" Jamal looked over his fingernails. Currie worked the loosened straps each time the Libyan averted his eyes.

Jamal said, "Let's be honest with each other. You're too intelligent not to know it's the end for you. But you have that martyr glow. If you don't start talking I'll bring Anna here. Oh yes, I know where she is. Mahmoud told us. You can save yourself pain. And help Anna."

Currie slipped his left hand free. The name "Anna" had struck him almost physically. The blood pounded in his chest. He saw Jamal bending over Anna with the lighter. He said, "What's to stop you from bringing her here anyway?"

"Nothing."

Currie changed tack. "Why should you waste time going after her after I'm dead? It's pointless for you."

Jamal tapped his chin with his forefinger. A slow smile spread on his face. "On the contrary. It's a question of reputation. The story would spread. Next time I have a talk with someone here he may have heard it. He'll be sure to tell me what I want to know right away. Last chance for Anna. *Why are you coming to Libya?*"

Currie said, "To kill Qaddafi." Jamal knew anyway, didn't he? But Jamal looked astounded. Currie said, "You've been hunting me, didn't you know why I was coming?"

Jamal started to laugh.

He brayed "AAAAAH" and coughed and laughed some more. He repeated, "To kill him." He was shaking with mirth. The bodyguards smiled. Currie thought they were crazy.

With a jolt, the halftrack stopped.

Gasping, Jamal said, "Now I will show you something before I ask the last question. What I do to people."

He pressed a small blue button and a six-foot steel section of wall slid away behind Currie. Turning, Currie looked out a picture window and gasped. The halftrack had reached an oasis, he saw dunes in the distance. But the reeds and palm fronds were alive with crawling insects, fire-red ants half the size of mice.

The other prisoner began moaning, "Jamaaaaaal."

Currie saw a human rib cage and pelvis half protruding from the sand.

The air-conditioning hummed steadily.

The moans grew louder, the prisoner kept crying Jamal's name. Currie was frozen with horror. As the larger bodyguard bent to untie the man the moans became screams.

Jamal raised his voice to be heard. "Hamid Ali was supposed to find you in the United States. He didn't."

Currie slipped his right hand free. He hid the hope from his face.

Jamal straightened, his excitement palpable in his posture, shiny on his face. He glowed with an almost sexual flush, an accentuation of the look he had had when burning Currie with the lighter.

He snapped an order to the Libyan guard, who mounted

a ladder and threw open a circular hatch to the roof. Broiling desert air filled the vehicle. Hamid Ali was pulled by one guard, pushed by the other up the ladder. Despite the fact that the Arab had been hunting him, Currie felt pity for the man. And disgust.

In English, Jamal said, "Push him off the top."

The slam of steel cut off Hamid Ali's cries. Both guards were out of the halftrack. The circulation was coming back into Currie's hands but he'd only have one chance at the ankle straps and Jamal was watching him. There was a wall intercom through which Jamal could call for help. Currie willed him, *Turn around.*

Hands behind his back, Jamal said academically, "I don't know what the ants eat when we aren't bringing them people. The vibrations of the halftrack brings them out. But they won't climb on the halftrack. They don't like hot steel."

Hamid Ali's body fell past the window. Then the hatch opened and the guards were coming back. No chance to reach for the ankle straps now. Outside, Hamid Ali rose and lunged toward the desert. He got five paces before he started dancing. Currie couldn't take his eyes away. At first Hamid Ali looked comic, a man swatting flies or hopping barefoot on a hot sidewalk. Then he started clawing at his clothes. He threw himself at the window, inches from Currie. He could see Currie's hands were untied and he pointed at them. He screamed but no sound was audible. He hammered at the glass.

The two guards came up to the window but the Eastern European had trouble watching.

The first ant appeared on Hamid Ali's forehead, clinging to his eyebrow. Then ants rushed onto his face from his robe. He wiped them off in handfuls. More took their place. Screeching soundlessly, he flailed, ants going into his mouth, his ears. Running blindly, Hamid Ali crashed into a palm tree.

Buried in ants, he fell.

"They'll strip him in five minutes," Jamal said. The wall was sliding shut again, the air-conditioner hummed. Jamal opened a bottle of Fanta, poured the contents into a glass and drank thirstily.

He came close to Currie. "I want to know about Tecala's paper you found in Washington," Jamal said. The intensity in the Libyan's voice pierced Currie's horror. It struck him that the paper was what Jamal had been interested in all along. The little date tree drawings. The drawings Nori had been murdered for.

Keep your hands behind your back. Don't give yourself away.

Jamal was watching him closely. Desperately, Currie tried to complete the puzzle of his senses. Why hadn't Jamal been concerned about Qaddafi's safety earlier? Because Currie had turned out to be so pathetic an adversary? Or because Jamal had no interest in protecting the man?

Third possiblity. Jamal had happily and accidentally stumbled upon a threat to Qaddafi, that was why he had laughed so much.

Currie tried an experiment. "Oh, the FBI figured out that paper."

Jamal's smile vanished. The gold specks in his eyes floated together. Behind Currie's back, his fingers curled into the death shape. Jamal was so close Currie saw the hairs extending from his nostrils. Pulse fluttered in the Libyan's neck. Currie thought of Anna strapped to the floor again, he battered down choking rage, he held the hand in check. He had no doubt he could strike the kill spot but he had seen no bulge of weapon under Jamal's tightfitting jacket. The guards would reach him in seconds if he wasted his one chance on Jamal.

Wait until a guard gets close.

"You're lying," Jamal said.

"Not at all." Currie went casual. Pain savaged his shoulders and spine. He added, "Israel, Saudi Arabia, Iran." He put knowledge into his tone. He thought, Give me something I can use against you.

Jamal sat back on his heels in sick fascination. But Currie was fascinated too because Jamal emanated fear. "Tell me more about the note," Jamal said. Even in his fright he gave nothing away. Currie remarked, "Why, Qaddafi is Israel." The flecks in Jamal's eyes were spinning. A strange thought gripped Currie, that Jamal had been trying to hide the paper from Qaddafi. Was that it? *Was Jamal doing something he did not want Qaddafi to know?*

But when Currie added nothing more, the Libyan began to relax. Jamal's fear shifted to speculation. Currie met the stare with a knowing smile but a victorious shine came into Jamal's eyes.

Jamal stood. "Bluffing," he said. "You never figured it out."

The steel section of wall slid aside again. Tinted glass colored the banded desert: blue sky, green oasis, sand. People don't come back from Jamal's oasis, Zarek had said. Aware that the guards were rising, Currie tried not to look at them. He willed one of them to step close to untie his ankles. The blood was hammering in his veins.

"I'll bring Anna here when I'm finished with you," Jamal said. "I told you I was vindictive."

He snapped an order in Arabic. When the balding guard lumbered close and bent to untie Currie, Currie brought his hand around, arching it viciously and feeling it strike the soft flesh over the carotid artery. There was a grunt of pain. The guard brought his hand to his neck, chin dipping and eyes growing wide. Currie sensed the second guard starting toward him. He was clutching the stunned man's lapel, knuckles on white cotton. He touched the shoulder holster but the blow knocked him sideways, away from the prize. He sprang back, using the heel of his hand to push his torso off

[271]

the floor. His ankles remained bound. His jaw crashed into the incoming heel. He screamed.

When his vision cleared, the hollow-cheeked Libyan stood three feet off, aiming a snubnosed revolver. Currie moaned, "My jaw, Christ."

Mindlessly, the blond rocked on the floor two feet away, blood oozing from his mouth and ears. Through his own hurt Currie heard the horrible whistling of air in a crushed human windpipe.

He ran his tongue over the bottom of his mouth. Teeth were broken, jagged. The blood taste was thick. Shining rubies dropped onto his chest and smeared his skin, sliding.

Jamal reached into the dying man's jacket and came up with a black automatic. Looking at Currie with annoyance, he said, "Neuman has been with me for years." He might have been chastising Currie for breaking a favorite appliance. His glance flicked out the window and the excitement was back. "You ought to provide a good show with such spirit," Jamal said. "Advice for you. Don't lose hope. If you don't lose hope, maybe you will be the first to escape here."

It was a ploy to keep Currie's fighting spirit up for what was about to happen. Jamal pressed another button. At a vibrating sound a hatch slid open on the ceiling and a ladder stopped two feet above the floor. The temperature rose about fifty degrees.

The Libyan unstrapped Currie carefully, ready to strike if Currie moved suddenly. He disappeared up the ladder to wait for Currie on the roof. "Up," Jamal said, jerking the automatic toward the ladder.

The sun broiled the top of Currie's head. Blinking, he emerged into the light. The earth was dazzling. Beyond the oasis the Sahara rose and fell, massive against his puniness, a five-thousand-year-old graveyard.

The end of Currie's adventure. The pulseless abyss of the desert.

The sky was bluer than he had ever seen it.

Currie smelled the rot of overabundant vegetation.

I had a good life, he thought.

Jamal joined them on the roof, the power washing out from him, practically humming in the air. "Look over the edge," he said. Sweat dotted his forehead.

The ants crawled everywhere, rippling over the reeds and grass, avoiding the hot steel tread and body. The mandibles were so big Currie discerned them from twelve feet up.

"They don't like the sand, it's too hot," Jamal said. "Reach the sand and you've escaped them."

Currie stretched, feeling the sun soak into his shoulders, his face. "Someone will get Qaddafi," he said, not threatening, just stating a fact. "And you. In the end." If he jumped right, he might land on his feet. Zarck had told him you should roll on the ground to break a jump but if he rolled the ants would be on him right away. He saw Hamid Ali's skeleton down there in the reeds, ants crawling from the eye sockets in his skull. With effort he pulled his gaze from the ants.

A hundred yards to the safety of the desert, he guessed.

Make it to the desert and the sun would suck him dry.

Then a new voice sounded from below, Arabic and urgent. The driver, Currie guessed. There must be a door from the cab to the interior. A head poked above the rooftop. The soldier spoke rapidly to Jamal, gesturning back into the vehicle. Currie heard the name, "Qaddafi."

Furious, Jamal looked between Currie and the driver. Prudence and instinct warred upon his features. Clearly, he was wanted back in the halftrack, probably on the radio.

From the way Jamal snapped orders to the guard Currie decided he wasn't going to have to jump right away.

Jamal disappeared into the halftrack. Currie started to sit

down but the roof was hot and he stood. He grinned at the sourfaced guard. "You look tired, why don't you climb down to the oasis and rest," Currie said. "I'll tell you when Jamal's coming back."

The man glared at him. A moment later footsteps came halfway up the ladder and Jamal's voice barked a command from inside the vehicle. Currie couldn't believe it but the guard jerked his gun to direct Currie back inside. "Down, up, down, up," Currie said flippantly. "Make up your mind." But his legs were weak with relief.

At the bottom of the steps Jamal's face was clouded, pale.

"Qaddafi wants to meet his assassin," he said. "We will take you to Tripoli and there you will die."

CHAPTER
19

SHEEP, I see sheep on the balconies, Currie thought. In Tripoli he rode as prisoner in a twenty-jeep convoy. Apartment buildings and date trees lined the ten-year-old boulevards. Libyans in embroidered waistcoats and baggy pants turned to stare.

His whole body throbbed from the beating he'd received. His feet were on fire, in the rearview mirror his face had swollen purple. Blood caked the corner of his mouth.

FREEDOM IS LATENT proclaimed a banner in Arabic and surprisingly, in English. The convoy had met Jamal's halftrack at the edge of the desert. The secret police chief sat behind Currie with a soldier whose Dragunov jabbed Currie's neck each time the vehicle lurched.

From overhead came the detonation of Tupolov fighter jets breaking the sound barrier. They left rapier trails in the blue. After the unbroken white of the Sahara the city had risen mirage-like, a jigsaw of imported treasures of the world, from the white box-shaped apartment buildings to the Mercedeses idling at intersections or smashed around telephone poles. Preoccupied, Currie saw the city in snatches. Already smells of decay seeped up from spanking boulevards. Buildings peeled from lack of maintenance and blistered in the sun. The desert had claimed far more magnificence than this, the planned obsolescense of assembly-line monuments to the new Ozymandias, Colonel Qaddafi.

"He likes to meet people we've arrested," Jamal said. He had regained his self-satisfied vindictiveness. Currie did not bother to turn around. There was fear in the speed with which the troops obeyed Jamal's commands and any hope Currie had felt that Jamal might be countermanded had disappeared. Zarek had said, *Jamal speaks with Qaddafi's authority.*

They swung onto an even wider avenue where a date tree park centered six lanes. Jamal added, "He talks with you, lulls you. It's his ego, I think. He likes to handle enemies by himself. You'll see. Even though I'm telling you this, he will make you think he is going to let you go. A magician with words. He enjoys trying out new weapons personally."

Still, Currie felt no fear. In the vacuumlike heat the convoy proceeded with the power of predestination. He floated in a calm of inevitability. At times his aching body even went detached and he saw his bruised and raw hands as if they belonged to another person. Nori was almost a physical presence beside him. And Asher. Anna. Zarek. Sperazza. All the people who had helped him, Currie's volunteer brigade, troops in a captured army.

The rooftops showed a battleground of higher and higher television antennas, and a crowd fought for sets outside a state store. Shutters were closed at midday but balconies were packed with livestock. Currie heard sheep over traffic noise. Boys kicked soccer balls under palm trees. Everything he saw — the balls, parks and rifles — was all new.

The Dragunov jabbed him. A cadence of images broke in on him: Zarek in the embassy in Iran, pushing close in the panicked crowd. "I owe you." Nori on the picnic blanket at Roosevelt Island. He saw his father, which surprised him, climbing from the bakery truck in front of his boyhood apartment house. Shirt ripped. Bruises visible even from the third-floor window. Thumbs-up signal for another petty highway fistfight victory. In the halftrack, Jamal's cigarette lighter came close. Currie armed himself with memories.

"He tested an antitank device on the last man I brought," Jamal said. "Went into some theoretical discussion, got the man talking, calmed him, befriended him. Then he blew him up like a rabbit, with a bazooka."

The voice was inconsequential, the droning of a fly. Currie's heart beat slow and loud and steady. So many things had happened that nothing surprised him. He'd run out of fear. Numb expectation remained. He left off the personal memories and found himself running through stories he'd heard since Nori's death. He remembered Ronni Moffitt who had been blown up by the Chileans in Washington, and her killer who had sent her husband a note saying he was sorry. She hadn't been the "military" target. He remembered the two little housewives from Argentina who had spoken at Catholic University, trying to get their sons out of prison. He remembered the London policewoman machine-gunned by Libyans from inside a diplomatically protected embassy. It did not occur to him that his calm might be a product of these influences. He merely felt connection although he was alone.

When he laughed the rifle slammed into his neck, the trooper behind barked a command, probably "shut up." Currie had had a funny thought. He'd remembered reading in high school about the Boxers. The Boxers were Chinese who had rebelled against the British in the nineteenth century. They'd believed their cause was so right bullets could not hurt them. By the thousands they had died charging British guns. Currie figured he must be crazy as the Boxers.

But now the convoy swung off the main boulevard. Beyond a green park submachine guns gleamed above a fifteen-foot-high wall. Currie recognized the whitewashed Bab Azizea barracks in which Qaddafi lived and worked. Zarek's descriptions were always perfect. Blank faced with antagonism, troops looked down from the wall. Qaddafi's influence hummed in the air. It was a vibration from a powerful generator and Currie sensed the man beyond the walls.

Then the jeeps rolled through the gate, barracks to the left. On the right, beyond a boiling guard-studded tarmac and maze of concrete barriers and steel tire-shredding spikes, a three-story stucco barrack dominated the fortress with its isolation.

He's there. The pounding in Currie's head grew huge.

Currie's jeep threaded the maze. Jamal's fingers were light on his shoulder. "His desk is equipped with buttons," Jamal was saying. Angered he'd been robbed of his prey, he tried to increase Currie's fear. "Underneath. He pushes a button and machine-gun fire sweeps part of the room."

But Currie was automatically recording the guards' locations. He recognized the Beretta submachine guns and Kalashnikov rifles. He checked for shadows in which he might hide if he escaped. Doorways. No sewer grates or manhole covers. Shutters yawned open on all windows. An antiaircraft gun gleamed on the roof.

Qaddafi keeps a helicopter outside Tripoli and a submarine off Benghazi in case he needs to run, Zarek had said. *He's pointed missiles at his own barracks if his troops rebel.*

Such a careful man would give himself more than one way out of here. Currie asked, "Are there tunnels?" Delighted, Jamal laughed. "Keep hoping, always."

The heat drove back at him off the tarmac. At Bab Azizea the troops wore maroon berets instead of the green of convoy soldiers. They had the tough look of elite guards. With a jerk the jeep halted by the steps. A red bereted officer stepped forward, AK-47 pointing at Currie. Jamal barked an order and the man jumped back. Currie was Jamal's personal prize and no one else could get custody.

Time sped up. Prodded by Jamal's automatic, Currie limped

along a third-floor corridor toward a huge door of polished mahogany. More red hats stood every ten feet. Each step sent waves of pain up his leg. He heard booted footsteps and the creaks of metallic bolts in a gun behind him. Gleaming brass knobs adorned the door like medals. Currie could feel Qaddafi on the other side of the door. There was a tingling draw on Currie's skin, the door was Qaddafi's flesh.

At Jamal's command the escort dropped back. The door slammed behind them, shutting them in, but there was no Qaddafi. The spacious square room was drenched in sunlight, cool from stone walls and floors, vaultlike from the curved ceiling yet eerily empty except for a cedar desk and lone wooden chair. A plain manila envelope lay on the desk. There were no pencils or pens or photographs. No paintings or commemorations, mementos, toys, calendars, cigar boxes. The only decoration was a six-foot Roman bas-relief pilfered from ruins along the coast, stadiums or ampitheaters. A carved procession of legionnaires started by a small back door and rode north in chariots. They appeared to be emerging from the wall.

It was a cell, not an office. A cave. No weapons visible but *there are buttons under the desk,* Jamal had said.

The small door opened and Qaddafi walked into the room.

There had been no footsteps, no warning. Currie caught his breath. Qaddafi was alone. The Colonel glided toward Jamal, legs moving almost independently, as if he were a puppet drawn across the floor. Physically he was smaller than Currie, who stared at the sculpted, pitted and slightly over-sized head, the oddly slack hands, the raised chin as if Qaddafi were listening to something nobody else could hear. Under a forest of black curly hair the zealot's eyes blazed but re-mained distant and detached.

It was the strangest feeling he had ever had, watching the man he had come to kill. Qaddafi couldn't be here. It was impossible. He existed only on airwaves or in newspaper photographs. The emotion surged into Currie's brain and froze him.

The Colonel came closer. Undeniable force, greater than any Currie had ever felt, poured from the man. Jamal had dipped his shoulders, made himself smaller. For the first time in his life Currie experienced the physical meaning of the word *power*.

Jamal commanded, "Back away, to the wall." Qaddafi was clad in a loose-fitting tropical safari shirt of white cotton which fell around a button-down leather hip holster. His gun was not drawn. He was pudgier than Currie would have thought. But it occurred to Currie that he had already been in the Colonel's presence for weeks. Qaddafi's presence was scattered over a globe of billions. His presence was graffiti on a Rome statue, a stock market report in the London *Times* and a debate on the East Side of New York. The price of wheat in a Nigerian village. A submachine gun rolling off a Prague assembly line. That was Qaddafi's presence. Currie had penetrated the armor and stood before the beating heart.

Jamal addressed Qaddafi boastfully, nodding toward Currie. The Colonel turned his gaze fully on the prisoner. From straight on Qaddafi showed the hollow-cheeked haggardness of an insomniac or workaholic. A scar nicked the right lower jaw. An assassin had almost killed Qaddafi, Zarek had said.

Looking at the face explained the starkness of the office. The man who worked in this room lived in his head.

Then Jamal said the name "Currie" and the bubble burst. Yes, here was Qaddafi, the hated and terrible Qaddafi in the same room. Hatred cascaded down on Currie. He began to push himself off the wall but Jamal jerked the gun. "When the Colonel is ready," he said. "Not when you are. Get back."

Air washed through the open window, it ran like liquid onto Currie's neck.

The Libyans began talking in animated Arabic.

Hoping for an opening, Currie felt a great pulse beating

inside him, a rhythm of rage that had begun when he was in Iran, which had built while he wrote useless protest letters for Watchers International, which had exploded when Nori died but *continud to grow* while Zarek educated him in the system of murder Qaddafi directed. In the whole dirty war that went on under the surface of normal life.

Here, in this room, he was face to face with the great evil. Master and servant. Currie's pain was gone. It was as if the pounding in his chest was the heartbeat of all the victims.

Jamal was willing him to try something, to make a move toward Qaddafi. He was furious that Currie had reached Qaddafi at all. If Currie could figure out why, he might have a wedge.

Now, waving a hand vaguely at Currie, Jamal continued his monologue to Qaddafi. Currie guessed he was saying, "Here is the assassin, Brother Colonel. Let me take him from your sight and finish it."

Qaddafi seemed to ask, "Who is he?" When Jamal said, "CIA," Currie knew he was interpreting the conversation correctly. He thought, Where are the buttons under the desk? The desk centered the room, ten feet off. He could not imagine where the hidden guns were unless they were inside the desk or wall.

At a muffled artillery *whump* to the south, Currie jumped. Jamal started to ask what was that but Qaddafi abruptly turned to Currie, switching to English. Currie had expected this. Jamal had said the Colonel liked to play with victims before dispatching them personally. Currie had seen Qaddafi use English on TV. Besides, the use of English was another triumph. The unspoken message was, I've mastered your language, I've even beaten you there.

"Maneuvers," Qaddafi said with a hint of French accent. "A simulated American attack with paratroopers. I don't think the Americans will do so well."

"We are ready for them if they come, my Colonel," Jamal

said, switching to English too. But he frowned. "I'm, eh, surprised I wasn't told about the maneuvers."

Qaddafi laughed. "Even you don't hear everything. Look at this!" With relish he pulled the gun from the holster. Another Ceska, Currie saw. Qaddafi produced an odd, square-shaped silencer from his back pocket. He screwed it on. Jamal had said, *He likes to try out new weapons.*

"From Kiev," Qaddafi said. "Watch."

Qaddafi swung the gun toward Currie. Currie leaped left. There was nowhere to hide. He hit the floor. He heard no shot, only a plaster-breaking sound to his left. The Libyans were laughing. The head of the lead Roman in the bas-relief had disintegrated. Plaster dust drifted in a sunbeam, coated the floor.

Lifting himself, Currie saw he was three feet closer to the desk.

Qaddafi had a low, throaty laugh. "Oh, that was good," he said. "He moves fast. But the silencer, Jamal. No one hears a thing! Marvelous! Not even the pop of a regular silencer. Think what you can do in crowds."

Qaddafi stopped laughing. He turned the Ceska on Currie. "Put away your gun, Jamal."

Jamal started to protest in Arabic. Qaddafi snapped, "Don't you think I can take care of myself?" Jamal holstered his gun. Qaddafi asked, "Do you believe there are accidents in life, Jamal?"

"Excuse me?"

"Accidents. Do you believe destiny determines even small events? A master plan? Or do you think fate unfolds on a case-by-case basis?"

Currie was five feet from the desk. *Where are the buttons?*

Jamal said, "Destiny, certainly, Brother Colonel. I believe in the destiny of our great revolution. Luck is the weak man's excuse though. Hard work to compliment destiny!"

Dryly, Qaddafi said, "Yes, that you uncovered the assassin,

the hand of God is in this. Divinity exists in the small twists of life. Remember that. It keeps people from making mistakes."

Currie was a little surprised. He thought he detected antagonism in the Colonel's voice suddenly. Anger at Jamal or contempt. A second artillery blast shook the building, closer this time. Jamal wet his lips. Whatever was going on, Currie was glad it was unnerving the man. He could see the swirls on the wooden top of the desk, by the unmarked envelope. If Qaddafi would only glance away for an instant he could leap for the desk. What the hell, Qaddafi would kill him anyway and maybe he could reach the buttons. But Qaddafi ordered, "Get away from the desk!" and went there himself, blocking all path to the buttons.

Qaddafi upended the envelope on the desk. A paper slid out.

"What are these drawings, Jamal?" he said softly.

Currie caught his breath. The xeroxed enlargement showed the date tree drawings Currie had found in Washington. Jamal backed up, now he stood beside Currie. The smile had left Qaddafi's face. "Your gun, Jamal," he said. With two fingers, Jamal withdrew his automatic from his pocket and kicked it toward Qaddafi. It slid under the desk.

In less than a second the mood had changed. Qaddafi radiated danger, covering both Jamal and Currie. He was no longer the philosophical leader but the soldier. Jamal had gone white with terror. The thunder of revelation beat in Currie's head. He could still see Jamal bending close in the halftrack, laughing with surprise. "You came to *kill* Qaddafi?" Jamal had said.

Currie burst out, "That's why you were relieved!"

Jamal snarled back in Arabic, he had no idea he used a language Currie did not understand. But Currie needed no translation.

Qaddafi was saying, "You brought me two assassins and

[283]

one of them is you." Jamal backed toward the window, widening the distance between him and Currie. Qaddafi said, "I've had this note for days. You thought you could fool *me*?"

There came a precise instant in time when Currie knew the dictator's attention had split, but Currie was still too close to Jamal to move.

"Brother Colonel, I . . ."

Qaddafi was saying, "Now Israel, that is me." Currie eased left, toward the back door.

"I am not so small I could not take a joke," Qaddafi said. "Iran. General Shweidi. Saudi Arabia. General Maher." Currie took another step. "Get back where you were," Qaddafi ordered in English. To Jamal he said, "All to be murdered by your troops so that Jamal al-Hawaz could become next president of Libya. Your men are being slaughtered right now." The force of the sonic boom overhead sucked the walls in and out and made Currie's teeth vibrate. "Do you actually believe I would remain ignorant of your plans?"

The three men formed an isosceles triangle, Jamal by the window, Qaddafi centering the room and Currie inching again by the bas-relief.

A tremendous series of explosions shook dust off the relief. "A plot, yes," Jamal pleaded. Sweat gleamed on his outstretched palms. "I learned of it recently. I'm not part of it. I joined to learn their plans." Currie recognized the staccato *wham* of Dragunovs nearby. Fighting was going on inside the city.

"It was the Russian's idea," Jamal said.

Jamal glanced out the window. A moan escaped his lips.

In the courtyard a Russian and a Libyan were being dragged before a firing squad.

Jamal gathered himself. "I was going to arrest them," he said. "I needed the complete list. Trust me, my loyalty has never been in question. Brother Colonel, pleeeeease."

Everything broke loose at the same instant.

The firing squad unleashed a volley outside.

The gun bucked in the Colonel's fist, a red flower sprouted on Jamal's forehead, his feet buckled and Currie was in the air. The Colonel whirled. Currie drove the side of his hand into Qaddafi's throat. With a gargling sound Qaddafi fell, clutching his windpipe. The gun went off when it hit the floor. Scrabbling, Currie reached it and swung on Qaddafi.

Suddenly he was looking past the gunsight upon Qaddafi. Smoke rose from the barrel.

It had been so ridiculously easy. The situation was reversed. Currie had a ludicrous thought: I didn't know his eyes were green.

For an instant they were immobile. Knocking started at the door. In Currie's dreams he had watched the awful realization of what was about to happen come into Qaddafi's face. Sometimes Qaddafi begged for mercy. Or they grappled by hand, Currie watching the bulging eyes, the sweat breaking out on the forehead.

Qaddafi merely looked dazed.

The knocking stopped, to Currie's relief. The soldiers outside were probably under orders not to enter unless summoned.

Jamal had fallen sideways by the window, knees drawn up, neck twisted. One sunglass lens had rolled away to stand upright on the floor, glinting. Jamal's right palm pressed against his forehead. Blood collected in cracks in the floor.

In death Jamal looked surprised.

The firing in the city had grown vicious. Currie heard the drone of heavy bombers.

Qaddafi's gaze went from Currie to the gun. His senses were returning. He glanced at the front door and Currie cautioned, "Don't."

"Guards out there," Qaddafi croaked, rubbing his throat.

Currie wondered what lay behind the smaller door. Escape? "Just don't."

Qaddafi winced in pain. "I saved your life."

"You saved yourself, I was just there."

Qaddafi shook his head vaguely. "Tell me one thing," he said, eyes flickering toward the desk. "Was the CIA working with Jamal or did they send you here independently?" His shirt had hiked up to expose a roll of baby fat around his middle, pale and vulnerable. Currie's eyes settled on a small fiery welt on Qaddafi's side, a red pimple like anyone might have.

This wasn't the scene he had rehearsed in his mind.

"You killed her," Currie said.

With the tips of his fingers Qaddafi pushed himself to a sitting position. He probed his shoulders and arms. "What are you saying? Who?"

"In Washington," Currie said. "Lipko killed Tecala, then Nori. She drowned from blood pouring into her lungs."

He struggled to keep his voice low, to keep the soldiers outside from hearing.

Fire, screamed Zarek's voice in his mind. *What are you standing around talking for?*

Qaddafi cleared his throat with a delicate cough. "Oh, that woman who died with Tecala," he said.

That woman. Massaging the back of his neck he said, "That's ridiculous. Jamal was responsible, I had nothing to do with it. After what just happened here you must realize he worked independent of me. You're here because of one woman? An agent too? Don't tell me your government would sanction a revenge killing."

"She was my fiancée."

Jamal's jacket was smeared with blood, it resembled a fingerpainting.

Qaddafi was silent; when the truth dawned, his mouth opened but no sound came out. "You?" he said. "Alone?"

Currie wanted to laugh. Jamal had reacted the same way, unable to comprehend action by a single man.

But the cynical curve of Qaddafi's mouth became more friendly, reasonable. He spoke with delicacy, as if to a jumper on a ledge. "Jamal planned to take over," he said. "He thought you were coming to warn me, you'd found the paper in Washington and he was afraid you knew what it meant. He thought you were on my side.

"That's not what you said before."

"I didn't understand then who you were. But you see we have both suffered because of Jamal and now you are free of him."

Stupefied, Currie heard the truth in Qaddafi's words. Qaddafi *had* saved his life, hadn't he? Hadn't he called Currie in from the desert just when Jamal was about to kill him? Qaddafi had shot Nori's killer. But Currie kept the gun up, his danger sense was screaming, there was some quantum leap he knew he must make, he had to think, to find what it was.

Qaddafi had modified his voice to the low and confidential ranges. Currie had never thought of the man as having any appeal beyond a raw and vicious affinity with the masses, yet the Colonel had transformed himself. The aloof posture was softened. Qaddafi radiated extraordinary charming persuasiveness. The power Currie had felt in the man earlier was now directed at himself.

Qaddafi swayed as he made points, moving back and forth before Currie. "Tecala was loyal to me. Working in our Paris embassy he discovered Jamal's plot. He wanted to warn me but he was afraid if he tried to get to Libya the insurgents would guess his intentions. He was afraid to use the pouch mail or phones and rightly so. He arranged a trip to the United States where he planned to pass his message through a friendly diplomat. But the diplomat worked for Jamal too. The diplomat has been recalled to Syria. So you see, I had nothing to do with her death. And now that I know the reason for your trip here, you're free, go home. What you have come to do has been accomplished."

Qaddafi moved another half-foot toward the desk.

The instant you lower the gun you're dead, said a voice in Currie's mind, not Zarek's voice but his own. Danger stood in the room like another person. The guards could enter momentarily.

But Qaddafi sounded so logical. A wave of grief staggered Currie. He had not wept for her since that night at Stonehaven which seemed years ago. He fought back welling tears, desolation swept over him. Dead, she was dead. She had felt alive while he plotted to reach Libya, but with the Colonel in his sites she was gone and the black abyss opened.

Qaddafi said, "You look ill. Our doctors should examine you." His voice was hypnotic, numbing. Qaddafi said, "The Russians put Jamal up to it. They send guns and become angry when I don't do what they say." He slid a step toward the desk. Jamal's gun had disappeared beneath it. *There are buttons under the desk.*

Currie said, "Stay where you are." But Qaddafi seemed to know exactly how far he could go. He stopped with one hand resting casually on the ridge of the chair.

Dazed, Currie saw the blood spots outside Georgetown Hospital. Spattered rings drying on the curb. The corridor doors swung shut. He saw Nori's bare feet receding on the orderly's cart.

Qaddafi massaged his own shoulder. "You hit hard, I'm dizzy," he said.

He sat down at the desk.

"You do not want to shoot me," he reasoned. "You've been blaming me for something and it's hard to let go." His hands lay six inches from the edge of the desk. "You know the truth when you hear it, that's why you have not fired. You're tired. Jamal was the man you wanted. I killed him for you. See me as a real person, the person I am and not the one you have imagined in your brain. I've done nothing to you. I want to help you."

See me as the person I am. Something in Qaddafi's own words penetrated Currie's fog. Under the torrent of argument his brain righted itself, lifted itself past Nori and Washington. His grief receded or at least he pushed it away. It would crash down later but for now he commanded his senses.

"I watched you on television the day she died," Currie said. "In the hospital, while she was being operated on. You announced reprisals against your enemies. That was your word, reprisals. You knew Jamal had ordered Tecala killed but you didn't know that he was on your side, not then. You were pleased Tecala had been killed. You were boasting about it. If Nori had to die too, then you were glad as well. Or worse, indifferent." Currie lifted the gun higher. "Jamal had done his job, what he was supposed to do. What he'd done for you before. In London and Israel. In Italy. What you paid him to do." There was a droning engine noise in the courtyard. Currie envisioned a truck outside, soldiers piling on corpses.

He said, "Now you tell me Nori was a mistake and I'm supposed to go away. And tomorrow you'll appoint a new Jamal and send him out to keep killing. You're right that without Nori I wouldn't have come here but now that I've come I can't go away, not yet. You and the people like you, the way you operate, that's what killed her. Jamal gave the order and Lipko carried the gun but you were behind the whole thing."

"Who are you to decide who lives?"

Currie shook his head. "Pain for pain, that's what will stop people like you. You set things in motion and blame others when they come to fruition. Besides, you have no intention of letting me go. You're waiting for me to relax so you can drop your hands under the desk."

Startled, Qaddafi moved back from the edge of the desk. "You can't blame me for everything subordinates do," he said. His voice had gone disdainful. "Your President is the same, all over the world. People do things for him he doesn't know about either."

"Then someone will shoot him."

For the first time the confidence drained out of Qaddafi. He said, "You really did come alone, didn't you. Nobody works alone."

"You want to say a prayer?" Currie said. "I read you were religious."

Qaddafi's right hand was edging back to the end of the desk but Qaddafi saw Currie watching him and stopped.

"Assassins have never changed a thing," he said. "That's all you are, plain and simple. An assassin. Disraeli said it after Lincoln was shot. Oh, I know your history. I could give you Islamic examples but you would not be familiar with them. Sirhan Sirhan killed Kennedy but nothing changed. The guards will shoot you if you harm me. Charlotte Corday was convinced she would stop the French Revolution by stabbing Marat. The Reign of Terror went on. Put down the gun. James Felton, who murdered the Duke of Buckingham, wandered the streets afterwards begging to have his hand severed. An offense against a ruler is an offense against God. I'm saying nothing you don't already know in your heart."

"Maybe you want to write a note," Currie said. "I read you were close to your parents."

Knocking began at the door again.

Qaddafi looked from Currie to the door. It struck Currie that the room was soundproofed. Otherwise guards would be listening to Qaddafi all the time. Qaddafi said, "Pay attention to what I am saying. I won't beg like Jamal but listen to me. Your reason for coming here no longer exists." The knocking stopped. "You think oil will dry up under the desert if I die? Or airplanes or cars will no longer require gasoline?

"Oil, this is what determines who we are. Men clamor for oil through the world, their need is stronger than any individual, than you or I or your fiancée. A thousand Qaddafis

[290]

live to serve them. I'm just the one in front of you, the one you see and focus on, the one you blame your problems on. Yet you will find Qaddafi Bedouins in the desert. In Green Square in Tripoli. Shepherds. A grocer. I don't know who the next one will be but it makes no difference. The oil won't be denied. It drowns its opponents. Maybe the next Qaddafi will have a name like Kaebi . . . let us say Kaebi will be his name . . . and the West will forget my name and cry out" — Qaddafi made his voice high and pitiable — " 'Oh, if there were only no Kaebi all our problems would be solved.' . . . And more years will pass while you decline and blame someone else. The West will forget Qaddafi and think him unimportant and *they will be right!* The real power will remain unchanged."

Qaddafi refused to be debased, refused to surrender. Oh, Currie knew he was right in blaming the Colonel for Nori's death but striking back at the man seemed useless suddenly. The fog was coming back. Currie had granted Qaddafi magical influence long before Nori's death, and this power had been fed by the public fascination with the man. As Qaddafi spoke Currie saw the oil under the desert, in vast tides. He heard the clamor of men and machines crying for it. Against the forces of nature and history his efforts seemed small and unimportant. He saw the effrontery of a lone human opposing oil itself.

One by one in ten minutes his blocks of reason had been stripped from under him, yet *still* blind unreasoning instinct kept him from lowering the gun. Had Zarek died for nothing? Both men were breathing loudly. The sweat stood out on Currie's temples. His legs trembled.

"I am a servant," Qaddafi was saying, half risen at the desk. "A conductor. I stand between the people and the dream. The oil flows through me to ships and machines and bank vaults. The guns come back to the people. I am utterly replaceable. I am a cog. If I tried to do anything differently, the people would oppose it. Do you hear? They would kill me."

The gun terminated four feet from Qaddafi's chest.

The dictator's eyes blazed.

Slowly, Currie lowered the gun.

"You're right," he whispered. Qaddafi's hand was moving on the desk. "You can't be blamed. And it's funny because I'm like you, a product of a force too."

Qaddafi's hand disappeared under the desk. "What force?" he asked, smiling in triumph.

Currie's gun came up again. There was a flash of light from the desk.

"Revenge," Currie said.

He pulled the trigger.

EPILOGUE

THE village had no name, marked no map. No phones served it, or postmen or roads leading anywhere outside the valley. No census takers or tax collectors appeared. The only policemen were private guards. If lookouts upriver spotted a private plane approaching, half the village went hiking in the mountains until the pilot was identified or gone.

They had waterfalls there, in the jungle. Currie lived in a cinderblock hut with air-conditioning and a refrigerator. The village maintained a generator and Currie, who kept it running, found his talents came in useful in the jungle. But the heat outside was brutal, it would kill a weaker man.

On Tuesday nights Currie played chess with a German named Stangl, except Stangl called himself "Protzer" when he was drunk. An American in the village lived alone in a mansion he'd had built. There was a Greek who listened to opera records all day. Nobody tallked about why they had come here. Nobody talked about home.

One year after the death of Muammar Qaddafi Currie walked down the rickety village quay to a fifteen-foot flat-bottomed river launch. He was stripped to the waist at seven A.M., he wore dirty khaki shorts and a blond beard. Humming, he unlashed the boat and started the motor. Toucans took to the sky at the noise. Pigs ate garbage near a shack on shore. A yellow-furred tail slinked into the jungle.

Adjusting the throttle, Currie headed downriver for the

weekly run for supplies. Trees crowded the shore, their branches bounced from monkeys excited by the boat.

Currie was thinking back to how he had reached the village.

After the exchange of shots in Qaddafi's office, which had left the Colonel slumped at the desk, Currie had remained immobile. He'd expected the door to crash open and troops to rush in. But then he'd realized both guns had been silenced. The firing outside grew louder, the building swayed from a rocket hit on the barracks. Jamal's troops were assaulting Bab Azizea itself.

Currie left the room using the small door through which Qaddafi had entered. He found himself in Qaddafi's private quarters, a small hallway led to a bedroom as sparse and sunny as the office. A double bed and a single dresser. Huge arched windows looked out on a walled in garden. No paintings. No decorations of any kind.

The only other door was a closet's, but through the rack of hanging uniforms Currie saw a *second* door, iron, barred, which opened into a long tunnel. A flashlight, canteen and knapsack hung on the limestone wall inside the door. Currie's heart began to pound. He'd known Qaddafi would have another way out of Bab Azizea and this had to be it. He barred the door behind him, using an inside bolt, and headed down the tunnel. As he proceeded it became clear why Qaddafi had taken so little trouble to hide the escape route. More iron doors had to be opened every five hundred yards. The doors were so heavy any effort to blast through them would bring the tunnel roof down on an attacker. And each door could be barred from either side, enabling Qaddafi to effectively control all access to the route.

The tunnel let Currie out in a private home in Tripoli, devoid of people but stocked with supplies and clothing. A faded Russian car, a Lada, sat in a garage. Dressed in a jacket and baggy Libyan pants, Currie had driven through the city, searching anywhere for an embassy so he could ask for asylum. The streets were either empty or packed with panic-stricken civilians or troop trucks. Lost, Currie found himself at the docks. Explosions were coming from the city. It was like Iran all over again. People were fighting to reach motor launches to ships, crewmen fought off refugees and the tankers were streaming from the harbor.

Currie had bulled his way to a launch and fought and boarded the boat. The European sailors, sympathetic to a foreigner, had let him stay. Once at sea it was easy. The ship was bound for Marseilles, had to pass Malta. Currie had stolen a life jacket, jumped ship and swum ashore.

In return for more of the Swiss money, which Currie had wired for, Zarek's friend Neville Smythe had arranged false credentials and passport to the village.

To Currie it seemed like a miracle that he had gotten out of Libya. As if ten years had passed.

Now Currie swung the wheel left and took the last turn of the river. Ahead he saw a thatched hut on stilts at the junction of three rivers. Boats were docked and loading supplies. A fat man with greasy black hair lifted himself out of a rocker on the veranda.

Currie said, tying up the boat, "Hello, Da Gama."

"Ah, Mr. Gillespie. I have a tape video machine for Stangl and more punk rock records for the Italians. You keep our boat running this week?"

Currie had bought half interest in the boat. Running it gave him something to do.

As Currie unloaded crates the fat man unfolded reading glasses and exhibited a six-month-old copy of *Time* magazine. The cover showed an angry-looking military man with a fist raised. The headline said, "LIBYA'S NEW STRONGMAN. THREAT TO MIDEAST PEACE?"

The fat man spat into the red water. "Qaddafi or Gosbaidat. They're all the same."

Currie shrugged, working. The sweat poured down his back. "Maybe there's a difference but we don't see it, Da Gama. Maybe Colonel Gosbaidat thinks twice before he sends out his killers. I believe that."

The fat man snorted. "What does anyone in this hell-hole know about optimism?" he said.

Currie laughed. He was satisfied with the way the loading was going. When he was finished, the fat man pulled a soiled white envelope from his breast pocket. Lots of stamps. "Letter for Gillespie," he said. "I could open it and find out who you are."

He added quickly, seeing Currie's expression, "I don't want to know who anyone is. I don't want to know anything."

The heat seemed to expand on the back of Currie's neck. But he didn't open the envelope until he was on the way home on the river, and then he saw with relief that it was from Smythe.

Anna Currie was in Malta looking for you. She tried the bars. She said she had a letter for you. I stole her pocketbook so she would think the thief wanted money, not the letter.

Smythe

Currie felt dizzy, looking at the second envelope. He'd steeled himself against thinking about home, it was stupid to think about what had been before.

But Anna had written:

Dear Tim,
Sperazza never came back. I heard about the death of [Smythe had blacked out Qaddafi's name]. You told Sperazza he should take you to Malta so maybe someone here knows where you are.

At least tell me if you're alive. Or let me come to you. I love
you. I'll be in Washington.

I love you,
Anna

On shore, a pig-footed tapir trotted up the riverbank, startled by the boat. Currie opened the hatch and looked down
at the engine. It had been running rough today, it needed a
valve job. Above the river ahead, clouds of mosquitoes swarmed
at a bend. He told himself he was home now. He had always
known what it would be like after Qaddafi, if he lived. Cut
yourself off from people and you can't go back.

Currie looked over the fine feminine loops in the hand-
writing. He told Anna in his mind, If I let you know I'm
alive, you'll try to find me. You'd hate it here. Two months
and you'd want to go home, but you wouldn't be allowed to
leave. I can't write you. The Libyans might be hunting for
me, they'd come to you, they'd read in your face that you
know I'm alive. They wouldn't believe you don't know where
I am.

Currie crumpled the paper and held it over the gunwhale,
ready to throw it away. The heat was awful, the water the
color of clay. The surface swirled from the boat's passage
and from fins of fish. She would loathe the heat and the
animals. Even the fish didn't look normal. They had whiskers
like catfish and tails like newts.

He pulled back his hand and spread the paper on the
bulwark. He should throw it away but he smoothed it out
and folded it into his back pocket instead. He had an urge
to read the letter again. He told her in his mind, It will never
work.

The engine coughed, he steered the boat. Somewhere in
the forest, birds were screaming.